A PROMISE SO BOLD AND BROKEN

MORE BY SOPHIA ST. GERMAIN

COMPELLING FATES SAGA

A Tongue So Sweet and Deadly

A Promise So Bold and Broken

A Bond So Fierce and Fragile

A Fate So Dark and Delicate

ECHO SERIES

Echo of Wings

Echo of Deceit

A PROMISE SO BOLD AND BROKEN

COMPELLING FATES SAGA

BOOK TWO

SOPHIA ST. GERMAIN

kensingtonbooks.com

Content Notice: Violence, Torture, PTSD, Death, Gore, Spice, Some Swearing, Imprisonment, Orphans

KENSINGTON BOOKS are published by:

Kensington Publishing Corp.
900 Third Avenue
New York, NY 10022

kensingtonbooks.com

All Kensington titles, imprints, and distributed lines are available at special quantity discounts for bulk purchases for sales promotions, premiums, fundraising, educational, or institutional use.

Special book excerpts or customized printings can also be created to fit specific needs. For details, write or phone the office of the Kensington sales manager: Kensington Publishing Corp., 900 Third Avenue, New York, NY 10022, attn: Sales Department; phone 1-800-221-2647.

The K with book logo Reg US Pat. & TM Off.

ISBN 978-1-4967-6473-7 (paperback)

First Kensington Trade Paperback printing: June 2026

10 9 8 7 6 5 4 3 2 1

Printed in the United States of America

Chapter illustrations by Antonia Ansgariusson

Electronic Edition ISBN 978-1-4967-6487-4 (ebook)

The authorized representative in the EU for product safety and compliance
is eucomply OU, Parnu mnt 139b-14, Apt 123
Tallinn, Berlin 11317, hello@eucompliancepartner.com

To the ones who keep fighting for a better world for everyone,
even when that world seems dark and far away—

I hope you find a light to guide you.

HAVLANDS
N
E
S
Ellow
Asker
Korina
Eiatis
Sea
Vastala

CHAPTER ONE

As she swallowed a mouthful of watery porridge, Lessia glared at the men around the timeworn table.

To her right, Merrick scrunched his nose as he lifted a spoon of the pale liquid to his lips, the disgust when it trickled down his throat as apparent as the stench of sweat and stale air permeating the small ship's cabin.

Before her, Ardow and Venko sat with blood still staining their clothing, and her gaze snagged on Venko's swollen-shut eye and the angry red line snaking its way from his forehead down to his chin.

The men's gazes remained fixed on the bowls the ship's captain had brought down for breakfast, declaring their contents was the only edible thing onboard, as their departure hadn't been planned. Not one of them looked up as they shoveled the soupy mess into their mouths.

Lessia ground her teeth as she continued to stare daggers at them.

It'd been almost a week since they escaped Ellow.

A week in which she'd given them time to rest and heal from the injuries Ellow's guards—and, in Merrick's case, King Rioner's soldiers—had inflicted.

A week in which they'd barely spoken more than two words to her, guilt building across their features every time they met her eyes.

A week in which Lessia had spent the time mainly outside, leaning over the railing and staring at the wrathful sea, trying to comprehend how everything had gone to shit.

How could she have missed two people so close to her being traitors?

She should have seen the signs with Ardow!

And Merrick...

Her gaze flicked up to the worn ceiling for a moment, following the cracks and warped beams weaving their way to the stairs leading up to the deck of the ship.

She'd assumed he was acting on orders from their king.

But whatever he'd been doing all those times he sneaked away must have been connected to the rebellion these idiots believed they were spearheading.

An ache started in her chest as she thought of Amalise—the fear she'd seen in her friend when they'd sat on that bed together on her final night in Ellow—and she clenched her teeth when Kalia's, Ledger's, and Fiona's faces flashed before her eyes.

What if Zaddock hadn't gotten to Amalise in time?

What if Amalise and Zaddock hadn't gotten the children out?

What if everyone she loved was rotting in Loche's cellars right this moment, believing Lessia had left them behind?

The wooden walls of the cabin seemed to creep closer, darkening the already dimly lit room and casting foreboding shadows on the males around her, causing a shiver to dance across her shoulders.

Lessia dropped her spoon when thoughts of Zaddock made Loche's smirk fill her mind, then the images of his cold, distant eyes as she'd taken every feeling he'd ever harbored for her away.

The spoon clattered to the floor, shattering the thick silence.

Still, when Merrick quietly bent down to pick it up, neither Venko nor Ardow reacted.

The constant pressure on her chest tightened as the men's eyes remained anywhere but on hers, and the air she forced into her lungs became heavier, filled with guilt and regret.

Her nostrils flared, and Lessia slammed her hands on the table so hard that her bowl toppled over and the gray mush spilled across the stained wood.

"Enough!"

Every pair of eyes in the room flew to hers.

Finally.

With magic pulsating under her skin, she snarled, "It's time for you to tell me what's going on! It's been a week, and I've tried to be understanding, but I'm done waiting! Absolutely. Fucking. Done."

Ardow's eyes lowered when she bore her own into his, and she slammed a fist on the rotting wood again. "Look at me!"

Lessia nearly vibrated from withheld anger, the breaths she dragged into her lungs turning choppy.

They'd put the people she loved in danger.

Could have ruined everything she'd fought for the

past five years.

And now they wouldn't even meet her eyes.

A large hand landed on her shoulder, and she turned her glare to Merrick's night-sky gaze.

She narrowed her eyes when something flashed in his dark ones, and when his mouth twitched, her magic burst to the surface, the golden glow of it reflecting in his silver flecks.

"Don't you dare laugh at me," she hissed, the shaking in her hands spreading through her body.

One of his brows quirked up, and the hand he kept on her shoulder tightened in warning.

Soft whispers responded to the magic buzzing around her, but there was no room for fear within her.

Not with the guilt and shame and worry that already festered like a disease on her every nerve and limb.

She should use her magic on every single one of them.

Force them to tell her everything.

Force them to face that guilt hunching their backs—do it as they looked right into her eyes.

But the longer she kept Merrick's gaze, the longer his whispers traced her skin, the trembles racking her body softened, the overwhelming emotions were soothed, and her eyes widened when she realized what she'd almost done.

Forcing herself to blink hard, she pushed her magic down, lowering her gaze when another wave of hot guilt washed over her.

She'd promised herself never to do that.

And now...

Now that she acted on her own will and not the Fae king's, she could actually honor that vow.

With her chin against her chest, Lessia drew a few deep breaths of musty air, and when she finally lifted her eyes, she found Venko and Ardow watching her with blanched faces.

Merrick's gaze, though, didn't waver when she met it again, the hand he'd kept on her shoulder squeezing it once more before releasing her.

"I'm sorry," she muttered when silence stretched on. "I'm just tired of being kept in the dark."

"I know," Merrick said quietly, and when their eyes locked again, she realized she believed him.

Something in the intense silver-sprinkled darkness made her trust he understood her completely, and her stomach flipped when Merrick continued to keep her eyes hostage.

"We'll tell you everything," Ardow broke in, and she reluctantly shifted her gaze to his when he continued.

"We couldn't before, Lia. It was too dangerous with your... your connection to the king." Ardow's eyes pleaded with her. "But we'll tell you everything you want to know. You only need to ask."

"How long have you all been working together?" Lessia, trying to keep out of her voice the sense of hurt that two males she'd trusted had kept this from her, made herself focus on the anger that swirled dangerously close to the surface of her skin.

Ardow's brows flew up, and shocked laughter burst out of Venko.

Even Merrick let out a choked sound beside her.

"What?" she growled, her eyes flitting between the other three pairs.

"As if I would work with these two." Leaning back in his chair, Merrick crossed his arms over his chest. "Their mess is theirs alone."

Ardow scoffed, but his mouth closed when Lessia raised a hand.

"Then why would you try to save them?" She eyed Merrick as he pulled out a ribbon of fabric from inside his tunic and used it to tie back his hair.

Her eyes lingered for a moment on the shiny strands, and she wondered whether it was a full-Fae trait that kept it looking as if it had recently been washed while her own was matted and smelled like death.

When he finished removing his hair from his face, Merrick rolled his eyes. "Someone needed to help them clean it up."

"I need more, Merrick," she hissed through clenched teeth.

"I don't have all the information, as our dear king made sure I couldn't be trusted with it," he hissed back, his eyes flaring.

She swallowed the snide remark on her tongue.

Like her, he'd been forced to serve King Rioner against his will, and she knew all too well the limitations that came with the blood oath.

And Merrick had been bound by it for centuries...

Blowing out a shaky breath, she managed to demand, "Then tell me what you do know."

"There is more to the little rebellion your friends think they're heroes for being part of. I don't know the full extent, but Alarin—your father—does," Merrick responded.

Lessia winced when her father's sorrow-filled eyes burst into her mind, the compassion that had filled his face as he stood behind Rioner that final day on Ellow.

He hadn't even known who she truly was when he'd hurt for her in Loche's office.

Hadn't known his own daughter was the one on her knees on the floor, begging the man who'd started to piece together her broken heart not to cast her out like trash on the street.

With a sharp inhale, she pushed the images away.

Threw them to the back of her mind as quickly as Loche had thrown her out.

"Alarin is your father?" Venko leaned forward, his uninjured eye narrowing.

"I—" she started, but Ardow interrupted her.

"King Rioner is your *uncle*?" Hurt twisted his dark features as the hands he'd placed on the table clenched.

"So what if he is?" she snapped, balling her own hands when they continued shaking. "He doesn't know I exist. At least not as his niece. My father kept us hidden from him my entire life, and he wouldn't dare look at me long enough to recognize the resemblance."

"Of course it matters!" Venko hissed. "You're of royal blood!"

"I'm a *halfling*, remember? I have as much claim to the throne as either of you. Rioner would sooner kill me than recognize the blood that flows through my veins," she snarled.

Ardow shook his head. "That's exactly why it matters! If he ever finds out, he'll stop at nothing to find you!"

A chill traced down her spine, but she shrugged angrily to hide it.

There was no point in worrying about King Rioner finding out who she truly was.

Not when she already had so much else to worry about.

Not when she didn't know if her friends were safe.

If they were alive.

"Then let's hope he never does," she said quietly before boring her eyes into Ardow's. "You've stalled long enough."

Tension strained Ardow's face as his eyes drifted toward Venko, and her magic pressed in her veins again when he remained quiet for a moment.

But then he sighed, his gaze returning to meet hers. "It started many years ago. Before you and I were even born... The books have it wrong, Lessia. Not all shifters were on their king's side, but they were slaughtered all the same. No man, woman, or child the humans and Fae encountered was shown mercy. Still, some survived, and they've been hiding out across Havlands ever since."

Lessia nodded slowly.

Geyia had told her the same thing back in that cave.

But she didn't want to stop him now that he'd finally started talking, so she waved for him to go on when he eyed her.

"Like you and me, they're outcasts... and they've grown tired of it. They can't return to rebuild their home for fear of discovery. They can't integrate into society..." Ardow leaned his chin in his hands, his gaze fixed on the battered table. "Their numbers started dwindling a few decades ago... until they ran into a group of half-Fae that had managed to flee Vastala. Initially, they fought for the small piece of land both sides wanted to claim, but they soon realized they'd be stronger together—that it would give them the numbers they needed to fight back."

"Wait—" Venko started, but when Lessia cast him a warning look, he sealed his mouth shut.

Still, a crease marred his forehead as he picked at the bowl before him.

With a quick glance at the merchant, Ardow straightened. "As they began planning for the rebellion, the half-Fae and shifters realized they weren't so different after all and that there were more people like them all across Havlands—living in Vastala and Ellow. Well... if you can call it living."

He shot her a penetrating glare, and Lessia had to look away when something stirred inside her.

What Ardow spoke of wasn't so different from what she'd told Amalise whenever she felt guilty for keeping the children locked up.

But this *was* different, wasn't it?

The children were innocent, while these... rebels were not.

The ancestors of the shifters amongst them might not have followed their king.

But the rebels had killed people.

Woven their way into an election to manipulate the process—the will of the people of Ellow.

Is that so different from what you did?

Lessia shook her head as the voice flitted across her thoughts.

She hadn't had a choice.

These people did.

Merrick was quiet—worryingly quiet—and she glanced his way, finding him glowering at Ardow, his long fingers impatiently tapping his knee.

As if he felt her eyes on him, his gaze shifted to hers,

and she nearly flinched at the thunderous darkness swirling in it.

After throwing a sharp glare Ardow's way, Merrick rasped, "I knew humans were slow, but your friend here has surpassed my expectations."

A muffled sound left Ardow, and one of Merrick's silver brows lifted, but his eyes remained locked on hers as he drawled, "What he—very slowly—is trying to say is that this group banded together to overthrow the leaders in Havlands and has been recruiting people across the realm ever since. Some, like Ardow here, believe in their cause, believe that they're working for a better world... and others, like that one"—he waved toward Venko—"are bribed to help them. That's what they tried with Loche as well, but apparently he wasn't as pliable as they'd hoped."

Lessia tensed when Loche's name left his lips, and Merrick's eyes slitted as they followed her raised shoulders down to the shaking hands in her lap.

Shifting so she sat on them, Lessia tore her eyes away and focused on Ardow.

"Is it true?" she whispered.

His nostrils flared as his gaze flitted between her and the Fae beside her. "In his world, perhaps. But he's right in that I do believe in our cause. We believe in a world where everyone is treated the same! Where part-Fae and shifters and outcasts can all walk the streets and into whichever establishment they want without worrying about being stared at, attacked, or even killed. It's time for a shift, and it needs to be now! We're done waiting around for a change that'll never happen."

"And you're trying to accomplish this by killing people who disagree with you? Aren't you doing the same thing you're accusing Rioner and L—" Lessia sucked in a breath when the regent's name stuck in her throat and pinched her thighs to relieve the pain in her chest.

"That you're accusing the leaders of Havlands of?" she finally got out.

Ardow shook his head, his eyes burning into hers. "I've been an outcast my entire life, and I'm done with it! I'm tired of being looked down upon as soon as people realize the heritage I bear. If we need to take drastic measures to get there, so be it! And you should be on our side! How many times have you been called names? How many times have you been hurt by humans and Fae alike?"

He leaned over the table and waved his finger in her face. "Remember why you're on this ship! Your king and the regent you desperately wanted to believe would treat you fairly forced you on here. How can you not see that we're the good ones, Lessia!"

Casting her eyes down, she pinched her legs harder as Loche's cold eyes flashed in her mind.

Take them away, he'd told her.

I only want to remember you as the spy who snaked her way into our election. Nothing else.

She swallowed a whimper as the coldness in Loche's eyes faded to mere boredom.

He'd finally seen her for what she was.

And *good* wasn't the word she'd use.

"Good ones..." Merrick scoffed. "You're so naive. I've lived long enough to learn the belief in inherent goodness is a delusion."

Ardow shot up. "That's why you're trying to stop us? Because you don't believe shifters can be good? What about halflings? You seem to have stopped trying to kill Lessia, but perhaps that's just another way to trick us into listening to you?"

"As I've been trying to inform your leaders, we also believe in a world where everyone is welcome!" Merrick growled, his hand gripping the edge of the table so hard it shifted with a loud squeak. "But bigger things are happening in Havlands than your little rebellion, and we all need to work together if we're going to survive them!"

A hollow chuckle left Ardow when Lessia's eyes snapped to Merrick, but Venko's injured face paled as he asked, "What do you mean?"

With a huff, Ardow threw himself onto the chair again. "He's making up wild stories to save that king of his and stop what he knows is coming. Don't believe a word he tells you."

Merrick let out a laugh that made Lessia's skin prickle.

Raising his brows, Merrick ignored the scowling Ardow, keeping his gaze on the increasingly flustered Venko. "How much of what Ardow has now entertained us with has he actually told you? Did you know who you were truly working for? Did you know they're planning an attack that will end up with more innocent blood spilled? Much, much more."

Venko shrunk into his seat at the intensity of Merrick's glare, his blond hair falling into his eyes as he cowered.

"That's what I thought," Merrick sneered.

"I couldn't tell you! Not with Lessia..." Ardow trailed off when Lessia's eyes found his.

"I'm sorry," he pleaded. "But it's true. I was supposed to be the one going into the election, but we had to adjust when we found out what King Rioner had planned for you. I knew too much, and while you hadn't used your gift on me... we couldn't risk it."

Her teeth slammed together as the urge to pound a fist into his face overwhelmed her.

"I told you I'd never," she gritted.

Ardow's eyes flashed with pity when hers glossed. "Perhaps not willingly. But you did it to Venko... and I'm guessing you did it to Loche as well, since—"

"I suggest you stop talking now." Merrick's voice was soft, but whispers began to reverberate between the walls of the cramped cabin, layering over her skin as they intensified.

"I don't care who you are! You don't tell me what—" Ardow started.

She couldn't stand the arguing, couldn't stand the raised voices joining the guilt and fear inside her.

And she really couldn't stand the whispers that seemed to state the same words again and again: *It's not your fault, it's not your fault, it's not your fault.*

It was her fault!

Of course it was her fault.

Lessia closed her eyes and pressed her hands against her ears to drown out the staggering whispers.

"Stop it!" she screamed when her hands did little to quiet them.

After a moment, Merrick's magic seemed to still, even though the air still flickered with the ancient gift that filled his veins, and Lessia drew a deep breath as she lowered her hands, ignoring the wide-eyed stares from the males around her.

"Stop it," she said again, quieter this time, but forcing her voice to remain strong.

It was her fault.

It was her fault Loche had banished her.

It was her fault that Amalise and the children had to flee Asker.

It was her fault for getting tangled up with the Fae king—the one thing her father had devoted his life to not happening.

And now she needed to do something about it.

Arguing on a stupid ship in the middle of the Eiatis Sea would be of help to exactly no one.

"None of you will talk unless I say so." She let the magic brimming under her skin shine through, her golden eyes casting bright shadows across the dark wood as they darted between the three males. "Otherwise, I swear I *will* break all promises I've made and use my damned magic to make each and every one of you tell me your deepest, darkest secrets and use them against you."

She wouldn't, but she refused to let them know that when Venko whitened further, and even Ardow leaned back in his chair, his eyes everywhere but on hers.

Merrick shifted beside her, and when she flicked her glowing gaze his way, he met it, but she didn't miss the flicker of unease in the silver swirls.

"Now that that's established... Merrick, what is happening in Havlands?"

The Fae hesitated momentarily, and it was enough to stop her from pushing the magic down again.

Instead, she tilted her head and raised a brow in the arrogant way he'd done earlier.

A vein in his neck bulged as he glared back at her, but the whispers didn't surface again as he finally responded, "We have reason to believe a neighboring realm is planning on invading Havlands."

A shiver racked her shoulders at the gravity of his tone, but she forced herself to ask, "Why?"

"I don't know much, only what your father could risk to tell me." Merrick pulled the cord from his hair, shaking his locks out. "A few years ago, a group of Fae that used to be ruled by a royal family called the Oakgards entered our waters, their ships bearing the mark of what we called the Old World—the realm our kind migrated from a few millennia ago. They asked to speak to King Rioner and informed him that their realm was dying, their lands rotting, their forests burning, their water turning poisonous, and that the people were at a loss for what to do. They asked him for sanctuary in Vastala... but he turned them away, forced them to leave and go back where they came from."

"So what?" Ardow sneered, but he quieted when Lessia glared at him.

With a low growl that vibrated right through Lessia, Merrick continued. "They were desperate. The king's brother even got on his knees and begged him to at least take the children... But Rioner refused. He told them they were too many—that he couldn't risk his own people to save another—one he didn't even remember."

Lessia swallowed when the memory of her on her knees before Loche in his office struck her like a dagger to the chest.

Stiffening, Merrick balled his hands on top of his knees. "We believe they're coming back. That they're not here to ask nicely but to take our realm by force. If we're right, Havlands can't risk not standing united. If we're in the middle of an uprising... it will be easy for them to pick us off one by one."

"Does Rioner know?" she asked, driving the image of Loche's office from her mind.

"He does, and he doesn't believe it." Merrick's lip curled, his sharp teeth rasping against the bottom one. "Your father has seen foreign ships when he's traveled from your home, but since he can't say exactly where... Rioner seems to believe it's L... it's the regent who somehow wants to intimidate him."

She realized her magic had faded from her eyes when she stared into Merrick's dark ones and fear wrapped around her heart like an icy hand.

The fact that her father had even mentioned being somewhere outside the castle Rioner had so graciously given him when he ascended the throne had erased any doubt she might have harbored.

Her father wouldn't risk the king's men stumbling across their hidden island—the sanctuary he'd discovered after meeting her mother, and the place he actually called home—the place Rioner knew nothing of, as he had no idea her father only visited the castle a few times a month to keep up appearances.

Especially not if Frelina somehow was alive.

He must be convinced in what he'd told Merrick.

And that meant the people she loved were in more danger than she'd realized.

Not just from the rebellion...

But from an entire other realm.

And Loche...

If Rioner believed he was behind it all...

He was in the most peril of all.

"Is he... is Loche aware?" she made herself ask, even

as the mention of his name made her rib cage feel as if it would cave in.

When Merrick's gaze fell and he shook his head, she couldn't stand being another minute in the musty cabin.

Shooting upright, she stumbled toward the latch, a cry rising up her throat when she couldn't get it open right away.

CHAPTER TWO

As she gripped the wooden railing and stared out over the furious waves crashing against the port, she struggled to hold back the scream building inside her from the emotions pressing against her chest, threatening to boil over like a pot left too long on the stove.

And when the faces of her loved ones—Amalise, her parents, Frelina, Kalia, Fiona and all the other children, and finally... Loche—consumed her thoughts, the sensation continued to mount until it felt as if she would break apart into a million tiny pieces if she didn't let some of it out.

So, with her eyes on the gray horizon, she did.

Lessia let every ounce of guilt and fear and frustration fuel the piercing cry as it drifted across the ripples of water.

She screamed for the family she'd left behind in Vastala, for the friends she'd abandoned in Ellow, for the regent she'd betrayed, for the king she'd been too weak to fight, for the contradictory emotions churning inside as she took in what Ardow had told her.

But most of all, she screamed for the helplessness she felt as Merrick's warning of war lodged itself in her throat.

She didn't doubt he'd spoken true.

That Havlands and those she loved in it were in danger.

And with her being banished and traveling with three fugitives...

There was little she could do to get King Rioner and Loche to believe it.

A sound from the upper deck startled her as she caught her breath, and she whirled around to find one of the men in the crew operating the ship staring at her with wide eyes.

Smoothing out the hair blowing around her face, she hissed, "Can I help you?"

The man nearly tripped as he backed away, the color of his face fading with every step, and she realized her eyes must have shifted into gold when a soft glow broke through the mist traveling across the wooden deck.

Sighing, she turned back toward the water, clutching the worn wood so hard splinters bit into her palms.

But she welcomed the pain.

Welcomed anything that could distract her from the crippling powerlessness that lay heavy on her chest.

A warm hand touched her lower back, and the smell of salt and wet wood mixed with Merrick's untamed scent as he took up the spot to her right.

When she glanced at him, the sheen of her eyes illuminated his hard features and the pearly hair trailing over his shoulders.

His eyes met hers briefly before they shifted out over the sea. "Did that make you feel better?"

She was nearly overcome by the urge to slap him, but as she lifted her hand, he moved faster than she'd ever seen anyone do, his fingers locking around her wrist before she had time to blink.

Pulling her against him, he glared at her. "Have you learned nothing of what I tried to teach you? You need to be in control. Of your movements. Of your emotions. Of your magic. Of yourself. If you're planning to take out your anger on me, do it right!"

When Merrick released her, she took a step back from his rumbling chest.

Moving her eyes to her boots, she drew a shaky breath, trying to rein in the emotions drawing up her magic.

She knew heightened states of mind drove magic to the surface to protect its wielder—had had more practice suppressing it than using it.

But right now, suppressing it was proving difficult.

When the light brightening the wood finally dimmed, she lifted her gaze again.

Merrick had shifted his glare to the dark clouds building in the north, the swirling white sheets beneath them betraying the snowstorm heading for Ellow.

She rubbed her arms when a brisk wind whipped around them, blowing Merrick's hair out of his face and the torn cloak he wore toward the stern.

"I'm sorry," she muttered when his tense shoulders didn't lower and the angrily set jaw didn't soften.

"I do not need an apology. You're entitled to be angry. Gods, you're entitled to be fucking furious. But you're not entitled to be reckless with it."

When she remained quiet, Merrick moved to lean his elbows on the railing, his eyes meeting hers again as he laced his fingers together. "Unless Raine kills us for entering his waters, we'll start training again as soon as we arrive. You need to learn how to *feel* your emotions, especially the negative ones—the sadness and grief and fear—and use those feelings to control what you do with them. You're Fae. Our emotions are too strong to be pushed down for long. Especially the negative ones..." Merrick sighed. "You have power, Lessia. More than you think. You just need to learn how to harness it."

Power...

She nearly scoffed, but then Loche's betrayed face flickered in her mind, and it felt as if someone ripped her heart from her chest and stomped on it, smashed it into a pool of crimson to allow it to drip through the planks they stood upon.

She sucked in a breath of salty air.

She couldn't let those emotions in.

No.

Not without breaking down.

And she didn't have that luxury.

There were people depending on her.

Perhaps more people than she'd expected, since she believed what Merrick had spoken was true.

Squeezing her eyes shut, she forced Loche from her mind—forced herself to focus on the anger that had consumed her before.

Merrick sighed again when she opened them, his features hardening when she didn't respond.

As he watched her for a moment, something she couldn't read flashed in his eyes. "It seems we need also to practice using your gift. You require more control over it if you plan to continue to threaten us with it."

She started shaking her head but stilled when Merrick's eyes narrowed.

"There may be a time when we'll need you to use it," he said softly.

Lessia didn't respond as he straightened and brushed off some drops of water that had landed on the green tunic he wore beneath his cloak.

She had threatened them in there, but only because her frustrations got the better of her.

She would never use it on a friend again.

Now that she was no longer forced to by the blood oath, she could choose never to use it on *anyone* again.

She gripped the railing once more when another wave of fury roiled inside her.

All her magic did was destroy and hurt and betray.

"Lessia." Merrick took a step toward her. "The gods gifted it to you for a reason. You do not need to be frightened of it. It's not evil or good. It's nothing but a power to be molded by its wielder. A power to be used carefully, yes. But not to be suppressed or forgotten about."

"The gods are gone!" she snapped. "They don't partake in our world anymore. They don't care for us! And especially not us *halflings*!"

Bridging the final distance between them and crowding her against the railing, Merrick stared down at her, a muscle in his jaw twitching as an angry tear snaked its way down her cheek.

Lessia furiously wiped it away, wondering how she'd ever wished to be able to cry again.

It was stupid.

Weak.

And she didn't have time for either of those things.

"If you believe that, you're not as clever as I thought," he said quietly as he lifted a hand and used his thumb to brush away another treacherous drop.

Merrick watched it for a moment before he let the tear fall into the dark waves.

Cupping her chin, he lifted her eyes to his again. "The gods may not show themselves anymore, but they're here. They're in every creature in our world, in all the beauty and the ugliness, in good and evil, in glory and flaws. And they are most certainly in you. They choose a person's gift for a reason, and I'd be lying if I said I didn't question mine for a long time. Truth be told, I still question it—but *I* wield it, Lessia. I decide what it is and what it isn't."

She swallowed as Merrick stepped back. "You didn't kill your sister. I don't know how she survived, but perhaps it was the gods' way of teaching you to respect your gift. Showing you the darker side should you turn to it."

Her brows drew together. "So you're saying I should be grateful for the gods forcing me onto the streets of Vastala? For making me live in darkness for years in Rioner's cellars? Perhaps for me getting banished from every home I've ever known?"

Merrick raised a brow when her magic stirred, and she snarled when light filled her eyes again and an urge to tell him to shut his mouth crashed through her.

When she stepped toward him, warning whispers boomed through the mist, and oily tendrils snaked their way around her arms, forcing her trembling body to a stop.

But he didn't avert his eyes as his glacial voice broke

through the fog overtaking her mind. "I won't pity you. We forge our own fates. While the gods might give us gifts, it's up to us what we do with them. We always have a choice."

"So was it your choice to chain yourself to Rioner, then?" she taunted as heat crept up her neck.

The air stilled, and a shiver skittered down her spine when Merrick's magic tightened its grip.

But just as fast it released her, the wind and the water hitting the sides of the ship soon the only thing filling her ears.

"It was my choice, yes." Merrick's voice barely traveled over the gusting breeze as he spun around to walk back inside.

Her stomach churned at the sorrow that seeped into his scent, and before she knew what she was doing, she gripped one of his large hands.

"I'm sorry," she whispered as he turned his head over his shoulder. "I shouldn't have said that."

He didn't respond, only stared at her with those star-filled eyes.

When his wild, mourning scent continued to whirl around them, she threw her head back and closed her eyes.

"I'm sorry," she reiterated. "It's been a rough few days."

She didn't dare look at him when she heard his feet shuffle, but a little bit of warmth clawed itself into her chest when they brought him closer, the sadness lacing the air fading.

"Enough with the apologies. And... I'd say you've had a rough few years."

Her eyes flew to his, and her heart leaped when a crooked smile brightened his features.

Pulling at her hand, he led her back to the railing. "While I won't pity you, I told you—you are entitled to be angry."

Merrick let go of her hand to lean his arms on the railing, letting out a breath as he stared down the stained wood of the hull. "Gods know I've been angry for a long time. Furious at my fate and the decisions I made. But I can't change the past. I can only use that anger to direct the future. You need to learn how to do that as well. How to direct your emotions before they direct you."

Her eyes wandered from the pearly strands of hair the wind played with, to his delicately pointed ears, over his high cheekbones and slightly parted full lips, and that feeling that he understood her, perhaps better than anyone else, layered around her.

Shifting so she mirrored his position, she listened to the waves hitting the side of the ship.

She was angry.

At her fate.

But also at herself.

Merrick was right—even if the gods had bestowed on her the stupid gift, she had made the choices leading to where she was today.

She was the one who hadn't listened to her father's advice to manage her emotions, especially as she neared the age when magic manifested, to avoid situations exactly like the one she'd believed she'd caused that day with her sister.

Stealing a glance at him, she whispered, "How do you know my sister is alive?"

Merrick's eyes drifted her way. "I saw her once."

He hesitated for a moment. "King Rioner had me follow your father a few years ago. He suspected he was hiding something, and it didn't take me long to find your home. It was easy, even."

He let out a low laugh as he shook his head. "But as soon as I stepped onto the island, Alarin trapped me. He'd intended for me to find him all along. Rioner didn't realize we'd gotten to know each other during the many years I was in his service... that we'd become friends, even. And apparently it was on purpose. Alarin needed someone close to Rioner, and I wanted out, so we decided to work together. We had to be careful with what he told me, but I learned of the stirring rebellion and the other threats against our realm, and Alarin provided me with enough secrets that Rioner was kept satisfied and I could leave out the other things I saw. Including your little sister."

Lessia shook her head, her thoughts whirling.

It didn't sound like her father to take such a risk, even if he considered Merrick a friend.

Rioner could have easily forced Merrick to tell him every detail he'd learned.

And he'd worked too hard to keep her, her mother, and Frelina hidden.

Merrick moved to face her. "It was a risk he had to take."

One corner of his mouth quirked when her eyes widened. "He wouldn't have done it if he believed another option existed. The threats we're facing are real, Lessia. He's protecting your family against them."

Glancing down at her laced fingers, she asked quietly, "Can we go see them?"

It was quiet for so long she wondered if Merrick had

left without her noticing, but then he finally cleared his throat. "I think it might have been your father who turned me in that night."

"What?" She slipped on the wet planks as she spun around. "He wouldn't do that!"

Her father was nothing if not loyal to those he loved.

He'd rather die than hurt them.

"He would if someone more dear to him was in danger." Merrick placed a hand on her shoulder to steady her, and his grip tightened as he continued.

"You were nowhere near to figuring out what King Rioner wanted to know. He knew that someone close to him must have been betraying him. Too much confidential information was leaked for him not to figure it out."

"What do you mean?" She stared from his hand to his eyes as her heart began pounding.

Merrick sighed. "We had to get the rebels to trust us if we would ever convince them to stand down so we could face the Oakgards' Fae together. And the only way was giving them something they wanted..." His hand dropped to his side. "Rioner would have never let you go unless whoever it was, was captured."

"But my father doesn't remember me," she whispered.

If Frelina was alive, she would have told them.

The small voice in her mind made a lump form in her throat.

But if they knew...

Why hadn't her father come for her?

Of course he wouldn't come for you.

He blamed you for what you did.

Rightfully so.

Lessia swallowed against the thickness, trying to tell herself that wasn't true.

"I don't think he knew, or at least suspected, until he saw you," Merrick said softly as pity darkened his eyes. "I told you before—you were a child. Even if you'd killed her, they wouldn't have blamed you. And I've seen the love Alarin holds for his family. He would have turned these lands upside down to find you if he knew."

She sniffed as Merrick picked up a lock of her bronze hair, twining it between his long fingers. "You are a mirror of your sister, Lessia. Alarin isn't dumb. He knew something was off the moment he met you."

A knot formed in her stomach when Merrick sighed again. "We need to go somewhere safe to figure out our next steps, and while Raine might not welcome us with open arms, I'm hoping he'll not turn us in as soon as he sees us."

CHAPTER THREE

When they finally made their way inside, the captain had brought down more watery grain.

Venko and Ardow sat at the table, picking at it with rusty spoons.

Shadows danced over the men and across the small cots covering the cabin walls, their eerie movements shifting when the ship tilted from the rising winds.

Lessia had to grip the side of one of the cots when a strong gust made the ship heel, and her stomach turned enough that she headed to her assigned bedding instead of joining the table and the unpleasant smell of half-rotten oats.

Sitting down on the bed, she drew deep breaths through her mouth against the nausea, her eyes tracking Merrick as he also opted to head to his cot.

Settling in the too-small cot opposite her, he unsheathed the sword always strapped to his back, its rubies glowing softly as he placed it beside him on the mattress.

Lessia picked at the dagger he'd given her, running her fingers along the identical red gemstones before laying it beside the one her father had gifted her.

She'd thought it strange King Rioner hadn't disarmed Merrick when they'd captured him.

But perhaps his faith in the blood oath was that strong.

Merrick had been in his service for centuries, after all.

Ardow rose, his chair scraping against the floor as he pulled it out.

Picking up two cups from the table, he closed the short distance to her cot, his eyes flicking to the spot beside her.

Lessia thought about refusing, but when his face strained, she sighed and shifted to the end of the bed.

Ardow offered her a small smile as he pressed one of the cups into her hands.

"Truce?" he asked softly.

She narrowed her eyes as another surge of anger swept over her, but when Merrick cleared his throat across the room and she shifted her eyes to his, a wheezing breath made its way into her lungs.

I can only use that anger to direct the future, he'd said.

Averting her eyes to the hands in her lap, she thought he had a point.

She could be angry at Ardow all she liked, but it wouldn't help their situation.

Flexing her fingers, she made herself meet Ardow's imploring gaze and groused, "For now."

He nodded as he bumped his cup against hers, and when he lifted it to his lips, she followed.

Tears sprung into her eyes the second the liquid touched her mouth, and she spat it out, gasping for air as the few drops that had made it down her throat burned like blazing flames.

"What is this?" she hissed, using her sleeve to wipe at her tongue when the scalding sensation continued. "Are you trying to kill me?"

Laughter exploded through the room, and she snapped her gaze between Venko's flushed cheeks, Merrick's turned-down face, and Ardow's wide eyes.

Lessia clenched her jaw when Ardow and Venko continued giggling, and when even Merrick's shifting shoulders betrayed him, she hesitated only for a second.

Then she poured the rest of the cup over Ardow's head.

"What the..." He stared at her with pale liquid dripping down his face and the strands of his hair turning darker as the liquor stained it.

She glared right back at him. "I told you not to laugh at me."

When Ardow lifted his own cup, she shuffled backward but stilled when whispers crashed through the cabin, the oily magic turning the air even more stale as Merrick flew to his feet.

"Don't you dare," he growled. "You had it coming for lying to her. She saved your life. Show some gratitude."

Ardow's features hardened as he glared at the Fae, but when the whispers grew louder, causing the hair on Lessia's arms to rise, he rested the cup on his knees.

Although the hand holding it shook so much the liquid spilled over the sides.

"I'm sorry," Ardow snarled when Merrick's magic continued roiling through the room. "Just stop it!"

Lessia held her breath as the whispers faded, but a low hum remained until Ardow turned toward her, fear reflecting in his eyes as he shakily got out, "I'm so sorry, Lessia. For everything."

When it finally quieted, Venko's face had returned to the pale coloring she'd gotten used to the past few days, and both she and Ardow jerked when he pushed his chair back and stalked toward the stairs.

Venko stiffened on the first step, and his finger trembled as he pointed it Merrick's way. "You're *actually* the damned Death Whisperer? I thought you were joking before! I wasn't even certain you were real or if it was only a story told to keep humans wary of the Fae."

His gaze sliced to Ardow. "The Death Whisperer, Ardow? What in the gods did you drag me into?" Venko shook his head, his face contorted with betrayal, before hurrying up the stairs.

Lessia flinched again when the hatch slammed shut, and she squeezed her eyes together when memories of another door shutting invaded her mind.

Gripping the rough blanket tight, she tried to push the thoughts away—tried to drown out the sounds of metal and dripping water.

"Lessia?"

Ardow's voice sounded far away, and a whimper fought to leave her throat when a Fae with blue eyes squatted down before her in a dark corner, a wicked smile on his face as he whispered her name.

You're never leaving this place.

No.

Enough.

She wasn't going back there.

Violently shaking her head, she let the fury of

Ardow's betrayal, of Loche's dismissal, and of the helplessness she felt thinking of her friends flood her veins, tinting the darkness before her eyes crimson.

A warning snarl escaped her when warm hands settled on her knees, and she pried her eyes open to dark eyes and an inhumanly tall form crouched before her.

Lessia scrambled backward on the bed, dashing for the daggers she'd placed beside her.

"Get away from me," she hissed as she tightened her grip on the hilts.

"It's me, Lessia," the figure said quietly.

"No!" she shouted. "Leave me alone!"

But the Fae didn't.

Instead, he shoved someone off the cot, the grunt from the person hitting the floor echoing in the cramped cabin.

"It's me. It's Merrick," the figure said.

She blinked hard.

But she could still only see the dim outline of the Fae in Rioner's cellars.

"It's me."

The voice rumbled through her as she blinked again.

Her vision sharpened, and the Fae's silver hair and familiar features kindled something within her.

Lessia blinked again as he climbed into the bed, taking the spot beside her.

Merrick.

Dropping the daggers, she pressed her shaking hands to her face.

Merrick wouldn't hurt her.

Not anymore.

She stiffened when the bed shifted, and strong arms wrapped around her, pulling her into a broad chest.

"It's me," he whispered into her hair, and as his low voice wrapped around her, her coiled muscles softened.

He held her closer, and his hair tickled her cheek as he continued. "I promise you, you're never going back there. I will never allow them to hurt you again. Do you hear me?"

When she didn't respond, Merrick repeated, "Do you hear me?"

Finally, she dipped her chin, and a low rumble vibrated in his chest.

When her body finally relaxed fully against his, her cheek resting against his soft tunic, and she breathed in the scent that reminded her of forests and wilderness, he shifted, gently unwrapping his arms and guiding her head to the pillow.

"You need to rest," he whispered.

She peeked at him through her lashes, and an involuntary sound left her when his feet found the floor.

Freezing, Merrick glanced back down, and whatever he found in her eyes made his nostrils flare as he nodded once.

"I'll stay here while you sleep."

It was all she needed to hear for her eyelids to flutter, and she sighed as she curled up on her side, facing the wall, but her feet still touched Merrick's legs as he sat down on the end of the bed with his back against the wall.

Fatigue seeped into her every muscle and limb, and she tried to focus on Merrick's slow breaths as sleep pressed down on her.

For a while, the only sounds filling the cabin were the sparks as the candles sputtered, the soft breaths of people, and the rustling of fabric as someone moved positions.

But as she was about to fall into darkness, a barely audible whisper broke through the musty air.

"Is she sleeping?"

She made herself lie completely still, keeping her breaths even, unsure whether she could handle another conversation right now.

"It appears so," Merrick responded.

"Is she going to be all right?" Ardow's words were laced with worry, and she could hear him adjust his position somewhere on the floor.

A low rumble shook the bed as Merrick hissed, "Yes."

"But... I've never seen her like this. She—she's so angry."

It was quiet for a beat, and Lessia didn't dare move a muscle as she drew air into her lungs not to allow her heart rate to increase.

"Are you surprised?" Merrick asked, his tone so cold she held back a shiver.

"No, but... I've never seen her react like that when she's reminded of those years. Sh-she usually breaks down," Ardow whispered.

Lessia tensed, but Merrick's low voice drowned out the memories threatening to surface.

"It's a good thing. She's fighting back. She *is* angry. And that anger is what's keeping her going. She's been through so much in her young life, and she's repressed all the resulting emotions for so long... But she can't anymore, not with all the hurt and disappointment. So she focuses on the easiest one to manage—rage."

"Sh-she only feels rage?" Ardow breathed.

"For now," Merrick responded quietly. "She might

only be half-Fae, but our emotions are much stronger than human ones. With everything that happened in the past week, I'm surprised she's even left the cot. I've seen full Fae break over less."

Lessia could hear Ardow shift, and she imagined how his face scrunched up the way it did when he was scared, and an unfamiliar feeling of irritation crept over her skin.

"But she'll be back to normal soon?"

Merrick moved again, and she could feel his eyes on her, the warmth of his gaze traveling down her face as he sighed. "Time will tell. For now, I suggest you stop riling her up, or you might find yourself in a dangerous situation. I certainly won't stop her if it comes to that."

A low muttering bounced between the walls before Ardow broke the silence again. "Can... can we help her get better?"

Lessia stopped herself from swallowing when Merrick tensed, feeling as if every beat of her heart slammed against her chest.

"She doesn't need *to get better*," he snarled softly. "If she decides to break apart this whole ship to deal with what happened, I'll help her. If she wants to kick your lying ass into the depths of the sea, I'll take your legs. If she decides to rip the world to shreds for what it's done to her, I'll cheer her on. And if you were a true friend... you would as well."

CHAPTER FOUR

She'd barely gotten any sleep last night, not even when Ardow and Merrick quieted and the former began snoring softly.

She'd been awake for hours, trying to understand Merrick's words.

Was she truly that angry?

The constant red cast clouding her vision certainly implied so.

Too many emotions swirled inside her... and none of them were good.

Bleary eyed, she dragged herself off the cot when the captain entered and put the usual unappetizing bowls on the rattling table.

He informed them that they were getting close to the eastern border of Havlands, that they'd recently passed Korina's waters and would be near Fae territory within a day or so.

Merrick followed him up to the helm to give him

instructions for where they needed to go to get to wherever Raine lived.

Her eyes lingered on his back as he stalked up the stairs, and she wondered if her own shoulders looked as taut as his did, if her gait was as high strung.

Avoiding Venko's and Ardow's gazes, she slumped down onto a chair and lifted the bowl to drink directly from it.

Perhaps if she ate quickly enough, it wouldn't taste as foul.

"How are you feeling?" Ardow asked hesitantly.

Setting down the bowl, Lessia lifted her eyes and wiped at a stray drop that escaped her mouth.

Ardow's eyes were guarded as he studied her, and another urge to punch him crossed her mind.

But she pushed it down.

You are in control.

She repeated the words to herself until the red hue tinting her vision dimmed.

Ignoring Ardow's question, as she wasn't sure how to respond, she turned to Venko. "What did the rebels promise you to get you on board with this... plan?"

Venko's face turned crimson, and his eyes lingered on Ardow briefly before moving to the grayish substance in his bowl. "They promised me monopoly over the trade."

The trade...

A bitter laugh escaped her. "Greed... is that what drives all males?"

"No, Lessia." Ardow sought her eyes. "Venko might have initially had dubious intentions, but after we got to know each other, he understood—"

Venko's hand slammed onto the table. "Stop! You didn't tell me there would be bloodshed, Ardow! I thought you were on the good side. That the rebels were fighting for something better for *everyone*! It's the only reason I stayed when I realized what was happening. But you didn't tell me you planned to kill Loche. Or innocent people, for that matter. It sounds to me like the rebels are as bad as those Oakgards' Fae Merrick talked of. They want to take our lands by force, and so do your damned rebels."

Ardow tried to reach out for him, but Venko sprang from his chair, taking the one beside Lessia instead.

Dragging his hands down his face, Ardow sighed. "I'm sorry. I'm sorry I hurt both of you. But it was the only way. Please, you have to believe me. We are the good side."

Lessia's eyes locked with Venko's uninjured one, and they shook their heads.

"You killed Stellia and her company," she snarled quietly.

"We would never," Ardow snapped. "Yes, we wanted to make it seem like she had some part in it—create mistrust within Ellow. But we didn't kill her or her guards."

"How can we trust that?" Venko still had his eyes glued on Lessia's as he spoke. "Some of her own guards betrayed her. They tried to kill Craven before he left!"

Ardow remained silent for a moment, and Lessia's eyes widened when guilt tugged at his face, pulling his dark brows down and emptying his gaze.

"Ardow?" she whispered, not certain if she wanted to know what thoughts swirled in his mind.

"He's dead, isn't he?" Venko's voice jarred her, and she sliced her gaze to the side, finding him clenching the table so hard his knuckles drained of blood.

When Ardow dipped his chin, she sucked in a breath.

"Was it you?" Lessia got out.

His jaw flexed, but he raised his downcast eyes to hers. "He hurt you, Lessia! He would have killed you, from what Venko told me. He was a danger to the Ellow we want to build!"

When she started shaking her head, Ardow let out a choked sound before he urged, "Lessia, you know how it's been for us! What the children we rescue have to face! Do you not want to give them a chance of a better life?"

Ardow's eyes glossed, and she let out a huff when guilt constricted her throat.

Forcing it away, she growled, "Of course I do!"

She wanted nothing more than for them to live like humans and full Fae.

But not at the expense of thousands perishing.

Not even at the expense of someone as vile as Craven.

She'd made herself a promise when she thought she killed Frelina: that no more souls would taint her conscience.

And that included innocent people, whatever heritage they might bear.

"We are on the same side," Ardow said quietly. "Perhaps the way I've gone about it is wrong, but if we work with them, we can figure out another way. I know Merrick seems to think we need to go to his gods-damned friend, but we should find the rebels. They will listen to me. I'm sure of it."

"Like they listened to you when you told them Lessia was off limits?" Merrick prowled down the stairs, a thunderous look on his face. "We're not going anywhere near them! Not until we have a plan. And my gods-damned friend is one of the most powerful Fae in our realm. You should count yourself lucky if we can get him to help."

"And when will we get the honor of meeting this almighty Fae?" Ardow sneered.

"Right now," Merrick snarled back. "And rein in that attitude of yours if you care for your life. I'm much more forgiving than Raine, and I'm already this close to ripping your damned head off."

Lessia couldn't stop the small snort that left her, and when Merrick turned to her and his dark eyes twinkled, the anger that had clawed so sharply at her lessened.

"Is he here?" she asked as she pulled at her tunic—a habit she'd probably carry for the rest of her life, even though only angry scars now covered her left arm.

Merrick shook his head, a muscle in his jaw twitching. "The captain of this ship doesn't have a brave bone in him. He will not take us farther... not where we need to go. We'll have to take a rowing boat from here."

"To where?" Ardow broke in, the loathing in his voice so palpable she could taste it.

Lessia tensed when Merrick's furious gaze focused on Ardow, and she rose to her feet when the Fae took a step toward her friend. "Let's just go."

She might be angry at Ardow.

Livid, actually.

But she couldn't let Merrick kill him.

And based on the whirring sounds building in the cabin, that was exactly what Merrick had planned, but as she brushed past him toward the roaring wind above, she felt him fall into step with her.

Fixing her eyes on the gray sky as she ascended the stairs, she watched as raging clouds revolved around the ship, but when she took the first step onto the deck, the wind was warm and the air tinged with the humidity she'd known from Vastala.

To the east, an impenetrable mist hovered, not a single island or part of land in sight.

And to the west there was only water stretched out as far as her sharp Fae eyes could see.

She almost opened her mouth to ask Merrick the same question Ardow had, albeit she would have done so less rudely, but when he stormed past her, barking at the crew to hurry up, she pinched her lips.

Merrick seemed on edge, and with the strange kind of friendship they'd formed the past months, she knew now was not the time to push him.

Behind his rigid stature, the crew fought against the wind to hoist a small boat over the railing, all the while screaming orders at each other not to fall overboard.

A shudder went through her when she looked out over the sea, over the choppy waves crashing against the stern, and Lessia pulled her cloak tighter.

Wherever they were going would be wet, and while the temperatures here had picked up from the freezing winter in Ellow, the wind would ensure they weren't comfortable.

"Venko, please."

Lessia spun around when Ardow's pleading voice floated toward her, and she found him pulling at Venko's hand, tears streaming down his face.

"No." Venko pulled his hand from her friend's. "I'm staying."

"Please," Ardow begged, and a small piece of her heart cracked at hearing his voice waver.

She clenched her hands, unwilling to let the feeling fester.

She couldn't go down that road, because if she did...

Hot breath hit her ear as Merrick leaned in behind her to whisper "He knows too much, Lessia."

Her forehead creased as she turned her head to look at him, and Merrick continued. "He knows where we're going... and he knows who you are. We can't leave him here."

She slowly turned back toward the two arguing men, realizing Merrick was right.

Venko couldn't stay behind.

Looking up at Merrick again, she swallowed.

He kept her gaze for a moment before nodding once, then bridged the distance to Ardow and Venko with a few long strides.

"You're coming." Merrick's demand rumbled through her, and her eyes widened when Venko dared glare at the Fae and shake his head.

He must be braver than she'd thought.

But Venko didn't stand a chance as Merrick let out a low growl, his hand clamping down on his arm, nearly lifting the man off his feet as he started dragging him toward the small boat.

"Let me go!" Venko looked like a child, his fist whirling in the air around Merrick—who only appeared bored as he dodged it—and dug his feet into the wooden planks of the deck. "I said, let me go!"

The crew stormed forward, but after a glance at Merrick's face, the men froze.

One by one, they backed away, keeping a safe distance as Merrick determinedly set Venko down in the small wooden boat.

Ardow's eyes were cast down as he passed her and quietly gripped the railing to haul himself into the vessel.

She fidgeted with the daggers in her waistband as she shot a final glance at the ship, and she nodded when the captain who had kept them fed lifted his hand.

"Lessia?" Merrick's voice was soft as he called to her, and when he reached out a hand, she took a shaking step toward him.

As she reached him, she didn't let herself look down into the wild sea, instead keeping her eyes on the small bench Merrick guided her to.

The rushing of water filled her ears as the crew lowered them, and she didn't move as drops of saltwater kissed her face once they cut the ropes, and the waves immediately took them away from the trade ship.

CHAPTER FIVE

The boat wasn't as vulnerable to the waves as Lessia had feared, moving smoothly over the choppy water.

It was challenging to steer, though, and every time she switched with one of the males to row in the direction Merrick pointed toward, she couldn't focus on anything else but pushing through the water, keeping her eyes on the thickening mist around them.

Lessia gripped the wooden oars tight when a current threatened to pull them from her hands, letting out a wheezing exhale when she managed to push through.

"Do you want me to take over?" Merrick slipped onto the wooden bench in the stern, shifting the boat's weight but helping her get a better grip against the water fighting her strokes.

Shaking her head, she forced another strong pull.

It felt good using her strength.

If nothing else, it kept all the thoughts and worry inside at bay.

"Those lazy humans are passed out back there," Merrick sneered.

She shrugged as she let a wave hit the boat before pulling another stroke.

Neither Ardow nor Venko had been very helpful when it was their turn.

Even Ardow, with his Fae blood making him stronger than most humans, had almost let the oars slip out of his hands, and she was certain Venko's muttering and venomous glares were the reason.

But there wasn't room in her to pity him.

Not with everything else going on.

Although she'd been on the receiving end of similar stares, so she understood why he'd barely been able to move the boat a few feet forward.

"Where are we going?" she dared ask when they'd both been quiet for a beat.

Straightening his cloak, he captured her eyes. "Midhrok."

The confusion must have been evident on her face because he continued. "It's the land between Havlands and the next realm."

She'd never heard of Midhrok—had only heard of a few other realms from the children's stories her father had told her growing up. "Have you been?"

Merrick shook his head. "I've not heard good things."

A cold sensation swept over her, and she quickly took another hard stroke. "How do you know Raine is there?"

"It's where he told me he'd go if everything fell apart," Merrick responded simply.

"So... so you don't actually know if he's there?" she whispered.

"He's there." Merrick stretched his arms over his

head, and his hands disappeared from view in the mist that now surrounded them like white walls closing in on the small rowing boat.

When he brought them down again, the white clouds lingered over his skin, and he swatted them off his hands. "Let's switch. You look ready to drop dead."

As she started shaking her head, the boat listed, nearly turning fully onto its side, and Lessia gasped as it slammed back down into the waves.

"What was that?" Ardow yelled behind her.

Turning her head over her shoulder, she could barely see Venko gripping the side of the boat through the mist, which seemed to thicken with each passing second.

She only just made out Ardow crouched beside him, his eyes wild as he stared back at her.

"I don't know," Merrick muttered, and they were perhaps the most terrifying words she'd ever heard.

A slight tremor worked its way into Merrick's usually hard voice, and she held her breath as he leaned over the side to stare into the water.

When it remained quiet for a few moments, Lessia relaxed slightly.

Then the boat heeled again, and it was so sudden that she lost her grip on the oars.

"No!" she screamed as she rushed to get a hold of them.

But it was too late.

The wooden oars fell from their oarlocks and crashed into the stormy sea below.

"Fuck!" Merrick snarled, his hair flying across his face as his back snapped straight.

"What is it?" Ardow shouted over the wind that began whipping around them.

"Sea wyvern," Merrick responded as he unsheathed the sword on his back. "And it doesn't seem to want us here."

Lessia's eyes widened as she followed Merrick's gaze into the water, and a reflection of something broke through the dark surface.

A reflection of something very large...

"What do we do?" she got out through gritted teeth as she pulled the daggers from her waistband, clutching them in her hands.

As she stared from the huge shadow beneath the boat to the daggers, her stomach twisted.

The blades seemed quite small in comparison.

"Fight for your life," Merrick snapped as the boat tilted furiously again.

"This isn't what I signed up for," Venko cried. "Do something!"

"Can't you whisper it to death or something?" Ardow screamed as he pushed Venko down onto the floor, standing over him as his wide eyes tracked the creature now swimming in circles around the small boat.

"No," Merrick growled as he clasped the gunwale so as not to fall into the water. "My magic—" His words clipped when the boat jarred again, the raging waves spilling into the hull and making Venko wail.

"Your magic what?" Ardow screamed.

"It has limits," Merrick hissed as the boat slanted to the other side. "Magic only works on humans, shifters, and Fae."

Merrick reached out for Lessia, but the boat turned so quickly that she slid backward, away from where he held on to the stern.

His dark eyes flashed when she scrambled to grip the

wooden ridge best she could with daggers in hand, and she didn't like the look on his face.

Not one bit.

Swearing to herself, Lessia squatted down when another hit nearly tripped her, and when she peeked over the side, her blood chilled.

A tail, twice the length of the boat and lined with purple scales and several thick spikes, rose from the water, whipping the mist viciously as it towered over the boat.

"Jump!" Merrick bellowed. "Now!"

When the tail slammed down, Lessia didn't think.

Clasping her daggers, she threw herself off the side of the boat.

The chill water immediately bit into her skin, and she kicked her feet to dive when wild waves crashed around her.

Something nudged her, and she snapped her eyes open to find shards of wood joining her descent.

With the daggers in her hands, she forced herself to swim faster, even as her lungs protested at the exertion and lack of air.

When the water cooled further, Lessia threw her gaze around, but she couldn't make out anything in the dark, murky sea.

Thrashing in place, she peeked upward—or at least where she believed the surface loomed—but no light broke through anywhere around her.

Lessia waited for a few moments, her eyes flying across the wet darkness.

When the waters remained calm, she decided to risk it.

It was either head to the surface or drown.

And hopefully she wouldn't get eaten on the way.

Her pulse roared in her ears as she started swimming to where she hoped was the surface, and her lungs screamed for the air she hadn't had time to draw before she dove—when something flickered in the corner of her eye.

Lessia whipped her head to the side, and when two huge violet eyes met hers, she let out a scream that was immediately swallowed by the water.

Only bubbles burst out of her mouth, shielding the wyvern from her vision for a moment.

Floundering backward, she kept her eyes open, her heart slamming so hard against her chest that each beat echoed in her ears.

When the bubbles floated upward, the violet eyes were no longer before her, but as she spun in the water, Lessia found them again, closer now and still fixed on her.

The wyvern began circling her, so tightly that its tail almost touched its mouth, and Lessia shuddered every time the violet eyes locked with hers.

She tried to remain as still as possible, moving her feet only when the lashing tail nearly nudged her.

Dread knotted itself in her stomach when the wyvern opened its maw, almost as if in a smile, displaying a row of sharp teeth the length of one of her arms.

Black spots flickered before her eyes as the little air she'd had left with a scream, and she realized this was it.

Either she'd die from lack of air... or this beast would eat her alive.

A whimper worked its way up her throat when the wyvern moved even closer, those cold eyes flashing with amusement when her face scrunched.

She wasn't ready to die.

She had too much left to do.

Too many people to make up to.

Frelina.

Her mother.

Her father.

Amalise.

Kalia and the other children.

Ardow.

Merrick.

Loche.

She wasn't ready.

A whisper of rage flushed her skin.

She wasn't fucking ready.

More fury lapped her skin, heating the water around her and driving the panic from her mind.

Lessia tightened her grip on the daggers.

She was done not fighting back.

Look at what good it had done her the past months.

If she was to die... it wouldn't be because she surrendered.

No, even if this creature swallowed her whole, she'd fight from inside it.

When her eyes flew open, a golden glow illuminated the water, and her features twisted into a snarl as she glared at the wyvern.

It slowed its speed until it finally stilled completely, its eyes tracking her slight movements.

You should be scared, she thought as her chest began caving in, pain shooting through her throat from the lack of air. *I have nothing to lose.*

The wyvern's maw twitched as it tilted its glittering head, the creature's violet eyes challenging hers.

It lurched forward, and while Lessia's heart stopped for a second, she refused to take her eyes off the beast as she lifted her daggers.

When the wyvern was a few feet away, her magic roiled inside her, more strongly than it ever had before, and she didn't care about what Merrick had said about magic not working on magical creatures.

Stop! she screamed in her mind. *You will not hurt me!*

The wyvern halted so fast that Lessia gulped down a few mouthfuls of water in surprise.

Coughing, trying to prevent more water from choking her, she stared at the wyvern with a hazy vision.

Its violet eyes still flashed, but a glassy hue tinted them.

Back up, she tried.

The wyvern inched backward.

She shook her head.

It worked.

But as a small smile spread across her face, her body convulsed.

With the adrenaline that had held her in an iron grip fading, black spots overtook her eyes, and panic once again chilled Lessia's veins as her lungs forced her to inhale more seawater in their need for air.

As tears flooded her eyes, mixing with the salty squalls of the sea, she begged, *Help me!*

CHAPTER SIX

"Stupid fucking wyvern. Wake up, Lessia!"

Something hard slammed into her back as a familiar voice broke through the darkness within her mind.

"Fuck! Wake up!"

Another strike had her chin slam into her chest, and as she came to, the sense of not being able to breathe made her eyes spring open, terror jolting through her blood.

Lessia caught a glimpse of beautiful swirling silver flecks for a second before a wave of nausea hit her and she expelled a grotesque mixture of seawater, algae, and whatever else the depths had forced her to consume.

A stifled sob escaped someone nearby, but she couldn't look up as someone yet again delivered a sharp blow to her back, causing her to splutter and relieve her stomach and lungs of more water.

Lessia shuddered as the disgusting mixture left her raw throat, keeping her eyes above the mess she'd made, the dark plants layering across the sand like the snakes sunning themselves on the white rocks that surrounded the capital of Vastala.

After coughing a few more times—and finally only vomiting bile, which she was grateful for even though it burned her throat further—she could draw a breath again.

Pulling in one more, savoring how the air lifted the fog in her mind, she'd started lifting her head when yet another blow landed on her back, driving out the few remaining drops of seawater.

Her head snapped up when she heard air rushing once more, and she quickly rasped, "Please, stop hitting me."

Merrick's face came into view, and his eyes hardened as he growled, "Stop fucking dying, then."

She wanted to snarl something back at him, but she swallowed the remark when his gaze flew across her body and a vein strained on his neck.

As she followed his furious eyes, her own widened when they snagged on her ripped clothing—on the large gashes in the black fabric.

Only one of her boots remained on her feet, and she cast a quick glance around her, finding the other lying a few feet away.

Her tunic was so severely ripped it barely covered her chest, while her trousers only had one leg remaining, and her cloak...

Nowhere to be seen.

Flying upright, Lessia quickly tugged at the ripped pieces to ensure all the essentials were covered before sweeping her eyes around their surroundings.

Mainly to avoid Merrick's sharp gaze but also to

understand where she'd ended up after the stare-off with the wyvern in the depths of the Eiatis Sea.

Eyes rounding further, she took in the white beach they stood upon.

She and Merrick were only a few feet away from where the sea lapped the coastline, the soft whispering of water vastly different from the violent waves she'd just escaped.

Behind them towered tall green grass, the blades rippling in the warm breeze, and as she drew another breath came the smell of summer: a sweet aroma of newly bloomed flowers and warm, dry earth mingled with the saltiness from the sea.

A small cottage stood a few hundred feet above the beach, and from the reflection behind it, Lessia guessed there was some type of river or stream weaving a soft path inland. When she followed the shimmering water, she glimpsed more buildings, these with straw roofs as yellow as the sun above them.

It appeared to be a small village or formation of houses, although she couldn't be too certain, as they must be a mile or perhaps even more away.

Another choked sound broke the soft rustling of the wind, and she tore her gaze away from the rhythmic swaying of greenery.

Her eyes locked on Ardow's where he stood next to Venko a few yards up the beach.

Both men were drenched, but their clothing was intact, and while Venko's hands shook by his sides, he offered her a relieved smile when his blue eyes landed on hers.

As she confirmed neither seemed harmed—or at least no more wounded than they had been on the ship

—her skin tingled from the seething presence behind her.

When she turned around to face Merrick again, it was all she could do not to cower under the glare he shot her.

The Fae's muscles were taut under the dark tunic sticking to his body, his pearly hair plastered around his raging face, and the lethal humming in his chest told her he was struggling not to yell at her again.

An urge to stick her tongue out at him rose within her—to replace that sour expression with a surprised one—but she forced it down. Instead, Lessia clenched her fists and asked roughly, "What happened?"

Merrick's nostrils flared as he stepped toward her and shoved her daggers into her hands. "Why did you swim downward, Lessia? Were you trying to get yourself killed?"

Her eyes narrowed as she stared at the shiny blades, at how the rubies and the amber stones mockingly glowed at her in the bright sunlight.

Lifting her slitted eyes to Merrick's burning ones, she snarled, "Of course I wasn't!"

Merrick stepped into her space, nearly fusing their wet bodies, and she had to bend her neck back to keep meeting his gaze.

"That was truly stupid," he said in that lethally low voice that always sent a shiver down her spine.

A muscle in his jaw ticked as he kept her eyes hostage, and she ground her teeth when another wave of anger roiled inside her.

She wanted to punch that stupidly chiseled jaw.

Perhaps leave him with a black eye to match the night-sky shade of his livid eyes.

It wasn't like she'd seen much when she dove into the water.

How could she have known the wyvern would dive too?

Merrick continued to glower at her, his broad chest heaving so close to hers that tiny droplets of water landed on her bare skin.

"There could have been more of them," Merrick hissed. "Wyverns like to swim in the depths of the sea. Everyone knows this!"

Not everyone, apparently.

Lessia tightened her grip on the daggers, wondering if lodging one in Merrick's gut would be worthwhile.

But when his eyes flicked down to her hand for a moment before returning to hers, and he arched a brow, she groaned.

She almost wished he still couldn't look at her—couldn't stand the unnerving scrutiny of his gaze, the reflections of understanding whenever she shifted an inch before him.

When she thought she'd combust from the tension, she snapped her gaze to the sand and grumbled, "Perhaps I am stupid, then!"

A growl roared through Merrick, so loud it felt as if the beach should shift with it. "Perhaps you are! Do you know what it was like, watching that beast carry you up from the sea? We thought it had chewed you up and decided to taunt us with your dead body!"

Lessia stiffened when his hand landed on her shoulder.

But he didn't throw her down the way he liked to in the training ring, as she'd expected.

Instead, Merrick slammed her into his chest, his arms enveloping her as he crushed her against him.

His heart raced against her body, thrumming through her, and another low sound rumbled in his chest as her body relaxed against his.

Blinking, she glanced up at him.

His eyes collided with hers, and apprehension whispered over her skin when she didn't understand what was swirling within the silver-flecked darkness as Merrick shook his head at her. "Don't do that to me again."

Before she could ask him what had his pulse so heightened, someone cleared their throat behind them. "M-Merrick?"

Lessia tried to wriggle free at the worry that laced Ardow's voice, but Merrick was too strong, his arms only tightening their grip when she shifted.

"What?" Merrick hissed as he continued to look into her eyes.

"There is someone over there. And that wyvern seems to know him."

Merrick's arms left her so quickly that a rush of air threatened to blow her ripped clothing off, and she pulled at it as she took a stumbling step after the Fae.

Ardow sidled up next to her, with Venko taking the other side, but Lessia froze when she glimpsed what Ardow had noticed over Merrick's broad shoulders where he walked ahead of them.

A copper-haired Fae, perhaps not as tall as Merrick but at least a few inches wider, stalked toward them on the beach.

Sunlight bounced off the jagged tooth-like edges of the crescent blades he held in his hands, and beside him glittered the wyvern she'd encountered in the dark waters.

Lessia caught the wyvern's violet gaze, and a quake shook her knees when it bore its eyes into hers before splashing its tail down so hard a wave of water crashed onto the beach behind the Fae.

The wyvern seemed to follow the Fae's lead because when the male lifted a large hand, both he and the wyvern halted about thirty feet away.

A jerk shook her body when Merrick also froze midstep, and Lessia's blood chilled when she realized she couldn't move either.

Her fingers were locked around the daggers she carried—her feet stuck in the sand.

Only her eyes could shift slightly, and she realized Ardow and Venko also stood still as statues beside her.

Who are you?

Fear roiled in her stomach as the unfamiliar voice boomed through her mind, and if she'd been able to move, she would have sprinted in the other direction when cold claws seemed to creep into her head.

We're friends of Merrick, she thought.

You lie. Merrick is blood-sworn to the king. He does not keep friends.

The voice floated and echoed through her mind, bouncing off the invisible walls she fought with everything in her to keep upright.

But it proved useless.

One gentle swipe of those claws broke through the barriers she'd spent years putting up.

Into all the memories she usually buried deep inside her.

Closing her eyes, she tried to fight—tried to find any

way to keep this Fae out of her mind—but the little magic she'd had left after facing the wyvern faded so quickly she thought she might not have had any to begin with.

The presence began prodding through her memories as if it were reading a book.

Stop! Please! she begged when an image of a bloodied Frelina formed in her mind. *I'm not lying!*

A dark chuckle reverberated inside her thoughts. *That's what they all say. I shall find out for myself.*

A silent cry tore through her when more memories flashed, splitting pain ripping at her chest as images began forming before her eyes.

Her mother smiling in the kitchen.

Her father gifting her the dagger in her hand.

Meeting Ardow in a dim tavern.

Walking into the warehouse with Amalise and Ardow for the first time.

Kalia stepping off the boat and running right into her arms.

Merrick threatening her in the tavern.

King Rioner on the cliff.

Lessia squeezed her eyes tighter when Loche's smug grin ripped into her chest as he told her she couldn't join the others during the festivities.

The memories started flipping faster.

Her sitting before that fire in the cabin.

The fight with Craven.

The attack at the castle.

The debates.

The cliff when the men surrounded her and Loche.

No! No! No! Please! Lessia screamed inside her mind.

But the library came next.

The kiss.

The conflicting feeling tearing through her as if she were living it again.

The ride, leaning against Loche's warm chest.

The cave.

A whimper burst out of her mouth.

Loche pushing her up against the wall.

The desire flooding her veins.

A choked breath left her when the memories switched to Ardow in the cell.

Then to the night the noble Fae visited Ellow.

The presence inside her mind lingered when she looked up at her father, the love she held for him whirling inside her, mingling with the guilt from what she'd done to him.

Then it switched to an opening door.

The whimper turned into a scream as she watched herself crawl toward Loche on the floor, the pain so raw she thought she might split right down the middle when his gray eyes emptied.

Merrick's battered body came into view, and curiosity flooded her.

But it wasn't her own.

No, the presence made her relive the full memory of forcing Merrick to look at her.

Of how uncertain she'd been that it would work.

Of how surprised she'd been at his eyes.

You're quite broken, aren't you, little Faeling?

She felt as if her legs would give out when the memories finally faded.

But the presence remained inside her mind, holding her body and mind hostage, and she could still only open her eyes, glimpsing the drop of sweat trickling down

Ardow's temple to her left and how terror filled Venko's expression where he faced forward to her right.

"Why are you here, Merrick?"

Lessia's gaze flew forward when the Fae finally spoke out loud.

Like the rest of them, Merrick stood rooted in the sand, but the air around him rippled, and she could almost feel how close he was to losing control over his whispers.

Gritting her teeth, she thought she might prefer the oily whispers layering over her body to these sharp talons holding her mind in a death grip.

At least Merrick couldn't read her mind, even though he seemed to pick up a lot just from studying her.

"Always a pleasure, Raine," Merrick said quietly, but the warning in his tone was as evident as the sea beside them. "You've seen it all in my mind, and you still need ask?"

Holding her breath, Lessia watched Raine flick the sharp blades in his hands before elegantly sheathing them across his back.

"I've heard it's the polite thing to do." Raine shrugged.

Merrick's teeth glinted in the sunlight when he bared them in a snarl, and Lessia's eyes widened when his taut shoulders shook from restrained anger.

"Get out of my head. I will not warn you again," Merrick hissed, his eyes squeezing shut for a moment before they snapped open.

"Threatening me, Merrick?" Raine's lips curled back to show off his own teeth as he crouched, hand shooting out to gesture toward the wyvern. "You know how quickly I could tell those weak humans to greet Ydren here."

Raine's gaze flicked to her for a moment, and her heart began thundering against her ribs at the look in his hazel eyes when a smile curved one side of his mouth. "And while the young mind-bender seems to have some power, she isn't strong enough to resist me."

A snarl burst out of Merrick, and whispers exploded across the beach.

If she could move, Lessia would have flinched from how thick the air became—like an oily shield wrapping around her, the soft wind almost shimmering—as if the air had somehow turned solid.

Venko let out a strangled cry when the oily ripples intensified, and Ardow's eyes seemed as if they would pop out of his head before they crashed shut.

Even the wyvern backed up an inch where she hovered a few yards from the shore.

"You know I could kill you in a second," Merrick growled. "We used to be friends, Raine. You've seen what is coming for Vastala in my mind! You've seen why we're here... We used to fight these threats together."

"That was a long time ago, Merrick." Raine shook his head. "I haven't seen you for years, and today you come to my sanctuary, bringing two angry humans and a Faeling who is so broken she might fall apart right here. For what? To ask me to fight for the realm that destroyed everything I loved?"

Lessia's eyes met Ardow's briefly, and she would have snapped her teeth at him if she could at the pity brightening his brown ones.

Forcing her gaze forward, she locked it on Merrick's tense back, watching how the curls of his hair slowly shifted in the wind—or perhaps within his whispers—she wasn't entirely certain what had them dancing around his face.

"No," Merrick gritted. "We came because we had nowhere else to go. We only need a safe place to stay until we figure out our next step."

A scoff left Raine. "Those two humans plan to escape you the first chance they get. The one over there"—Raine nodded toward Ardow—"is planning to convince the others to join those ignorant rebels and leave you behind. The other one seems content finding somewhere far away from all of you."

Ardow sucked in a breath beside her, and he refused to meet her eyes when she sought his.

She slowly exhaled through her nose.

How had Ardow become such a stupid bastard?

She'd saved his life.

The life the rebels had gladly sacrificed.

And now he wanted to go back to them?

Had he not heard what Merrick had told them? Did he truly not grasp the danger they faced if an entire nation of Oakgards' Fae descended upon Havlands?

The rebels might have a few shifters and half-Fae with magic, but...

Like in the previous war, they'd not stand a chance against full Fae.

"Perhaps," Merrick responded quietly, and Lessia was certain from his tone he'd already suspected as much of Ardow. "But you owe me, Raine. I will not ask more of you than to shelter us. Once we have a plan, we'll leave you be, and you can choose to go as many years as you like before seeing me again. Or forever, if that's your choice."

Raine sighed as he slipped a hand into his white shirt.

Tensing, Lessia watched closely as he dug around for a while, wondering if he'd perhaps bring out another lethal weapon, even worse than the jagged blades on his back.

And when he took a step toward Merrick as he did it... everything before her eyes turned a vivid red.

Raine glanced her way, his mouth curling into a cold smile that didn't touch his eyes as he took another stride.

Overwhelming fury built inside her, a feral snarl working its way through her throat, and she could see the talons, the presence inside her mind, clearly for the first time.

It was like a shadow version of Raine.

Only it wasn't a Fae form; it was more similar to the wraiths Preysaih, the god of death, had used in his warmongering when he still walked this realm.

She'd seen drawings of them in her father's books growing up, and if it hadn't been for the anger coursing through her blood, she might have shuddered.

But like the wraiths, Raine's eyes were clear as day within her mind, and when she shut her own, she let her Fae intuition guide her.

Her eyes turned inward, almost as if they peered out of her soul, and when she met the hazel ones in her mind and a golden sheen reflected in them, a low laugh left her.

Get the fuck out, she purred.

The presence evaporated.

Snapping her eyes open, she didn't hesitate before storming toward Raine with the daggers in her hands, sand flying around her feet as she pushed herself to run as fast as she could.

"Lessia!"

She ignored Merrick when he hissed at her, able only to focus on the still-smiling Fae before her.

She didn't even care that the wyvern let out an ear-splitting shriek or when it splashed its tail so viciously that a stream of water fell over her.

Raine shot a glance toward the beast, the cold smile giving way to an amused one. "Stand down, Ydren."

The wyvern let out another cry, its hostile gaze fixed on Lessia when she flashed her teeth at it as she continued charging toward Raine.

He snickered as she stormed up to him, and when the thing he pulled out was merely a flask, her strides slowed, confusion weaving a crease between her brows.

Unscrewing the cork, Raine grinned at her before drawing a large swig.

When he finished, he wiped his mouth with his white shirt, staining it with a brownish tint, and reached out the flask toward Lessia. "You might need this more than me. You seem a bit high strung."

A hiss left her, but Merrick's voice broke in from behind before she could tell him to shut his mouth. "Back off, Raine."

"Very well." Raine shrugged. "Perhaps this might be more interesting than I thought. It's been a while since someone could escape my hold."

Huffed breathing sounded behind her, and when she spun around, Venko stood with his head in his hands while Ardow brushed off some hair that had stuck to his flushed face, the magic that had held them in place finally releasing them.

Merrick stalked right up to them, pushing Lessia out of the way.

Getting into Raine's face, he dragged the Fae to him by his shirt. "Do not threaten any of us again. Especially not her. Do you hear me?"

A dark chuckle left Merrick when Raine raised his brows in challenge. "We've fought before, Raine. Remember the outcome."

Rolling his eyes, Raine patted the hand twisting his shirt. "I see your temper remains intact."

But when Merrick continued to glower at him, his steely eyes burning into Raine's, the latter nodded. "Fine. You have my word."

Raine glanced toward the still-snarling beast, and when he jerked his head, Ydren disappeared into the clear water, barely leaving a ripple on the smooth surface —almost as if the wyvern had never been there at all.

"I see you were able to control Ydren as well. She didn't like that." Raine gave her a lopsided smile over Merrick's shoulder.

Lessia only glared back at him, still unsure whether his promise not to hurt them was sincere.

Releasing him, Merrick seemed about to turn around to face Lessia when Raine spoke again. "Do you know who she really is?"

Merrick froze mid-turn, his magic roiling in the air once more.

"She's Alarin's daughter, yes," he growled.

Raine lifted his hands. "Just making sure you know what you're doing. Come on, I'll take you to my place." He glanced at Lessia and wiggled his brows. "Seems like some of you might need something to wear. Unless you prefer to walk around naked, that is. Not that I'd mind."

Her lips curled back when a laugh bubbled out of Raine, but before she could slam a dagger into his stupid face, Merrick lifted her and threw her over his shoulder.

"Let. Me. Down," she snarled when he started walking after Raine, Venko and Ardow cautiously following. "I swear, Merrick, I will kill you."

"No, you won't," he said simply as he adjusted her and lengthened his strides to follow Raine up a sandbank.

CHAPTER SEVEN

Lessia stared at the leathers folded on the chair in the corner of the room she'd been shown.

Raine had reluctantly given them to her while mumbling something about how they'd probably fit, but with a strange expression twisting his features.

Lessia shook her head.

She knew Fae usually dressed differently—had seen the clothing her father would wear upon returning from spending time with his brother.

Their clothing was usually more elaborate, with different and more daring cuts, using colors humans usually deemed excessive.

But this?

Hesitantly lifting the brown vest, she examined it, wincing at the cutoff sleeves.

Even if she was no longer forced to hide the tattoo, these sleeves were nonexistent—not the capped ones the women in Ellow preferred, but leaving everything from her mid-shoulder to her hands bare.

And while the intricate lacing in the front was beautiful, it ended just above her chest... revealing much more skin than she was comfortable with.

When she unfolded them, the breeches weren't any better.

She might have lost some weight during the election, and the leather was supple, but these would be skin tight.

Groaning to herself, with a rough towel, Lessia rubbed off the last drops of water from the quick dip she'd taken in the creek behind Raine's house.

Her fingers absentmindedly traced the scars on her arm when she finished, whispering over the raised skin where the outline of the snake remained, only now in a slightly lighter shade than her skin.

As she peeked at it, her chest constricted.

While it no longer bound her to the king, it was a permanent reminder of what had happened a week ago.

Of the people she'd let down.

Of the people she'd hurt.

Of how her heart had broken.

Perhaps beyond repair.

A sob lodged itself in her throat, but she quickly started pulling on the trousers, refusing to allow herself to dwell on that darkness.

She didn't dare glance at herself in the mirror—didn't want to meet the hollow amber eyes she was sure would stare back at her.

And she definitely didn't want to see how ridiculous she looked in these leathers.

After years of hiding beneath layers, primarily to hide her tattoo, but perhaps also—the tiniest bit—to hide from the stares she gathered anyway, being half-

Fae, she wasn't used to wearing anything this exposing.

Even before her capture, living at home, she'd mostly worn human clothing.

Her mother loved to sew—one of the few things Lessia didn't have in common with her—and she'd created the most beautiful flowing dresses and clothing that allowed Lessia and Frelina to play in the forests behind their home without worrying about being restricted.

Rather than play or comfort, these leathers seemed to have been made for fighting.

Or at least training.

Patches covered the knees of the breeches, there were loops to hold daggers and other weapons by the waist, and the vest was padded over the heart with a material she was unfamiliar with.

Lessia fastened her two daggers into loops on each side of her hips and, after a glance at the room—which, honestly, was more of a cupboard with a small rounded window, a tiny bed, and a chair—opened the creaking door and walked down the short hallway leading into the living room.

Merrick and Raine stood by the vast bar extending across the entire back of the room, seemingly deep into a hushed conversation, each with a glass of clear liquid with a bluish tint.

An unlit fireplace occupied one of the corners. Even without the flames that she expected often burned bright within it, based on the soot covering the gray stone, the large windows on either side of it allowed enough light.

At least for now.

Wherever Midhrok was, it seemed to be early summer, and though evening had fallen, the sun still hovered over the cliffs leading down to the beach before the house.

Neither male turned around when she walked in, so Lessia strolled up to a large painting to her left.

It depicted a wyvern raised tall over the dark waters from which it emerged.

The wyvern faced four Fae, one of whom held in one of his outstretched hands something that sparkled in the darkness surrounding them.

Her finger trailed over the wyvern, and she wondered if this was Ydren, and whether Raine controlled it the way she had, or if he'd somehow formed a friendship with the terrifying creature.

"Is there anything to eat?"

Lessia jerked when Ardow's voice jarred her out of her thoughts, and when glass shattered a moment after, she spun around, her pulse quickening.

Her eyes collided with Merrick's, and hers widened when she realized blood dripped from his hand, staining the shards of glass beneath him.

And her heart beat even faster when Merrick continued to stare at her, his full lips parting as his eyes trailed down her body, and an urge to hide swept through her.

Tearing her eyes from his, she met Raine's gaze, and heat crept up her cheeks when she found his eyes glossed, the hand holding his cup trembling.

Raine quickly downed the drink in his hands, refilled the glass to the brim, and turned toward Ardow and Venko, who'd seated themselves on the large couch before the fireplace.

Clearing his throat, he responded. “There is bread and some meat. I don’t keep any extravagant food here.”

The tension in the room crawled over Lessia’s skin like Merrick’s magic liked to do, and she shook her head to clear it of Merrick’s and Raine’s strange behavior.

“Thank you. We do not need anything lavish,” she forced out when Ardow’s face betrayed his disappointment.

Raine stared at her for a moment too long, and the uneasiness within her grew with each silent second.

Finally, he lifted the cup to draw another gulp, and she shuffled behind the couch, trying to keep as much distance between them as possible, since she wasn’t certain if it was anger that flashed in his eyes when she met them.

Refilling his glass for the second time, Raine said quietly, “What you need and want are different things.”

Frowning, Lessia started to ask him what he meant, but Merrick interrupted her.

“Raine, why don’t you get us some food? Then we can discuss our next steps so we can get out of your hair.”

Nodding, Raine slipped out of the room, but not before staring at Lessia again, that glossiness in his eyes returning.

A shudder went through her as she slumped down in the chair beside the couch, and she pulled up her legs and wrapped her arms around them, trying to shield as much of her body as possible.

She was used to Fae staring, after her years on the streets of Vastala, but somehow, she’d expected a friend of Merrick’s not to be so blatant about it.

“It was his mate’s,” Merrick whispered as he took a seat in the chair beside her.

When Lessia frowned, he continued. "The clothing you're wearing. It was Solana's."

A knot formed in her gut. "She's... dead?"

Merrick nodded, a muscle in his jaw flexing. "A long time ago. He's not been the same since." He let out a sigh. "But who would be? Finding the soul that mirrors yours, only to lose them... I expect it's worse than never finding them at all."

The cracks in her heart widened when something worked its way into Merrick's voice, and she was certain from his tone that he hadn't found his mate yet.

It was loneliness, she decided, that sneaked into the deep rumble.

Lessia wasn't so sure that never finding them was preferable.

Half- or part-Fae didn't always have one, so she'd never been too concerned, but her mother was her father's mate, and she couldn't imagine them without each other.

Two pieces that fit so perfectly together—like two melodies harmonizing with each other or two hearts beating in the same rhythm.

Even her mother being human and her father a Fae of royal blood hadn't stopped them.

Apparently it was impossible for the male Fae to resist being close to their mate once they'd smelled them, the scent driving them to near madness unless they could be near—be with—their fate-bound.

Her father had caught one whiff of her mother and realized what she was.

And that was that.

When Raine returned with a tray of food, she realized she'd been staring at Merrick, and she busied herself with picking up small pieces of somewhat stale bread and popping them into her mouth, even though she wasn't very hungry.

She hadn't really been hungry since they left Ellow behind.

With so many emotions choking her, it felt as if it would be too much, stuffing anything else inside her body at this point.

"So what's the grand plan?" Raine kept his eyes on Merrick when he spoke. "You're taking on the rebels and then the Oakgards' Fae by yourselves?"

"No," Merrick snarled. "We need to—"

"We need to go to the rebels!" Ardow dared urge.

When Lessia released a frustrated breath, Ardow turned her way. "I know you disagree with our ways, but we all want the same thing. A free Havlands—free from the corrupt and evil men that rule it—allowing all species to live freely." He reached out a hand toward her. "We can convince them together, Lessia. Change their ways if that's what it takes for you to join us. You're of noble blood—they'd surely listen to you, especially the half-Fae."

The chuckle that left Merrick rattled her bones. "You stupid, ignorant human. If you tell the rebels what she is, they'll kill her on the spot. I don't know of all your plans, but if the rebels are planning on taking down Rioner and Loche"—Merrick cast her a glance when Lessia swallowed loudly at the mention of Loche—"do you truly think they'll let their families and friends live?"

Ardow's face flushed. "I have a high standing with them. I can convince them to spare her."

Venko laughed hollowly. "Such a high standing that they left you to rot in Loche's cellars."

Lessia couldn't stop herself from nodding.

He'd been unable to stop them coming after her during the election.

What could have changed now?

"Venko," Ardow started, but Venko turned away from him, pointing to one of the cups on the table, and when Raine nodded, he downed the entire thing.

"I don't want to hear it, Ardow. I don't want to be part of whatever you're planning on unleashing on Havlands. You lied to me, and I'm starting to believe you're lying to yourself," Venko rasped once he'd swallowed.

Ardow's face twisted, but he remained silent as he leaned back on the couch, eyes dropping when Venko moved farther away to refill his cup.

"Humans," Merrick grumbled under his breath as he also lifted a glass to his lips.

Lessia watched him swallow a small mouthful, his tense features softening slightly as he set it down again. "I have to admit, I've missed your liquor, Raine."

Raine grinned at Merrick as he swept his arm toward the bar. "There is more where that came from."

When he shifted his hazel eyes to hers, she was relieved no tears glistened in them, but she shook her head when he raised a brow and offered her a glass of blue-tinted liquid.

"Suit yourself." Raine shrugged and downed that cup as well. "I think you'll need it, based on what's to come."

"What's to come?" she echoed.

Raine inclined his head. "Those scoundrel rebels came by here a few weeks ago. Wanted to see if I or any of the others here wanted to join in."

"What did they say specifically?" she asked, her

fingers digging into the fabric of the seat. She ignored the mention of others. They hadn't seen anyone else on the short walk from the beach, but since they hadn't seen the entire island, that didn't mean there weren't more sad recluses residing here, perhaps drinking away their worries like she'd started to realize Raine did.

It didn't matter anyway.

"Oh, they said many things." Raine grinned, his eyes glossy again—not from tears, but from the fifth glass he'd downed while she spoke.

"Raine," Merrick snarled softly.

Raine crossed his arms over his chest. "You two are no fun."

Flying from her seat, Lessia stepped up so close the stench of alcohol wrapped around her, making her nose scrunch, and slammed a finger into his chest. "You might have given up on this world, but we haven't."

Her magic vibrated under her skin, and when Raine only yawned, it burst through her, her eyes brightening his face.

"Tell. Me. What. They. Said," she purred, every limb tingling from magic flowing freely through her veins.

Raine laughed, and a hiccup sneaked its way into the deep chuckle. "Oh, you're so young. That magic of yours —" He hiccuped again. "Doesn't work on me. But the gold is pretty. Better than other half-Fae tells that you have magic. I once met someone—"

Snarling, Lessia lifted her fist, but Merrick was faster, and his arm wrapped around her waist, pulling her flush against him.

"Don't," he hissed in her ear. "He'll only enjoy it."

When she tried turning her head to glare at Merrick,

he clasped her tighter against his chest, forcing her to keep facing forward.

"Raine," Merrick snarled over her head. "She's right. Unless you prefer we stay here forever, tell us what you know."

"You're truly no fun," Raine whined, but then he straightened.

"They told me they're planning an attack in the next few weeks and that if we weren't to join them, we should stay out of Vastala and Ellow." Raine shook his head. "As if any of us would return to Havlands," he scoffed.

She could hear Merrick grinding his teeth behind her before he asked, "What else?"

A deep sigh left Raine. "They've been working on this for decades. They have rebels all over Vastala and Ellow. Regular townsfolk who are preparing to launch the attack from the inside, while the shifters will attack from the sea. It will be quick. And ruthless."

Unease roiled in her gut.

The rebels were all over Havlands?

Her stomach dropped as she thought back to the past few months.

It made sense.

The attacks on the castle had been from within, not from a small group of rebels out at sea.

"When?" Merrick growled when she released a shaky breath.

Raine picked at his nails. "They were here a fortnight ago, so I assume in the next months or so? They weren't particularly eager to share once I laughed in their faces. And... I didn't care to ask too many questions."

Merrick released her, and when she spun around, his

eyes locked onto hers. “We don’t have much time, then. What do you want to do, Lessia?”

Her mouth fell open as she stared back at him.

He wanted her to decide?

She was in a room with two of the most lethal Fae warriors ever to set foot in Havlands.

A rebel with insight into the plans.

Even Venko knew Havlands better than she did, with all his travels.

But Merrick continued to look at only her.

Her heart began thumping in her chest as silence endured, and Merrick’s eyes briefly shifted down before continuing to burn into hers.

Lessia swallowed audibly.

She wanted to see her family.

She wanted to make things right with Loche.

She wanted to get Amalise and Kalia and the rest to safety.

But where was safety?

Even if they somehow managed to subdue the rebels, the threat of the Oakgards’ Fae who planned an attack still remained.

Her eyes flew across the room, trailing across Ardow’s still-flushed face, Venko’s glazed eyes, and Raine, who drank from yet another cup.

“We need to stand united if we’re going to take on an army of Fae,” she said, her voice quivering slightly. “We need to convince Rioner and L...” Lessia bit her lip when pain struck her heart. “And Loche,” she forced out.

Jaw twitching, Merrick nodded, his eyes encouraging her to go on.

Clenching her fists, she continued. “We need to see my father. He might be the only one who can convince

Rioner. And… and when we've done that, we need to return to Ellow."

Reaching out to grip her hand, Merrick dipped his chin. "Then that's what we'll do."

Merrick turned toward Raine. "Do you still have your eagles?"

Raine groaned as he shifted on the chair, his eyes half shut. "I do."

Squeezing her hand, Merrick said quietly, "We send for Alarin tonight. And I'll see if a few other friends might also answer a summons."

CHAPTER EIGHT

Lessia stared up at the ceiling of her small bedroom.

The moon cast silvery shadows that danced across the thin wooden beams, tangling with the firelight that reflected from the small lantern she'd placed on the floor.

The group had finished their drinks in silence after the decision to reach out to her father, and the liquor must have been strong because Venko first, then Ardow, fell asleep on the couch, their snores echoing through the living room.

A trail of drool twisted down Ardow's chin by the time Lessia quietly bid Merrick and Raine goodnight, and she'd hesitated for a moment, wondering if she should try to help him to bed.

Then she'd thought better of it.

Perhaps waking up stiff from the uncomfortable sleeping position and with what she expected to be a violent liquor sickness would shake some sense into him.

She couldn't understand why he wanted to return to the rebels so badly.

Ardow had never been violent.

From the moment she'd met him, she'd trusted him because of his gentle nature.

Even being part-Fae, he didn't have the temper she sometimes struggled so hard to rein in herself.

Dragging her hands down her face, she groaned.

She should have accepted the cup Raine had offered her.

There was no way she'd be able to sleep.

Not with all the thoughts that vied for dominance in her mind.

How her father would react when he found out.

How they'd get back to Ellow.

How they'd get Loche to see their side.

How she'd get the children to safety once more.

She held back another groan, wishing she could drag the worries from her mind as easily as she could pull at the blanket lying across her legs.

Lessia listened to the quiet house, and when no voices floated over the soft breathing and the wind tapping the windows, she sat up and pushed the cover off.

After picking up the lantern, she tiptoed to the door and eased it open.

The house was dim, and only the moon shone on Venko and Ardow, who still half sat and half lay on the couch.

But to the left, soft light flickered out of a cracked door.

Making her way over, she made sure her steps remained silent, having no energy to deal with the two men she could barely look at without rage fluttering inside her.

Not that she had the energy to deal with the other two males either.

Raine was nothing like she'd expected.

She wasn't sure what she'd hoped for when Merrick suggested they go here, but a barely functioning drunkard wasn't it.

And Merrick infuriated her to no end.

The grumpiness she'd gotten used to...

But she couldn't read him.

Didn't understand why he pushed her, then growled at her, his moods shifting within seconds.

Damned broody males.

A frustrated sigh escaped her as she slipped into the lit room.

It appeared to be some type of office.

A large wooden desk stood before a floor-to-ceiling bookshelf, with a square window to the right and more shelves lining the wall to the left.

Lessia shook her head at the half-empty bottles littering the racks as her bare feet sunk into a plush carpet.

She was no stranger to heartbreak.

She hadn't even been sure whether she had any pieces left to shatter after everything.

After her sister.

After the years in the king's cellar.

After having to keep it together for the broken souls she'd brought over from Vastala.

But after that last day with Loche...

A choked sound traveled up her throat as the memories invaded her mind.

Squeezing her eyes shut, she tried to push his betrayed face back into the dark abyss where she preferred to keep painful experiences locked up.

But it was pointless.

Her shoulders hunched at the shame that tore through her as she thought of what she'd done to him.

To them.

"He doesn't deserve your guilt."

Heart flying into her throat, she spun around.

Raine leaned against the windowsill, his eyes still dimmed but his back surprisingly straight as he sized her up.

"Get out of my head," she hissed.

"I'm not in your head." A corner of Raine's mouth lifted. "Right now."

She gritted her teeth as she turned back toward the shelf, eyeing the objects lying there so as not to have to look at the Fae behind her.

A beautiful dagger, curved and jagged in the same way Raine's swords were, lay in an intricately decorated mount, and she trailed her finger over the sharp edge.

"That was my mating gift to Solana."

She winced at the grief that laced every word of Raine's quiet declaration.

"It's beautiful," she murmured.

Turning around again, she leaned against the shelf, careful not to shift any other strange artifacts—a few crystals, shells, and other things of which she had no idea what they were.

"I heard she died. I'm sorry," Lessia said softly.

Raine's eyes snapped to the floor, his shoulders tensing. "She was killed."

Lessia remained quiet when Raine's mouth opened

and closed a few times, her chest aching at the agony playing across his features.

Loche hadn't even been her mate, and she could barely hear his name without wanting to fall into a heap on the floor.

She couldn't imagine the excruciating pain Raine must be in.

"I'm sorry," she whispered again when the silence became too loaded, the air so thick from sorrow she struggled to draw it into her lungs.

"She'd have liked you, I think." Raine walked up to the chair, sat down, and poured himself another glass. "She always fought for what she believed was right too."

Lessia's eyes trailed his hand as it shakily set down the flask on the desk, where stains, probably from the contents of the many bottles in the room, marred the beautifully carved wood.

"I saw what he did to you."

Her eyes flew to Raine's, and she couldn't stop herself from flinching, her arms wrapping around herself to keep whatever pieces were left together.

Raine shook his head as he observed her.

"So broken," he whispered before swallowing more of the liquid, a drop trickling down into his unkempt stubble. "You won't always be, though. Not like me..."

Lessia frowned as she hugged herself tighter.

She wasn't so sure of that.

Every breath she'd drawn since that last night in Ellow felt as if it might be her last.

Not just because of Loche.

While what happened between them had nearly killed her, there were so many others she needed to do right by.

So much damn guilt to live with.

Rubbing his eyes, Raine continued. "When Solana died, so did I. I'm merely a wraith in Fae form at this point. But you kept moving—kept walking. I saw how you saved Merrick and your friends. You didn't give up. You haven't given up."

"I had no choice," Lessia responded quietly.

Raine's head jerked up. "Of course you had a choice. Everything you've done in your young life has been the result of a choice, whether you believe it or not. I can see you think all things merely happened to you, but each heartbreak, every moment of pain, of happiness, of love, happened because of the paths you chose."

Tears burned behind her eyes. "I guess I chose all the wrong ones, then."

Raine slammed a hand against the desk. "There are no wrong paths! Dark ones, sure. I nearly drove myself mad thinking about the choices that led to Solana's death. But if I hadn't chosen them, I wouldn't have met her in the first place."

"Was it worth it? Meeting her just to lose her?"

When Raine remained quiet, Lessia wondered if she'd gone too far, but then he cleared his throat, tears glistening in his own eyes. "I will never regret meeting her. Not for all the pain in the world."

Lessia nodded, her eyes fixed on the carpet.

His words sounded so similar to the ones Amalise once had spoken about her lost love, pain emphasizing every letter.

She heard Raine lift the bottle yet again, the splash of more liquor hitting the glass.

"I wanted to thank you."

She whipped her head up at Raine's words.

Her forehead creased. “For what?”

“For saving Merrick.” Raine took another sip. “I wasn’t strong enough. Not after Solana.”

Shrugging, she kept Raine’s gaze. “He saved me too. Several times.”

A sad smile pulled at Raine’s lips. “Sounds like Merrick. Ever the martyr.”

“What do you mean?”

Raine leaned back in the chair, the low scrape of the legs dragging against wood reverberating through the room. “He swore that blood oath because of me. Well, me, Thissian, and Kerym.”

Her brows knitted. “They are the other two in your brotherhood?”

A raspy laugh left Raine. “Brotherhood?”

He shook his head before she could respond. “I guess you can call it that. And yes. We fought together for centuries. Grew up together. Bastards all of us, so we were raised in a soldiers’ camp. Probably for the best—we all harbored so much anger and resentment, so letting it out on the battlefield helped.”

“I didn’t know,” Lessia mumbled, her aching chest hollowing further when she thought of a young Merrick, the one with the face she’d seen when he’d slept after the attack.

He’d seemed so peaceful then.

But hearing this, she wondered if he’d ever seen peace.

She at least had years of a loving family, a warm home and bed, and as much safety as her father could muster while trying to keep them out of Rioner’s claws.

“I’m not surprised,” Raine said. “Merrick isn’t one for small talk.”

Despite everything, she giggled softly. "You don't say."

Raine's lips curled further. "He doesn't pity himself, even when he should."

"What happened to him?" Lessia asked, even though she was still unsure whether she really wanted to know.

Whether she could handle more devastating information.

Raine's smile fell. "The damned king, of course. We'd fought for Rioner's father for decades when he realized how strong we were. He started paying more attention to us. At first, we relished it. He made each of us commanders—let us roam as we pleased as long as we came when he called. But then he passed on the crown to his oldest son, and Rioner wasn't as... trusting."

Goose bumps peppered her arms when Raine's eyes darkened.

"He wanted something on us to ensure we'd never go against him. I'd found Solana by then, and Thissian and Kerym had also met their mates. Rioner took them from us. Kept them locked in that castle of his for us to pay off the debt he believed we owned the crown, for ensuring we had a roof over our heads growing up."

Raine's teeth slammed together. "We got worse at fighting after that. Nearly died several times because we couldn't focus when worrying about them. Merrick, being the fucking idiot he is, couldn't stand it, so he took it upon himself to try to set them free. He swore that damn blood oath right in front of us for Rioner to release them."

A growl rumbled through the room. "Rioner couldn't resist having the Death Whisperer at his beck and call. The strongest Fae in Havlands bound to him?"

A bitter scoff escaped Raine. "He kept his promise of setting them free, only to hunt us all down a few days later… He doesn't take well to anyone turning their back on him. So Solana and Thissian's and Kerym's mates paid the ultimate price."

Tears spilled down Lessia's cheeks when Raine's hand pressed against his chest, his eyes fixing on the swirling liquor in the glass in his hand.

Not just for Solana and the others who'd died.

But for Merrick, who'd sacrificed everything.

And for what?

"He blames himself, you know," Raine got out in a thick voice. "Even though none of us do. He believes he is as evil as the stories about him. That he's cursed. I think a small part of him was relieved to swear that blood oath—that he had a reason to keep everyone at arm's length. Live up to the reputation of the Death Whisperer."

"Wh-why would he ever think that?" Lessia stuttered.

Raine tilted his head. "Do you know what his magic truly is?"

She shook her head.

"While a vile name, the Death Whisperer rings true. Those whispers you hear? It's your mind opening up to the other side. It's the souls of those who passed before you speaking while they prepare to bring you over—to claim you as one of their own."

Lessia's brows knitted. "B-but that's not possible."

"And why is that?"

"Because…"

It couldn't be possible.

Could it?

"Because he is a mental Fae, is he not? I've never heard of such a power."

A wry twist tugged at Raine's lips. "Isn't the world how we perceive it? Isn't the world how we think and process and imagine? Isn't it our mind that shapes us, directs us, guides us toward our fates? Why wouldn't the afterlife be the same?"

Dread chilled her bones—like an icy wind sweeping through the room.

But not for fear of Merrick.

No.

For the fear of what he thought of himself.

She knew what it was like to hate her magic, believe she'd been gifted it because she was inherently evil.

I'd be lying if I said I didn't question mine for a long time. Truth be told, I still question it.

That's what Merrick had said to her on the ship.

Raine stretched his hands over his head and sighed. "Well, this was a tad heavy for a late-night conversation. I shall try to get my hour of sleep. You should probably do so as well. I heard Merrick muttering something about training in the morning before he went upstairs."

When Lessia nodded, Raine rose from the chair, and she followed him out of the room.

Venko and Ardow still snored on the couch, and with a final glance at them, she slipped into her brightly lit room.

Her brows snapped together when she glanced around, finding lanterns placed every few feet of the short walls, and two in the windowsill.

She strained her ears, but she couldn't hear anything besides Raine's thudding footsteps as he stomped around the room next to hers.

Releasing a deep breath, she slipped into the bed.

He might wield death magic, but Merrick was no Death Whisperer.

He wasn't evil.

And if he wasn't...

Perhaps neither was she.

CHAPTER NINE

Lessia questioned her conviction that Merrick wasn't evil when he stormed into her room at dawn, after she'd only gotten a few hours of sleep, and barked at her to "get out of the damned bed."

With a yawn, she dragged her tired body out of the warm sheets.

While small, she thought it might have been the most comfortable bed she'd ever slept in.

Or perhaps anything was better than the rigid cots on Venko's ship.

She winced when her back ached at the memory of the hard planks, and bile burned in her throat when the smell that seemed to permeate every inch of the cramped cabin, making her eyes tear every morning when she opened them, stung her nostrils.

Scrunching her nose, she pushed the memory away, and after rummaging around the room for a hairbrush—and finding none—Lessia ran her fingers through her tangled hair and straightened her leathers.

She'd slept in them, since Raine hadn't offered her a nightshirt and there was no way she'd sleep undressed.

Not with Merrick's penchant for slamming open her door anytime it pleased him.

Making her way into the kitchen, Lessia found all the men standing around the tall island in the middle of the room, steaming cups of coffee in their hands, although when she passed Raine to get her own, she suspected his cup was laced with something stronger, judging from the fumes wafting over her.

As she took a sip, she couldn't stop a flinch from flitting over her face when the scalding liquid hit her tongue, and she slammed the mug down on the island harder than she'd intended, all heads snapping her way at the loud thud.

Trying to stop the heat threatening to flush her face, she offered them a weak smile. "So what's the plan today?"

Her words came out clipped, but she tried to attribute it to morning grouchiness, not the simmering rage that seemed to want to take over every time she met Ardow's remorseful eyes.

"I sent for Alarin last night." Merrick's eyes lingered on the hands she'd clenched atop the wooden countertop before he continued. "I've asked him to meet me, so we'll need to wait for his response."

Lessia swallowed.

She wasn't sure if she was ready to face her father.

Even if Merrick suspected that he knew something was amiss when he met her, she wasn't sure how he'd react if she undid the magic that made him forget her.

If he found out what she'd done...

Not just to Frelina—even if the incident wasn't as severe as she'd believed—but to him...

To her mother.

For a moment, she wondered if it was best to leave it be.

But then her mother's kind face, her father's deep laugh, and Frelina's teasing fought through the darkness in her mind.

She could have that again.

Have her mother braid her hair.

Join her sister on rides in the forests behind their home.

Train with her father like she did with Merrick.

She fought for the breath she'd tried to draw when dread tightened her chest.

She could have that again.

But first, they'd need to find a way for Havlands to withstand the threats it faced.

Make sure there would be a home for her to return to.

Lessia squared her shoulders when she met Merrick's eyes again.

She'd have to be strong for them.

And for the family she'd left behind in Ellow.

Merrick's chin dipped an inch as he eyed her, and that feeling—the feeling that he understood her better than anyone—caused a sense of awareness to prickle over her skin.

Rubbing her arms, she fixed her gaze on the slightly swaying Raine when Merrick spoke again. "I also sent eagles to Kerym and Thissian."

Ardow's eyes widened. "The Siphon Twins? I thought they'd left this realm."

Raine broke in. "They have. They won't come,

Merrick. Last I heard, they tried to get as far away from here as possible."

"Siphon Twins?" Venko asked.

Lessia shot him a grateful look.

The nickname sounded vaguely familiar, but she knew little about the warriors Merrick had fought beside.

Only that the four of them were absolutely lethal.

"They drain the emotions—the energy—of others, making themselves stronger." A chilling smile spread across Raine's face, making Lessia question her wish to know more about them. "People think Merrick is terrifying, but it's those two that you should have nightmares about."

Venko clenched his jaw as his eyes shifted down, and he murmured something incomprehensible.

Lessia didn't blame him—they didn't sound like Fae she'd want to encounter if she didn't have to.

"Why did you ask them to come?" Ardow asked with eyes fixed on the cowering Venko.

Merrick sighed. "We need anyone we can convince on our side. If we're to try to convince Loche and Rioner, we need numbers—as many as we can to make them stop and listen."

Reaching over the table for a nearly empty bottle, Raine shook his head, his reddish hair flying around his face. "I told you they won't answer the call."

"Then so be it," Merrick snarled.

When Raine rolled his eyes, Merrick slammed his hand down on the table. "We used to face these threats with a smile, Raine. We used to believe in protecting our people. Doing what's right. Do you think these

Oakgards' Fae will stop at Havlands? They'll come here too."

Raine shrugged, an infuriating lazy smile that reminded her too much of Loche spreading across his face. "Ydren will keep them out. Besides, the others here have some tricks up their sleeves, should it come to that. We can protect our sanctuary."

The anger boiling inside Lessia turned hotter at Raine's indifferent tone, and she couldn't stop herself from hissing "Your *sanctuary*? From what I can tell, this is merely a hiding spot for cowards and drunkards. I used to savor the stories about you growing up! You used to be a hero, and now you're nothing more than a bitter shell."

"Look at you fighting back." Raine grinned at her, the smile a little lopsided from finishing yet another cup. "If you survive this, come back in a few centuries, and we'll talk about cowards."

Her nostrils flared as she bore her eyes into his hazel ones, which seemed almost green now, turning lighter from the alcohol perhaps. "If I survive this, I'll never go anywhere near you again."

"Thank gods." Raine lifted his cup toward her. "You're quite irritating."

"Raine," Merrick warned in a low voice.

"And you're a coward," she snarled back, her pulse thundering in her veins.

"Perhaps. But there are more of them in this room. Aren't there?" Raine raised his brows as he shot a glance at the seething Merrick.

Leaning over the table, she opened her mouth to argue, but then Merrick flew from his spot, and his hand slipped across her face, silencing her.

Dragging her backward so forcefully she stumbled into his chest, he growled at Raine, "That's enough."

Raine winked at her. "Don't tell me I didn't warn you."

She shook from restrained anger, her entire body itching to charge at him.

"Save your energy for training. Raine has offered to help us, and since he's drunk about ten of those cups already, you might even get a hit in," Merrick hissed into her ear.

Shaking her head, she pushed against him, but when Merrick kept his hand over her mouth and continued to drag her toward the door, she didn't think.

Lessia bit into it as hard as she could until the taste of iron flooded her mouth.

"Fuck!"

When Merrick dropped his hand, she spun around and stormed out of the house, her body buzzing with energy and heart pounding so hard she didn't hear if anyone called out for her.

CHAPTER TEN

She didn't stop running until she reached the shoreline, where the crystal-blue sea mocked her with its tranquility.

Not even a stupid wave ruffled the glassy surface, and no damned cloud floated across the cerulean sky.

Completely in contrast to the storm that raged within her.

Panting, Lessia finally slowed to a stop when water lapped her feet, and she realized she hadn't put shoes on before bolting out of the house.

Gods, that made her even more furious.

Her head spun—the anger coursing through her causing her body to thrum with energy and warmth to flood her blood, making it feel as if it were blistering through her veins.

Lessia flexed her hands as she stared out over the sea, barely able to remain still from the emotions pounding through her body, and she didn't even flinch when Ydren popped her head through the calm surface.

As she met the sea wyvern's glittering eyes and Ydren began swimming toward her, Lessia's lips lifted into a warning snarl.

There wasn't room for fear within her.

She was done being scared of damned creatures.

And... damned males.

Rushes of clear torrents dripped off the wyvern's long neck as she closed the distance to the shoreline and towered over Lessia, casting long shadows over the white beach.

"Not another inch," Lessia hissed between her teeth. "I won't warn you again."

The wyvern tilted her large head, her purple scales reflecting the morning sun as she eyed Lessia.

But even though her spiked tail lashed the water, Ydren slowed to a stop, head still cocked to the side and eyes firmly locked with Lessia's.

With magic buzzing in her ears, Lessia glared right back at her.

But there wasn't anger, or even fear, in the wyvern's eyes as she continued to meet them.

Something else brimmed in the violet gaze.

Something that made Lessia swallow audibly as the pressure she'd gotten so used to in her chest tightened, driving some of the rage away and replacing it with the same feeling reflecting in Ydren's eyes.

"You're lonely," she whispered.

Ydren blinked, her head dipping for a moment.

Drawing a few deep breaths, Lessia tried to soothe the emotions tangling inside her—tried to push down the anger, the sense of loneliness, and whatever other emotions she struggled to identify within her.

But filling her lungs did nothing to calm the energy sparking through every nerve.

She frowned as she glanced down at her feet, finding them shaking with held-back vigor, then to her tightly clenched hands and taut muscles.

What was happening to her?

When Ydren let out a low growl, her eyes flew up to find that the wyvern—despite her warning—had moved even closer.

Ydren's warm breaths mingled with the mild breeze blowing through Lessia's hair, and the wyvern's eyes were glossed, a sheen covering the deep purple as she cocked her neck.

But as the wyvern's snout nudged her, it didn't fill Lessia with fear.

Instead, her own eyes misted with tears.

Clenching her jaw to stop them from spilling down her cheeks, Lessia got out, "I am lonely, too, sometimes."

Most of the time.

Especially now.

When there was too much weight on her shoulders.

Too much she needed to do to make everything right again.

Ydren inclined her head and nudged her again.

"I miss my friends and family," Lessia croaked as the pressure in her chest nearly stole her breath. "I miss them so much. I-I don't know how to save them. I… I don't know if I can."

She did miss them so damned much.

She wasn't just angry at Ardow…

Or even at herself.

She was angry because she'd finally felt that sense of

home she'd craved for a small moment—barely a day—during the election...

And then it had been ripped away from her the same way it had that day when she hurt Frelina.

And now?

She wasn't sure how to get it back.

A large tear rolled down the wyvern's sparkling scales and splashed onto Lessia's shoulder.

She hesitantly lifted a hand, and after meeting Ydren's sorrowful eyes, Lessia placed it on the wyvern's snout.

Pressing into it, Ydren let out another muted sound, her broad chest rumbling softly.

"Do you miss your family as well?" Lessia murmured as she stroked the surprisingly soft scales.

A cry worked its way through the wyvern's throat, each note striking Lessia's cracked heart.

"I'm sorry," she whispered.

She had no idea how Ydren had ended up here.

From what she had read, the wyverns had left a long time ago, for somewhere far, far away.

Ydren butted her hand, another tear spattering onto the sand by Lessia's feet.

They stood like that for a moment, quiet in their sorrows, until footsteps reached Lessia's ears.

With a jerk, Ydren flew backward, sending a wave of water over Lessia as she dove deep into the sea, leaving large ripples on the calm surface, which twisted the sun's reflection.

Drenched and with that strange energy still flushing her skin, she spun around.

Merrick stalked toward her, sand whipping around his boots and dark eyes flashing, and she quickly averted hers, snagging on the small bandage wrapped around his hand.

Despite the furiousness of his gait, a smile tugged at her lips at the sight.

He deserved it.

But when she felt the rage simmering in the air, she quickly bit it down.

Best not to rile him up further.

"Most people take off their clothes to bathe," he growled.

Her eyes clashed with his, and when she noted his furiously lowered brows, she squared her shoulders, forcing back a wince when the wet tunic shifted uncomfortably as she did so.

"Are you trying to get me undressed?" she taunted, ignoring the small voice in her mind warning her that she'd just decided not to agitate him more.

A vein throbbed by his temple. "If I were, you'd already be splayed out on the sand beneath me, begging me to join you."

He...

What?

Heat flooded her face, and she groaned to herself when he lifted a silver brow.

"Whatever you need to tell yourself," she forced out, using every ounce of willpower within her to keep meeting his eyes.

The corner of Merrick's mouth twitched, and she sighed again as the smile she'd repressed earlier pulled her lips upward.

A low chuckle left Merrick when she lost the battle to keep them down, and she couldn't stop a muffled laugh from escaping her as they continued to stare at each other.

She shook her head as more laughter bubbled up.

Stupid Fae.

She wanted to be furious at him.

Not laugh.

Merrick lifted his wrapped hand. "Don't worry, I'm aware."

She could smell the iron staining the white bandage, and when an ember of guilt clawed its way into her chest, her lips finally dropped.

Wincing, Lessia took a step toward him. "I'm sorry. I don't know what came over me."

She'd been so damned angry at Raine.

And when Merrick tried to keep her quiet...

Merrick offered her a crooked smile. "Not many have managed to draw blood from the Death Whisperer. You should be proud."

More shame tore through her.

After what Raine told her last night...

She hated that he called himself the Death Whisperer.

He was so much more.

But she didn't know what to say.

Didn't have the words to tell him that's not how she saw him.

Not anymore.

Merrick's smile fell as well as he studied her, his gaze narrowing as it swept over her face, down to the hands she'd begun twisting.

Lessia opened her mouth to say something—anything—but no words left her lips as Merrick's eyes snapped back to hers.

The air grew heavy, the wind dying down around them, and the intensity of their locked gazes became too much.

She didn't understand the indignation swirling in his darkness, why a crease formed between his pearly brows, why his jaw locked and unlocked.

When a shiver of worry danced across her shoulders, she glanced down at her feet, the warning from earlier not to anger him echoing in her mind.

Merrick finally cleared his throat as she stared at the sand seeping between her toes. "The others are on their way down to train. You should probably get some boots. Raine fights dirty, and he'd not hesitate to stomp on them if it came to that."

With a quick nod, Lessia started walking back to the cabin, unable to meet Merrick's eyes again—even when she could feel his lethal presence all around her as she passed him.

CHAPTER ELEVEN

When Lessia returned to the beach with her worn boots securely laced up, that nagging feeling still unsettled her, and it didn't help when all four males stared at her as she made her way through two dunes.

She picked at the raised scars on her arm as she approached them, avoiding Merrick's gaze when its warmth followed her hand's movement before it landed on her face.

Instead, she kept her eyes on Venko, who sat in the sand, head tilted toward the sun as he ignored Ardow hovering beside him.

"You're not training?" she greeted them as she approached.

Venko shook his head. "I am a tradesman, no soldier."

"V, you should r—" Ardow started, but Venko interrupted him.

"No! You dragged me into something I didn't sign up

for. You're keeping me as a prisoner, Ardow! I will not engage in this silly quest for revenge nor attempt to save our world when it's clearly beyond saving. I will not fight, so I do not need to learn anything."

Venko's eyes landed on Lessia's as he spoke. "Neither should you. Do you think you can go up against rebels *and* all of these Oakgards' Fae, Lessia? It is sure death. We should get out of this realm, try to find somewhere safe to hide out."

"Look at that. I'm clearly not the only coward here," Raine drawled as he slumped down in the sand beside Venko, angling his already flushed face so that the rays hit it fully. "He's right, you know. You should take a page from my book. Life is ever so much easier when you stop caring."

"You—" Lessia seethed but quieted when Merrick's scent flooded her nose and the warmth of his body brushed her back.

She didn't want to risk biting him again.

"Just keep your damned mouth shut, will you?" Merrick snarled over her shoulder.

Something within her whirred when Merrick's hand landed on her back, and for a moment, she wondered whether the rushing in her ears was his whispers, but then she realized it was her own rage crashing through her like a tidal wave.

"If I didn't know better, I'd think you scared, Raine," Merrick taunted, and she could sense the smirk that must have twisted his features.

"Ah, you got me! Seems like it's going around. All of us scared and broken and ever so lonely..." Raine laughed.

A growl boomed through Merrick, and he stepped

around Lessia to drag Raine to his feet, their faces barely an inch apart as he glowered at him. “Enough. Let’s settle this like we used to.”

Raine shrugged, nearly hanging limp off the sand from Merrick lifting him. “Care to make a wager?”

Merrick’s eyes flitted between his before he shook his head. “You know you’ll lose. You always lose.”

The grin Raine flashed sent a chill down Lessia’s back. “We’ll see about that.”

Merrick bared his sharp teeth at him before turning toward Lessia and barking, “Watch. You might learn something.”

Brows pulling, Lessia stared after the two Fae warriors as they stomped a few feet away, the fury rolling off Merrick’s shoulders as clear as the liquor Raine clung to like a newborn to its mother.

Raine was apparently trying to agitate Merrick, but she didn’t understand why.

The way he’d spoken about him last night had been with love.

But whatever was happening now definitely wasn’t love.

Or even friendship.

At least not the friendships she was used to.

“Come on, let’s sit over there.” Ardow’s fingers wrapped around her wrist, and she almost pulled out of his grasp, ready to snap at him, until she accidentally met his eyes.

Pain touched his brown gaze as it traveled to Venko, who’d shuffled backward toward one of the taller dunes by the edge of the beach—where the tall grass met the white sand—and a knot formed in her gut at the emptiness of his eyes when he met hers again.

With a sigh, she let Ardow pull her with him to sit next to the merchant.

She could taste the hurt in the air when Venko moved to sit on her side, and Lessia fixed her gaze ahead, where Merrick and Raine now circled each other, each with a terrifying expression contorting his face.

As Merrick reached for the sword on his back, her eyes trailed the bright reflection bouncing off it.

She wasn't surprised they trained with real weapons. Merrick had refused to let her train with wooden weapons in Ellow.

Apparently the wood would throw her off.

She knew Fae healed quickly, but still… that blade was sharp.

Lessia shook her head as Raine pulled out a small flask from his tunic. "Shall we make this more fun?"

Only the slightest downward movement of his mouth betrayed Merrick's second of hesitation.

It was so fast that Lessia was certain neither Venko nor Ardow had noticed.

But the grin on Raine's face told her he hadn't missed it.

"We can do it the easy way if you're out of shape." Raine winked.

"Just give it to me," Merrick hissed.

When Raine offered him the shimmering bottle, he swiped it out of his hand and swallowed something red-tinted so quickly that his movements almost blurred.

"What was that?" Ardow breathed.

Hushing him, she observed Merrick closely as he licked his lips, letting his tongue drag across the top row's canines while Raine took a sip—a much smaller one than what Merrick had downed.

The Fae stared at each other for a moment.

Then Merrick's shoulders grew taut, and Raine's features twisted.

Not with anger, but...

Pain.

Whatever was in that drink was causing them pain.

She wasn't sure if the men on either side of her realized, but she could see it in every hard line of Merrick's face, in the way his boot-clad feet sunk into the sand, in the slight tremble of his hand as it reached for the sword once more...

Despite the warm day, a biting freeze crawled over her skin.

Was this how they had been trained growing up?

"Sh-shall we?" Raine stuttered as he unsheathed the twin blades.

When Merrick's chin dipped, both males leaped.

Lessia's eyes widened as Raine rushed forward, those lethal blades glittering in the sun as he charged Merrick head-on.

Merrick didn't even lift his sword as he spun around, sand spurting around his feet, and easily shifted out of the way of Raine's massive body and sharp steel.

After letting out a roar as he skidded to a stop in the sand, Raine's eyes slitted as he faced Merrick again.

Without even drawing a breath, Raine lunged, thrusting both blades fiercely before him, but Merrick sprang into the air, his body seemingly flying for a moment before he landed behind the crimson-haired Fae.

Raine nearly fell on his face from the force of his own attack, and he remained upright only because he managed to use one of his swords as a cane, the blade splitting through the sand beneath him.

A huffed laugh left Merrick as he flipped the sword in his hand, watching Raine breathing raggedly as he regained his balance. "That's all you got?"

A snarl was the only warning of Raine's attack.

Flying forward, he anticipated Merrick's shift to the left, and sparks showered the sand as Merrick was forced to parry the blows from Raine's curved weapons.

Lessia's heart pounded as she watched the two males fight each other, their sharp breaths mingling with the clash of steel and occasional groan, either from getting a hit in or from whatever they'd ingested.

She took a shallow breath when the Fae males continued their dance of death, moving with inhuman swiftness and force, whipping up sand and sea as they spun, twirled, and collided.

Raine relied on brute force, using his weight and body mass to his advantage as he tried to strike wherever he could reach—again and again.

It was terrifying, and she knew without a doubt she wouldn't withstand a second in a duel with him.

But Merrick...

Merrick was something else.

He moved with a skill she'd never seen before.

A skill she'd probably never see again.

It was as if he was truly dancing.

His every movement was agile and calculated, and his weight expertly shifted with every step, keeping him steady on the uneven sand as he struck back with lightning-fast movements.

Still, a sheen of sweat covered his forehead when Raine forced him to face the huddled group, and when she met his eyes and flickers of pain burned bright in them, she pushed her hands into the sand to get up, the energy from before fueling her.

Merrick's gaze flew to hers.

That was all it took.

The hardness usually masking his face warped into agony as the hilt of Raine's sword slammed into the back of his head, and the silver-haired Fae stumbled a step forward.

She cried out when Raine lifted the other sword, the light dancing over his wicked smile making him seem like a madman.

Merrick's eyes remained locked with hers, his sword hanging limp by his side.

"No!" she screamed, fear slithering along her spine at the cruel twist of Raine's mouth as he let the blade fall.

Then Merrick grinned.

A crimson-stained, lethal grin that did nothing to drive away the dread within her.

On the contrary, frost settled in her bones at the shadows deepening his eyes.

Something flickered across his features as he took her in, but then he tore his gaze from hers, and with a speed that should be unlawful, he threw himself to the side, out of the way of Raine's second strike.

Lessia blinked as Merrick crouched low, taking out Raine's legs with one of his own, so the latter fell to the sand with a loud thud.

After disarming him with one hand while the other held his ruby-decorated sword steady by his throat, Merrick said quietly, "I told you you'd lose."

Raine only grunted, but he took the hand Merrick offered him, and after brushing some sand off his clothes, he pulled out another flask—the one she'd seen yesterday—and took a long sip.

"I forgot how much this shit hurts," Raine muttered as he waved the flask Merrick's way.

Ignoring him, Merrick's eyes sliced to hers again, and she realized she was shaking when they flew over her body, his mouth tightening into a thin line.

As Merrick stalked up to her, she tried to lock down her uncooperative muscles.

But it was useless, and she was certain he noticed when his eyes flicked down for a second before he nodded toward the daggers dangling from her waistband as he reached her. "Your turn."

Lessia reached for them with trembling hands, but she mustn't have moved fast enough for him, as Merrick swiftly sheathed his sword and slipped them out of her belt.

Shoving them into her hands, he stated, "You're scared of me."

She thought of arguing, but she wasn't sure if her voice would betray her, so instead, she pressed her lips together as she tried to muster up a glare.

She wasn't actually scared of Merrick...

She was scared of having to fight those like him.

Anyone with even half his skill would take her out in mere seconds.

Merrick's tongue flicked one of his canines as he nodded. "You should be."

Without sparing Venko or Ardow a look, he gestured for her to follow him, and Lessia didn't dare glance at them, either, as she staggered after him.

She might just run back to Raine's cabin and hide if she also saw fear in their eyes.

CHAPTER TWELVE

"What was it you drank?"

Lessia's voice was still shakier than she'd like, but she tried to push the apprehension away as she trailed a step behind Merrick down toward the shoreline where he and Raine had fought.

"You're not having any, so you don't have to worry." Merrick's tone was his usual surly one, but she didn't miss how he stiffened, perhaps still feeling the effects of the liquid.

A raspy voice broke in. "The little Faeling can't handle some pain? How ever is she going to save the realm?"

Lessia barreled into Merrick when he halted, her nose filling with his wild, untamed scent as it pressed against his leather tunic.

Pushing off him, she glared at Raine. "I know Fae males can't handle a blow to their pride, but can you please just shut your mouth?"

Raine threw his head back and cackled, and disgust pricked her skin at the drops of liquor running down his stubbled chin and the bloodshot eyes staring back at her when he lowered it again. "Training will be good for you. Put some of that anger to use. Even if you can't do it like us real fighters."

"Lessia," Merrick warned when she snapped her teeth at Raine.

"No!" She switched her glower to Merrick. "He's right! If I can't handle what you just did, I won't be able to handle whatever we'll face when we leave this stupid island."

Raine was right.

There must be a reason they trained like this.

And if she was to survive even a minute in battle, she needed to do everything she could during practice.

It wasn't like it would kill her.

Right?

"You have nothing to prove to him," Merrick said quietly. "We've trained for centuries. You're only just beginning."

She bore her eyes into his. "So when you started, you didn't do this?"

Merrick's silence told her enough.

Stalking over to Raine, she shot out a hand.

"Give it to me," she demanded.

"Lessia! What are you doing?" Ardow called out, and when she turned, she found him and Venko staring at her with wide eyes.

"I'm doing what I must, unlike you bastards," she hissed under her breath.

Merrick let out a shocked chuckle from her side, and damn if the sound of it didn't try to curl her own lips.

But she bit down the smile, waved dismissively at Ardow, who'd begun approaching her, and snarled at Raine, "What are you waiting for?"

The Fae grinned at her and plucked the small vial from his tunic.

But before she could grab it, Merrick yanked it from his grip with one hand, the other wrapping around her arm and pulling her across the beach until even Raine couldn't make out his words.

"This is no child's play." Merrick's stare burned so hot across her face she couldn't stop her eyes from rising to meet his, and some of the conviction that she needed to do this wavered at the stark silver flecks whirling in his gaze.

As he relieved her of one of her daggers and placed the small bottle in her hand, he closed his own around her fingers. "I know you can handle pain, but you should know what you're getting yourself into. Rioner's father developed this so we could fight Fae that could quell our magic—fight them while injured and near crazy from agony. So that nothing could stop us from winning."

Lessia swallowed as she glanced from the red-hued liquid in her hand to Merrick's eyes.

But she couldn't stop the small voice inside her from reminding her how the physical pain during those years in Rioner's cellars had silenced the guilt, the fear, and the terror from being stuck within her own mind.

It had been a relief whenever the guards who preferred physical torture showed up.

A reprieve from the emotional pain threatening to break her.

She winced as Loche's face flashed in her mind.

The hate in his gray eyes.

The disgust as he watched her on her knees, his name falling from her mouth.

With her eyes on Merrick's, she uncorked the vial and lifted it to her lips.

As the surprisingly warm liquid trickled down her throat, a muscle in Merrick's jaw twitched, and his whispers joined the wind whipping across the beach.

Lessia narrowed her eyes at him as she wiped her mouth, but the whispers continued, charging the air with magic, and the hair on the back of her neck rose as the tendrils caressed her bare arms.

It wasn't until she rubbed them that Merrick's eyes snapped down, his hands clenching, and the whispers slowly faded.

"What are you doing?" she asked when his forehead creased, his fingers continuing to flex by his sides.

"What happened in that room with Loche?" Merrick gritted.

It was like taking a punch to the gut.

Lessia opened her mouth to tell him to shut his mouth.

Tell him she couldn't speak of it.

Not now.

Not yet.

Perhaps not ever.

But instead of the words she'd intended, a gasp caught in her throat.

Something warm and sticky flooded her veins.

Not like the oily sensation of Merrick's magic.

No.

It was more like old honey that clogged every pore, every nerve, every blood vessel, muting any ounce of magic inside her.

Then, white-hot pain tore through her skull.

Lessia dropped the vial and dagger, pressing her hands to her face as a cry broke through the air.

It sounded as if from far away, and she wasn't certain whether it was actually her own when it bounced within her mind.

It got worse.

Blinding pangs of agony shot out from her head into her arms, her legs, her gut, her back, until she wasn't sure whether the world around her still existed.

She tried to focus on the air she could feel flowing into her lungs.

On the salt she could taste on her tongue.

On the presence beside her—a silhouette in the darkness that was this painful reality.

She drew another breath.

Focus, she screamed at herself—out loud or in her head, she didn't know—as her eyes tracked the shadow's movements.

Something pulled her toward it.

Told her it was there to help.

Her eyes trailed the flickers of silver sparking around the figure.

It looked like one of the angels she'd seen in her father's books growing up.

As if one of them had left the pages and now was here with her in the pit of agony.

Another breath made its way into her body.

The pain didn't ease, but with every breath flowing into her lungs, she began to feel the world again.

The sand under her feet.

The wind brushing her skin.

Merrick's voice softly calling her name.

"Lessia."

She pried her eyes open, finding him crouched before her.

"H—" she tried, but she needed to suck in one more breath against another wave of pain.

"It's not real," Merrick said.

Right.

She'd drunk something.

She drew another breath.

A red vial.

Another breath.

She'd chosen to do this.

Another breath.

Lessia managed to straighten her hunched back.

While the pain was still there, those pangs still shocking her body, when she blinked, she could take in the beach again.

Merrick was still on his knees before her.

Raine was a few yards away, a worried expression marring his drunk face.

Venko and Ardow had also inched closer, identical looks of fear deforming their features.

"G-give me." Lessia's eyes dropped to the dagger in the sand, then to the one in Merrick's hand. "P-please."

He seemed as if he was about to argue, but then a low rumble vibrated in his chest, and he did what she asked, although he shoved the daggers harder into her open hands than he needed to.

Squeezing the hilts, Lessia drew more air through her nose.

It helped, gripping something—had her focus on something other than the pain.

Placing her feet a few inches wider, she scowled at Merrick. "Go on."

Merrick's pearly hair flew around his face as he shook it, another growl rolling through him, but he unsheathed his sword.

She didn't wait for a signal to start.

Flying forward, Lessia focused every part of her mind on Merrick's unguarded gut.

But as he'd done with Raine, he sidestepped her.

"Good," he rasped into her ear, tapping her back with his sword. "But not good enough."

She hissed through her teeth as she spun around, forcing her mind to ignore yet another jolt of pain, but found Merrick's sword pointed at her heart.

"Stay behind your daggers at all times," he growled at her, his face an inch from hers. "You're making it too easy."

Sweat stung her eyes, but she charged again, ensuring her daggers moved first.

Merrick danced around her, his sword lining up with her gut, the edges of it scraping against her arms as she spun again.

And again.

When she cried with frustration, Merrick's lips brushed her ear. "Switch up your pace. If you use the same tactic, your enemy will learn your approach from the first blow."

Lessia snapped her teeth together, and before she could overthink, she crouched, crying out when it made the pain in her head worse but managing to shove one of the hilts into Merrick's knee.

When he swayed, she shot up, both daggers raised and ready to sink into his muscled torso.

She hesitated for only a second.

Still, Merrick's free hand clasped her wrists, pulling her flush against him before she could finish what she'd started.

Glaring down at her, he hissed, "You do not falter. Ever! It's fight, flight, or die! That second just killed you!"

Her nostrils flared as she glared back at him, a blood-red hue filling her eyes.

And when he released her wrists, she didn't hesitate.

She drove a dagger right into his shoulder.

A loud laugh burst across the beach behind them, and when she blinked and noticed Raine slamming his hands on his knees, she realized what she'd just done.

Lessia dropped the daggers as if she'd burned herself.

"I'm sorry!" she cried as she watched the blood trickle down Merrick's tunic and stain the white sand beneath them red.

Stumbling the step she needed to reach him, she pressed her hand against the wound.

"I'm so sorry," she whispered as the warm blood coated her palm.

"Look at me," Merrick said in a glacial voice.

No.

She couldn't.

What had she done?

She'd stabbed him, for gods' sake!

Overwhelming guilt—worse than she'd ever felt—chilled her blood, and she wanted nothing other than to be back in the king's cellars, taking whatever punishment they saw fit.

What was wrong with her?

"Lessia, look at me," Merrick rasped.

Her bottom lip trembled as she finally lifted her eyes.

But there was no anger in Merrick's gaze.

Instead, a grin brightened his face, and his eyes glittered as he said "Good."

His smirk widened when she stared at him with rounded eyes. "But you missed my heart."

CHAPTER THIRTEEN

Lessia sighed and rolled over on the bed when someone knocked on her door.

She'd spent the afternoon staring at the wall of her room as she tried to muster up any courage she could for what was to come and not let fear fester from the rebellion and the full-blown Fae war she expected they were to face.

After making sure Merrick was all right and stopping herself from stabbing Raine as well when he couldn't stop laughing at her, she'd left the males on the beach and returned to the cabin to hide in this room, the energy that had kept her moving this morning dwindling with every step she took on the snaking path.

"You need to speak to me." Ardow's eyes sought hers as he opened the door, slipped in, and thudded it shut behind him. "You need to, Lessia."

She was about to snarkily respond that she definitely didn't, but when that emptiness from earlier glossed his gaze, she made herself sit up and pat the mattress beside her.

She might be furious with Ardow...

But he was still her friend.

Perhaps if she tried to understand him instead of blaming him, she could get him to see that what he was doing was wrong.

The bed creaked as Ardow sat down and leaned against the wall, nervously pulling at the ill-fitting clothing Raine had given him.

While Ardow wasn't a small man by any means, he only had a fraction of Fae in him, and Merrick and Raine must have several inches on him.

Another surge of guilt swept over her.

Like her, Ardow was out of his depth here.

And he was all alone.

She had the—somewhat strange—friendship with Merrick.

And Venko would at least meet her eyes, even if they held doubt for what she was trying to achieve.

"Talk to me," she said when he continued pulling at the gray tunic.

"I know you... you disagree with me." Ardow grimaced when she nodded forcefully. "But please know, I only got involved because of how people like us are treated, Lessia. I need you to understand that."

"Ard..."

"Please let me finish, then you can judge me as much as you'd like," Ardow pleaded.

Flames of anger licked her veins, their constant presence becoming worryingly familiar, but she nodded, gripping the blanket tightly when her fingers twitched.

"I became part of the rebel movement before I met

you. As you know, I left my family at sixteen to try to help my father, as our land wasn't providing enough to sustain us and the workers my father employed. So I thought I'd go to the capital, find employment, and be able to send home some silvers for them so they could at least take a day off once in a while. That didn't work out. No one would employ me when I showed them my papers and they realized my grandfather was half-Fae. I couldn't even find anywhere to live... It was like the few coins I'd brought weren't good enough for the tavern owners to keep Fae under their roofs at night."

Lessia bowed her head, her eyes falling to her clasped hands.

She knew all this—had learned already, during the first days after meeting him, why Ardow had been so quick to approach her that first day on Asker.

It hadn't been only because he carried Fae heritage, but because he also was burdened by devastating guilt toward his family.

Although his was less warranted than hers.

Ardow hesitantly touched her knee, his voice growing stronger when she didn't swat it away. "I got drunk one night in the same tavern I met you, and some bastard started spewing shit about Fae, so I knocked him out in my frustration. Unfortunately, he had a whole group of men with him. After they'd nearly turned me into carrion and thrown me into the alley behind the tavern, a woman found me. She helped me onto a small boat, cleaned me up, and let me stay until I recovered. Whenever I was awake, she'd tell me stories. Stories about a united people, where Fae, humans, and shifters all worked together. I thought she'd just made them up to give me something else to think about other than my broken bones, but on the last day, she asked me if that world was something I'd like to be a part of."

Ardow sighed as he dragged a hand through his hair. "I said yes without hesitation. Over the next few years, I was slowly introduced to more and more of their plans. In exchange for me bringing on more recruits, they helped me get that shabby apartment I had when we met, and they even sent funds to my family to help them get back on their feet. And once they were certain I could be trusted, I got to meet their leader. She is amazing, Lessia. A visionary. She believes what we believe—wants what we want! I know you'd love her if you met her."

Lessia stopped herself from rolling her eyes.

She wasn't so confident of that.

Someone who'd willingly sacrifice innocent people didn't sound like someone she'd call a friend.

But she swallowed her argument and asked, "Who is she?"

Ardow squeezed her knee. "She is a shifter. I've never seen her real form. Honestly, I don't think many have. But she has a vision for a world where Ellow, Vastala, and Korina work together—with no borders separating us. She has this whole plan for how it'll all work—for how the people will choose their rightful leaders, and all will thrive under a new rule. It's exactly what we used to dream of, don't you remember?"

Lessia clenched her jaw.

They had dreamed of that.

On nights where they'd sipped on wine before the fireplace in their living room, they'd let themselves dream up a world where their loved ones were with them, where no one had to hide, where Amalise's lover was alive and Lessia hadn't hurt her family beyond repair.

But nowhere in that dream had innocent people had to die for it to be true.

"But you would spill blood—the blood of people we know... of children... to achieve it? Did you even consider our children? You've put them in harm's way now," Lessia said, her tone eerily similar to the lethally low one Merrick preferred to use.

Ardow's eyes flew down.

"We don't want to," he grumbled. "We will not harm those who join us, and we believe few will decide against becoming one of us when they realize just how many will stand against them otherwise. Especially once we've taken down their leaders..."

Ardow snapped his lips shut when she threw his hand off her knee.

She couldn't believe him.

Rioner she didn't particularly care what happened to.

Uncle or not.

But Loche...

"You haven't even given him a chance to stand by you!" Lessia snarled. "How do you know he wouldn't work with you? He believes in the same world we do."

"We tried!" Ardow raised his voice. "When he stopped taking the bribes, our leaders tried to reason with him, but he's too headstrong!"

"Try again!" Lessia glared at him. "I am sure he will listen if you explain."

Ardow's eyes narrowed. "Are you? He was ever so quick to throw you to the streets! You think we don't notice how you can't even hear his name without looking as if you've seen a ghost? What did he do when he found out your connection to the king? Tell me, did he listen to you?"

Her chest caved. "It wasn't like that..."

"It was. That *I* am sure of." Ardow threw his head back, his gaze flying to the wooden-beam-lined ceiling. "Lessia, we've been friends for a long time. I've heard you the past few days, and I agree that the planned attack is perhaps a bit hasty. I don't want to see blood spilled any more than you do, and I worry about Amalise and the rest as well. I am willing to speak to the rebels and try to stop it—try to find another way. But I am telling you, I don't think Loche will listen."

Pity pulled at his features when she flinched, even as she tried to stop her body from reacting.

"Lia," Ardow said softly. "You can talk to me."

"There is nothing to talk about." Her nostrils flared as she let the anger brimming under her skin wash away the hurt.

She was responsible for what happened.

She didn't deserve pity.

But she'd make it all right again.

"Please, just talk to me. I know how you're feeling," Ardow said as he glanced at the door.

"What happened between you and Venko?"

She doubted she'd find out much more than what she'd gathered from the merchant's hostile glares: that he and Ardow had been involved, that Ardow had lied to him, perhaps even worse than he'd lied to her.

But there was no way she'd speak about Loche.

Not just because it felt as if she would break apart every time his face appeared in her mind... but because she couldn't afford to shut down.

Not like Venko was doing.

Because if she did...

There was no way she'd have the strength to endure the challenges she suspected awaited.

"H-he just sneaked up on me," Ardow said shakily, and her eyes locked with his glazed ones. "I didn't mean to fall for him. He was only supposed to be our source in the election. But I did, Lessia. I fell hard. He's so different from anyone I've ever met."

Ardow cleared his throat. "I didn't want to lie to him, but it was too dangerous. Especially... especially with you there. I couldn't risk it. But I grew careless, and that last night... I was going to tell him everything, I swear! But then Loche's soldiers found us. And... you know the rest."

Lessia shook her head. "Ard. What have you gotten yourself into?"

Her eyes widened when a sob shook Ardow's body, and when his face scrunched, wetness touching his cheeks, she couldn't stop herself from crawling over and wrapping her arms around him.

She knew the pain gleaming in his eyes all too well.

What Ardow had done to Venko...

It wasn't so different from what she'd done to Loche.

Tears trickled down her arm as Ardow cried against her shoulder, and she hugged him tighter when he whispered, "I'm sorry, Lessia. I promise I want to make it right."

Resting her chin on his head, she whispered back, "We'll make it right together."

As his body shook against hers, she prayed that she could keep that promise.

CHAPTER FOURTEEN

She wiped her forehead as she walked beside Merrick and Raine up the small path from the beach.

They'd been training every day for a week, and while she'd not stabbed Merrick again, she'd gotten better at handling the Vincere—which she'd gathered was the name of the liquid Rioner's father had invented.

Not that Merrick had held her stabbing him against her.

On the contrary, he urged her daily to do it again.

But she couldn't.

Anger might be the only thing keeping her upright right now—especially with all the emotions draining her, thanks to waiting for her father's response, not knowing how Amalise and the rest were faring, and wondering how her family would react when she undid her magic...

But Merrick didn't deserve to be on the receiving end of it.

While she couldn't necessarily describe him as kind —not with how he growled and barked at her when she lost focus trying to withstand his or Raine's attacks—he at least didn't push her outside of training.

Not like Ardow, who, after that night when she'd let him sleep in her room like old times, hadn't stopped asking her about Loche and what happened in that room.

He believed she needed to "talk it out."

Relive the memories so that she could move past them.

As if her dreams at night weren't filled with cold gray eyes, stolen moments in a cave, and the shattering of her heart as a wooden door slammed shut behind her.

It had gotten to the point that Lessia flew up from bed every day at the first trickles of sunlight through her window, grabbed something to go from Raine's quickly emptying kitchen, and spent the morning running up and down the beach until Merrick and Raine showed up to continue painting her body black and blue every time they overpowered her.

She stretched her arms over her head, wincing at their soreness.

Each night, she'd stumble into bed, exhausted and with every limb aching.

Lessia sighed.

And they hadn't even begun incorporating their magic into training yet...

A gagging sound ripped Lessia from her thoughts, and when she glanced to the side, Raine was doubled over, his hands pushing into the tall dune beside them as he emptied his stomach onto the powdery sand.

Her nose scrunched when the harsh stench of alcohol

assaulted her senses, and she backed up a step as he continued retching.

Raine very unwillingly participated in her training, and even while circling her, he'd take sips from that beloved flask of his.

At least she wasn't in as bad a state as he was, she thought as she retreated farther to avoid getting sprayed by the droplets of his expulsions.

"Don't judge him too harshly."

Turning her head over her shoulder, she met Merrick's eyes, and warmth spread over her cheeks at the look in them. "I wasn't—"

"You were," Merrick said quietly.

Gripping her shoulders, he turned her back toward Raine, who'd sat down against the dune, panting as he scrambled to pull the cork on the flask and take another drag of it.

"He used to be one of the most powerful Fae in Havlands," Merrick whispered, his warm breath tickling her neck. "So powerful even Rioner's father didn't dare stand against him."

Stepping closer so his chest lined up with her back, Merrick continued, his voice barely carrying over the salty breeze. "No war, no torture, no pain could break him. That's love. That's what it does to you. To love someone and have them love you back... only to lose them..."

Lessia's breath caught in her throat when Merrick shuddered behind her.

"Did you... did you lose someone?" she whispered, keeping her eyes on Raine as he stuffed the flask into his sweat-stained tunic.

She wasn't sure if she'd be strong enough if she saw

Merrick's darkness fill with pain, like the pools of agony that were Raine's eyes whenever he saw her dressed in Solana's clothes.

A breeze traveled across her skin when Merrick hesitated.

It was quiet for so long that she would have suspected that Merrick had stormed off if his soft breaths didn't continue to drift through her hair.

"You can't lose someone if you've never had them," he finally responded.

A lump formed in her throat at the sorrow lacing his voice, and something brushed her senses, sending a prickling sensation across her skin.

Lessia bit back the question at the tip of her tongue, thankful for the screech that burst through the air, interrupting the strange silence.

She whipped her head up at the same time as Merrick stepped back, the coldness he left behind forcing her to stop herself from shivering.

An eagle soared through the air from the sea, circling a few times before it landed on Raine's outstretched arm.

Her eyes widened when she realized the feathers covering its body were the usual brown—like the eagles she'd seen in both Ellow and Vastala—but those lining its head were bright gold, shimmering in the afternoon sunlight.

Raine patted the eagle's wing before plucking a small white parchment tied to its leg.

"Looks like Alarin responded." Raine held out the letter to Merrick, who'd stalked up to him.

After reading it, Merrick rolled it up again, and she thought her blood might freeze to ice when he said, "They're coming here tomorrow."

Raine wiggled his brows. "Didn't trust you to come to his island?"

"He didn't say," Merrick responded.

It felt as if her knees would buckle.

Her father was coming here.

Tomorrow.

Tomorrow, she'd have to face what she'd done to him.

To her mother.

To Frelina.

Black spots danced before her eyes and she thought she might faint, when a strong arm snaked across her back.

Glancing up, she could barely make out Merrick's tight face as he mouthed something.

She shook her head as she stared back at him, the blood rushing in her ears drowning all other sounds.

Clasping her chin to stop the movement, Merrick glared right into her eyes. "I've told you before. You're stronger than you think."

Lessia only blinked.

"After all you've been through, you're strong enough to handle this." Merrick captured her with his gaze. "You made it out of Rioner's cellars. You escaped the blood oath. You even survived the election and L..." He trailed off, his eyes hardening when she stiffened.

The fingers holding her chin tensed, but when he moved them to cup her heated cheek, they were gentle.

"Trust me," he whispered. "You are strong enough."

She wanted to look away from the swirling flecks, the silver reminding her too much of another pair of eyes, darker, which had once held the same conviction of her strength.

But when some of that certainty flowed into her, the hushed words working to pierce the shell of doubt that pressed on her chest, she squared her shoulders.

It wasn't like she had a choice.

She had to be strong enough.

There was no other way.

"Well, she needs to be strong to handle tonight." Raine smirked.

She moved her gaze his way. Her face must have betrayed her confusion as he offered, "It's Zehmkell tonight, and the Fae living on the other side of the island like to celebrate."

A groan left Merrick as he dropped his hand from her cheek. "I'd forgotten you still celebrate."

"Wh-what is Zehmkell?" she asked hoarsely, pushing the dread deep down into the dark abyss that held on to all the pain and hurt and fear she'd experienced through the years.

When Raine's lips curled into a mocking smirk, she frowned.

She recognized the name but couldn't place where she'd heard it before.

"It's a tradition amongst Fae soldiers." Merrick sighed. "It's said the gods encouraged it to strengthen the bond between Fae before battle."

"But now it's merely an excuse to drink and fuck once a month." Raine snickered.

She fought with everything in her to keep a blush from spreading across her face when Raine wiggled his brows.

But she mustn't have succeeded because Raine burst out laughing, and when even Merrick let out a muffled sound, she gritted her teeth.

Stupid males.

Stupid damned bastards.

While she waited for Raine to calm down, her fingers flexed, twitching toward the daggers by her waist, and she wondered whether her decision not to stab any of them again had been a bit hasty.

"Perhaps you should stay back?" Raine asked when he stopped laughing. "If you can't even hear the word *fuck* without looking like you stayed out a little too long in the sun, Zehmkell isn't a place for you."

The thought had also crossed her mind, but being alone in her room with only the thoughts of her father arriving with the next sunup keeping her company made her shake her head.

Raine chuckled again. "You sure? I know some of my friends back there will be happy to see Merrick, and I'm quite certain they won't mind the two humans either. They're handsome for not being Fae. You might have to face the night alone, little broken one. I'm not so certain you can handle it."

Rage struck her like a bolt of lightning.

She felt like punching Raine's smug face as heat, and not from embarrassment, flooded her veins, and a growl built inside her as she took a step toward him.

"She'll be fine," Merrick snarled, gripping her arm. "Enough."

"I'm merely stating facts." Raine innocently rounded his eyes. "In fact, I know someone who will be *very* happy to see you, Merrick, so you won't be able to babysit her for long."

There wasn't anything human about the growl that burst through her.

The vicious sound traveled across the beach and

crystal sea, and only because Merrick's hand locked around her arm did she not rip Raine's damned head off.

Ydren popped her head over the calm surface, and her screech was enough to snap Lessia out of the haze that had overtaken her mind.

Staring at the terrifying creature, she drew a shaky breath.

Her body continued fighting against Merrick's hold as she drew another one, but when she got to the third, she could finally feel her muscles relax, the sand swirling around her feet trickling down to join the millions of other grains across the beach.

"So angry, even after a full day of training." Raine smirked, but when Merrick growled in warning, he rolled his eyes. "You might want to rein in that temper tonight. My friends do not take well to being threatened."

"I said enough, Raine." Merrick's whispers emphasized his edged tone, and the gentle wind filled with oily vibrations.

A shudder made its way down her spine when the air around her began gleaming, and she wondered if those shimmers were some type of veil, keeping the dead souls from their world.

Pushing the thought out of her mind, she focused on Raine again.

Perhaps she didn't want to know.

"Fine." Glancing at the wyvern swimming by the shoreline, Raine rolled his neck. "Ydren tells me you were quite angry when you used your magic on her as well." He tsked. "Compelling a poor, innocent wyvern... That wasn't very nice of you."

Lessia flashed her teeth at him, trying to quench a

new wave of fury directed at the Fae warrior. "It wasn't very nice of her to try to kill me either."

"She protects me." Raine shrugged. "She didn't know you; you could have been a threat." His eyes traveled over her, even with another warning snarl from Merrick. "I haven't met anyone who could control wyverns before."

"You must have done it to make her so loyal to you," Lessia hissed through her teeth. "She is lonely here. I'm sure she wouldn't stay if you weren't forcing her."

"Lessia," Merrick warned quietly.

Raine snapped his eyes to hers, his jaw tensing. "I am not forcing her to do anything! Her family is dead."

Lessia swallowed as she shot a look at the still-swimming wyvern.

"Yes, it hadn't crossed your mind that I am protecting her right back?" Raine took a step toward her. "I saved her life when some shifters slaughtered her family. They ripped her mother's head off right before her eyes and struck her sister with so many arrows that the weight of them made it impossible to recover her body."

He took another step, and Merrick's fingers tightened around her arm.

"When those rebels came here, she was so frightened by their shifter leader, it took me days to find her. She'd crept into a cave so small she nearly couldn't leave it. I almost drowned getting her out of there."

"I didn't know," Lessia whispered, the greasy feeling of guilt that lathered across her skin worse than any dust and sand sticking to it from training.

"No, you just assumed." Raine's hazel eyes were so cold that she stepped back into Merrick's chest. "Our dear gods gave the Fae royals stones: fucking sparkling stones that were meant for us to communicate—bond—

with the wyverns. They abused what was meant to be a sacred bond—lied to the wyverns to get them to fight for us in whatever damn war was going on. Thousands of them died out of loyalty to a family that wouldn't care if their enemies plucked off every single scale on their babes' bodies."

Merrick's chest heaved against her back, each breath moving in rhythm with her breaking heart, and she might have fallen to the sand in a heap of shame if his arms hadn't wrapped around her waist.

When a tear slid down her cheek as she glanced at Ydren, who'd begun swimming away, Raine nodded. "Don't assume you know me, or anyone for that matter, because of what you see."

"I'm sorry," she got out in a choked voice.

Anger flared inside her again.

But this time, it was directed at herself.

She knew better than this.

Raine uncorked his flask and swallowed a few mouthfuls before he responded. "We should all be sorry that we were born into the cruel world. But we have to make the best out of it." Waving at them, he started up the beach. "Come on, you must clean up and change before Zehmkell."

When Lessia only stared after him, unable to move, Merrick's hand slipped into hers, and he gently tugged on it so she would follow him toward the cabin.

"I told you not to judge him too harshly." Merrick's eyes were soft as they followed his friend's swaying steps.

She stared at her dusty boots as they made their way up the narrow path.

She *had* judged him.

She'd done what she'd asked—no, begged!—people in Ellow not to do to her.

As he slowed his strides, Merrick's warm gaze landed on her. "Don't judge yourself too harshly either. You don't deserve it."

Lessia didn't respond—only forced her feet to continue moving, one step after another.

She wasn't so sure Merrick was right this time.

Not when the suffocating sense of shame followed her all the way to the house.

CHAPTER FIFTEEN

Lessia sighed as she tried to wiggle into the dress Raine had unceremoniously thrown her when they reached his wooden cabin.

Like the leathers, this dress must have belonged to Solana, and she knew better than to speak ill of the dead, but...

Raine's mate had truly lived by wearing as little as possible.

The dress was made of satin, similar to the black one Lessia had left at the castle back in Ellow, but its similarities to her own dress ended there.

This one was bright scarlet, sleeveless, with two straps connecting at the nape of her neck and a neckline that wound its way down to her stomach, barely covering her breasts.

It shouldn't have been possible, but somehow, the dress plunged even deeper down her back, leaving most of it bare.

With the garment coming just below her mid-thigh,

Lessia thought she might as well go to Zehmkell in her birthday suit.

The few buttons that kept the fabric together were, for some reason, sewn into the back of it, and she groaned as she squirmed to reach them, the sore muscles in her arms protesting as she stretched them.

A low chuckle lifted her gaze into the mirror she stood before, and she grimaced when she found Merrick leaning against the doorframe, a crooked grin pulling at his lips.

"Do you need some help?" Without waiting for a response, he strode into the room, towering over her as he bridged the distance.

Still staring into the mirror, Lessia shrugged. "I'm not certain these buttons will be of any help."

Merrick's eyes met hers in the mirror. "Solana had specific taste."

"You don't say," Lessia muttered.

Another low laugh escaped Merrick as his fingers grazed her back. "She swore like a soldier and never backed down from a fight, but clothing was her weak spot. She loved dressing up, and she'd always make poor Raine do it too. I'll never forget his face when she showed up with a violet shirt and trousers for him for their mating ceremony." Merrick shook his head, his slight smile widening. "Of course, he couldn't say no to her, and we teased him endlessly for it."

Lessia watched in the mirror as Merrick continued to button the dress, the tip of his tongue sliding between his teeth as he focused on the tiny loops.

"Were you close?" she asked.

Merrick's eyes remained on the last button as he nodded. "I stayed with them when they first met."

Sadness crept across his face, dimming the light that the smile had brought. "She was wonderful. Except when she tried to set me up with every single one of her friends."

He rolled his eyes. "When she got something in her head, there was no talking her out of it. But she was warm and kind, and she loved Raine so much. It was almost unbearable to watch them look at each other."

"She sounds wonderful," Lessia said quietly, sorrow casting shadows across her face when she thought of the unimaginable pain Raine must carry.

She couldn't fathom it.

Even with the liquor, he must feel as if he were dying every day.

"She was." Merrick's eyes locked with hers as he straightened, and a jolt shot through her when she realized he'd also changed.

Even though his shirt and breeches were black, they shimmered against his tan skin, the silver threads running through the tunic mirroring the starry night sky of his eyes and the newly washed hair tumbling down his shoulders.

He looked almost regal, with the dark fabric snugly hugging his muscles, the pearly hair softly layering around his face, and the polished sword with the bright rubies sticking up over his shoulder.

Lessia realized she'd been staring when one of Merrick's brows quirked up.

"She... she must have also been very beautiful if she chose to wear this dress voluntarily. I could never," she joked, pulling at the hem of the short dress and desperately trying not to blush at having gawked at him.

It was quiet for a beat, and goose bumps raced across

her skin when she realized Merrick's fingers still whispered over her back, his eyes trailing down her body, then back up and clashing with her own.

"I-I think you're done," she whispered as warmth bloomed across her chest from the nervous energy sparking inside her, the weight of Merrick's stare making her almost lightheaded.

When Merrick leaned in, his strong jaw brushing the exposed skin on her shoulder, she held her breath, not entirely sure what was happening.

Her eyes remained on his as he gently swept her hair over one shoulder and fastened a button she must have missed at the neck.

Lessia let out a shaky breath when his hands fell to his sides, but Merrick didn't step back.

Instead his presence surrounded her, and she couldn't stop her blush from deepening when she noticed her wide eyes in the mirror.

"Thank—" she started, but then she noticed a movement behind them.

Lessia couldn't stop herself from flinching, and she didn't miss how Merrick's eyes widened, his hand twitching toward the sword on his back, before he realized it was only Raine's head popping into the mirror's reflection.

"You ready? Or am I interrupting something?" Raine's brows pulled as he watched them, the frown deepening when Merrick stepped back but kept his eyes locked on hers.

"We're coming," Merrick snarled, the impossible darkness of his eyes deepening as his glare shifted to Raine.

Nodding once, Raine spun on his heel, the scowl on his face still present until his reflection disappeared.

"I... I'll just..." She couldn't even devise an excuse as Merrick's hard eyes burned into hers, and she only pointed vaguely toward the bundle of clothes on her bed.

Merrick's jaw twitched, and she thought he might yell at her like he did during training, but instead, he averted his gaze and began walking out of the room.

"Keep your wits about you tonight," he rasped as he slipped through the unlatched door.

Lessia blinked a few times.

What had just happened?

Bringing her hands to her heated cheeks, she drew deep breaths until her hammering heart slowed and her reddened face shifted back into her usual color instead of mirroring the dress she wore.

She shook her head at herself.

What was she doing?

Merrick had only been kind to her—tried to help her with the dumb dress.

And while it perhaps wasn't something she was used to...

She'd just managed to make it awkward.

Lessia nervously went to pull down her sleeve as she met her own wary eyes in the mirror, her heart rate increasing when her fingers only found bare skin.

"Get it together," she hissed at herself when her breathing became choppy.

She didn't need to hide the tattoo anymore.

She didn't need to be scared of Merrick anymore.

She repeated the words as she left the room, forcing herself not to fidget with the dress as she approached the sitting room.

"What are you doing, Merrick?"

Lessia froze when Raine's harsh tone drifted toward her.

"I'm fighting," Merrick responded in a furious whisper.

The clink of a bottle hitting glass reached her ears before Raine responded in an equally raging whisper. "You don't have to. You know that, right?"

Her heart slammed against her rib cage in the silence that followed.

"You're wrong," Merrick finally hissed.

"Why? You could make your life so much easier."

"Because it's the right thing to do."

The stairs behind her creaked, and she pushed off the wall she'd been pressing her body against and walked over the threshold as loud steps reached the bottom of it, heading toward the room.

"Damned martyr," Raine griped as he caught her gaze while downing the glass of liquor in his hand.

"Just because you don't want to fight doesn't mean you get to judge others for it." Lessia kept her voice even, the guilt from earlier still ringing in her mind.

But she wasn't about to have Raine fault Merrick for doing what was right.

Especially when Havlands needed him.

When she needed him.

"Assuming again, are we?" Raine taunted.

When Raine took a step toward her, Merrick slammed his arm into his chest, his eyes flitting her way.

"Don't make eavesdropping a habit," he said quietly. "You might hear some things you'd rather not."

She almost wavered under his cold stare, and only

when she nodded did his gaze fix behind her. "Seems like we're all here. Let's get this over with, shall we?"

When Lessia turned her head over her shoulder, Ardow and Venko lingered by the back wall, looking as reluctant as she felt to join the festivities tonight.

"You all act like you're going to a burial, not a feast." Raine sighed. "Zehmkell is supposed to be exciting."

She and Merrick groaned at the same time, eliciting another sigh from Raine.

While Merrick's features remained hard as he followed Raine out the door, the flecks in his eyes twinkled when they briefly met hers, and embers of warmth—not the uncomfortable ones she'd experienced before the mirror, but something more akin to safety—spread in her chest as she fell into step with them, Ardow and Venko on either side.

CHAPTER SIXTEEN

They walked the twisting path deep into the island mainly in silence.

Ardow had asked her a few questions about today's training as they left the house. Still, both his questions and her answers became shorter and farther apart with every jerk of Venko's head and every deep sigh that wove its way through the tension surrounding the group whenever Ardow broke the silence.

The air became so thick from the strain between Ardow and Venko that it was almost a relief when they finally reached the edge of a small stone town and the sounds of people washed over them, even as apprehension thrummed over her skin at meeting a group of unfamiliar Fae.

She hadn't really spent any time with Fae outside her own family and the half-Fae children back in Vastala, and later Ellow.

A knot tightened in her stomach.

Apart from King Rioner's guards, of course.

Steps, singing, and the clattering of dishes echoed between the low gray buildings, and the farther into the village they walked, the more Lessia's pulse heightened, her ears perking and body tensing with each step.

Merrick cast a glance over his shoulder, and when he met her eyes, he slowed his strides until she caught up with him, ignoring that he pushed Venko out of the way.

"These Fae aren't loyal to Rioner," Merrick said under his breath. "You have nothing to fear from them."

Nodding, she glanced down at the worn boots she'd had to pair the dress with, since Solana had had larger feet, and none of the ones Raine had offered her fit.

They might not be loyal to Rioner, but she was still half-Fae.

And she'd seen how the Fae in Vastala treated those like herself.

Even if they hadn't outright bullied and threatened them, like Rioner's guards liked to do, the look in their eyes when they accidentally met the gaze of any of the half-Fae was enough.

They'd purposely walk to the other side of the street, as if being half-Fae was somehow contagious, and the scrunch of their noses when they couldn't escape getting close was burned into her memories.

She huffed a breath when Raine stopped before a gray stone building with a thick straw roof. Lampposts towered behind it, shining their soft light on the yellow roof from what seemed like a large outdoor terrace.

Merrick's hand landed on her shoulder, and she met his eyes when he squeezed it quickly before dropping it to open one of the wooden doors.

Bright light, loud voices, and the clinking of glass spilled onto the gravelly path, and Lessia realized she wasn't alone in the urge to turn around and run away when she met Ardow's rounded eyes where he hovered beside her.

But when Merrick waved for them to follow, she blew up her cheeks before slowly letting out the air and following him over the high doorstep.

If she was to face Rioner and Loche... she could face a group of Fae.

It was like being met with a wall of warmth, the small room filled with Fae, most standing around a worn counter, yelling their drink orders at the two barkeeps behind it.

Others, all with cups and glasses in their hands, filed out of the room onto the terrace she'd spotted upon walking in, where a large fire burned in the middle and benches were placed in a circle around it.

Lessia kept her gaze down as she followed Merrick and Raine to the bar, but blocking out the hushed conversations around them was impossible as they pushed through the crowd.

"Is that the Death Whisperer?"

"Yes, look at his eyes! I heard they're a window to the sky of the otherworld."

"Two of the lethal brotherhood together? This can't be good."

"Are those two *human*? They're a long way from home."

"Half-Fae... I didn't think there were many of them left."

An elbow slammed into her side, and she was about to flash her teeth at whoever had done it when Ardow's face popped into view.

"They don't seem that friendly," he whispered,

shoulders raised high and eyes darting to the sides as they squeezed through groups of more Fae to keep up with Raine and Merrick.

Lessia bowed her head as more stares burned into the side of it. "No, they don't."

"It doesn't help that they're all so damn tall either," Venko hissed as he slipped up on her other side.

Lessia's eyes widened, and when she met Ardow's guarded ones, a giggle burst out of her.

Ardow's lips lifted as well, and soon, they had to hold on to each other as they shook from quiet laughter.

"Stop it," Venko grumbled, but the stern tone she assumed he'd tried for gave way to a choked sound, and when he stormed ahead of them, she could swear he bit down a smile himself.

"He seems to have warmed a bit. A tiny, tiny bit." Lessia hugged Ardow's arm, the smile from the laughter remaining when Ardow's eyes softened as he watched Venko take up a spot next to Merrick by the counter.

"What do you want?" Raine asked gruffly as he shoved a gawking Fae out of the way to allow Lessia and Ardow some space, then leaned over the sticky surface.

She observed Merrick pointing toward a golden liquor filling a carafe to the brim and suspected it was the same one he'd drunk that night in Ellow when he told her Rioner was coming soon.

Catching her eye, Merrick raised a brow, and when she nodded, he waved for the barkeep to fill another glass.

"Merrick!" a melodic voice called out.

Lessia stumbled when she was pushed to the side, and only because of Ardow's tight grip on her arm did she not slam face-first into the wooden floor when a Fae with fiery orange tresses barged past them.

"I can't believe it! I thought I'd never see you again." The female wrapped her arms around Merrick's neck, and Lessia dug her fingers into Ardow's arm when a surge of rage roiled in her gut as she steadied herself.

"Are you all right?" Ardow mumbled.

"I'm fine," Lessia grumbled as she straightened the dress, her gaze tracking the female as she stepped back and turned her bright blue eyes in their direction.

"Oh! I'm sorry." The woman's hand flew to her chest when her eyes found Lessia's. "I didn't mean to push you. I just couldn't believe my eyes when I saw Merrick."

She moved her gaze to Merrick's again. "I do hope you're staying for a while. We haven't caught up in... what is it, a few centuries?"

"I'm sure you didn't, Iviry," Raine scoffed before patting Merrick's back. "Merrick is only passing through. Unless someone can convince him to stay, that is..."

Rolling his eyes, Merrick pressed a glass of liquor into Lessia's hands. "This is Iviry. She was a captain in the Rantzier fleet. Iviry, this is Lessia, and the humans are Ardow and Venko."

Iviry tossed her flaming hair to the side, a smile brightening her beautiful face as she reached out a hand toward Lessia, the other wrapping around Merrick's waist. "It's lovely to meet you, Lessia. We don't get many half-Fae here." She threw a wink Ardow's way. "And I don't think I've ever seen a human on these isles. You must be not only handsome but brave as well."

"I'm part-Fae," Ardow murmured.

He was rewarded with another blinding smile from

Iviry. "I knew your looks were too good to only be human! Although your man there is quite mesmerizing."

Ardow grinned beside her, and Lessia pinched his arm harder until the stupid simper slipped from his face.

She wasn't sure what it was about this Fae, but even though the smile on her face seemed sincere, there was something off about her eyes, a slight twitch telling her she was sizing up Lessia the way Lessia was her.

When Lessia only glared at Iviry's outstretched hand, Raine chuckled. "It's their first Zehmkell. I did tell them the people here would be friendly, but alas..."

Dropping her hand, her smile never wavering, Iviry nodded. "You'll enjoy it! There is food and music, and they're just beginning to tell the tales of the Old World out there." She gestured toward the terrace where Fae filled almost every single bench, the flames from the fire flickering on their faces. "I've heard them a thousand times by now, so I intend to dance."

As if she'd conjured it, a few Fae in the corner behind them unpacked instruments they must have brought with them, and soon, the soft beat from a drum hummed across the room, joined by a deep voice beginning to sing a song of war and love and loss.

Fae all around them paired up, brushing past Lessia as they took to the makeshift dance floor forming before the musicians and singer and started swaying from side to side, some spinning slowly in rhythm with the song.

Watching them, Lessia jerked when the memory of her and Loche dancing on that final night of the election ambushed her.

She slammed her eyes shut, trying to push away the feeling of his arms around her, the sound of his strong heartbeat thumping when she leaned her cheek against his chest, the fingers that caressed her neck tingling over her skin.

She couldn't think of this.

Not now.

Lessia swallowed a whimper fighting to leave her.

She wouldn't have that again—have what the people in this room so easily found.

What had taken her twenty-five years to stumble across.

And only days to destroy.

"Lessia." A hand brushed her cheek, and she opened her eyes to Merrick's dark ones—to his tense jaw and drawn-down brows.

As she looked into his darkness, following the sparkles swirling in the shadows, some of the turmoil inside her eased, and when she finally tore her eyes from his and glanced around, her cheeks heated upon realizing everyone was staring at her.

Ardow with a worried expression.

Venko with sorrow.

But it was Raine's glossed hazel eyes, which flitted between her and Merrick, that had her nearly shut her own again.

Agony.

It was pure agony flickering across his face.

"Are you all right?" Ardow whispered.

Her bottom lip trembled as she tried to say yes, but no words came out.

"She will be," Merrick said quietly, and she shot him a grateful look. "Let's join the storytellers." He cast a pointed look at Ardow and Venko. "I am sure you haven't heard all of our history."

Iviry, who'd been openly staring, her eyes narrowing

as they locked with Lessia's, turned toward Merrick and placed a hand on his chest. "You owe me at least one dance after being gone for so long."

Merrick began shaking his head, but Iviry only stepped up closer to him. "Please. Raine won't ever do me the honor, and we never get any fun guests. It's Zehmkell, Merrick."

When Iviry gripped the hand Merrick had just used to cup her cheek and began to drag him toward the other dancing couples, Lessia didn't think.

"Leave him alone," she snarled, boring her eyes into Iviry's. "He doesn't dance."

Iviry spun around, and whatever she saw in Lessia's face made her brows pull. "Everybody dances during Zehmkell, young one."

Young one...

Lessia's vision darkened when Raine stepped in between them. "Iviry, you know Merrick never dances—we barely used to get him to join us on these celebrations. Leave the poor male alone. Besides"—he gestured toward Lessia—"he's on babysitting duty."

Iviry's eyes flew to Raine's, and Lessia could see she wanted to argue, but after a second of silence she finally shook her head. "Fine. But then *you* owe me one, Raine."

After he nodded, Iviry waved to them, then elegantly shifted between couples, finding a blond Fae leaning against the wall and offering him a broad smile as he bowed.

"Why are you so angry?" Venko's brows knitted as he stared at Lessia, but she didn't respond; she was busy watching Raine battle one of Merrick's icy glares, the latter having stepped forward, right into Raine's space.

Nausea welled within her as she watched Merrick

hiss something into Raine's ear, and she wondered if she'd gone too far with all her snarling and being rude to their friend.

Somehow Iviry had really gotten under her skin.

It had been clear Merrick didn't want to go with her, and she hadn't missed him shifting to get away from the arm she'd decided to wrap around his waist.

But the furious expression currently twisting Merrick's face made her wonder if she'd imagined it.

Perhaps she'd just stopped him from enjoying Zehmkell with an old friend.

Or... an old lover?

"Fuck!" She whipped her head around when Ardow slapped her hand off, his own wrapping around his arm where small dark stains appeared on the white tunic he wore.

Right where her fingers had just been.

Glaring at her, he whispered, "You drew blood. What is wrong with you?"

"I—" she started.

But she didn't have time to finish before Merrick forcefully gripped her arm, dragging her after him as he growled at all of them, "Let's just get this night over with."

CHAPTER SEVENTEEN

Every seat on the wooden benches was taken when Merrick hauled her out of the brightly lit room, and she was relieved when he guided her to lean against the tavern wall instead of trying to squeeze down between any of the unknown Fae.

Only a few eyes tracked them, some of the Fae who faced them on the other side of the fireplace noting the small group gathering in the shade of the stone building.

But most kept their attention on the brown-haired Fae with a thick beard of the same color who paced back and forth before the orange flames.

Some kind of leader, she guessed.

The Fae seemed older, the gray streaks touching his temples telling her he must be several thousand, if not tens of thousands, years old.

From what her father had taught her, Fae looked up to elders.

If there weren't any royals, nobility, or famed

warriors in the room, age typically determined who could claim authority.

Lessia drew a breath of smoky air, her eyes trailing the embers sparking above the large fire as Merrick took up the spot next to her and Raine leaned against the wall on her other side.

"Are you drinking that?" Raine nodded toward the glass she still held in her hand as Ardow and Venko placed themselves beside Merrick.

When Lessia shrugged—not particularly eager to drink the liquor upon remembering the cup she'd tasted on the ship—he stretched out his hand, and she unbent her stiff fingers to offer him the cup.

After downing it in one go, Raine croaked, "Thank you," and rested his head on the stone, his eyes closing.

Merrick's fingers brushed hers as he flexed and unflexed them, and when she stole a glance at him, he was faced forward, his features strained as he glared at the group of Fae.

She was just about to ask him what was wrong, or perhaps even apologize, when the bearded Fae began speaking.

Not wanting to draw any more attention, she quickly pressed her lips shut.

"Tonight is Zehmkell."

The Fae around the fire began drumming a low, steady beat by clapping their hands on their thighs, like an eerie melody in the dusky light.

The fire flickered in tune with the sound, amplifying the Fae's throaty voice, and a shiver shook her body when he continued.

"While the gods created Zehmkell, we do not celebrate Zehmkell for them. Zehmkell is for us. It's for unity.

For friendship. For lost ones and loved ones. For those that are here and those we left behind."

When a wolflike cry echoed over the terrace, Lessia started, her eyes flying across the group, snagging on the faces contorted by the flames—on the two males who cupped their hands around their mouths, crying up toward the moon, which had begun rising over the island.

A low humming accompanied the thumping rhythm and the harsh cries, and her legs began shaking when something whispered over the skin.

Not a chill, but like soft, warm caresses that prickled everywhere across her bare skin.

As if the gods, or perhaps those that didn't walk this realm anymore, still wanted it known they were there.

That they were listening.

When Lessia jumped again at another otherworldly howl, a warm hand wrapped around hers, and she met Merrick's eyes as he intertwined their fingers.

Lessia offered him a weak smile, and he dipped his chin before shifting his gaze forward once more.

The bearded Fae began circling the fire with slow, deliberate steps, his hands clasped behind his back. "Zehmkell is a time for remembrance. It's to remember the bond between us, not just when facing an enemy but every day we walk this realm. It's to remember those who came before us, those who sacrificed for us, those who ensured we could live in peace."

Lessia couldn't take her eyes off him as he walked up to a stack of branches and threw a few onto the fire, the flames furiously reaching for the sky for a moment, with sparks shooting toward the darkness as the pace of the drumming quickened.

"The first Zehmkell was held by the gods in the Old World: Preysaih, the god of death. Zharra, the god of life. Evrene, the god of mind. Killem, the god of earth. Orshine, the god of water. Lodem, the god of sky. They'd gifted us different magic and abilities, and a divide was forming between our people. They needed us united to protect our world. And so Zehmkell was born."

Merrick's hand tightened around her own when she trembled at the Fae's booming voice, how he emphasized the name of each god in sync with the mounting force of the tapping, and the strength of it steadied her as she continued to listen.

"But there was a bigger divide." The Fae paused to throw more branches at the roaring fire. "Between us and the gods. For millennia, they'd forced us to do their bidding, follow their rules, fight their wars... and our ancestors grew tired of it. Thousands of lives were lost as they forced the gods to leave our lands, but in the end, they stood victorious."

Another wail pierced the air, with sorrowful lower whimpers echoing softly after it.

A jolt struck her.

Not from the haunting sounds but from surprise.

She knew the gods had left the Old World, but she hadn't known it was at the hands of their ancestors.

Her father had conveniently left that out of the history lessons he used to force her and Frelina to attend in the mornings growing up.

Leaning forward, Lessia found a wrinkle between Ardow's brows as he watched the Fae halt with his hands lifted toward the sky, but before she could mouth something at him, Merrick tugged her back, casting a sharp stare her way when she opened her mouth.

Snapping it shut, she followed the speaker's gaze toward the sky as he called out, "And so the four kingdoms were born. Our own, ruled by the Rantziers, the travelers and emissaries and soldiers. One ruled by the Oakgards, the ones who answered the call to the earth. One ruled by the Himmlah, for those who sought the sky. And the final one ruled by the Wrehns, for those who didn't fear a path guided by darkness. Free to choose our calling, our people split up. But without the threat of the gods, what they had feared unfolded. War broke out between kingdoms. Mistrust and wariness spread like wildfire. Not even Zehmkell was enough to unite us; the bonds were too fragile... So our broken people dispersed across different realms. The Rantziers took their people the farthest, the travel urge in our blood driving us to Havlands, a land shared with humans and shifters."

The drumming stopped.

Lessia held her breath as the wind whispered across the ground, mingling with the crackling from the fire, gripping Merrick's hand so hard she was certain he would snap at her.

But he only clasped her hand back when the Fae sat down and crossed his legs on the ground before the fire.

Staring into the flames, he said quietly, "But although Rantzier's people shared traits, the iron fist that the royals ruled with, the thirst for power tainting their minds, drove a deeper divide between us. That's why we created this sanctuary. That's why Zehmkell is the one holiday we still honor. We must remind each other never to fall into the darkness of the Rantziers and those who follow them. We must remind each other that while we are different—we are one. That regardless of the blood that flows through our veins or the lineage we carry, we are equals. Equals in standing up against the evil that is the Rantziers."

Her heart started beating so hard that a few Fae in the back row turned their heads her way. However, they quickly shifted when a warning growl rumbled in Merrick's chest and his teeth glinted in the fire as he flashed them.

As he released her hand and stepped forward, covering her from sight as the people rose from their seats, she met Ardow's wide eyes, and fear wrapped around her like a lead-lined blanket.

She hadn't questioned Merrick's conviction that she needed to train, assuming he was only preparing her for what they might face trying to stop the rebels and maybe even the Oakgards' Fae he believed were headed for Havlands.

But perhaps he was also preparing her for what would happen if people discovered who she truly was.

What blood flowed through her veins.

What family name she bore.

Lessia doubted she'd be able to hide it much longer.

Not with what she suspected they'd have to do to convince Loche and Rioner of the threats against their realm.

Her eyes slammed into Merrick's when he spun around, and she nearly cowered when he stalked up to her, crowding her against the wall.

But his voice was gentle as he whispered, "You do not carry that darkness. You may bear a name, but that name does not define you. You may share his blood, but that blood does not dictate who you are. And I promise you" —his eyes bore into hers as he stressed each word—"I. Promise. You. I won't let anyone hurt you. Rioner, Loche, the rebels, the Oakgards' Fae, or any of these fucking people won't come near you. Ever again."

Her mouth went dry as the sounds around them receded into the background.

Only Merrick's sharp breaths, her own thumping heart, and the low humming from a held-back growl in his chest reverberated in her ears.

When Raine stepped up beside him, she jerked, and the sounds of people holding low conversations, of liquid being swallowed, of Ardow clearing his throat boomed through the air once more.

"That's a bold promise, brother," Raine said softly, eyes locked on hers. "Let's hope you do not have to break it."

His eyes dipped for a second before he beckoned to the group. "Let's just go home. I don't expect any of us will be able to enjoy this night as we should."

Merrick reached out with his hand again, and once Lessia took it, she held on to it the whole way back to Raine's cabin.

And Merrick's promise echoed in her ears with every steady step across the small island.

CHAPTER EIGHTEEN

Her hands dug into the sand as she stared up toward the darkening sky, and Lessia tried to catch her breath from once again having crashed into the ground after misinterpreting one of Merrick's impossible-to-anticipate moves.

As she pulled a wheezing breath into her lungs, a shadow blocked the sun, and her eyes narrowed when Merrick rasped, "You plan on staying down there all day?"

Ignoring his outstretched hand, she pushed herself to her feet, wavering slightly as the effects from the Vincere still lingered within her.

They'd been out here since dawn, when she, as usual nowadays, awoke before the others and repaid Merrick for all the times he'd stormed into her room.

Dragging off his cover, she'd jumped out of the way of his death glare and asked, "Are we training or not?"

He'd growled something back about rest also being

important, so Lessia had pulled his quilt entirely off and brought it with her as she sprinted out of the room.

She couldn't rest.

Her mind wouldn't let her.

If she got even an hour of sleep these days, she was lucky.

A yawn crept up her throat as she glared at Merrick, who stalked in a circle around her.

But an involuntary hiss replaced it when one of his brows shot up, and his sword lowered an inch, a question in his eyes.

She could almost hear his voice in her mind as she violently shook her head.

You should rest.

She might not have gotten any sleep last night, and it wasn't because of the dread she'd felt when she realized just how much the Fae here hated the Rantzier family.

Her family.

No, it had been the swirling guilt clogging her throat as she tried to imagine how she'd tell her parents why she'd left.

What if Frelina had told them, but they'd been so furious that her father decided not to come looking for her?

What if they'd decided Frelina was enough?

She shook her head again as doubt danced across her skin.

They couldn't know.

Her father had loved her too deeply to leave her to fend for herself.

Hadn't he?

"You done?" Merrick asked.

Eyes snapping to his, she shook her head again. "No."

The Vincere had been a respite today.

A painful one.

But its effects were fading quickly.

So the only thing she could do to keep her mind occupied until her father's ship arrived was to fight.

Keep her eyes fixed on Merrick's lightning-fast movements, his glinting sword as it tapped every weak spot she left open, and let his grumblings when she didn't follow his exact orders fill her head.

"Good." Merrick gave her a smile that sent a shudder through her.

On most, a smile would have been encouraging.

But on Merrick...

It was more like a lethal promise.

Lessia's hand shook as she wiped the back of it over her forehead, the sand sticking to her damp skin scratching her, but she made herself crouch, gripping her daggers tightly as Merrick charged her.

The clang of her daggers blocking his sword echoed across the beach, and she stumbled backward when he pushed against the cross she'd made with the blades to stop him from tapping her gut.

A growl left her when Merrick spun around so fast that sand danced around him, and she lost her vision for a moment as she straightened and blood rushed from her head.

As she blinked against the dark spots, Merrick's arms circled her, and the cold of his sword soon rested against her bare neck.

"You're getting sloppy," he hissed into her ear, blowing a few of her sweaty strands into her face. "You need to surprise me! Not use the same movement you've done the past three times. I've said it before!"

"I know!" she gritted through her teeth.

"It doesn't seem like you do!" Merrick snarled.

She fought the frustration urging her to bite him again. Bite right into his golden skin, letting iron mix with that wild scent of his. "Let me go, and I will show you!"

"Hasn't she trained enough for today?" Raine asked as he strolled down to the waterline before them. "She looks a tad tired."

"No!" she and Merrick hissed in unison.

Raine raised his hands. "No need to snap at me."

His gaze swept over the sword at her neck before it lifted to just above her head, leveled with where Merrick's eyes must be based on where his chest heaved against her back. "You have a few weeks at most, Merrick. With how much sand is tangled in her hair, I assume she's not gotten much better than she was the past few days. What is the point?"

Releasing her, Merrick stalked up to him, his every step slow and steady.

If they hadn't been on a beach, Lessia imagined each stride would bounce off the ground with icy precision, like a thunderous storm preparing to unleash.

"What is the point?" Merrick repeated as he halted right before Raine, the latter's eyes widening at whatever he saw in Merrick's face.

Merrick's arm flew out behind him, and a long finger pointed her way. "The point is to survive, Raine. The point is to fight back. To not let evil win. You might have forgotten the point... but I haven't. And neither has she. You know as well as I do that skill only goes so far. It's that burning passion, the fever to do what's right, that matters. And she has that!"

Rolling his eyes, Raine pulled out his flask.

But Merrick wouldn't have it.

Slapping it out of his hand, he leaned in further, his furious whisper drifting toward her. "Solana had that fever as well, Raine. She wouldn't have stood idly by, drinking herself into a stupor each night if it had been you who died. She would have fought beside us, regardless of how futile it might be. You're betraying her memory with your actions."

A buzzing began in her head as Raine's face went ashen, guilt pulling at his drunken features.

Tearing her eyes away, she stuffed her daggers into her waistband and forced her tired legs to move faster than they liked, taking her down to the water, away from the arguing Fae.

Lessia clasped her hands over her face when Loche's deceived face flashed before her eyes.

"Stop it," she mumbled to herself. "Stop it!"

She hadn't chosen to betray him.

But the same guilt that slumped Raine's shoulders drove the air from her lungs.

She might not have chosen it, but she'd done it all the same.

Like Raine, she'd given up.

There must have been a way for her to tell Loche of her oath to King Rioner before the king told him himself.

But she had barely tried...

A sharp slash of water made her eyes dart to the side.

Ydren swam dangerously close to the shore, her violet eyes fixed on Lessia and her large body gliding through the water like the snake that had once marred Lessia's arm.

The wyvern's head jerked up and down, and Lessia

dug her boots into the sand when Ydren's long tail whipped toward the horizon.

Something white glinted where the sky met the sea, and Lessia swallowed loudly when she realized it was a ship.

Her father's ship.

A stifled sound left her.

She wasn't ready.

Her eyes crashed shut.

She didn't know how to do this.

How did you tell someone you were their daughter?

How could they forgive her for the thirteen years she'd robbed them of that knowledge?

She couldn't do this.

As her mind began spinning out of control, Lessia heard something slosh, and she didn't have time to react as a wave of water fell over her—drenching her tunic and trousers and making her hair fall down her shoulders like a heavy curtain.

Eyes flying open, she glared at the wyvern. "What was that for?"

She swore the wyvern gave her a pointed stare back.

Pushing some wet strands of hair out of her face, Lessia was about to flash her teeth at Ydren, perhaps even use her magic to tell her never to do that again, when she realized...

The water had forced her out of her spiraling.

Lessia brushed her arms, savoring the smoothness—it had also washed away the sand from her failing to heed Merrick's instructions—and gave the wyvern a small smile.

"Thank you," she got out.

With a dip of her large head, those terrifying spikes

pointing in Lessia's direction for a moment longer than she liked, Ydren spun in the water, swimming swiftly to the side.

Then the wyvern sent another wave of salty water over the still-quarreling Merrick and Raine.

Despite the ominous vessel growing larger on the horizon—the only silhouette disturbing the clear sea, apart from Ydren's whipping tail—Lessia giggled when Merrick spluttered and Raine's mouth fell open.

She was starting to like this beast.

Merrick's head snapped toward her, and she tried to quench the laughter when he began walking her way, his silver hair plastered around his stern face and dark leathers shining from drops running down them.

But it proved challenging when Raine screamed something incomprehensible at Ydren, and her only response was to splash him with more water.

A wheezing sound escaped her lips when she took a stumbling step backward to escape Merrick's glower, and for some reason, that made her laugh even harder.

Not even clamping a hand over her mouth could drown out the bubbling laughter.

Staring at her as if she'd lost her mind, Merrick asked, "This? This is what makes you laugh?"

Another wheezy giggle left her, and he shook his head.

Then he took one more step, threw her over his shoulder, and as she made a startled sound, he flung them both into the calm ocean.

"What the fuck, Merrick?" she spat as she broke the surface.

Saltwater stung her eyes as they widened upon finding Merrick grinning back at her.

Actually grinning.

Not the menacing curl of his lips that she'd seen before.

But a genuine smile.

Merrick's hands shifted beneath the surface as he moved toward her, and she realized a second before he did it what he was planning.

"No!" She threw herself to the side when he sent a spray of water toward her. "Merrick!"

A low chuckle escaped him as she stared at his bright face.

Moving before he could anticipate it, she dragged her fingers through the water, pelting him with a surge of it.

His eyes crinkled as he shook his head, sending his hair flying around it, and she couldn't help but smile back when he began swimming toward her, looking more like a young boy than the menacing Death Whisperer.

"What. Are. You. Doing?" Raine stared at them from the shore. "That's Alarin's ship, if you hadn't noticed."

Lessia's smile fell.

And a moment after, so did Merrick's.

Keeping her eyes down, she swam the few strokes needed to get to the beach to drag her weary body to a spot next to Raine.

"Merrick?" Raine hissed as the Fae followed her up the beach.

Merrick set his jaw. "What?"

Raine's eyes were wild as they sliced from her to Merrick.

"You're playing with fire," he mumbled before he shook his head. "They'll be here in a few minutes."

Her eyes flew to Merrick's as her heart began pounding against her rib cage.

"You are strong enough," he said, sidling up beside her.

She gave him a shadow of a smile when his lips curled, trying to let the gratitude for the way he'd tried to take her mind off what was to come shine through.

Closing her eyes, she tried to let the conviction within him flow into her as she listened to the soft waves and wind whistling across the sea.

When she opened them again, the vessel had docked.

CHAPTER NINETEEN

Lessia couldn't breathe as the ramp from the small boat landed on the beach, and the thud of wood hitting sand reverberated through her so loudly it drowned all other sounds.

The sun had already begun its descent behind the house at their backs, and she blinked in the dappled light when a hand landed on her back.

"Is that your father?" Ardow breathed.

Without turning around, she nodded.

"Are you all—"

Ardow's question was cut off when someone—she suspected Merrick—slapped their hand over his mouth.

Regardless, she was grateful for it when her father's golden-brown hair came into view, and the lump that seemed ever present in her throat grew.

Her father reached out a hand, and when a smaller figure emerged from the boat's head to be helped off, she thought she might tumble to the ground.

Her sister's eyes found hers, and she didn't hesitate as she overtook their father.

Frelina's skirts billowed in the breeze as she stormed up to them, and Lessia took a stumbling step toward her, drinking in the sight of her round face, the amber eyes that were identical to her own, and the hair that had flowed nearly down to her waist—like Lessia's still did—but was now cut short, coming just beneath her ears.

Lessia opened her arms when Frelina was a step away, her eyes closing as her sister's flowery scent floated toward her, and a small piece of her broken soul seemed to fuse together.

Then, her head slammed to the side.

"Well. Shit," Ardow gasped somewhere behind her.

Eyes flying open, Lessia touched her burning cheek and met Frelina's furious gaze.

"How could you, Elessia?" she hissed as she lifted her hand once more.

"I'm so—" she started, but Frelina slapped her again, so hard the taste of iron filled her mouth, and the words were clipped by a sob.

"Enough!" Merrick stepped in between them, his glare fixed on her sister. "Do not hit her again," he warned quietly.

Or perhaps the maddening noise in her ears made his voice seem soft.

Her blood roared inside her, heating every inch of her skin, not just the cheek her sister had struck, as devastating grief filled her to her core.

Her sister's blazing gaze became blurry as Lessia's eyes burned with tears.

She had been so occupied with the guilt toward her parents when she found out Frelina was alive...

She hadn't even considered what she'd say to her sister.

The sister she'd compelled to jump off a roof.

Her father rushed to their side, but as he tried to pull Frelina behind him, she ripped her arm free and slammed her finger into Merrick's chest. "The Death Whisperer, Elessia? Really? That's what you've been doing all these years?"

Upper lip curling back, she turned to Raine, who'd stepped up to Lessia's side. "Get the fuck out of my mind. I won't tell you a second time."

"Frelina..." Her father reached out for her sister again.

Spinning toward him, she snarled, "No! I lied about Elessia to protect you! You do not get to lecture me." Her burning eyes flew across the group before she stalked off toward the cabin with a loud "Fuck all of you!"

Lessia breathed in through her nose and out through her mouth as she tried to stop the pressure building in her chest and the familiar black spots flickering in the corner of her eyes.

Staring at the rest of the group, she fought with everything in her so as not to succumb to the panic.

But as Ardow, Venko, Raine, and even Merrick looked back at her with pity, her legs went out.

Dropping down beside her in the sand, Merrick reached out to pull her against him, but she pushed his arm off, incapable of standing the gentle gesture.

She wasn't the one who deserved comfort.

She couldn't even meet Merrick's eyes.

Not with the sympathy she expected to flare within the darkness.

This was her fault.

Frelina hating her was warranted.

Like it was warranted for L...

She dragged her hands through her hair, pulling at the roots and squeezing her eyes shut.

It was all her fault.

"I thought I was called to battle, not a catfight."

The foreign voice had Merrick jump to his feet, his sword in his hands in less than a second.

But Lessia couldn't muster more movement than tilting her head upward, the tears that filled her eyes spilling over and tracing down her cheeks.

A Fae with ebony hair and crystal-blue eyes smirked at Merrick's tense stance before lazily shifting to meet her eyes and offering her a wave. "Hello, little Faeling."

Merrick shook his head as he sheathed his sword. "Kerym."

"That's all I get?" Kerym wiggled his brows. "I know you're not usually one for hugs, but it's been a few centuries. I thought I'd get at least a handshake."

She couldn't take in any more information, her mind feeling as if it'd been struck by lightning, so instead of listening to Merrick's response, Lessia's eyes traveled toward her father.

She immediately wished they hadn't.

Tears spilled down his own cheeks, his face crumpling as he stared back at her.

"Raine," Merrick barked.

Nodding, Raine grabbed Kerym by the arm, and after a glance at Venko and Ardow, he made them all venture back to the house—the same way Frelina had stormed off.

Lessia's gaze flitted from Merrick, who eyed her closely, to her father, who looked as devastated as she felt.

"So… it's true. You're my daughter," her father whispered, his voice raw.

When Lessia only stared back at him, Merrick cleared his throat. "It is."

He reached out a hand, and when she allowed him to pull her to her feet, Merrick continued. "Alarin, there is much we must discuss, but you two need to talk first."

As he motioned to follow the others back to the house, unease coiled around her neck, and she reached out to grip his hand.

"Please," she whispered when Merrick met her eyes over his shoulder.

He hesitated for only a second before he nodded.

Turning back around, Merrick firmly laced their fingers as he took the place by her side, with her father opposite them, his eyes falling to their joined hands.

She followed his gaze to the large hand enveloping hers for a moment before lifting her gaze again, and if Frelina's slap still didn't burn on her cheek, she might have laughed.

How had she ended up here?

Needing comfort from the Death Whisperer to speak to her own father.

"E-Elessia? Is that your name?" her father asked, his gaze flitting to Merrick for a second before meeting her own.

Thankfully, the tears she'd found there before were gone.

She swallowed. "Yes, but I go by Lessia now."

Dragging his hands down his face, her father sighed. "I should have known. I couldn't believe my eyes when I met you in Ellow. You look so much like Frelina a-and Miryn."

"It's my fault. I..." Her voice faded away like the breeze over the sea.

Merrick squeezed her hand when she shook her head, wondering if she could continue.

But that conviction—his conviction—seemed to flow freely between their linked hands, and as she drew a breath, she was able to get out a few more words.

"I thought I killed Frelina. It was horrible. And I..." Her voice broke once more as the memory of her parents' devastated faces, the blood marring their clothes and hands as they told her Frelina had jumped from the roof, surfaced in her mind.

"She told me what happened when I received your letter." Her father nodded toward Merrick. "I can't believe she kept it to herself all these years. I just wish..."

Tears began spilling down her father's face again, and it felt as if her chest were splitting wide open when his tall frame began to shake from the sobs.

This was worse than she'd imagined.

A lot worse.

"I'm so sorry," Lessia whispered. "It's all my fault."

"No." Her father shook his head. "It isn't."

Lessia's face broke as she stared back at him.

Of course it was.

She was the cause of these tears.

She was the cause of their family being broken apart.

Of Frelina having to live a lie.

"You were a child. Twelve years old! Nothing was your fault. If it's anyone's, it's mine."

Her bottom lip trembled as her father took a step toward her, opening his arms.

When she faltered, Merrick gently nudged her forward, and she nearly collapsed when her father's leathery scent cloaked her, his arms as strong as she remembered them.

"It wasn't your fault," her father whispered into her hair when a low cry left her. "You were just a child."

"I thought..." Lessia hiccuped. "I thought I lost you forever."

"We're here now." His arms wrapped tighter around her. "We're not leaving you again."

As she let herself hug him back, even with the guilt berating her, telling her she didn't deserve it, she asked shakily, "Where is Mother?"

Her father froze.

And so did her blood when she pulled back to look at him.

She could sense Merrick stiffen behind her, his unnerving presence moving closer.

Her father stared at her, and she bit her cheek at the devastation in his eyes.

"I'm s-sorry. She's... she's dead."

Lessia shook her head as she took a step back, shaking off his warm embrace.

That was a lie.

Her mother couldn't be dead.

The woman with the softest hands.

The woman with the kindest smile.

The woman with the most beautiful singing voice.

No.

"She's— No!" Lessia violently shook her head again. "She's not old enough to die yet."

She hadn't been more than a few years past forty when Lessia left.

Humans could live to at least eighty. Perhaps even ninety if they were lucky.

"She was sick." Her father's eyes pleaded with her as she continued to back away. "I brought a healer to help your sister after... after the accident. When she was updating us on her progress, she realized almost immediately that your mother... that she was ill as well."

Lessia's back collided with Merrick's chest, but she couldn't even feel his arms around her as her father continued.

"There was nothing we could do. It's... humans, they get diseases we don't. She'd been so happy, it had masked its progression, but when everything happened—"

Lessia pushed Merrick off and sprinted away, her hands flying up to cover her ears.

No.

No.

No.

She repeated the word with every step she took.

Her legs didn't take her to the cabin but toward the cliffs on the other side of the island—their darkness and lonely position mirroring the empty abyss within her.

She might not have killed Frelina.

But her mother had died because of the worry she'd brought into her life.

And...

She'd died not knowing Lessia existed.

CHAPTER TWENTY

The moon hung high in the sky as she lifted rock after rock and hurled them onto the calm surface.

The low splashes didn't do anything to soothe the chaos churning inside her, the feeling so suffocating she wanted nothing more than to crawl out of her skin—to become someone else...

Or perhaps become nothing at all.

Opening her mouth, she screamed her devastation across the darkening reflection of the sky.

Lessia screamed for her mother, for her useless death, for the regret that she'd never be able to rid herself of, until her throat was raw.

She cursed the gods.

She cursed fate.

She cursed every single decision that had led her to this moment.

And most of all, she cursed herself.

Out of breath, she fell to her knees and slammed her hands against the hard rocks, glad when they pierced her skin and blood began staining the gray stone.

What was the point?

What was the point of all this pain?

What was the point of it all?

The gods' gifts were supposed to be the foundation a Fae needed to wander the path to their fate.

But hers?

Her "gift"?

It was poison.

It was cursed.

It might not have ultimately killed her mother, not in the way she thought it had her sister, but given what her father had said, it had surely shortened her life.

And it *had* been directly responsible for the disaster with Loche.

While fury—white-hot fury—built within her, golden light cast back from Ydren's scales as she swam by, and Lessia blinked hard to repress the magic brightening her eyes, her nails pressing into her palms as she stared at the large wyvern.

Ydren had swum by a few times in the hour or so Lessia had stood atop the cliff, and she was sure the wyvern reported her whereabouts to Raine and the others.

Perhaps she'd even reported that Lessia had screamed and screamed and screamed at the sky until her voice drifted away like the mist floating atop the waves in the distance.

But so far, they'd left her alone.

She guessed Merrick might have stopped anyone

who'd thought of checking up on her, and a tiny ember of gratitude wrangled with the rage pressing on her chest for the Death Whisperer.

Watching Ydren as she sailed through the water, droplets trickling down her long neck like heavy teardrops gliding down a child's cheek, Lessia thought again on the strange path her life had taken her.

It had been filled with darkness and sorrow and fear, yes.

But then more faces joined Merrick's in her mind—Amalise and Ardow, Kalia and the children, Soria and Pellie, her family and even Loche, although shadows still mingled with his hard features—and she realized there was light as well.

She'd been happy.

Up until her twelfth year, she'd been more than happy.

And after that...

She'd found friends.

Unlikely, strange friendships that still managed to warm a small part of her chest.

She'd even found love.

She might have lost Loche, but...

She wasn't alone.

She still loved.

She did.

Even if she might not want to, she loved those damned children. She loved Ardow and Amalise. She loved her family in the way her mother had—unconditionally. And she even loved the broody Merrick.

Her eyes followed Ydren's movement in the water, the ripples that formed around her huge body, how the spikes lining her back reflected the moonlight.

The wyvern didn't have a single part of her family left.

The only person she had was a drunkard.

Lessia, on the other hand...

She *had* a family, even if her mother had passed.

She had a father.

A sister.

Friends.

With a sniff, Lessia straightened her stiff legs.

There might be much regret in her life.

Choices she'd make differently now.

But there wasn't time for her to wallow in it.

Her father and Frelina were alive.

So were her friends.

And she needed to ensure it stayed that way.

Numbness settled within her, driving away the pain and the fear and the helplessness.

Letting out a harsh breath through her teeth, she stared at the moon's reflection in the sea and unleashed every ounce of anger that had kept her moving so far.

Energy—wild, untamed energy—sparked within her, and her magic kindled across her skin, the light from her eyes brightening the polished stone beneath her feet once more.

She couldn't break down.

She couldn't even suppress her magic anymore.

Not if it could right the wrongs it had made.

If it could make sure the people she loved were safe.

She'd made so many stupid decisions in her short life.

Had believed the path the gods sent her on was inescapable—that it was out of her control.

But this wasn't one of them.

Havlands was in danger, and the people on this island were perhaps the only ones who could ensure it was saved.

It wasn't about her anymore.

It wasn't even about her mother.

Or Loche.

Or any other single individual.

With a final glance at the winking stars, Lessia spun on her heel and began walking back to the cabin.

She wasn't surprised to find Merrick waiting for her halfway there, but as she fell into step with him, he didn't speak, only nodded once as his steps slowed to keep her pace.

Lessia halted with her hand on the doorknob when they reached the cabin.

Turning her eyes to Merrick's, she stated, "We need to make sure they believe us. And that they'll help. With whatever means necessary. I... I can't fail again. I won't."

Merrick's hand touched hers as fiery determination sparked within his eyes. "I know."

She eyed him for a moment—it seemed as if he wanted to say something else—but when he remained quiet, Lessia pulled the door open and stepped into the warmth.

Her resolve wavered for a second when she took in the cramped cabin.

Raine stood by the bar, a surly expression on his face as he poured liquor into a dirty glass.

Her father sat in one of the chairs, with Kerym beside him, his thick sword lying across his lap.

Ardow and Venko shared the couch, and she noted that their distance appeared to have shrunk compared to the past few days.

Frelina was nowhere to be seen, but as her ears perked, the rustling of clothing reached them, and she realized her sister must be in one of the rooms adjoining this one.

Merrick nudged her over the threshold, and when his hand remained on her back, her voice sounded steadier than she felt as she spoke. "F— Alarin, we don't have much time. As you know, Havlands is in danger, and we must ensure Rioner and Loche see it before it's too late. We need them to set aside their differences, with each other and us, so we can withstand the threats to our realm."

Her father met her eyes, but Kerym spoke before he had the chance. "I was wondering why a fleet of Oakgards' Fae was traveling this way. The sound of their war drums still has my ears ringing."

"Where?" Merrick snapped.

"Oh, they're several weeks away. Perhaps a couple of months, depending on the weather they'll face." Kerym grinned as he traced a finger over the sharp edge of his blade. "I haven't fought Fae in many decades, and the constant traveling was getting quite dull. I was already on my way to investigate when I received your letter. Seems like I made the right choice." He slapped Raine, who'd sat down on the armrest of his chair, so hard on the back that the Fae choked on the sip he'd just taken. "We get to fight together again!"

Raine bared his teeth at him. "I am not fighting for Rioner. All of Vastala can fall for all I care."

"You wouldn't fight for Rioner," Merrick snarled. "You'd fight for our family and friends who still live there. Or have you given up on everyone you care for?"

"You, out of all people, should agree with me!" Raine

flew from his seat, his finger jabbing in Merrick's direction. "After what he did to you?"

Without thinking, Lessia grabbed a bottle from the table beside her and smashed it on the floor, forcing all eyes to hers. "Enough! We do not have time to argue. It's not about any of us. It's about the people in Havlands! The rebels are planning an attack soon, and it'll weaken the whole realm. We need to get Rioner and Loche to speak to the rebel leader—make sure we're united before those Oakgards' Fae arrive."

"Even better." Kerym leaned back in his seat, his grin creeping wider. "A little warm-up fight before the big act."

Ardow let out a low sound of disapproval but kept his mouth in a thin line when Lessia glared at him.

Rising from the chair, her father shook his head. "It's not that simple."

He raised a hand when Lessia opened her mouth to argue. "Please... Just listen to what I have to say."

Walking up to the painting of the wyvern and dragging a finger over the Fae holding up the glowing stone, he spoke in a hushed voice. "I'll be executed if Rioner finds out I even thought of telling you this. But Elessia is right. The realm will be weakened, but it's not Vastala that is in danger."

"What do you mean?" Merrick stepped closer behind her, the warmth from his body keeping her feet firmly in place when a shiver raced down her spine at her father's haunted face.

"I couldn't tell you this before, Merrick... But Rioner knows all about the rebels and the Oakgards' Fae, and he has a plan to keep Vastala and his rule intact." Her father sighed as he sought Lessia's eyes. "This goes back to before any of us in this room were born. Back to when our ancestors lived in the Old World."

"What scheming shit has Rioner come up with now?" Kerym scoffed but quieted after Merrick growled softly.

The low rumble rolled through Lessia, and she wrapped her arms around herself when goose bumps pebbled her skin.

"It wasn't Rioner who came up with it." Alarin wrung his hands as his gaze swept over the room. "When we drove our gods from this world, they didn't leave peacefully."

"We know," Raine sneered. "Our race was nearly extinct from the war."

"Not just that," her father responded. "It's rumored that they left each royal family with a curse as revenge for their treachery. My father didn't believe it, nor did his father or the king before him. But when those Oakgards' Fae arrived to speak to Rioner... he wasn't so sure anymore."

"Curse?" Ardow asked as he leaned forward, his eyes wide.

Alarin nodded. "Curse or prophecy... whatever you prefer to call it. Each of the four royal families was supposedly bestowed with one. The Fae planning to invade us are bound to the earth—used to be under the Oakgards' rule—and only through the connection to the elements can they draw up power to wield magic. They told Rioner their lands are dying because the Oakgards were cursed to kill their lands if they ever used magic again."

Lessia's breath hitched, and from the silence at her back, she guessed Merrick held his breath as well.

Wincing, her father cast a glance their way. "Supposedly, the Rantzier family—which back then was known for our emissaries, our eagerness to travel and to form new alliances—was cursed to be dethroned, our people's lives torn apart by an ally. It wasn't until recently I heard part of the curse, and..." Alarin swallowed. "While I don't agree with Rioner's plans, I can understand his reasoning as a leader of his people."

It felt as if everyone in the room stared at her chest, where her heart beat so hard it echoed in her ears when Lessia opened her mouth. "What... what did the curse state?"

Her father's eyes dropped to the floor. "As I said, I only heard parts of it..."

"Alarin," Merrick warned when he hesitated.

"Very well." Alarin leaned against the wall, and when Lessia's gaze traveled across the room, all eyes were glued to him as he spoke in a low voice.

"The Rantzier rule will end, its people disband, by the hands of the reluctant ally—the ally that should have stood by their side, that should have fought with them, that should have protected them. It's the one loved by Fae and human, the one you may not slay for the war that fragile death would bring, who will finally bring the Rantziers to their knees."

Everything went silent.

Everything but her pulse, which seemed to sing a song of fear within her.

"Fae and human..." Raine mumbled, his eyes flying over her for a moment.

Lessia violently shook her head as Ardow whispered, "It's Loche, isn't it?"

Alarin nodded. "Rioner wasn't sure at first, as Loche seemed to be a true ally. It wasn't until... that last night of the election with Elessia."

Lessia swallowed, the sound bouncing between the walls of the silent house.

"For those of us who just arrived, what happened with the human ruler and the Faeling?" Kerym's eyes sought hers, and she quickly averted them when curiosity filled his sea-blue ones.

"Well?" Kerym demanded when thick tension layered across the group.

Loved by Fae and human.

Betrayed gray eyes filled her vision.

Herself crawling toward him on the floor.

I think I'm falling in love with you.

Her father remained quiet, but the pity in his eyes was as evident as the shaking in Raine's hands when the latter offered him a glass of liquor.

When Raine's face also twisted with sympathy as he glanced her way again, she couldn't stand it anymore, every muscle within her body going taut as she cast her eyes down.

"I told him I loved him," she said in a monotone, refusing to let the images of Loche's disgusted face surface.

A muffled cough made her whirl around, and her brows knitted when Merrick's face drained of blood as he stared back at her.

Mind spinning, she stepped toward him, but Merrick's features quickly slipped into his usual mask, and he waved her away.

Her frown deepened as he instead stalked up to her father and Raine and grabbed the glass in Raine's hand to drain it.

Lessia looked on as he threw his head back, more realizations slamming into her.

That's why Rioner had been so adamant Loche had something to do with the strange things happening, even when she told him he didn't...

That's why he'd needed eyes on him from the inside.

That's why... he'd sent her.

A half-Fae.

As a test.

She bit back a growl.

No one hated anyone as much as Lessia hated the king then.

A loathing swept through her like poison—filling every nerve and vein.

"So." Merrick's tongue darted out to lick a stray drop off his lips as he slapped the glass back into Raine's hand. "Rioner believes Loche is about to dethrone him. What has he planned to do about it?"

Her father's eyes narrowed as he sliced them between her and Merrick before responding, "Rioner doesn't believe he can kill him himself—not with how the curse was outlined. So, he's made a deal with the Oakgards' Fae. They have sent some soldiers to help quash the rebels who plan to attack Vastala. And once that's done, and Loche and his men are still occupied with what we expect to be a fragile aftermath of the rebel attacks in Ellow, he will provide Vastala soldiers to take Ellow for their own."

"Amazing!" Kerym clapped his hands as a wicked smirk lifted his lips. "So there is no chance of us succeeding in saving Havlands, then? Thank the gods. I've tired of this world anyway. Perhaps I might finally find rest."

A smile pulled at Raine's features as well. "When you put it that way... this might be more interesting than I thought."

Lessia's nostrils flared as her eyes flitted between the two grinning Fae, then to Merrick, who'd grabbed another glass to down it.

The fucking gods.

Always the damned gods.

They'd done nothing more than wreak havoc.

"There must be something we can do!" Lessia snarled. "Stupid fate cannot be the reason Ellow is destroyed. Loche doesn't have any interest in taking Rioner down. Even if Rioner is a stubborn bastard, we must be able to convince him!"

They would have to.

Amalise was in Ellow.

And so were the children.

The children she had brought over from what now seemed to be the safe isle.

Her father shot her a sorrow-filled look. "Rioner will not listen. I've tried. Some of his other council members have even tried to calm him. He believes he is protecting his people. And... what if he is right? The curse does speak to our people being disbanded."

Lessia snorted.

Protecting his people...

There was no way.

"Merrick?" Stalking up to him instead, a snarl ripped from her lips when he didn't immediately meet her eyes. "Merrick!"

When he finally tilted his head down and met them, a current whispered over her skin.

The inky black was impossibly darker, the silver flecks more pronounced, his cheeks flushed with color, and if she didn't know better, she might have thought his hand shook as he gripped her arm—to keep her steady or to keep her from getting more into his face, she didn't know.

"We'd need an army if we're to take on Rioner *and* a fleet of Oakgards' Fae. A much bigger army than those flimsy ships the humans call their navy." Merrick pulled her closer, his breaths fanning over her face as he leaned in. "We'd all die, Lessia. We'd die for this. For..."

She heard the word he swallowed.

Him.

They'd die for Loche.

But it wasn't about him.

At least not only him.

It was about every person who'd visited her tavern.

Every person who'd smiled at her during the election.

Every person who'd hoped for a better life under Loche.

Sure... they could try to get the children out and just take off—hide somewhere and wait this out.

But she'd made a vow that day she'd hurt Frelina.

And damned if she wouldn't keep it.

She refused to break their stare off.

Refused to believe there was nothing they could do.

She'd made a choice.

And if that choice led to her death?

Well, then, so be it.

She was so tired of the gods.

So tired of fate.

So tired of being helpless.

No.

Fuck that.

"Then we find an army!" she hissed. "I thought you all had taken down companies of soldiers by yourselves!" Lessia threw her arm out toward where Raine and Kerym still grinned at each other as they refilled their drinks. "Did the stories lie?"

"They do not lie," Merrick snarled back, his face an inch from hers, and she nearly stumbled back when his eyes flared. "If you want to fight... I'll fight for you."

"So will I."

Both their heads whipped toward Raine when he spoke.

Raine winked at them. "Don't look so surprised. I won't fight for Rioner, but I'll fight for the humans. If they're all like those two"—he waved toward Venko and Ardow, who sat with their mouths open and stared at them all—"they can be quite amusing."

"Count me in." Kerym studied his nails. "I meant it. I am bored with this world. And I enjoy these odds."

"I will fight as well, Elessia." Alarin took a hesitant step their way. "It's what Miryn would have wanted."

Lessia closed her eyes when raw despair etched across her father's features, and Merrick's grip on her arm tightened until she opened them again.

Ardow cleared his throat from the couch while he threw Venko a quick look. "I will stand by you. I believe we need to warn the rebels, but I will follow your orders if you do not wish to do so."

Venko chewed on his lip for a while, his cheeks reddening as the others' gazes landed on him, but he finally said, "I can't promise I will fight. But if you can get me back to Ellow, I will provide you with weapons and other resources you might need from my ships."

Lessia gave him a small smile, then moved to meet the males' eyes one by one. "Then I guess our first step is to warn Loche."

CHAPTER TWENTY-ONE

"It's getting late." Her father stretched his hands over his head from where he was perched on the chair by the fire Raine had lit, his mouth rounding into a yawn.

They'd all quieted after Lessia's declaration, their eyes drifting to the raging flames as they sipped on whatever drink they held in their hands, and the energy that had sparked in the room had vanished as quickly as the light in Loche's eyes when he found out why she was truly in the election.

Rising from the squeaking seat, Alarin gave her a sad smile. "I should go check on your sister."

Lessia rose as well. "I'll come with you."

If she were to take on a whole army, she could face her sister—the girl who'd once been her best friend.

Well, her only friend.

But even though she'd met Amalise and Ardow, and perhaps even Merrick now, Frelina would always come first.

"Elessia." Her father lowered his voice as he walked up to her. "She needs time when she gets like this. I think it's perhaps best to wait until morning. We'll need to stay at least a day to plan. There is time."

"But..."

Alarin shook his head. "Trust me."

When she remained quiet, he patted her shoulder, and with a soft "Good night" to the rest of the group, he walked into Frelina's room and closed the door.

Lessia winced as Frelina's soft voice traveled through the thick wood, her father's soothing rumbles following soon after.

It had been thirteen years since she last saw her.

Frelina hadn't liked being alone back then.

She'd always come to seek Lessia out whenever they fought—even when Lessia was at fault.

But Lessia had also changed in the past years—the happy memories from her youth mere whispers whenever she dreamed of them—so it wasn't that surprising her little sister had as well.

With a sigh, she threw herself back on the couch, eliciting a low moan from Ardow, who'd fallen asleep on Venko's shoulder beside her.

Her foot tapped the ground as she watched their sleeping faces, but not even when Venko snuggled closer to her friend could she relax.

"Here." Raine shoved a cup of brown liquor into her hands. "It's battle nerves. This helps."

It wasn't just nerves, Lessia thought as she lifted the cup to her nose, which scrunched at the harsh smell.

It was the damn weight of the world on her shoulders.

Amalise and the others didn't even know what was coming.

What if Loche didn't believe them?

He'd told her he'd kill her if she ever returned to Ellow...

Her fingers clenched around the glass, and without a second thought, she lifted it to her lips and downed the whole thing.

"Shit."

Unable to hold back a grimace at the burning sensation, she lifted her eyes to Raine's wide ones.

"What?" she asked after she licked her lips.

"I didn't think you'd drink it," Raine said as a smirk replaced his surprised expression. "This will be fun."

"What will be fun?" Merrick stalked into the room from the kitchen, where he'd done his usual brooding or whatever else he did when that sour mask hardened his features.

Lessia giggled as she studied his drawn-down brows and the muscle that twitched in his jaw.

He was so damn broody.

Merrick's eyes slowly moved from the glass in her hand to her eyes, and she giggled again when his expression went from sour to murderous. "What the fuck, Raine?"

Raine quickly slipped behind the couch, and Lessia tilted her head back, finding him with palms out and shoulders raised. "It's fine. She's half-Fae. It won't be so bad."

"I swear, one of these days, I will kill you," Merrick snarled.

The world began spinning, so Lessia quickly dipped her head back down.

As she eyed the few drops left in her glass, a wave of warmth embraced her, the feeling eerily similar to her mother's hugs, and Lessia braced herself for the stab of pain at the image of her mother.

But it didn't come.

Instead, another rush flooded through her.

She blinked as the colors around her softened, the sounds in the house muting.

Oh.

She was drunk.

Or something like it.

She didn't exactly feel like she did when she drank wine with Ardow and Amalise.

She'd mostly get nostalgic, and then the guilt from what she'd thought she'd done would ruin the buzz.

But this felt good.

Better than good.

Merrick's grumblings before her touched her ears, and when she stared at him, his entire body vibrated from the vicious sound in his chest.

Reaching out a hand, she placed it on his stomach, and another laugh bubbled out of her when all those muscles he was made up of flexed.

Merrick gripped her hand, removing it from his quivering body. "What are you doing?"

She stuck out her bottom lip. "Come on, Merrick. Don't ruin this for me."

"You don't drink," he seethed. "This is strong stuff, Lessia. Raine is the only one who can handle it. And that's because he's been drinking it for years!"

"Not true." Kerym tsked as he raised his glass from the chair opposite her. "I'm thoroughly enjoying myself over here."

"She'll be fine, Merrick. Look at her. She's actually smiling." Raine rested his elbows on the couch so his face leveled with Lessia's. "Let her have some fun."

"Yes, Merrick. Let her have some fun," Lessia parroted as she snatched the glass in Raine's hand and drank that as well.

"The—" She couldn't stop a rough cough as the drink burned her throat, but more giggles soon joined the hacking.

Wiping her hand over her mouth as more warmth welled within her, she tried again. "The world is ending. And everybody hates me. Let... let me have some fun. I never have fun."

Merrick glared at her for a moment while dragging his hands through his shiny hair.

As she watched him, an urge to drag her own hands through it seized her.

It was so sparkly in the firelight.

It'd probably be very soft.

Soft like one of the wolf pups she'd found in the forest when she was younger.

Crouching down before her, Merrick gripped her chin to ensure she stared into his eyes. "Everybody doesn't hate you."

"Yes, they do." Lessia laughed. "My sister does. Loche does. And I can see my father blames me for my mother's death. I left Amalise and the children I'm responsible for —they must also hate me."

She was sure of it, but the liquor didn't let any of the guilt or sorrow fester.

Lessia found Raine's dancing hazel eyes when he grinned at her.

She was beginning to understand why he refused to go a second without this.

It helped.

Maybe she shouldn't have been so quick to judge him.

Moving her face back to his, Merrick said softly, "You're wrong."

"It doesn't matter. I feel amazing!" As she shrugged, Lessia offered him a broad smile, and Merrick's eyes widened.

"That's great and all, but some of us are trying to sleep," Ardow muttered from her side, and she slapped a hand over her mouth not to burst out laughing when one of his sleepy eyes opened to glare at her.

Raine's hand clasped her shoulder. "There are some kind of festivities every night at the tavern. I say we go. I'm sure the weeks ahead of us will be all but festive."

The tavern.

It sounded perfect!

She'd been too worried last time.

But now?

She wasn't afraid of some dumb Fae.

"Can we?" she begged Merrick, adding, "Please?" when he hesitated.

When he threw his head back with a groan, his silver hair billowed across his shoulders, and she watched in wonder as the pearly strands caught the light, dancing freely in contrast to his sharp features.

"Fine." Merrick sighed. "But do not blame me for how you'll feel tomorrow."

Lessia flew up from the couch and was about to hug him when he stepped back, something she couldn't read fighting over his features.

With another shrug, she hugged herself instead, savoring the warmth softening her limbs.

Kerym also rose, and the thumps as he patted Merrick's back echoed through the room. "We've known each other for centuries, and I was never able to convince you to join us in our drinking escapades! I'm unsure whether I should be upset or happy for you."

"Kerym," Raine warned as he ushered them all out the door.

Lessia's eyes sliced between the two Fae males, but then the chill breeze brushed her arms, and she nearly squealed as the saltiness tickled her bare skin as she walked out into the night.

Every step through the island was one of wonder.

How could she not have appreciated the smooth rocks that formed a pathway through the swaying hip-height grass?

Or the birds: the eagles and the hooting owls that peeked at them from the tall trees strewn out as they ventured further inland?

Even the somewhat crumbling stone wall surrounding the small town was beautiful in the dim light of the lantern Merrick carried as he walked beside her.

"You ready?" Raine's brows danced as he reached to open the door to the tavern.

Nodding, Lessia skipped by him, stepping right over the small step and into the warmth.

Her wide eyes took in the bustling room.

It wasn't as busy as it had been during Zehmkell, but it was still filled with Fae, and she was happy to find the eyes that snagged on her quickly moved along, although she could see they lingered on the three males behind her.

Spending time with the lethal brotherhood, or whatever they were called, apparently had great benefits.

Without waiting for the others, she sprinted up to the bar.

"Can I have something that will keep me feeling like this?" Lessia pointed to her smile when the barkeep nodded toward her.

"Certainly." A grin spread across the Fae's face as he poured the golden liquor she'd seen Merrick drink into a tall glass.

Placing it on the sticky surface before her, he reached out his palm, and Lessia slapped her hand over her mouth, her eyes rounding. "Oh no. I don't have any silvers!"

Another breathy giggle escaped her as the Fae looked over her shoulder and waved his hand.

"Put it on my tab." Raine sidled up next to her. "And get three more of those."

After spinning around, Lessia leaned her elbows on the bar and took small sips of whatever the barkeep had given her.

It tasted much better than Raine's brownish liquor.

Or maybe she was just getting used to it.

It didn't matter either way.

If she could feel like this just for a little while longer—whatever the taste, it was worth it.

Her eyes drifted toward the packed dance floor, where most Fae danced by themselves, not in couples as they had during Zehmkell, and before she could second-guess herself, she exclaimed, "I'm dancing!"

Swallowing the last of the drink, she pressed the

empty glass into Merrick's hand as he joined Raine by the bar and made her way over.

A few people moved out of the way as she approached, but it didn't seem it was because she was half-Fae.

No, the smiles on their faces were welcoming, and she beamed back at them.

They were making room for her.

With a happy sigh, Lessia closed her eyes, stretched out her arms, and let the music take her away.

The melody was unknown to her, the tunes drifting high for a moment before lowering—building the anticipation—until the sound swelled, growing richer and richer, as if the music was gathering strength until it reached its peak.

When the climax boomed through the room, she spun—faster and faster—ignoring the beads of sweat forming at her temples and how her cheeks began aching from laughing.

It didn't even make her nauseated, so she pushed her body to whirl faster, a delighted squeal leaving her when her feet obeyed.

As the song faded, she slowed her movements until she halted in sync with the music.

The sense of happiness filled her entirely, as if stopping had bottled it all up inside her.

Lessia opened her eyes and joined in the clapping from the Fae around her, then moved to lean her back against the wall to catch her breath as the music shifted into a slow song and the Fae around her pulled each other close.

She shook her head when a blond Fae eyed her questioningly, throwing him an apologetic smile as she gestured toward the wall and mouthed, "Maybe later."

She didn't want to dance with anyone else.

Not right now.

Doing it by herself felt... freeing somehow.

As if she could do this.

Not just the dance but... life.

A prickling sensation whispered over her face when she drew a happy breath, and as she lifted her eyes, Merrick's dark ones collided with hers, knocking the breath right back out of her again with their intensity.

A frown pulled at her features.

There was something different about him.

She continued meeting the unsettling darkness that was his eyes as she tried to understand what it was.

Softness.

It was softness, she decided.

While his face would always be sharp, with that strong jaw and high cheekbones, that boyishness she'd seen when he'd been sleeping after she helped clean his wounds or when he played with her in the water peeked through.

He was beautiful.

She'd always known he was.

He was Fae, after all.

But tonight?

He was every bit the strong Fae warrior she'd heard of.

But he was also a male.

A friend.

He was Merrick.

A fire kindled within her the longer he held her gaze

captive, those starlike flecks in his eyes sparkling from across the room.

It was as if they were talking to her...

But she couldn't hear what they were saying.

At the same time she took a step toward him to ask—to understand—Merrick jumped down from the chair he'd sat upon, their movements so synchronized a shocked laugh bubbled up within her.

Her eyes didn't leave his as he walked toward her, and she held her breath until dizziness made her vision blurry.

Shakily releasing it, she reached out a hand when Merrick halted before her.

When he glanced at it for a moment, she whispered, "I'm not making you dance, I promise."

The low chuckle leaving him rumbled through her, and her body trembled when his warm hand wrapped around hers.

"But I am."

Merrick's gravelly response made her sway, and he had to steady her when she stared up at him.

"You... you're what?" Lessia asked, that lightheadedness returning when Merrick tugged at her hand, turning her back toward the dance floor.

"Dancing."

"But..." Lessia frowned at him, bringing them both to a halt. "You don't dance."

She must be drunker than she'd thought.

Merrick laughed, a rough, quiet laugh. "I'll make an exception."

She was about to ask why when the question stuck in her throat.

Something dangerous flashed in Merrick's eyes.

And it wasn't the danger of battle or even magic but... something even more perilous.

Something she wasn't sure she was ready for.

So instead, she nodded, expecting him to drag her out to the other dancing couples.

But Merrick nudged her back to the spot by the wall where she'd rested after her first wild dance.

When her back was nearly touching it, he stilled and pulled her into his arms so gently her mouth would have fallen open if she hadn't caught it.

Wrapping her own arms around his neck, she let him align their bodies so every inch touched the others, and when he began moving from side to side, the movement so slight it was barely making her shift her weight, she smiled into his shoulder.

It wasn't the dancing her father had taught her growing up.

It wasn't Loche's elaborate moves.

It was Merrick.

It was trust.

It was assurance.

It was friendship.

It was...

Her breath hitched when Merrick's cheek brushed hers, and she could feel his muscles growing taut as her heartbeat surged.

His stubble scratched against the sensitive skin just beneath her chin, and she tried to suck in a breath—tried to breathe, but it proved impossible.

She needed air.

That must be it.

It was so warm in here.

Dragging Merrick with her, she led them toward the

back of the tavern, toward one of the empty benches that still stood around the lit fireplace, stopping only to allow Merrick to pick up his cup from the bar beside Raine and Kerym.

Once they got out, air traveled into her lungs again, and Lessia plopped herself down on the wood with a soft sigh.

When Merrick only hovered before her, she gave him a pointed look.

As he rolled his eyes and went to sit, she playfully snatched his glass out of his hand and took a large sip, grateful when the eerie heat continued to push any unpleasant emotions she might feel away.

It was nice not caring for once.

The alcohol was a distraction.

She knew that.

But she needed one right now.

Especially since she wouldn't be able to afford them once they set off for Ellow.

Lessia released another breath as she gave the near-empty glass back, and her eyes once again snagged on the soft waves layering across Merrick's leather-clad shoulders.

They looked so soft.

And now the moon played in them...

Or perhaps they played with the moon?

"What are you thinking about?" Merrick asked after he drained the rest of the glass.

"Whether I'm allowed to pet you."

Her mouth fell open when she heard herself utter the words, but no heat crept up her cheeks, and she once again thanked the drink swirling inside her.

"You... you're asking if you can pet me?" Merrick

asked, and she knew she should have been worried about his low tone, but still, no sense of apprehension rippled across her skin.

"It's just your hair looks so soft and shiny, and I thought it would be nice to pet," she tried to explain.

A muscle in Merrick's jaw ticked—in the same way it did before he contemplated slamming her into the ground when they trained—so when he said "Fine," her brows nearly flew up to her hairline.

But she wasn't about to risk him changing his mind by asking if he was sure, so instead, she lifted her hand and cautiously ran her fingers through the inviting strands on the side of his head.

She'd been right.

They were as soft as they were beautiful.

Like warm butter drifting through her fingers.

When she moved toward his neck, her fingertips brushed his scalp, and she stilled when a shiver went through him.

Peeking at him through her lashes, she realized Merrick had closed his eyes, those wrinkles usually twisting the skin between his brows nowhere to be seen.

Her heart began beating so hard she glanced down at her chest.

And when she looked back up...

Her entire body froze at the look in Merrick's eyes.

The black was all-consuming, but it wasn't like a great fall right into their depths.

It was subtler, more gradual.

Like the sky that swirled there wanted her to surrender.

Willingly.

The world around them blurred at the edges, and

Lessia didn't think as she leaned forward and pressed her lips against his.

His lips were even softer than his hair.

Full, smooth, and melting against hers.

She couldn't stop herself from pressing her own harder against them, even as bells began ringing inside her mind, warning her against what she was doing.

She wasn't sure what she'd expected.

But Merrick letting out a low moan and weaving his hands into her hair... wasn't it.

His soft kiss was like a fever blooming across her skin, and a raw need, a need to be close to him, possessed her—consumed her.

Crawling into his lap, she locked her legs around his waist and deepened the kiss, desperate to get closer—to fuse their lips further, to merge their bodies as one.

If the alcohol had been a distraction...

This was something else entirely.

It didn't even matter when the memory of Loche kissing her that first time surfaced.

If she could just have this, she could forget everything else.

She didn't even care about Loche anymore.

Merrick was the greatest distraction.

"What did you say?" Merrick rasped against her mouth.

She tried to quiet him by brushing her lips against his once more, but Merrick pulled back, the hands in her hair holding her steady—and refusing her when she tried to look away from his hard eyes.

"I-I didn't say anything," she whispered.

Merrick's jaw locked as he shook his head. "You did."

He swore quietly as he moved her off his lap and back

onto the bench. "You said I was the greatest distraction. That you didn't even care about Loche anymore."

"I didn't..." Lessia started, but when Merrick raised his brows, she sealed her lips.

Shit...

She must have said it out loud.

And... she had used him as a distraction.

Hadn't she?

"I—" Lessia swallowed as the warmth drained from her veins, crushing, cold guilt surging in its stead.

"I'm sorry," she whispered in a shaky voice.

Merrick dipped his chin as he rose, his hands so tightly clenched that she wondered if he was contemplating slamming one into her face.

But Merrick only shot her a final glance that chilled her blood.

Not from fear...

No.

From the pain simmering in his black eyes.

Then he spun on his heel, his long strides quickly taking him back into the light of the tavern.

CHAPTER TWENTY-TWO

Fuck!

Lessia angrily wiped at a tear fighting its way down her cheek as she stumbled through the island, a throbbing beginning in her head as her body quickly—too quickly—burned through the alcohol she'd ingested.

She hadn't dared return to the tavern.

After meeting Merrick's somber eyes, she'd climbed over the wooden fence surrounding the tavern garden and sprinted down the darkening path back to the cabin.

Or, at least, moved as fast as she could with the cups of liquor she'd drunk.

Lessia pressed her hands against her face, stopping at the fork where one path led to the cabin and the other to the beach.

Against her will, the kiss etched itself into her mind, dimming all other thoughts until she could hear only Merrick's low moan, her own fast breaths, and whatever the sound was called that had left her as she desperately tried to get closer to him.

It had been a good kiss.

Better than good.

It had been amazing.

As in mind-blowing, earth-shattering amazing.

A mortified groan left her, and Lessia dug her palms harder into her eyes, not even caring about the darkness when crushing shame ripped into her.

She'd kissed Merrick!

Worse, she'd liked kissing Merrick.

And perhaps worst of all—he'd kissed her back.

Why?

Why had he kissed her back?

Heat shot up her neck.

Because he pitied her?

Because he couldn't stand her being rejected again?

She had just told everyone what happened with Loche...

Dropping her hands to her sides, Lessia stormed down the path to the beach instead of returning to the cabin, where soft light peered out of the rounded windows.

"Fuck!" she screamed again as she reached the shoreline, her frustration building when the water seemed to swallow the curse.

Lessia fell to her knees, her hands slamming into the sand.

Again.

And again.

But it still wasn't enough to quell the burn inside her.

Not until a wave of water fell over her.

Squinting as drops of salty water that clung to her

lashes teased her eyes, Lessia found Ydren's large shape snaking its way onto the beach.

Soon the beast surrounded her, and her heart skipped a beat as she wondered whether Ydren perhaps thought it time to punish Lessia for using her magic on her that first day.

But as Ydren curled closer, she was gentle, her thick body not crushing her but...

Hugging her.

The wyvern was hugging her.

A shocked giggle broke through the haze of panic that had threatened to take over as Lessia wondered whether she'd driven away yet another person she loved, and it wasn't the alcohol that made her wrap her arms around Ydren's long, wet neck.

Her brows furrowed at how soft Ydren's scales were.

And her body was so... warm?

Not what she'd expected from a creature that usually lived in the depths of the sea.

Ydren growled softly when Lessia trailed her fingers over her scales, and when the creature pressed her neck against Lessia's body, she couldn't help another sob escaping.

"I messed up tonight," she whispered.

Ydren didn't make a sound, so Lessia continued.

"I don't know what happened. I just... I was having fun, and he was there. And... I don't know... I think I liked it? But now I am afraid he also hates me."

Lessia sniffed.

She wasn't sure if she could stand Merrick hating her.

If she could return to how they'd been before growing close during the election.

Gods, why did she make a mess out of everything?

Throwing herself at every person who showed her an inkling of warmth, like a desperate child...

It was humiliating.

And wrong.

Ydren let out a rumbling sigh as Lessia let her arms go limp, and when Lessia met her eyes, the wyvern jerked her head toward the small spot of sand surrounded by her body.

"You want me to sit?" Lessia gestured toward the spot, and when Ydren nodded so vigorously that drops of saltwater stained Lessia's cheeks like her tears had before, she slumped down with her back against the wyvern.

Probably best she stayed out here for a while anyway.

She wasn't sure she could face Merrick and the rest yet.

With another deep sound, Ydren rested her head on her own body opposite Lessia, keeping one eye open to follow Lessia's movements.

Lessia shot the creature a skewed smile when Ydren continued eyeing her, something like curiosity reflecting in the wyvern's violet eyes.

"I messed up tonight." Lessia threw her head back as she repeated her declaration, wincing when her hair got caught in Ydren's scales. "I really did. It seems like I just keep doing it. Like I just can't get it right."

Ydren blinked at her, and Lessia interpreted the flicker in her eye as a sign to go on.

"I keep hurting those I love." Her hand flew to her chest, a fist forming over her aching heart and her voice thickening as she continued. "My sister, my parents, Loche... and now Merrick. They all hate me now. I—"

"You're wrong again." Merrick's voice floated over the wyvern, and her adrenaline surged as she whipped her head up to find his eyes staring straight into hers.

Her tense shoulders lowered an inch.

They were his normal eyes.

No hurt lacing the edges like it had back at the tavern.

Ydren winked at her as she started unraveling her body, and before Lessia could even say good night, the wyvern slithered down into the water with only a soft splash betraying her descent into the depths of the sea.

"What am I wrong about?" Lessia rasped as she fought the lump in her throat.

"Everyone doesn't hate you." Merrick gracefully folded his legs as he sat down beside her, his gaze wandering out across the sea. "I don't. And I doubt your sister does either. She's angry because she loves you so much. It's... it's easy to turn to rage when love stabs a dagger right through your heart."

"Sounds like you speak from your own experience," Lessia mumbled, but she couldn't help the whisper of hope that began fluttering in her stomach at Merrick's words.

"I do."

Sympathy roiled in her gut, but before she could say something, Merrick spoke again.

"You know that pain too. I can see it in your eyes every day. You need to tell me. Did Loche turn you away after you—" Merrick cleared his throat, the rest of his words coming out clipped. "After you told him you loved him?"

Lessia swallowed.

But they'd find out what happened soon enough, now that they were heading back to Ellow.

"He forced me to erase all memories of us together. To erase his feelings for me."

It was quiet for a beat, and Lessia didn't dare look up as rage tinged the air around them, Merrick's whispers softly skimming across the sand.

"Why would he do that?" Merrick mumbled, almost as if to himself.

"I betrayed him," Lessia whispered. "It... it wasn't that I was a spy. He didn't care about that—he seemed to have even suspected it. It was because I used my magic on him that night we were attacked on the cliffs. It's the same night he came to me and trusted me..." She drew a shaky breath. "He kissed me that night. And he never would have if I hadn't manipulated his memories."

She felt like slamming her hands into the sand again.

She should never have let Loche kiss her.

She'd known it was wrong.

She'd known their entire relationship—or whatever it was—was on borrowed time.

Silence stretched so long that Lessia finally peeked at Merrick through her lashes.

He appeared deep in thought, something fighting across his features as he dragged his hands down his face.

It was as if he was trying to solve a puzzle from memory, his eyes darting back and forth until they finally met hers again.

Lessia stiffened when that thought... the thought that he was beautiful... slammed into her chest once more, and a torrent of heat flowed through her, exactly like it had when she'd climbed into his lap.

Casting her eyes to the hands she wrung in her lap and trying to ignore her surely red cheeks, Lessia mumbled, "I am sorry for what I did to you tonight. I swear, I do not know what came over me. And... and I'm sorry for saying you were a distraction. I didn't mean to hurt you."

"Lessia." Merrick cupped her cheeks with his hands, forcing her eyes to his. "Stop. Fucking. Apologizing."

Her eyes widened when he inched closer, and the blush that had warmed her skin must now have been near purple.

"The world is painful." Merrick's gaze drilled into hers. "Yours perhaps more than most. But it's time for you to stop cowering before it. Make mistakes, and forgive yourself for them. Get hurt, and fight back. You're a good person. A fucking great person. Stop letting guilt dim your light. I told you once, it's time to shine..." His hands tightened their grip, and Lessia's breath caught in her throat.

"It's time to fucking burn, Lessia. If we're taking on the threats of this world, you'll need to be willing to burn it down. Love. Lose. Hate. Win. They all come together in the end. Use them to fuel that passion to make this wretched world a little better."

Warmth shot through her veins.

Not like the warmth from the liquor.

But courage, determination, and fiery conviction that Merrick was right sparked through every nerve when he dropped his hands.

If she didn't know better... she might have thought it was Merrick's emotions flowing through her, for how quickly they drove any lingering worry away.

But... he didn't manipulate or manage emotions.

Her muscles relaxed as she placed her hands on the beach, leaning her weight on them.

"You're right." Lessia nodded to herself. "Still, I'm sorry... I didn't mean to kiss you."

Merrick's brows twitched. "I know."

Lessia inclined her head, and as she pushed her hands into the sand and got up, Merrick did the same.

Walking in comfortable silence back the short distance to the house, that gratefulness she'd felt the past couple of days provided comfort against the nightly wind beginning to pick up, and a small smile tugged at her lips as she reached for the doorknob.

But before she could twist it, Merrick's hand gripped her own.

Confused, she glanced over her shoulder at him.

"You should know." Merrick's breath hit her mouth when he leaned in over her. "I don't regret it."

"Regret what?" she asked.

"Kissing you."

Lessia's eyes rounded so much she was surprised they didn't pop out of her skull.

"I know you didn't mean it. But..." Merrick's gaze drifted over her. "You don't need to feel guilty."

Her mouth fell open when Merrick's hand squeezed hers as he opened the door and threw a curt "Night" over his shoulder before stalking off toward his room.

Her jaw remained slack the entire time she got out of her clothes and washed her face in the bathing chamber, and when she slipped into the cool sheets of the bed.

CHAPTER TWENTY-THREE

Lessia realized why Raine never let go of his bottle as she gripped the wooden bucket with both hands, vomiting bile and whatever liquor remained in her stomach.

Wiping her mouth with a shaky hand, she forced her equally trembly legs to straighten.

She needed a bath.

Preferably an ice-cold one to drive the thickness in her head away.

Without bothering to put anything else on besides the undergarments she'd slept in, only grabbing a towel from the small closet in her room and half-heartedly holding it against her chest, Lessia sneaked out of her room.

It was still early, dawn probably an hour or so away.

But she'd awoken with a racing heart, and even though a somewhat hazy memory of Merrick telling her she didn't need to feel guilty floated around in her mushy mind, she couldn't help but still feel it.

It wasn't as overwhelming as it had been, though.

As Lessia slipped through the squeaking back door and headed toward the rippling creek behind the house, she thought perhaps guilt was necessary to do what was right... to stay on the right path.

It was the reason she hadn't given up on Loche and the rest of Ellow and just tried to get Amalise and the children out.

It was the reason she hadn't used her magic to get riches and fame but instead had understood the responsibility that came with such a "gift."

It was the reason she'd taken in the children in the first place and risked her own and her friend's lives to give others a better one.

You're a good person, Merrick had said.

Another voice flickered to life in her mind—one she'd spent years repressing.

But now she could hear her mother so clearly it was as if she stood beside Lessia.

Good people also do bad things, but it's how you handle yourself after that matters.

Her mother had told her that once, when Frelina had destroyed one of Lessia's bracelets on purpose because Lessia hadn't wanted to play with her just that second.

The weight on her chest lifted.

Just an inch.

But it was enough for Lessia to draw a breath of dewy morning air, the warm smell of the yellow flowers lining the creek bed filling her nose as that determination—that conviction from last night—ran like a current over her skin.

She needed to pay the debt she owed to Ellow.

Not just because of Loche.

Or the children.

Or her friends.

But because of her mother.

The kindest human she'd ever known, whose light she needed to remember, whose light she needed to ensure could continue to shine on the lands where she'd been born.

While her mother might not have known of Lessia when she passed... Lessia would do everything she could to live up to her memory.

To make her proud.

And to do that, she needed to be strong now.

Fight for what was right, even when it hurt.

Perhaps especially when it hurt.

Lessia smiled as she dropped the towel on the grass and walked into the cool water.

It had been decided.

She'd do whatever she could for Ellow and Vastala.

And if she died...

Then at least she could move on to whatever came after this life with her head held high—right into her mother's waiting arms.

Diving into the clear water, she relished the cold coating her skin, how the water caressed her body and drove the lingering murkiness from her mind.

Lessia stayed beneath the surface until her lungs screamed, and even then, she waited a few additional moments, unwilling to leave behind the sense of purpose and clarity swirling within her.

When she finally broke the surface, a tired voice drifted over the ripples she'd caused.

"Thank the gods. I thought I would have to get in." Raine waved his bottle toward her. "If it's humiliation that made you nearly drown yourself, it's better not to stop drinking."

Heat stained her cheeks despite the cool water surrounding her, and she dipped down again, wishing for the peaceful rushing of water to instill the same stillness in her as she popped up again.

"No, thanks," she mumbled when Raine raised his brows, the bottle still extended.

"Suit yourself." Raine shrugged before he slumped down with his back against one of the birch trees lining the creek.

She eyed him as he lifted the bottle to his lips. "Is it better to live in an illusion of happiness with artificial emotions keeping you going?"

"Happiness," Raine scoffed. "I don't live in happiness. The liquor doesn't create emotions that don't already reside within us. It can dim the negative ones but can't create happy ones. And I don't keep any."

Lessia frowned. "But... but that would mean—"

"You danced because music makes you happy? Yes."

Her brows pulled in further.

Music always made her happy—that wasn't a surprise.

It was the gravitating to Merrick—kissing Merrick!—that was confusing.

He makes you happy.

The low voice in her mind made her jerk upright.

Did he?

They were friends.

You wanted to kiss him...

She had wanted it. But only to distract herself.

Right?

"You should probably grab your towel." Raine

covered his eyes with the arm holding his bottle. "I do not want to get killed if Merrick finds us here."

"Why would he..." Lessia's words trailed off when her eyes snagged on golden-brown hair sticking out from behind another tree, a bit further back from the one Raine leaned against.

After moving so fast through the water that it splashed around her, Lessia grabbed the towel, wrapped it around herself, and started toward the tree she'd seen her sister hide behind.

As she walked past Raine, the Fae grabbed her hand. "Be careful with him, Lessia." His gaze flicked toward the cabin for a second before returning to hers. "He does not need more pain in his life."

She was about to pretend she didn't understand what he meant when concern, genuine concern, etched itself across Raine's features.

Merrick had spoken about love and pain last night.

She'd heard the agony in his tone as clearly as she'd felt the urge to kiss him.

So, instead of denying that she understood what Raine meant, Lessia nodded. "I will."

Raine's hazel eyes softened. "Good. Now, I think your sister is making a run for it."

Lessia whipped her head up just in time to see her sister weaving her way through the tall grass leading inland.

Without thinking, she cast a final glance at Raine and followed her into the thick green, ignoring that she was barefoot with only a towel wrapped around her body.

"Frelina!" Lessia called out when she glimpsed her hair between the whistling grass. "Please!"

But her sister didn't stop, and the greenery quickly

swallowed the figure, the blades swaying back and forth in the warming breeze.

Halting, Lessia cocked her head to the side, training her ears as she listened to the spears of grass rubbing against each other, the shrieks of wind as it brushed the stems.

There.

There was a shuffling of feet to her left.

Without making a sound, recalling the training she'd had sneaking through the streets in Vastala to avoid drawing the attention of Rioner's guards, Lessia swept some of the tufts to the side.

When she heard the sound again, she lunged.

Slamming right into her sister, who'd started creeping up behind her, Lessia straddled her and gripped her flailing arms, pushing them down beside her body.

"Stop fighting," Lessia hissed through her teeth when Frelina slithered like a snake beneath her, her white canines glinting in the sunlight that broke through the grass. "I just need you to listen to me."

"Why should I?" Frelina snarled. "I heard you were taking off again anyway."

Lessia stiffened when tears flooded her sister's eyes, even as she blinked furiously to rid herself of them, and she quickly released her arms.

She was immediately flung to the side, crashing into the ground beside Frelina, and her towel dangerously close to falling off.

Readjusting it, Lessia glared to her side.

Frelina's chest heaved, but she remained lying on her back, her short hair splayed out with grass sticking up between the strands.

"I'm sorry, Lina," Lessia said softly as a tear rolled

down her sister's cheek, hoping Frelina wouldn't snap at her for using the old pet name. "I'm so sorry for what I did to you. And I am even more sorry I left you. I promise, there hasn't been a day when I didn't think of you, when I didn't hurt for what I did to you... you and Mother and Father."

Frelina clenched her jaw, her eyes staring straight into the brightening sky. "I have been so angry with you! You don't understand what it was like waking up, seeing Mother and Father completely broken... And when I asked for you? They called back the healer because they believed I hit my head so hard I was hallucinating. *I* even started to believe them—believe that the memories of you were fabrications of my mind."

Lessia closed her eyes for a moment, digging her fingers into the ground.

Frelina was right.

She couldn't even imagine.

"I'm sorry," Lessia whispered again.

"I know," Frelina clipped. "When I was finally healthy enough to get out of bed, I overheard my mother and the healer talk and... that's when I realized they weren't just broken for me..."

A distressed sound left her. "Mother was dying. I stopped talking about you then. They were barely functioning as it was, and Father could only focus on taking care of her. He got so careless we even had several of Rioner's men pay us a visit, as Rioner wondered where he'd disappeared off to."

Lessia's eyes widened, and she turned to her side, eyeing her sister closely.

Something about her tone—the monotone coldness of it—sent a chill racing down her spine.

"I killed them." Frelina also turned on her side, her gaze hard. "I had to."

Lessia bowed her head. "Of course. I-I have done the same thing."

How she wished neither of them had to, though.

That her innocent sister—the girl who used to chase Lessia through the woods on her pony, laughing so loud she almost fell off the horse, and who started every day by singing with their mother in the kitchen—remained.

But Lessia could see there was something new in Frelina's gaze.

A darkness she knew all too well herself.

Frelina's eyes flitted between hers, the amber in her sister's deepening to almost pure brown. "You have changed as well."

A weak smile spread across Lessia's face. "You're a mind reader?"

"Kind of." Frelina grimaced. "I don't read your mind, not like that drunkard Raine does. I get glimpses of memories, almost as if I were that person—as if I am living it."

"What did you see just now?" Lessia wasn't particularly eager to relive many of her memories, but her sister's features had softened, and she'd talk about anything—even her time in Rioner's cellars—if that's what it took to continue seeing the angry lines fade.

"It was blurry, maybe two memories mixed? One you were terrified in, but the memory was almost pure darkness, arms holding on to you as they strapped you into something. The other hurt, like stepping onto a sharp rock and being unable to get it out of your foot. A beautiful man—a human man—stood above you, saying something while you called out his name."

Frelina's brows knitted when Lessia winced. "Who was that?"

"Loche," Lessia forced out. "He... he was someone I cared for."

Frelina crossed her arms over her chest. "He doesn't seem very kind."

A low laugh bubbled out of Lessia. "No, perhaps not. But I betrayed him, so I'm not sure I deserved kindness in that moment."

"Because of what Rioner made you do?"

When Lessia raised her brows, Frelina clarified. "I didn't get it from your mind, but when Father explained where we were going, that Merrick knew someone he'd probably like to meet, I tried to convince him again of what happened that day—of who you were—and Father told me of the blood oath, the spying Rioner forced you to do. I didn't realize, though..." She cleared her throat. "I didn't realize you cared that much for him. But I felt it just now. I felt your heartbreak."

Lessia reached out to grip her sister's hand, the slight smile on her face widening when Frelina clasped it tightly.

"My heart was already broken, Lina. It never repaired itself from that day I thought I lost you..."

Lessia drew a breath, the words she'd held in for so long tumbling out of her. "I-I did care for him. He understood me in a way few have before, and we had many similarities—we wanted the same things. But I don't think I could ever let myself love someone, not fully, unless... unless you forgive me."

Lessia's voice began shaking at the end, and she was grateful when Frelina squeezed her hand.

"I do," Frelina said in a choked voice. "I do forgive you if you promise not to leave me again."

Lessia nodded. "I promise I won't. I will need to leave..."

She held up her hand when her sister's face scrunched. "Wait, let me finish! I will need to leave for Ellow. There are more people's forgiveness I need to seek, relationships I need to mend. But... will you come with me?"

A rush of air escaped Frelina. "Of course! I've always wanted to see Ellow. Father still doesn't let me go anywhere, so I've only seen our damned island. And this one, I guess."

Releasing Frelina's hand, Lessia pressed her own down into the soft grass, pushing up to sit. "It'll be dangerous, Frelina. As in life-and-death dangerous."

Her sister wiggled her brows. "I was wondering why you had all these broody Fae males around. They're bodyguards, aren't they? The Death Whisperer, the Mind Capturer, and one of the Siphon Twins? Probably the best there are. I'm sure we'll be fine."

Lessia clamped her lips together so as not to burst out laughing.

Frelina wasn't entirely wrong.

She might have learned a little about fighting, but she was still no match for Merrick or Raine.

Probably not Kerym either.

"Perhaps do not call them that. As you said... they're broody most of the time, so best not to rile them up further unless you want to deal with all the sighs and growls." Lessia winked, warmth clawing into her chest when her sister grinned back at her.

The warmth spread to her limbs when Frelina fell

into step with her as she headed back to the cabin, and that determination, that fire, burned even brighter as they stepped over the threshold and the males' heads all snapped their way where they stood gathered around the kitchen table.

She could do this.

They could do this.

Lessia's smile didn't waver as she made her way into her room, quickly dressed, and then returned to the table to take up the spot Merrick had stepped aside to allow her as her sister slipped in under their father's outstretched arm.

It didn't even waver when all eyes sprang to hers.

She could do this.

CHAPTER TWENTY-FOUR

"We need to act quickly." Lessia met the eyes of each person in the room, lingering for a moment on Merrick's when something flickered in them.

Fighting a dumb smile that threatened to break out when she realized it was pride, she cleared her throat before she continued.

"We must get to Ellow and inform Loche about what is happening. Perhaps he can do something to quell the uprising coming from within Ellow if he can convince his people of the threat coming their way."

"Raine, do you still have that ship?" Merrick's presence beside her grounded her, and she couldn't help but steal another glance at him, immediately slamming into his distracting eyes, and she nearly tripped at the intensity of them.

"The ship you stole?" Raine answered slowly.

"That's the one," Merrick said without breaking eye contact with Lessia.

"Yes."

Raine's voice sounded as if it came from far away.

As if Lessia were falling right into the depths of the dark pools staring back at her.

You make me happy.

A corner of Merrick's mouth lifted.

And it felt as if her fall increased in speed.

Someone cleared their throat.

Merrick's lips lifted even higher when she continued to stare at him, and her eyes dropped down to the fullness of them.

The room's sounds returned, and when someone coughed discreetly again, she turned back toward the group.

Flames of heat shot up Lessia's neck as they all stared from her to Merrick.

"Are you done?" Raine raised a brow as he moved his glare to Merrick.

Merrick's hand brushed hers as he leaned over the table. "No."

Kerym broke in. "All right then. We have a ship. What next?"

Lessia shook her head before also leaning her arms on the table, using it to stabilize herself and, perhaps the tiniest bit, to stop herself from glancing again at the Fae warrior beside her.

"We need to divide into two groups once we get to Ellow. I do not know where to anchor, but we can't sail right into Asker's harbor. Not with me, Merrick, Ardow, and Venko being considered traitors. We'd be killed on the spot."

"They can try," Merrick rasped, his whispers rushing to life so fast Frelina stumbled back, and even Venko—

who should have been used to them by now—let out a low squeak.

"We're not going to kill anyone, Merrick." Lessia fixed her eyes on Ardow when Merrick sighed deeply, refusing to risk getting sidetracked again.

"Ardow, we need to get Amalise and the children out regardless of what happens. If everything went as I hoped, they're staying in a cave in the eastern part of Asker." She moved her gaze to Venko. "Can you get a ship to transport them here?"

"Yes, but... children?" Venko asked, turning toward Ardow.

"They're ours." Ardow's face reddened when Venko's eyes widened, and he stuttered, "I-I meant..."

"They're not their biological children," Merrick hissed, his whispers flickering to life again.

Lessia frowned at him. "How do you know?"

It was as if a shock jolted her body when his eyes captured hers, and she realized she'd swayed backward when Merrick gripped her arm.

"I followed you for four years." Merrick's eyes dropped for a moment. "I tried my best not to go by your house, to learn as little as possible about what you were doing, but you were careless sometimes. I was in the harbor when you greeted some half-dead Faeling and wrapped him in a blanket. I immediately understood why you refused to follow my orders of showing your face every night." He shook his head. "I stayed far away from your home after that to try to make sure Rioner didn't ask me a question that would force me to tell him."

Lessia blinked at him.

He'd known?

He's been protecting you the entire time.

She took a step closer to him as she whispered, "Thank you."

Remaining by Merrick's side, she turned back to Ardow and Venko. "I think it's best if you go get them. Ardow, you know them all. And..."

She glanced at the three giant Fae warriors and her father, who might not be as well built but who was still full Fae, with that intimidating stature they carried themselves with. "The children don't have the best experiences with Fae. I fear they might not come if you're there."

Ardow met her eyes and nodded. "We will make sure they get out."

She shot him a small smile, more embers of warmth settling in her chest.

They might not be all the way back to the friendship they'd formed the past years, but the cracks in their relationship were slowly repairing themselves.

"Elessia," Frelina said, her voice low but not soft. "I could go with them. If they're half-Fae like us, they might find it easier to trust me."

Their father looked as if he was about to argue, but when she and Frelina shot him a dark glare, he raised his hands, a smile playing across his lips. "Very well."

"We'll keep her safe," Lessia vowed when Frelina jumped up and down, and worry flitted across their father's features.

Alarin met Lessia's eyes. "Thank you. I shall go to Rioner to ensure he does not get suspicious. Try to see what information I might get out of him." He nodded toward Raine. "If you don't mind lending me one of your eagles, I can keep you updated—give you information from the inside."

When Lessia inclined her head, her father continued, his voice thickening with every word. "Miryn would have been so proud of you for what you've done. Saving those half-Fae..." Alarin sighed as his head slumped forward. "He hates them because of the curse, you know."

"Rioner?" Kerym asked.

"Yes. He believes they play a part in the destruction he fears will be unleashed upon our people. Since the traitor is loved by Fae and human—or half-Fae—he blames them for merely existing." Alarin threw her and Frelina a sad glance. "Even though it's wrong."

"Perhaps we can convince some of those still left in Vastala to fight for us?" Raine asked. "We do need the numbers."

"They're living on the streets," Lessia hissed. "They won't be in a state to fight."

"The rebels already got to most of them," Ardow offered hesitantly. "They're to attack the capital in Vastala."

Lessia's wide eyes found her father's, and he nodded forcefully. "I'll warn them, Lessia. I promise."

She ground her teeth at the thought of the rebels.

As if the half-Fae living on the streets of Vastala were any match for Rioner's guards...

The rebels were willing to sacrifice so many in their quest.

They might have aims similar to those of the people in this room...

But the path by which they meant to achieve them was vastly different.

Raine shrugged and lifted his flask to his mouth, a scowl overtaking his face when he found it empty.

As he stalked toward the bar, Frelina stepped into his path. "You need to stop that if we're to win."

Raine grinned at Lessia's sister before lifting her off her feet and placing her back behind him.

"We won't win," he stated as he uncorked a new bottle and brought it to his lips.

Merrick's fingers brushed hers as she watched her sister stare daggers at Raine, and the hair on her arms rose, the sensation tingling across her body.

With a quick smile at him, she walked over to the painting of the wyvern and the Fae, her finger skimming over the thick paper, over the unyielding faces of the males, over the small stone one of them clutched in his hand.

The thought had touched her mind before, but she'd been too preoccupied with everything else going on.

A sparkling stone.

That's what the Fae in the painting held in his hand.

The memory of the ride with Loche surged within her.

The warm, glowing stone he'd given her to keep the darkness at bay.

"What if I said I might have a way for us to get that army?" Lessia spun around to face the others.

"How?" Merrick's eyes were glued to her as he walked around the table, not stopping until he stood next to her again.

She glanced up at him. "Those stones that control the wyverns? I think I know where we can find one."

"Wyverns!" Kerym's voice broke through the haze that had formed as Merrick stared back down at her, his eyes glittering. "Thissian is missing out. He used to love fighting beside them. Although, come to think of it, it was probably because siphoning their energy made us quite high."

Merrick rolled his eyes when Lessia snorted.

As they stared across the room, a humming, vibrating energy soared through the house, spiking every nerve in Lessia.

Ardow and Venko stood straight-backed, their fingers interlocked.

Her sister smiled at her, something akin to freedom brightening her eyes.

Raine pretended to be busy by the bar, but she didn't miss how he stroked the dagger dangling from his belt.

Looking half crazed where he stood, Kerym muttered something about his "damn brother."

Her father looked at them all, and although his eyes were worried, there was something in them that everyone in the room shared as her gaze locked with each of theirs.

Something that Lessia felt mounting within her.

Hope.

CHAPTER
TWENTY-FIVE

"So... you stole this ship?"

Lessia leaned one of her elbows on the railing, peeking over the wood at the spectacular warship, then moved her eyes back to Merrick where he stood on the deck beside her.

They'd bid goodbye to her father earlier in the afternoon, and Lessia could still feel his embrace, the warmth of his arms as they wrapped around her, holding on so tight it felt as if he never wanted to let go.

When silence had fallen in the room after their discussion of what to do, Lessia had pulled her father and Frelina aside to ask him if he wanted her to return his memories.

He'd hesitated, and when the first word out of his mouth was "no," the sense of hope that had filled her nearly vanished before he pulled her into an embrace, whispering that he didn't want to risk it when he was to return to his brother's side.

As Alarin sniffed against her hair, a pearl of emotion escaped down her cheek.

And that was that.

Tears had begun falling down Frelina's face as she watched them, and the rest of the group had backed away when Lessia pulled her into their hug.

Her father had sobbed as he held on to them, whispering how proud their mother would have been, how she would have stood beside them on that ship if she could.

She and Frelina still had dampness coating their faces as they waved at their father's ship, which was quickly disappearing into the thick white blanket that kept the island hidden.

As soon as it vanished from view, they went to join the others as they boarded the ship they were meant to travel on.

But while the rest had headed into the cabin to get everything set up—and probably also to pick the best beds, based on Raine's mutterings—Lessia had stayed on the deck, needing the crisp wind to fuel the fragile hope and resolve that had ignited within her.

Merrick had joined her without a word.

"I did steal it. A long time ago," he responded as his sharp gaze traveled across the mist beginning to surround them—the mist that had already shrouded the island from view.

As Lessia followed it, Ydren's head broke the surface, and the cry she let out tugged so hard at Lessia's heart that she had to look away—and force herself not to cover her ears.

Raine had ordered Ydren to stay back until he called for her.

Apparently, she'd been so young when her family was slaughtered that she'd never been trained in battle, and Raine didn't want her anywhere near Rioner, should he somehow find them.

Lessia hadn't argued, having grown quite fond of the terrifying creature.

"Tell me how you stole it, then." Lessia went to elbow Merrick to keep her mind from lingering on the sorrowful sound, but he was faster.

Gripping her elbow, he pulled her against his body, his face stern as he stared down at her.

"How many times do I need to tell you not to lose focus?"

"Hmm, many?" Lessia's voice wavered a little as she became acutely aware of how hard Merrick's heart slammed against his chest, its beats echoing through her, quickening her own rhythm.

Placing a hand on his chest, right over his heart, she let out a soft breath when it drummed against her palm, its beats so wild she thought they might shake the ship if they hastened further, and an idea formed in her slightly clouded mind.

"Lessia?" Merrick asked hoarsely as he released her arm.

"Mm?" she hummed as she snaked the now-free arm around his waist.

Merrick's muscles went taut as her hand skimmed over his back, fingers dragging over the hard muscles playing beneath his tunic.

"What are you doing?" he rasped.

"This."

A triumphant grin spread across her face when she

jumped back, holding the sword she'd eased out of its scabbard, and lifted it between them.

Her smile widened when Merrick stared at it, his body frozen for a moment before his hand grasped at the empty belt by his side.

"Who needs to focus now?" Lessia teased, fighting with all her might to hold back the giggle eager to burst out of her.

Merrick looked furious—his dark eyes so wild she wondered for a moment if she'd gone too far.

Swallowing, she thought it best to keep her mouth shut right now.

Taking a deliberate step toward her, Merrick's voice lowered into a deep, purring growl. "A few weeks of training, and you think you know it all."

Lessia shrugged, shifting the heavy sword into her other hand.

The movement was a little clumsier than she'd wanted, the sword much heavier than her daggers.

Still, it had the desired effect when Merrick's eyes followed it instead of her shuffling back, positioning her feet wide, anticipating the attack she was certain he was planning.

But Merrick didn't lunge at her.

Instead, he took another slow step forward.

Another.

And another.

Until he finally stood with the tip of the blade pressing into his leather-clad chest.

Her hand shook as she glanced from the sword to his eyes.

"What... what are you doing?" she whispered.

"What you should have done as soon as you got the

sword away from me," Merrick growled. "You. Do. Not. Hesitate."

Lessia tried to plaster the smile back on her face. "I was just playing around."

Merrick's eyes captured hers. "There is no playing in war."

"I know." Lessia tightened her grip on the sword. "But you and I aren't at war."

"Aren't we?" Merrick raised a brow, and Lessia's face heated.

When she remained quiet, silently cursing the cheeks she expected to be bright red, Merrick shook his head.

And within a second, he'd disarmed her, his chest pressed against her back as he breathed into her hair.

"You should finish what you start, Lessia." Each word came out on an exhalation, the warmth of his breaths brushing her neck. "Or you might find yourself in a... tricky situation."

Her body reacted instantly, melting against Merrick's, before she regained control over her muscles and straightened her weak legs, although she still had to fight against her frame's wish to merge with the one behind her.

It apparently wanted to find itself in whatever tricky situation Merrick referred to.

"Are you teaching her to flirt her enemies to death, or what is happening here?"

A snarl escaped Merrick as his head snapped up.

After blinking for a few moments, her blurry gaze following the swirls of mist that now completely swallowed them, Lessia also lifted her gaze.

Kerym grinned at them both from where he was

perched on a wooden mast, legs dangling out over the sea, which had begun foaming around the ship.

Releasing her, Merrick took a step back and sheathed his sword. "Whatever will save her life."

"Right." Kerym arched his brows as he hoisted himself off the beam, landing gracefully before Lessia and Merrick.

"So... I've heard you're a pretty strong mind-bender." Kerym strolled up to her, his finger dragging over Lessia's collarbone, the nail scratching against her leather tunic. "That you were able to keep even Raine out of your head."

Lessia shot a quick glance at Merrick, who followed Kerym's movements closely before looking back at her.

Don't lose focus.

She could almost hear his growl in her mind.

Snapping her gaze back to where Kerym pranced around her like a wolf assessing its prey, she nodded. "I can only control one person at a time, but my magic also worked on Raine's wyvern."

"Ah, so not just on humans, shifters, and Fae, but also on magical creatures. That's interesting."

Kerym smiled at her, and she couldn't help but smile back as warmth crawled over her scalp, the feeling similar to the warmth of the alcohol she'd ingested the night before.

"It is," she said softly as her breathing slowed, the frantic beat of her heart, which never seemed to dull, finally easing.

Kerym hummed somewhere around her, but she was too tired to continue following his movements.

Sleep.

She wanted to sleep.

Maybe she'd sleep right here?

The wooden planks beneath her looked quite welcoming.

Someone cleared their throat before her, and a voice rolled through her like a gentle wave lapping the white beach of Raine's island.

Don't lose focus.

When Kerym halted before her, she met his crystal gaze, and it felt as if she were dreaming.

His golden skin brightened, his dark hair started shining like newly polished leather, and his blue eyes became clearer than the summer sky that should be hovering somewhere above the fog.

A wrinkle formed between her brows as she tried to rack her tired brain.

Kerym's white canines glinted as his lips curled into a smile.

But it wasn't a nice one.

No, even if her features itched to mirror the man before her, something inside her made her uneasy—a feeling of dread coating her body, joining the droplets from the mist that danced over any bare skin.

Lessia shuddered when she sluggishly tried to rub her hands over her arms to get it off.

It wasn't dread coating her skin.

It was magic.

Clamping her eyes shut, Lessia tried to feel where and how Kerym's magic connected with hers.

Siphon Twin.

Like Raine, he also wielded mental magic.

Which meant...

She forced her gaze inward—like she'd done when she believed Raine threatened Merrick.

Even if she moved slower, her energy worryingly low, she soon could open an eye within her mind.

Staring back at her were two sapphires, glittering within the darkness that was her mind.

She'd been too rushed when Raine had stalked toward Merrick—hadn't really given whatever she saw a second thought.

But now she wondered whether this was actually her mind or if she somehow subconsciously had decided these shadows, the hard floor that reminded her of Rioner's cellars, was her consciousness.

She pushed the thought away when her knees went weak, her arms blindly moving behind her to try to find the railing she knew existed somewhere in the real world.

Instead, she glared right into the gemstones before her, ignoring the deepening shadows around them.

"G-get out," she stuttered as she pulled on her magic.

But no golden glow reflected in the vivid blue.

Instead, the stones, as if in defiance, sparkled brighter, seemingly growing within the dark room.

You lost focus, you idiot.

Lessia's thought echoed within the thickening shadows, and pressure built upon her chest when they crept closer, sounds that she never wished to hear again mounting within them.

Dripping of water on stone.

Metal scraping against the floor.

A damp blindfold being wrapped too tightly around her eyes.

No.

She'd told herself she wasn't doing this anymore.

Enough!

Focus on the anger.

The memory of Merrick's voice broke through the sounds, and with a snarl, Lessia pulled up every ounce of magic left within her.

Eyes flying open, she screamed, "Get out! Get the fuck out!"

The sapphires evaporated.

And so did the darkness.

Waves brushing the side of the ship joined the deep voice whispering "Good" into her ears, and when she lifted her eyes, out of one corner she caught Merrick hovering behind her left shoulder.

Kerym grinned at her when she found his blue gaze. "You held on longer than I thought you would."

She couldn't stop herself.

Taking a step forward, she flashed her teeth at him.

"Isn't it quite stupid of you to drain my energy when we're heading out into dangerous waters?" she hissed.

Kerym popped his shoulders. "Needed to see if you'd be of any help."

Lessia tapped her boot on the wood when he didn't continue. "So?"

"So... what?"

"Am I going to be of help?" she gritted through her teeth, the urge to punch Kerym's satisfied face nearly overpowering the heavy tiredness on her limbs.

He seemed to mull it over for a moment, and it wasn't until Merrick growled under his breath behind her that he threw out his hands. "Sure. With more training, you could be an asset. Right now, you're... ah! What's the word? Unpolished."

Merrick's growl became more menacing.

Kerym's eyes lifted above her head. "I'm not saying

she isn't strong or that she couldn't be of help. It's just... she probably won't be able to withstand for long when it comes to the Fae. I don't know these rebels, but if there are shifters and half-Fae amongst them as well... She didn't even realize I was using my magic initially."

"*She* is right here," Lessia snarled. "I might not have trained for centuries like you old bastards, but I am trying! I am willing to train for as long as we have. And if I can help take one—just one!—enemy down, that's a win, right?"

Curiosity fought across Kerym's features. "You're willing to die for this? For these people?"

"Of course I am," Lessia responded. "They're my people. And Ellow is my home."

"Your home..." Kerym mumbled as his eyes flitted between her and Merrick—she assumed—behind her, his forehead creasing before he nodded once. "All right. Then we train for as long as we can."

"My turn?" Raine strolled onto the deck, and her sister followed close behind, a surly expression twisting her face.

"N— Yes."

She'd almost told him she needed to lie down first, but after her declaration...

She probably needed to ensure she lived up to her words.

With a sigh, Lessia planted her feet and glared right into Raine's eyes, praying he wouldn't drag up every embarrassing memory she could think of if she failed.

CHAPTER TWENTY-SIX

Lessia rubbed her temples, trying to relieve the ache that throbbed through her head from Raine, Kerym, and even her sister probing into her deepest thoughts the past few days.

Slumping down against the mainmast of the ship, she thought she might prefer the training Merrick had her do at dawn—even with the bruises she collected and with him growling at her for not following his stupid orders.

She also didn't mind practicing defensive magic by blocking Kerym's magic too much.

At least then she could sleep after.

But with Raine and Frelina...

A shudder wove its way down her spine.

They'd made her relive her worst memories.

Again and again until she figured how to keep them out of her mind.

Lessia didn't know what was worse—having to remember the torture in Rioner's cellars, the faces of her parents when she told them to forget about her, Loche losing whatever feelings he had for her...

Or the others' faces when they lived her memories for the first time.

Her days were now filled with pitying eyes and disagreements whenever Frelina or Raine got choked up from her memories and tried to stop the training.

That was worse, she decided.

She couldn't stand the pity.

Lessia yawned as she stared at the clouds building over the horizon, then sniffed at the wintery tang that now permeated the wind whistling across the sea, savoring how the breeze peppered her body with goose bumps.

The cold felt good.

Raine and Merrick had made her practice fighting the two of them simultaneously this morning, making her use her magic on one while fighting off the other.

She had to admit it was quite satisfying when she managed to make Raine freeze.

Although she had perhaps taken it a bit far when she flicked his nose...

But Merrick had thankfully stepped between them when she finally let him go.

"You're getting better." Merrick ducked under the pole and wrangled into the small alcove she'd squeezed her body into.

Lessia rolled her eyes as he navigated the small space, folding his long legs and lowering down so elegantly beside her that she felt like smacking him.

Did he ever do something clumsy or rash?

"What?" Merrick's brows narrowed as he turned her way, sitting so close their legs aligned.

Lessia elbowed him. "I was just wondering if you're good at everything you try?"

"Yes."

She snorted when his face remained serious, his dark eyes tracking her movements as she shook her head.

"Seriously." She nudged him again. "There must be *something* you're not good at?"

Staring into her eyes for so long that she started to get a little flustered, Merrick seemed to mull it over, his silvery brows pulling and forehead creasing as what seemed like millions of thoughts crossed his mind.

"Being nice?" he finally responded.

Lessia burst out laughing.

Merrick wasn't the warmest person she'd met.

Not like Ardow, who liked to hug every person he could.

Not like Amalise, who at least pretended to be warm when you first met her.

Not even like Loche, who underneath that cold shell was actually quite sweet.

Her laughter faded when her mind snagged on Loche, and Lessia waited for the stab of pain she'd become accustomed to.

But it didn't come.

Instead, that warmth that had started to spread within her back on Raine's island remained, softening the blow by surrounding the memories of gray eyes and hurt features with padding—like a cotton wall protecting her heart against the rejection.

Lessia released a breath.

She'd learned from what happened with Frelina—what happened in the cellars—that the pain from such memories would fade.

But for some reason, she hadn't expected this one's to.

Not when that small crack in the wall she'd put up around her heart had disappeared as quickly as it had materialized.

Not when all the memories reminded her of what she'd long suspected...

That she wasn't worthy of that type of love.

The love that was as pure as a winter night where no boots had yet to mark the newly fallen snow.

But perhaps...

Perhaps... there was a different kind of love out there.

One that wasn't untouched snow, but that was strange and wild and uncontrollable.

That was tainted and broken and... all the while perfect.

"Where did you go?"

Her gaze focused again when Merrick spoke, and before she could think, she lifted a hand to brush one of his shoulder-length pearly strands off his forehead.

"You are nice," she whispered. "You're kind and thoughtful and, yes, truly damned broody sometimes, but... you are nice."

Merrick stared back at her as he caught the hand she'd dropped from his face.

Bringing it to Lessia's chest, he placed his own over it, pressing over her heart.

"You about to disarm me?" she joked weakly when he leaned in farther, and it wasn't the chill air around them that caused more goose bumps to rise across her skin.

Merrick didn't respond.

Instead, he lifted his other hand and cupped her cheek with it.

"*You* are brave and clever and wildly loyal. You have such fight in you—even after everything. And you love so fiercely... so boundlessly. Don't let your past convince you that you aren't worthy of it in return."

Lessia frowned at him before she realized.

"Raine told you, didn't he?"

The slight twitch of the muscle in his jaw told her she was right.

Today Raine had managed to isolate every moment of her life when she felt unworthy, using it to unsettle her while they fought.

And the final night with Loche wrapped up the journey like a beautiful bow.

"He is an idiot," Merrick said as his fingers whispered over her cheek, moving slowly down until his thumb brushed her bottom lip. "A fucking idiot to let you go."

Lessia's eyes fell to her crossed legs as she whispered, "Who knew the Death Whisperer had a soft side?"

Merrick's fingers wrapped around her chin, tipping her head up and leveling her eyes with his. "You know. That's enough."

She was about to respond, but the words caught in her throat when Merrick's eyes shifted to the side and widened before he flew to his feet.

"Ship!" he called. "Incoming ship!"

Lessia stumbled into his chest when he forcefully pulled her up beside him, her blood pumping harder when he dragged her out to the port, and she noticed what Merrick had already warned the rest of.

A ship—one that once had belonged to Stellia, Lessia realized with a sinking stomach—was headed their way, its hull pointing right at their own.

The air around her filled with heavy breathing as

Ardow and Venko sprinted to her side from where they'd been resting in the cabin, and Lessia pulled Frelina close when she also ascended the rickety stairs, her eyes slightly puffy from just having woken up from the nap she must have taken after her turn training with the Fae warriors.

"Who are they?" Frelina breathed as she wrapped an arm around Lessia's waist.

"Rebels," Lessia mumbled. "And given what they did to get that ship, I don't expect them to treat us kindly."

"What do you want us to do?" Raine asked from behind them.

Lessia turned around, her stomach churning as all three Fae males looked at her.

They... they wanted her to decide?

"There are about thirty of them on that ship," Raine continued. "Twelve on deck, and the rest gathering weapons. A few humans, but most are shifters. A couple of half-Fae are with them as well, but two of them could be prisoners... I am not sure of their allegiance."

Lessia's eyes flitted between the group and the approaching ship.

The rebels had become bolder if they openly sailed this close to Ellow.

But if there was a chance to speak to them... to convince them of the dangers heading toward Havlands.

Shouldn't they take it?

Merrick flexed his hands as he walked up to her, not especially gently shoving Ardow to the side. "Do you want me to kill them?"

Lessia pursed her lips when Merrick's earnest gaze met hers, and she didn't miss Frelina's pretend cough, the sharp elbow digging into her side.

"I..."

Lessia hesitated.

Was it better not to risk it?

But they'd need all the people they could spare if the threat of the Oakgards' Fae from the other realm materialized...

"No," she got out. "We should try to convince them of the threat that's coming. Besides, they might have information that we could use."

Kerym batted his lashes in her direction. "Can I at least make them more agreeable?"

"I can do it from here, Kerym," Raine interrupted.

"They're good people!" Ardow barged into the middle, his gaze slicing from Lessia to Raine and Kerym. "We can't hurt them!"

"He's right." Lessia nodded. "We can't force people to join us."

"But—" Kerym started.

"She said no," Merrick snarled.

Raine and Kerym shared a look that had Lessia's top lip curling back.

Slipping away from the hand she somehow knew Merrick would extend, she stalked up to the Fae, pressing a finger into each of their chests.

"I do not agree with what the rebels are doing. But like us, they are fighting for something they believe is better. We have the same end goal; it's just our means to get there that is different. You will not hurt them. Not unless they become a threat."

The snapping of their jaws was so loud that Lessia was surprised none of their canines cracked, but finally, they dipped their chins.

"Good."

Lessia spun around and grabbed Ardow by the shirt to line him up with Venko.

She cast a quick glance to the side, where the ship was closing in.

They only had minutes now.

"And you two." Lessia wagged her finger at them, mainly toward Ardow, but she also kept a watchful eye on Venko's reaction. "You will not try to sneak away with those rebels. Do you hear me? You have a mission."

"We won't," Venko said quietly, but when his hand squeezed Ardow's, a hiss tore from her throat.

"Don't lie to me. Or"—she pointed to the Fae—"I'll have them practice their magic on you."

"You have our word, Lessia." Ardow placed his free hand on her shoulder. "I promise."

She wasn't so sure of that, but when she looked out toward the sea again, the crew on the ship had opened the gate on their side and were preparing the brow—a huge one with spikes that would seal their two vessels together until they decided to pull it up again.

She met Merrick's eyes, and they glittered when she stated, "Time to burn."

CHAPTER TWENTY-SEVEN

Even being a warship, the vessel lurched violently when the wooden brow connected the ships, and Lessia was grateful for Merrick's strong hand folding around her own, keeping her steady.

And she was even more grateful for it when the first person climbed onto the brow and the wind brought the smell of shifter with it—that ever-changing scent of winter and summer and spring and fall and birth and death.

Her senses sharpened, the walls she'd practiced around her mind slamming up, and she could tell from the thickening tension layering across the group that Merrick's and the rest's did as well.

Lessia wasn't sure she'd ever get used to that smell.

It was as if you'd bottled unpredictability, and she reminded herself not to trust a word that came out of their mouths.

At least not without verifying it first.

Merrick pulled her closer when more people followed

the woman in the front, and she glanced up at him, offering him a quick smile before she fixed her eyes on the small group that had now reached their side of the brow.

The woman standing in the bow had one of those faces where it was difficult to tell whether she was young or old—free of lines but with soulful eyes that seemed to be full of stories.

Inky-black hair, nearly violet in its richness, framed her face, and she wore simple clothing—scarred leathers and boots that, like Lessia's, had a few holes from use.

Behind her stood a mixture of shifters, one human, and... a half-Fae male with ivory hair and skin so fair it was almost translucent.

A half-Fae male Lessia recognized.

"Bowen?" she asked when the group halted before them.

His pale eyes widened as they locked with hers, and Bowen took a step toward her. "Lessia?"

Raine and Kerym inched closer, tightly gripping their weapons, judging from the metal clangs reaching Lessia's ears.

Merrick also shuffled to the side, almost imperceptibly putting himself a step ahead of her.

The group ahead responded immediately: hands subtly moving toward weapons, bodies tensing, weights shifting, and eyes darting everywhere they could reach.

"It's been a while." Lessia forced a smile, trying to break the unspoken warning that filled the air around the two groups.

"Merrick." She squeezed his hand. "This is Bowen. We met briefly when we both lived in Vastala."

Merrick nodded, but his eyes did not once leave the group before them.

"It has." Bowen gave her a smile back. "Are you joining us? Is that why you waited for our ship?"

"We want to talk." Lessia made sure her smile remained.

It proved easy when Merrick breathed, "Good."

"The time for talk is over." The violet-haired woman nudged Bowen back into the group. "You're traveling with one of us. He must have informed you already."

Lessia stared at Ardow for a moment, happy to find he didn't seem inclined to run over and switch sides before she tugged on Merrick's hand and walked toward the woman who must be some kind of spokesperson for this group of rebels.

Reaching out the hand not holding on to Merrick's, she drew a shallow breath, her thoughts fighting over how to approach this.

But as she met the shifter's guarded eyes, she decided there was only one way.

"I'm Elessia Rantzier, and... I have information that should make you reconsider your plans. Urgent information that you need to share with your leaders."

She'd been prepared for the gasps from the group before her, but it was her sister's shocked inhale that stirred something within her.

Stealing a look at her, Lessia's smile came easier when Frelina grinned back, bobbing her head for Lessia to continue.

"Elessia Rantzier..."

The woman only stared at Lessia's hand, so with a sigh, Lessia dropped it.

"I thought you went by Lessia Gyldenberg now."

Lessia's eyes narrowed, but she worked to keep the rest of her face expressionless.

She wasn't sure whether this woman was trying to unsettle her or if she actually knew who Lessia truly was.

"I didn't claim the Rantzier name until recently, when someone told me that just because I carry a name, it doesn't mean I carry the darkness that comes with another with the same one." As Merrick's thumb stroked the back of her hand, Lessia observed the woman, trying to see through the mask of indifference that painted her features.

"A name is powerful, Elessia. As you must have known, denying your own for so long." Her eyes traveled over Lessia's face. "And how do I know you don't carry the darkness of your family?"

Lessia waved her hand toward the group. "Surely you all, out of anyone, must understand? What with the actions your leaders took back in the war times?"

"Ah, that was all so very unfortunate, wasn't it?" The woman didn't appear to think it was unfortunate at all, as a slight smile drew at her lips as she peeked behind Lessia. "I assume that's your sister clinging to the mind-bender? You have the Rantzier hair. I heard the Death Whisperer traveled with you already. Oh! And that's one of the Siphon Twins, isn't it? I thought you and your brother were inseparable… I guess love can truly break us all."

The shifter pierced Lessia with her dark brown gaze as she straightened again. "I am the leader of the rebels. My name is Meyah, and I know more than you think I do, princess of Vastala."

Her stomach flipped, but she fought to hide it.

They'd stumbled across the *rebel leader*?

Moving her eyes to Merrick's, Lessia found his brows drawn down, thoughts working across his face as distrust brightened his dark eyes.

It all seemed very convenient, didn't it?

As Lessia turned back toward the rebels, she forced a laugh when she realized Meyah was staring at her. "I am no princess. Like you, I want Havlands to be a better place, but if you don't listen to me, there will be no Havlands—at least not how we know it—left, including any of your rebels. There is another threat coming. One that is much worse than the fight you're planning for."

Some of the people behind Meyah began mumbling, the whispers brushing Lessia's ear, but she made herself hold the rebel leader's gaze.

"But you're not like me." Meyah's lips lifted into a cold smile. "It's as easy to see as the bonds tying this broken group together. You won't do what's necessary to win—to drive actual change. I know all about you, Elessia Rantzier. Or is it Lessia Gyldenberg? You ran for regent in Ellow and, according to my sources, even managed to get the infamous Loche to take a liking to you... which I guess isn't too hard, as someone who can control minds."

Something sinister glinted in Meyah's eyes. "But you weren't strong enough to use it to your advantage—to your people's advantage! Instead, you ran. Like a coward."

Merrick snarled softly beside her, and Lessia struggled not to bare her teeth at the shifter herself.

With a glance at Lessia, Merrick took a step forward.

"Careful how you talk to her, shifter." Ice dripped from every word leaving Merrick's mouth. "She might not want to hurt any of you, but I certainly have no such qualms. I've killed your kind before, and I'll do it again if I must."

Meyah's eyes flared for less than a second, but it was enough for Lessia to understand Merrick's words had landed precisely as he'd intended.

"Me and my brothers"—Merrick gestured toward Raine and Kerym—"lived through the last war. Fought in it. Your people were slaughtered. How many of you remain now? A couple of hundred spread out across Havlands? There will be none—none!—left if you do not listen to her."

Meyah turned around to hush some of the louder people behind her, and Lessia decided this was the best moment they'd get.

"There is another race of Fae traveling here on their warships. There are thousands upon thousands of them, and they're as desperate as you are. Perhaps even more. And Rioner has struck a deal with them." Lessia moved her eyes from Meyah's to meet with those of a few of the others behind her as she continued. "If they help Rioner keep Vastala safe from rebels, he will help them take Ellow once it's weakened from the rebels' attack. There will be no human or shifter left in Havlands after that."

The whispers grew louder and more worried until Meyah screamed, "Silence!"

As she took a step to get into Lessia's space, her eyes narrowed. "Why should I believe you?"

"Why would I lie?" Lessia slitted her eyes right back. "I have nothing to win by deceiving you."

"Why would you lie, indeed." Meyah sucked her teeth when her gaze snagged somewhere over Lessia's right shoulder. "Ardow, it's been too long. Come greet me."

There was a wrinkle between Ardow's brows as he stepped up to Lessia's side.

"Oh! Forgive me. You've never seen me in this form." Meyah smiled sweetly, although no warmth touched her eyes, and within a second, the air filled with rushing wind.

The scent of shifter wrapped around them, masking the salty tang of the sea and the leathery aroma of clothing and sweat that had filled Lessia's nose over the past days.

Before Lessia's wide eyes, Meyah's image blurred, almost mirroring how Merrick's magic sent ripples through the air—like oil spilling on water with the soft colors of the rainbow tangling with each other.

When the magic drifted away with the breeze, another woman stood in the raven-haired's stead.

This one was younger—perhaps in her early twenties—with curly blond hair, amber eyes eerily similar to Lessia's and Frelina's, and a much shorter stature.

Lessia would almost have to bend her neck if she wanted to meet the girl's eyes.

When the shifter opened her arms, Ardow stormed into them, his muscular body nearly swallowing the girl whole.

"I didn't realize it was you! I've missed you so much! I thought of you every day," he whispered, and Lessia couldn't help but wrinkle her nose at the admiration and awe seeping into his voice.

What had this woman told him for him to act as if she were a deity?

Finding Venko's eyes, she noted the same confusion rounding his blues, and she shook her head when Raine and Kerym stared at her with raised brows.

"Ardow," Lessia urged when her friend stepped back from the shifter, still hovering closer to the other group than she preferred. "Tell her."

He shot her a nod before clasping one of Meyah's small hands with his own. "I believe she speaks the truth. There is another threat, so perhaps... perhaps we need to listen to her." Ardow swallowed loudly. "Perhaps we need to speak to Loche again... see if he'll accept our demands if we stand together against the threat against our lands?"

"Ardow." Meyah placed the hand he wasn't holding on his cheek. "You know as well as I do, that is not how it'll turn out. The humans will sacrifice us—use us—to die for them! And should any of us survive, they'll go back to what they've been doing for the past century: ignore the ones that don't fit in, shun the shifters and drive them off their islands... harass the half-Fae." Meyah shook her head. "No. We will not fight beside the very people who forced us to live in hiding. If Ellow is wiped out... then so be it."

"How can you say that?" Lessia released Merrick's hand to get into the rebel leader's face, ignoring the sharp hisses of warning coming from the people behind Meyah. "Many of the rebels come from Ellow! It's their home!"

"Their home is with their family." Meyah picked at her nails. "We are their family. We'll rebuild Korina, let those Fae take over the rest of Havlands, and stay out of their way. Perhaps we'll get lucky and have the races of Fae turn on each other. It's happened before, I've heard."

No.

Lessia couldn't believe this woman.

She'd sacrifice a whole land—all the people in it—for what?

Revenge?

"What about the families still left there?" she snarled. "What about your family, Ardow?" She spun around, pointing to Venko. "What about his family?"

Ardow's face whitened. "I—"

"We'll get them out. We have enough ships." Meyah smirked. "Since you've offered us this kind warning, we can begin already now. Probably for the better, anyway. Fewer loyal people who might get caught in the crossfire from our attacks."

She turned to the group behind her. "What say you? Shall we weaken the human defense so that they can get a taste of what it's like to almost be wiped out?"

The shifters behind her cheered, and Lessia's nostrils flared when even Bowen let out something akin to a howl.

She couldn't believe it.

They'd fought for their lives on the streets of Vastala together.

Had cursed the Fae together.

Had cursed them for being so cruel and leaving people—children!—to die just because they were different.

And now he supported the same thing?

"Please!" Lessia pleaded. "If you're truly fighting for a better world—do it with us. Let's speak to Loche. I know I can convince him to work together with us! I can convince him to meet whatever demands you have!"

The sly grin twisting Meyah's features chilled Lessia to her bones. "That's not what I heard... I heard he spit on you as you crawled on the castle floor, begging him to love you. If he wouldn't even forgive *you*—someone he claimed to care for—he would throw all of us into his dungeons as soon as we stepped over the castle threshold."

Mocking laughter and hums of agreement rose behind Meyah, but the buzzing that had begun within Lessia's mind quickly drowned the sounds.

She nearly vibrated from restrained anger, and when her magic stirred within her, she didn't leash it.

No, she let it completely free, her eyes filling with warmth, its glow reflecting in Meyah's gaze as Lessia gripped her arm.

Enough trying to be nice.

If everyone else was going to fight dirty...

Then so would she.

The corners of her mouth tilted upward as she opened it to tell Meyah that she followed Lessia's orders now.

Then everything went black.

Lessia's heart banged against her rib cage as she blinked.

Then blinked again.

But it was useless.

Someone slipped up behind her, and as familiar arms wrapped around her, pressing her against his body, a whimper escaped Frelina, with low snarls from Raine and Kerym following.

"I can kill every man and woman here in seconds," Merrick snarled so loudly that his chest rumbled against her back. "And so can Raine and Kerym. The only reason we haven't yet is because Lessia found it in her heart to spare you."

"I know you can," Meyah responded with a little laugh. "But you won't."

"Why not?" Lessia hissed, trying to push at the panic clawing at her as the darkness pressed in further. "You won't work with us, so I don't have any more need for you."

"Bowen," Meyah ordered. "Give them their sight back."

Lessia lifted her hand to shield her eyes when the bright wintery light ambushed them.

Squinting, she found Ardow standing in the same spot before Meyah, his hands rubbing his eyes.

As she tried turning, Merrick dropped his arms, and she didn't know why, but a sense of unease crept up her neck as she met Kerym's eyes, then moved to Raine's, finding them wide and filled with...

Fear.

There was fear in Raine's eyes.

Her eyes flew to the side where Frelina had been standing.

She wasn't there.

Lessia spun the other way.

She wasn't beside Venko, who held onto the railing as he stared daggers at the rebel leader.

No.

This was not happening.

"Where is she?" Lessia screamed.

"Somewhere you won't reach her. And if any of you" —Meyah shot a glare behind Lessia, her eyes probably trailing over her friends—"try to use magic, I can promise you'll never see her again."

A huge grin spread across Meyah's face when Merrick's whispers, which had danced through the air, faded until only breathing and the squalls of the sea against the vessel could be heard.

A soulless, freezing smile that, despite what had just happened, made Lessia's magic burst to the surface.

Bowen took her sight once more.

Lessia didn't care, and storming up to where she could smell the shifter, she grasped for her.

But only air met her furious hands.

"You coward!" she cried. "You fucking coward!"

"Lessia." Raine's voice drifted toward her as Merrick's strong hand pulled her to him. "One of the half-Fae was a voider."

"I don't know what the fuck that is, Raine!" She struggled against Merrick's grip, desperate to claw Meyah's damn eyes out. "Where is she!"

"Listen to me," Merrick hissed into her ear. "A voider is someone who can move between places in seconds. As in between Vastala and Ellow in seconds. They took Frelina."

"That's not the only problem," Raine said.

Lessia didn't like his tone.

Not one damned bit.

"Bowen," Meyah almost sang. "Give her her sight back. I believe her bodyguard will keep her from doing something stupid. He seems to have understood already."

Lessia lunged as soon as she could see again.

But Merrick was too strong.

Holding her against his chest, he hissed, "You need to calm down."

She panted as she glared at Meyah, who only looked back at her with a mildly bored expression.

Ardow shook his head as he stared at the leader, and

he started to back away, trying to get to Venko, when Meyah's fingers dug into his arm, stopping him.

Tilting her head, she smiled at him. "Ardow, you know we must make some hard decisions during war. You've executed some of them... Remember dear Craven?"

"Th-that's different," Ardow stuttered. "Frelina is innocent! She doesn't have anything to do with this."

"No one is innocent." Meyah tsked. "Especially not someone with the Rantzier name."

She shot Lessia a look that had her growl, her canines rasping against her bottom lip, wanting nothing more than to rip out the shifter's throat.

"Lessia," Merrick warned, and she nearly bit him again before she got ahold of herself.

She wanted to scream.

Hurt someone.

Kill someone.

She'd just gotten Frelina back!

"You should be proud, Ardow," Meyah cooed. "You're the one who made this possible."

Ardow blinked at her before spinning back toward Lessia. "I promise, I have no idea what she's talking about."

She didn't know why... but she believed him.

"Spit it out, Meyah," Lessia got out through clamped teeth.

"She's been tracking us," Merrick said when Meyah took too long.

Meyah winked at him. "Good, Death Whisperer."

It was Merrick's turn to snarl—a snarl so vicious it made Lessia's bones shake.

"Do not test me, shifter," he hissed. "One more word, and I'll rip your fucking head off."

That was not the right thing to say.

Snarls erupted behind Meyah, and Lessia's heart skipped a beat when several of the men behind her shifted into different terrifying creatures: three wolves with fangs as long as Lessia's arms; two birds that resembled eagles but were as large as the wolves, with jagged beaks that looked as if they could snap a person in half.

But they weren't the worst ones.

No, the massive ebony snake coiling up the mast beside them was.

Even Merrick stiffened behind her as he noticed it.

The serpent was identical to the one Rioner kept as a companion.

The one he modeled the mark of the blood oath on.

The one he liked to feed his enemies to.

Raine and Kerym stalked forward to join Merrick, and while the latter dragged her back so that she stood between Kerym and Merrick, Venko slipped behind them, his breathing heavy as he peeked over her shoulder.

Ardow cast her a desperate look where he stood frozen, Meyah's hand still wrapped around his arm, and mouthed, "I'm so sorry."

"Stand down." Meyah raised a hand, and while the wolves still paced back and forth behind her, the snake continuing to lap the air with its cruel tongue, they didn't charge.

Kerym let out a cool laugh that shuddered through her. "Why? This was beginning to look like fun."

"Shut up," Lessia and Merrick snarled at the same time.

Raine leaned forward so he could roll his eyes at Kerym. "I told you—they're equally boring."

"I will show you how boring I can be if you don't shut your mouth," Lessia hissed. "Now." She switched her glacial stare to Meyah. "Tell me what the fuck is going on."

Meyah dragged a hand through her hair, making the curls even wilder than they'd been before. "You didn't think you just happened to cross paths with us today, did you?"

When Lessia only glared at her, Meyah let out a pitying sound. "Oh, you did! I'm sorry to break it to you, but we've had eyes on you since you left Ellow."

Lessia's eyes flew to Ardow.

"He didn't know." Meyah patted his arm as she released him, and Ardow quickly returned to the group, taking up the spot beside Kerym. "But one of us on this ship has a very special kind of magic that allows us to use whoever we please as a spy... And who better than dear Ardow here."

"A mind seer," Merrick muttered. "I should have known."

"Well, fuck." Raine grasped within his shirt, making everyone standing ahead tense before they realized he was only bringing a bottle to his lips, his swallows echoing in the thick silence.

Lowering his voice, Merrick leaned in, whispering into Lessia's ear. "It's a type of mind-bender, but instead of reading your thoughts, he or she only needs to connect with a mind once, and then they can see through the person's eyes. Rioner's family used them as spies, but I thought they went all but extinct in the war when the shifters found out about them."

"Yes, one of the dear half-Fae on the vessel is a mind seer." Meyah rolled her neck. "It's been quite helpful to gather intel. The only thing we've struggled with is getting intel from Rioner... See, his guards are quite well versed in protecting their minds against this type of magic." Meyah shrugged. "We needed someone who wasn't—someone who would be able to get close to Rioner."

Lessia's stomach sank.

She didn't mean...

"Look at you catching on." Meyah placed a hand on her chest, her head cocking. "We knew you were special, Elessia, but finding out you are the king's niece? Amazing! And then your father and sister join the party?"

Meyah clapped her hand over her heart, the slow beat drumming through Lessia.

"We didn't particularly care who of you we'd send back, but alas, your father isn't here, and you seem to have learned something from the tedious training these Fae put you through. Your sister, on the other hand? Apparently, it was quite easy to connect to her mind. Our dear voider was a prisoner desperate to get back to his master, so with that very special skill of his own he brought your sister back as the perfect spy in Rioner's midst."

The smells and sounds of Rioner's cellar slammed into her, but it wasn't panic that roiled in her gut as she took a step toward the rebel leader.

"You..." Lessia shook her head as her vision flickered, her voice dangerously even as she continued. "I'm going to kill you. All of you."

Merrick's magic wrapped around her as she spoke, the whispers echoing the rage filling every inch within her.

Meyah only smirked. "No, Lessia. See, I have rebels ready within every single one of your taverns. We couldn't find those little Faelings of yours, but your loyal staff, on the other hand... Well, my people have orders to execute every single one should any harm come to me or my people."

Throwing her head back, not bothering to smother the growl shooting up her throat, Lessia cursed to herself as Merrick's magic drifted away once more, the fury rolling off him fueling her own.

This fucking woman.

"Why? Why risk this?" Lessia looked down again to stare at Meyah, unable to comprehend how this leader—the one who wanted a better life for those not esteemed by society, those like herself and Frelina—could do this. "My sister won't be able to be a spy for you. They'll kill her on the spot."

Tears burned behind Lessia's eyes, but she couldn't let them fall.

Especially not with the smirking shifter staring right at her.

Another damned leader trying to find a way to make her submit.

"I don't think so," Meyah responded as she began retreating backward, the people behind her falling into step as they kept watchful eyes on the group.

With one jerk of the leader's head, the animals shifted back into human form, straightening their clothes as they followed her back across the brow.

The rebel leader halted once she'd reached the other

side, and as a few people began pulling the brow up, she called out, "The king finding out his own brother produced the creatures he hates the most? *And* that he's kept it a secret! Oh! I think he'll keep her alive just to get to you and Alarin. Your sister doesn't look like she'll do well with torture. But"—Meyah threw her a pointed look —"neither do you, and from what I've heard, they did quite grisly things to you. We'll see—but I still think it'll keep Rioner busier than he expected, and that's exactly what we want for this next step."

The brow rose with a loud creaking that had Lessia slam her teeth together, shielding the rebels from view for a moment.

When it landed with a thud on Stellia's old ship, Meyah raised a hand. "It was nice to meet you, princess of Vastala. I don't expect to see you again, so... farewell!"

CHAPTER TWENTY-EIGHT

Lessia stared after the ship as it retreated into the fog that had started gathering across the surface of the sea.

The empty silence as the wind died down mirrored the feeling within her, and she dug her nails into the wood of the railing, feeling as if she might jump off if she didn't hold on.

The others had tried to talk to her—apart from Merrick, who, as usual, understood that she needed some time to process what just happened—but she hadn't been able to form words and had shaken off every soothing hand that tried to rub her shoulder or back.

She'd just gotten her back...

She'd promised to keep her safe...

But now her sister was on the way to, or already in, the one place their father had spent his whole life trying to keep them hidden from.

The place that had nearly broken Lessia herself.

Lessia's hands tightened around the railing, so hard that shavings of wood pierced her skin.

She didn't care.

She was so sick of these leaders who only took and took and took, not caring who they hurt in the process.

Meyah didn't care for her people!

Like Rioner, she only wanted power.

As Lessia stared out over the calm sea, small islands broke through the white clouds dancing across the dark water, some with thawing snow still peppering their cliffs, and Lessia realized they were in the outskirts of Ellow.

Loche...

He was perhaps the only leader who truly had his people's best interests at heart.

She knew he'd cared for her, and still, he'd turned her away because of what she'd done to his lands...

To Ellow.

Had taken the hurt himself for his people.

A cold hand gripped her heart.

Loche was selfless in a way she hadn't learned yet.

Every nerve within her screamed at her to turn around—to sail to Vastala as fast as possible and waste whatever lives she needed to get her sister out.

But...

It was bigger than her and Frelina.

Wasn't it?

She was doing this for herself and for her family, yes.

But also for her friends.

For her staff.

For the people in Ellow—the innocent people unwilling to join a ruthless rebellion against a leader they loved and respected.

A people that would bleed with the rebel attack.

Then bleed again once the Oakgards' Fae ships reached their borders.

Gritting her teeth, Lessia thought this world had truly learned nothing.

Meyah was happy to sacrifice a people like hers had once been.

Rioner would turn against an ally that had fought with his people, suffering great losses, not too long ago.

But Loche...

He'd listened.

He'd changed his priorities when she'd shared her experiences with him.

He'd accepted the half-Fae children without question—even with the illegal ways they'd been brought to Ellow.

Her blurred vision cleared.

She would get Frelina out.

By whatever means it took.

But there were other things that needed to fall into place. Other people to save. A whole realm to protect.

Lessia's gaze remained fixed on the islands they sailed past when Merrick silently joined her, resting his arms on the railing to level his face with hers.

"The plan hasn't changed," Lessia stated, surprised at how strong her voice sounded. "We need to convince Loche, perhaps now more than ever. And... after that, we'll find her. If I have to kill Rioner to do so, then so be it."

"I will help you get her back." Raine walked up to her other side, his eyes hard when she briefly met them. "I should have kept a closer eye on her. It's my fault. I've already sent one of my eagles to inform your father of what happened, but if he can't get to her, I will do everything in my power to."

Lessia gave him a sad smile as she shook her head. "It was no one's fault. I'm starting to think the damn fates are forcing us to face what my father tried so hard to keep us shielded from. But do you know what I think about that?"

She glanced from Merrick to Raine when they turned toward her. "Fuck fate. Fuck these leaders who think they can control us by threatening us. Fuck the gods who started this endless fight for power. I will not let them tell me how my life will end up. We are in charge now, and we will make the decisions we damned well please."

Merrick's lips lifted into a smile.

One of those smiles that knocked the air right out of her with how surprisingly bright and beautiful it was and how little it made him look like the terrifying Death Whisperer.

Raine, on the other hand, surveyed her for a long while, a wrinkle deepening his usual frown as his gaze sliced from her to Merrick.

"What?" she finally asked when the silence stretched too long.

"Nothing," he muttered.

"Just tell me," she hissed, unable to control the irritation in her voice.

She'd felt like Raine had kept something from her for a while now, and she was getting tired of it.

"We're almost there!" Kerym called out as he swung himself down from the mast, landing with a grin before Lessia.

After offering her a little bow, he grabbed her hand and pressed his lips against it. "I agree with you. Fuck fate. Fate let me meet my mate only to take her from me. I am in the mood for a little revenge. And if that revenge includes taking out Rioner... count me in."

Lessia couldn't help but grin at him, the frustration melting off her like the droplets of cold rain that began to pepper their faces as she let him pull her into a half embrace. "You and me both."

"And me," Merrick grumbled as he nudged Kerym out of the way and tucked Lessia against his body.

Kerym began laughing, and Lessia raised her brows as she glanced from Merrick to him.

When Merrick gave her one of those glacial glares, she tilted her head. "Do you know how annoying it is when you finally have that beautiful smile on your face only to revert to the broody male you always are a moment later?"

As Kerym's laugh turned into a howl, Raine spit out the liquor he'd just poured into his mouth, and even Merrick's jaw dropped an inch before his face hardened again.

Shifting her so she stood before him, Merrick aligned their bodies so she was pressed against him, and his nose nearly touched hers when he leaned in.

"Stop angering me, then," he said softly.

Angling up her head so their faces got even closer, sending a tingle down her spine, she rasped, "I am not trying to anger you."

Merrick's mouth twitched. "And yet you're so good at it."

Fighting the smile pushing to lift her lips, she shrugged. "I have had a lot of practice."

Merrick's nose brushed along hers, slowly, deliberately, and her knees went weak. "Maybe I need to train you to please me instead of piss me off."

Lessia's response stuck in her dry throat.

Was that...

Did he mean?

Yes.

His onyx eyes went impossibly darker, and when she nervously licked her lips, his gaze flew down, a sharp breath leaving him.

Heat pooled within her, and the urge to jump up on him—crawl into his lap and wrap her hands into his hair like she'd done by the fireplace on Raine's island—nearly took over.

Especially when a challenge burned in Merrick's eyes.

A challenge asking her if she dared.

If she wanted to play.

You make me happy.

Lessia blinked.

And he definitely made her *something else* as well...

Only because Ardow's sorrow-filled voice sliced through the heavy air could she tear her eyes away.

But her legs still nearly gave away when she turned around to approach Ardow where he lingered by one of the masts, especially when a dark chuckle left Merrick.

Turning her head over her shoulder, she threw him a glare.

Merrick only grinned back—the smile so wide her own mouth snapped into a mirroring one before she could stop herself.

What was happening?

Lessia's face burned when she realized Kerym and Raine still snickered, and when Ardow's brows rested almost by his hairline, she dragged him with her to the other side of the ship.

"I know," she said when they were out of earshot. "I know. Frelina just got kidnapped, the world is ending, and I'm flirting with the Death Whisperer. I've lost my mind."

"Actually." Ardow rested an arm on the railing. "I think your mind has never been more clear."

Lessia narrowed her eyes.

Lifting a hand, Ardow used his thumb to smooth out the wrinkle between her brows. "Look at you. Your sister *was* just kidnapped, but instead of dropping everything and hurtling after her, you're thinking like a leader." Ardow shook his head. "I'm so sorry I didn't see it before. You were right. The rebels are approaching this the wrong way. But you're not, Lia. You are a real leader. Someone who truly cares about this botched world—even cares about the people that treated you like trash."

"I don't know..." she started, but Ardow shook his head again.

"I do. You were born for this, Lessia. Your compassion and loyalty will make you a great ruler should that be the path you'd like to start down. And even if not, I believe people will still follow you in this war."

Lessia swallowed the lump in her throat.

She had no desire to lead.

It was true that she wanted a better world—that she'd fight for it.

But she did not want to be the one to lead it.

Especially if it forced her to make decisions like that of today—where she couldn't forget everything she had planned and follow her sister.

"We're almost there." Ardow gestured toward the tall

cliffs skirting the eastern part of Asker, glimpsed through the fog in the distance. "Raine was able to drive the mind seer from my mind, so Venko and I will go to the cave, but..." Ardow hesitated, his eyes wandering from the island to her and back again.

"Tell me, Ard." Lessia eyed him, noting the conflicting emotions fighting across his features.

"I don't think we should flee with them." Ardow sighed as he turned to face her fully. "It's not what they'll want. I propose we allow the children to help us in this war."

"I don't know..." Lessia rubbed her face.

Some of them were only twelve, thirteen...

They couldn't ask this of them.

Not after what they'd seen already in their young lives.

"Lessia, you rescued them for a better life. What if we tell them they're going into hiding again while we fight for others to have the same? We do not force them; some are too young, but we should give them a chance if they want it. Also... some of them have abilities that could be very useful."

Throwing her head back, she stared at the darkening sky.

She'd have wanted the choice if it had been her in their place.

Her mind traveled to that night with Ledger—how he'd cried and asked her why they'd killed his friend.

How he'd taken his name in honor of the sacrifice.

Many of them still had friends on the streets...

And who was she to tell them what they could and could not do?

Inclining her head again, she stared into Ardow's

brown eyes. “You’re right. But they will get a choice. Bring those who want to fight back to the capital—but wait for my signal to come to the castle. If they capture and kill us... you get as far away from Havlands as you can. Do you hear me?”

When he nodded, tears glimmered in Ardow’s eyes, and she cleared her throat to quell the ones pricking her own.

When she reached out to squeeze his hand, Ardow smiled through the tears. “Also... I don’t think Merrick is the worst choice. Even if he scares me to death.”

Lessia rolled her eyes. “It’s just flirting. I think he’s trying to distract me—keep me from getting overwhelmed.”

“I doubt that.” Ardow rolled his eyes. “And I think it’s about to get quite messy once Loche is back in the game.”

Smacking his arm, Lessia responded, “Loche hates me. He’ll never care for me again.”

“I doubt that too,” Ardow said as he took the lead down the stairs into the cabin, where the others were already packing the bags they’d brought with them, preparing to get off the ship that wove through the small islands peppering the water outside Asker.

CHAPTER TWENTY-NINE

"Tell me again why we couldn't just have stolen those horses?" Raine groaned as he pulsed through the wet snow ahead of her, and Lessia had to slap a hand over her mouth when he let out a tirade of curses as snow tumbled from one of the pine trees towering over them and drenched him.

Once the ship had docked by a small beach, they'd quickly disembarked and made their way into the woods to stay out of sight.

Ardow and Venko had bid goodbye soon after that, but since they'd agreed they would return to the castle with those who wanted to join the fight, it hadn't been too tear-filled.

The thought of hugging Amalise—of hugging Kalia, who Lessia was sure wouldn't hesitate to come—had kept Lessia warm the entire time they trekked through the forest, heading directly toward the capital.

As night had fallen, they'd passed the small farm where Loche had left his stallion last time she'd been in these parts, but even though the house was dark, Lessia wasn't able to convince herself that "borrowing" their horses was fair.

What if that was all they had?

Instead, they'd continued by foot in the soggy whiteness, and as darkness had continued to fall—the light that would come in the spring not yet breaking through the lingering winter—Lessia's breathing had become increasingly shallow.

She tried to blame it on the challenging journey, but every time one of the Fae walked into her line of sight, she couldn't help but shudder, remembering another darkness—another Fae—and the hurt and fear that had come with them.

Still, she hadn't shut down.

Hadn't given in to the tightness in her chest, nor the sounds that echoed softly in her ears.

As she pushed through another bank of snow, her muscles screamed, and Lessia let out a hissed gasp through her teeth when she stumbled, throwing out her hands to catch herself.

But she didn't have to.

Merrick, who'd been walking behind her, caught her at the last moment, pulling her back against his warm body.

Glancing up at him, she expected a snarled *Watch where you're going!* but instead Merrick searched her face, then ordered, "We're stopping for today."

Guiding her toward a copse of trees that stood more snugly than the rest, the ground beneath them not as wet—although it was still covered with snow—Merrick pulled out a blanket from his satchel and gestured for her to sit down.

Raine slumped next to her, and if she hadn't learned her lesson last time, she would have taken a sip to feel some ounce of warmth when he offered her the flask.

But she couldn't risk it.

Not out here.

And... if she was truthful with herself, she had no idea what was happening between her and Merrick, and she didn't want to confuse it further by drinking from Raine's never-ending supply of liquor and doing something stupid.

So after shaking her head, she rested her eyes on Merrick as he made quick work of finding any dry branch there was and lit a small fire.

"Is that the best idea?" Kerym asked as he sat down with his back against a tree. "Seems like a risk."

"It is." Merrick shot her a look. "But so is freezing to death."

"I'm not complaining." Raine pulled out another blanket, laying it on the other side of the fire and curling up. "This is why I hate war. It's so damn uncomfortable. People think it's all glory and fighting, but it's mostly freezing your ass off and eating stale bread."

"You've lost your edge, Raine." Kerym closed his eyes as he pulled his jacket tighter around him. "Thissian and I have seen far worse than this on our travels. Seems like all Fae realms are struggling—not just the one planning on taking over Havlands."

"Whatever," Raine muttered. "My life was fine before all of you came to destroy it."

Opening an eye, Kerym stared at him. "Was it fine? Doesn't seem like it, given how you hold on to that flask as if it were your newborn babe."

"Are you one to talk? You've thrown yourself into any

fight you can since they died. And what about Thissian? Where is he, Kerym? Is he so badly gone you had to leave him?"

A growl left Kerym, the sound traveling across the snow—way too loud for Lessia's liking.

"Keep your mouths shut," Merrick snarled as he joined Lessia on the blanket. "Your petty argument is worse than the fire. They'd both be ashamed of you."

"They'd be ashamed of you as well," Raine snarled. "I know exactly what they'd say if they were here right now."

Merrick flew to his feet at the same time as the two others.

And for the first time since meeting Raine and Kerym, Lessia could see why they'd all been the mightiest warriors ever to live in Havlands.

The air around Merrick shone, the darkness within his eyes seemingly seeping from him in harried whispers, and as he glared at the others, he was every bit the lethal predator she'd seen those first few years he watched over her.

Raine's massive body vibrated from restrained anger, his hazel eyes so sharp within his furious face that Lessia would have backed up if she hadn't been sitting down.

Kerym—though smaller than the other two—shifted his weight from foot to foot, his hardened face snapping between them, anticipating or perhaps planning an attack.

A storm of fury built within Lessia as well, and she balled her hands into fists as she sprang to her feet.

Stalking into the middle of the death glares—ignoring the warning blaring within her, telling her not to get in the way of these males—Lessia met each pair of raging eyes.

"Stop. This. Right. Now," she got out through tight lips. "I swear, I will go on alone if you continue. We do not have time for dumb arguments."

She focused her stare on Merrick, whose jaw twitched as he met her eyes.

But as she lifted her chin, a harsh breath left him, and his taut shoulders lowered a fraction.

Then, his hands flexed.

And finally, he rolled his neck.

"You're right." Merrick threw a glance at the others. "We need to stick together. One final time."

"It's definitely the last," Raine mumbled as he sheathed the sword he'd pulled from his back and dropped to the ground with a thud.

"It is," Kerym confirmed as he slumped back down against the white-peppered stem.

Lessia rolled her eyes as she started back toward the blanket again, the cold from earlier sweeping through her, making her teeth chatter.

Stupid broody Fae males.

If Rioner, Meyah, or Loche wouldn't be the death of her... she suspected the three of them might be before this was over.

She turned to the side, an urge to complain to Frelina coming over her.

An urge to shoot her an eye roll like she'd done every time one of these males growled or snarled when they talked amongst each other or to either of them on the ship.

But the space was empty.

A consuming ache spread through her veins, shortening her breaths once more.

She'd only had her sister back a few days, but she'd already gotten used to it.

Lessia stared so deep into the fire that the orange-and-red flames were the only thing filling her vision.

She'd get her back.

And...

She'd get her revenge on Meyah.

And Rioner, should she need to.

Not for herself...

No, while she hated him with a vicious intensity, she didn't care about what he'd done to her.

But if he harmed her sister?

The taste of iron filled her mouth, and she realized she'd bitten her cheek so hard, blood pooled within it.

"You all right?" Merrick eyed her as he finally sat down, his nostrils flaring, probably picking up the scent of blood.

Lessia swallowed.

Swallowed the blood.

Swallowed the hurt.

Swallowed the small ember of helplessness that fought within her.

Lifting her eyes to Merrick's, she stated, "I want to kill them."

Merrick remained quiet as her eyes burned into his.

Lessia nodded. "I... I want to. But I know I shouldn't."

Merrick kept her gaze, and for some reason, her vision blurred with tears.

Pulling her to him, Merrick wrapped an arm around her shoulders, and she couldn't help but curl into him, tucking in her legs so her knees rested over his.

"You'll get your revenge," Merrick said hoarsely. "I promise."

Lessia nodded as she stared into the fire while Merrick's hand drew circles on her back.

"Tell me something," Lessia whispered when Raine's and Kerym's soft breathing betrayed that sleep had taken them, and the world around her seemed to become too quiet—too gentle to keep her spinning mind distracted.

"What do you want me to tell you?"

Peeking up at him, she met his eyes, and one of those jolts—the ones that seemed to run through her more often when her eyes collided with his—hit her like a spark of electricity.

As she shivered in response, Merrick held her closer, a slight wrinkle appearing between his brows when she placed her hands on his chest.

"Tell... tell me what changed between us?"

He hesitated for a moment, and despite the cold night, Lessia's cheeks warmed.

But then one of Merrick's hands landed over her own.

"Everything," he said.

Her eyes followed his hand as it moved to her face, a finger gently trailing from her temple to her chin.

Cupping it, he brushed his thumb over her heated skin. "I see you, Elessia Rantzier. I see how you fight to live through each day. I see how you fight to better yourself—whether it's through training or understanding of others. I see how you fight to love so freely and so deeply. I see how you fight for a world that's only mistreated you, because you believe it's the right thing to do."

Lessia's pulse quickened as Merrick's hand drew down to her neck.

Gently cradling the back of it, he pressed his thumb against the vein thrumming on the side, and her breath caught in her throat when his voice lowered, the words coming out gruff. "You wouldn't have to fight for me. I… I can't say it would be easy, given what we're facing, but I'd make sure this—us—would be the one place you can rest, where you're always safe, where you never have to put on a mask to conceal your true feelings."

He makes you happy.

Merrick's words slammed into her heart, and as his other hand came up to cup her face, she leaned into his touch.

His eyes asked her a question, and while thickness clogged her throat…

It wasn't from sorrow.

He already felt like… home.

Dipping her chin, she waited.

And she wasn't disappointed.

A smile softened his hard features.

And then… he leaned in.

Lessia closed her eyes, her body humming from the nearness, and a low moan fell from her lips when Merrick's hot breath hit her mouth.

Then a branch snapped, and Lessia's eyes flew open.

Merrick was already on his feet, his eyes wild as he whipped his head from side to side.

"Get up," he hissed at Raine and Kerym. "We're surrounded."

Something whistled by Lessia's ear.

As her gaze snapped toward it, she realized it was an arrow that lodged itself in the tree beside her, and vigilance had her fly to her feet at the same time as Raine and Kerym, the two males' gazes frantic as they stared into the darkness.

"Behind me. Now!" Merrick ordered, and when she didn't move swiftly enough, he grabbed her so forcefully she had to hold on to his jacket not to fall.

Spinning around, Merrick steadied her, and her hands gripped for her daggers when he jerked.

Her eyes shot to his, and fear struck her heart when what shone there mirrored what she'd seen when he drank the Vincere.

Merrick jolted again, his face scrunching before he caught himself, and the sound that left her throat was like nothing she'd heard before—the growl so wild and untamed she wasn't entirely certain it was actually her own.

Ripping her gaze from his, she started overtaking him, her mind only able to focus on hurting whoever caused him pain, when a whirlwind of snow wove its way through the small clearing, its meandering path raising the hairs on Lessia's neck even before Merrick screamed, "Get away from it!"

But it was too late.

The twirling heap of white that moved against the wind whipping across the ground surrounded her, and she screamed when white-hot pain exploded within her mind.

"Merrick, no!" Raine bellowed somewhere in the distance—somewhere far, far away from the world of torture Lessia now lived in.

Blinded, she dropped to her knees, and Lessia barely understood what happened when arms wrapped around her, shielding her from something that made the shape groan as it pressed her against the cold ground.

More screams floated somewhere outside the ringing in her ears.

Still, as she felt her consciousness slip, they weakened until only a low crooning broke through the haze of agony, and when the world pressed against her—pressed everywhere until it all went silent—she let it swallow her, praying that that might somehow end the torment.

CHAPTER THIRTY

Mumbles sounded somewhere outside the muddled darkness that was her mind, and Lessia tried to perk her aching ears to make out what they were saying.

"That was fucking Vincere. But it was worse. I still can't feel my magic."

Must be Kerym's gravelly voice, she thought.

"Why would Rioner have gifted Vincere to Ellow? It's the one thing that keeps us subdued."

Raine.

"No fucking clue." Chains clinked as Merrick snarled somewhere to her left.

"Lessia," he called, his voice softening. "I know you're awake."

She squeezed her eyelids shut when another wave of pain stabbed at her, the sense that her every nerve was on fire rippling through her.

She really wished she hadn't awoken.

Especially when more sharp pangs of agony—agony

that reminded her of a severe toothache she'd had when little—shot through her skull.

"Lessia," Merrick said again, his voice worryingly gentle. "Do not panic. But—"

Whatever he said was drowned out when she finally gave in and opened her eyes.

To nothing.

It was utterly dark—not a single ember of light filling the space before her.

Jerking her head, Lessia felt a strap of fabric tightly bound around it shift.

Her heart started racing.

No, no, no.

"Lessia." Merrick's voice got sterner, but she ignored him as she tried lifting her hands to pull it off.

A whimper built within her when she realized shackles encircled her wrists, allowing her to move her hands only a few inches from where they lay in her lap.

Her feet were also bound, and metal grated on her skin where her trousers had slipped out of her boots.

You're never getting out of here.

No.

This couldn't be happening.

Her breathing became erratic as the musty scent of stone and waste permeated her senses.

Water began dripping somewhere in the darkness.

Metal scraped against the floor.

"No!" Lessia scrambled backward as much as the chains would allow, but it proved futile.

A wall stopped her retreat, the force of her back slamming into it wrenching a gasp from her lips.

You're not there, she tried to tell herself when she

managed to draw some air back into her lungs. *You're not there.*

But the shriek of metal only came closer.

A bone-chilling laugh echoed in her ears, and she couldn't hold back a scream as the memories of what would soon follow flooded her mind.

The pain of knives cutting through flesh.

The air she'd have no access to.

The memories they'd make her relive.

"Merrick, you need to do something."

Lessia flinched at the gravelly voice, and she started begging despite the promise she'd made to herself not to let Rioner's guards get to her anymore. "Please, I'll do anything... Please, j-just don't do this!"

"Merrick, she's panicking."

"I know! Fuck!" The curse brushed her ear, and she braced herself when the screeching quieted, the fabric over her eyes dampening as tears spilled from her eyes.

Then soft lips pressed against hers, a gentle voice breathing words into her mouth. "I need you to focus on me. Nothing else."

Her body reacted before her mind, her lips parting to let the hot air in—let the person before her help her struggling lungs.

It was like the sun peeking through a thick cloud bank.

Her heart leaped before its beats slowed, becoming more even.

"Good," the person rasped. "Only you and me."

When Lessia nodded, the pressure of the kiss deepened, and she couldn't help but return it, a feverish urge blooming across her face when a groan slipped through the lips playing with hers.

A gentle sweep of a tongue brushed her bottom lip, and it was all she needed to crush her lips harder against the others, fusing their mouths together, letting their tongues dance and tangle and play within the kiss.

"I need you," she whimpered.

"I know," he said as he nipped at her bottom lip, just enough to break through the mess that was her mind but not break the magic that seemed to wash away the sense of dread within her.

Of course he knew.

He always knew.

"Merrick," she whispered.

The voice she heard hadn't been Rioner's guards.

It had been Merrick.

Merrick's friends.

"I'm here," he whispered right back. "I'm always here."

Air continued to travel into her lungs, and with each breath, her mind cleared, but she couldn't stop herself from intensifying the kiss, her lips clinging to his as if every second could be the last.

And he gave her as much—if not more—back.

A tingle of delight shot up her spine when he growled against her mouth, and lust sliced through her like the pain had done before.

Pressing up against him, she tried to align her body with his, but the chains she was bound in—and that he was bound in—got in the way.

An involuntary sound escaped her when the urge to merge their bodies—to merge their souls—overtook all other thoughts, and she struggled against the restraints with everything in her.

"My little fighter," Merrick whispered, a low laugh

rumbling through him as she let out another unbidden moan when his lips left hers.

"Stay still," he ordered quietly. "I'm going to get this off you."

His mouth whispered across her cheek, leaving jolting kisses in its wake as it traveled upward toward the fabric covering her eyes.

After kissing her temple, he spoke again. "I'm sorry. This might hurt."

Lessia nodded, and she dug her nails into her palms when Merrick's canines scraped her skin, ripping into the blindfold.

With a sharp jerk, the fabric tore, and low light reached her eyes.

As she glanced upward, Merrick's eyes were the first thing she focused on.

And that sense of falling gripped her again.

But it wasn't frightening,

No, it was a fall she wanted.

A choice.

A decision.

A surrender.

A movement in the corner of her eye had her snap her head to the side, and she couldn't stop the blush burning up her neck when she met Raine's and Kerym's eyes from where the males rested against the wall opposite her and Merrick.

The wall that was perhaps a few feet away...

She quickly moved her gaze back to Merrick.

The half smile that had pulled at his lips fell when her wide eyes flitted between him and the other two, and something cold twisted in her gut when uncertainty glimmered in his night-sky ones.

Pushing down the embarrassment, Lessia leaned forward and pressed another kiss against his mouth, that all-consuming need flickering to life once more.

"Thank you," she said shakily as she sat back down again.

Merrick's eyes flashed. "Anytime."

"I'm sure," Kerym muttered. "Now that that's done, how are we getting out of this place?"

Lessia let her eyes travel around the small cell for the first time.

The space couldn't be more than eight feet square, the three large Fae males taking up most of it, and the only light filling the room trickled in from a thin gap beneath the thick stone door Kerym leaned against.

Her eyes moved to Merrick as he sat down next to her, and as she drew a deep breath to calm whatever he'd awoken within her from that kiss, a metallic scent joined the musty smell of cellar and sweat that hung heavy in the air.

Lessia stiffened.

"Are you hurt?" she asked, eyeing his constrained movements as he tried to fold his tall body comfortably in the small space.

It wasn't the chains that had that muscle in his jaw flex, his shoulders rising an inch as he stared back at her.

"Merrick," she demanded quietly when he dismissively jerked his head.

"He took ten arrows in the back for you."

She moved her eyes to Raine when he spoke.

Even in the dark she could tell he was paler than she'd ever seen, and a sheen of sweat layered across his face, a drop of it trickling down his temple and falling to the floor.

A surge of anger roiled in her stomach when she turned back to Merrick, and she realized the dark stains on his tunic weren't sweat.

"It's fine." Merrick nudged her with his leg. "They ripped them out before throwing us in here. I'm healing."

"You're healing slowly. Those heads were laced with Vincere." Kerym lifted a shaking hand. "I'd forgotten how much that stuff fucking hurts. Vincere? In Ellow... I don't understand."

"We... we're still in Ellow?" Lessia shifted closer to Merrick, trying to make out whether blood still dripped down his back and avoiding his gaze when he rolled his eyes at her.

"We are," Merrick said as he positioned himself so she'd have no view of his back.

"Where did you think we were?" Kerym glanced at her with a wrinkle between his brows.

"I-I... Maybe in Vastala," she mumbled.

She was an idiot.

She'd thought she'd gotten better at handling the reminders of Rioner's cellars...

But apparently she'd made little progress.

Kerym's eyes searched hers, and for the first time, his face softened.

"It gets easier," he said quietly. "I should know."

Lessia frowned as she stared from him to Merrick, and when Merrick nodded, she winced.

"How long?" she asked.

"Long. I wasn't the most obedient soldier." Kerym pulled at the chains encircling his wrists so the sound echoed through the small cell. "And neither was Thissian, so Rioner's father figured out if one of us was kept in his wonderful dungeons, we'd be more *agreeable*."

"I'm sorry." Lessia's eyes fell on her own chains, the muddy hands in her lap.

"Don't be." Kerym shot her a smile that didn't reach his eyes. "It's how I met my mate. She liked to anger the Rantziers as well. All the way to the bitter end."

A shuddering breath left her.

The Rantziers were the cause of so much hurt.

Not just for everyone in this cell.

But all half-Fae who'd ever been mistreated...

Or who'd had to hide...

All the soldiers that died for them...

All the Fae who weren't nobility...

Her sister.

Her father.

Her nostrils flared when she lifted her gaze again.

Merrick's eyes brightened with understanding at what swirled in her mind, and she could almost hear his voice.

You'll get your revenge.

She would.

If it was the last thing she ever did, she'd get her revenge.

Merrick's forehead creased the longer he watched her, and something she didn't fully understand flickered across his features before he moved his eyes to Raine and Kerym.

"We need to get out of here. I'm pretty sure there is a kill-on-sight order for me and Lessia, and I doubt Loche will listen to either of you brutes if we die," he said as he flicked some tangled strands of hair out of his face.

Raine dragged a finger down the wall, grimacing as he brought the white dust to his nose. "I'm pretty sure they've figured out a way to cover the walls in Vincere. I at least still cannot wield my magic."

Kerym frowned as his eyes landed on Lessia, but she didn't sense the energy pull—the slowing of her thoughts—that she usually did whenever he decided to train her to stop him from siphoning. "Me neither."

"None of you Fae bastards are going anywhere. Especially the traitor. We have special plans for you."

Raine and Kerym froze at the voice drifting through the door, but Merrick moved quicker than should be possible, with him being injured and in a room he wouldn't even be able to stand upright in.

Chains screaming, he moved into a crouch before her, his entire being vibrating with the growl leaving him. "The only plan you'll have is walking right into the arms of your dead loved ones if you touch her."

A glacial laugh bounced between the stone walls. "Oh, we won't touch *her*. At least not yet. We saw her during the election. She responds much better to others'... suffering."

A chill raced over her skin, but she didn't let her mind linger on his words.

Instead, she tried moving so Merrick wasn't blocking her—although he immediately shifted as well, so that proved entirely useless.

Shaking her head at him, she cleared her throat. "We need to speak to Loche. He is in danger. All of Ellow is in danger."

That laugh rang again. "You just won me one silver. We were betting on what your excuse would be to see Loche."

A hand tapped the door, the rhythmic thuds quickening Lessia's pulse. "We know you've come to kill him, and unlike you, we don't need a blood oath to be loyal to our leader. You won't get anywhere near him."

"Please!" Lessia called. "We're not lying! Just bring him here—you can keep him outside the door, but we need to speak to him!"

"No." The voice sounded farther away, receding footsteps joining it. "We'll be back in a while... I would say stay up, but I think I'll let you stay in here for a few days. Even with the handy powder to block your abilities, I've heard of your companions. The Death Whisperer... Tsk, tsk. We will not take any risks."

Another door slammed somewhere outside, and as icy silence layered across the cell, Lessia desperately pulled at her chains again, but it was of no use.

They were fastened with the thickest bolts she'd ever seen, deep beneath the stones lining the floor.

Noting that none of the males even tried, she finally gave up, allowing Merrick to nudge her back into the spot beside him.

"That went well." Kerym closed his eyes as he rested his head on the wall. "I'm taking a nap."

"Damn chains," Raine snarled as he twisted his arm in what looked like a very painful angle. "I can't even reach my flask."

"They took it anyway, you idiot," Kerym scoffed.

With a deep groan, Raine struggled into the spot next to Kerym, banging the back of his head against the closed door a few times before his eyes angrily squeezed shut.

Lessia flicked her gaze up to Merrick's. "What are we going to do?"

He captured her eyes. "Survive. Escape. Kill Loche and his guards."

Despite the situation, her lips twitched, and she pursed them so not to smile. "We can't kill him, Merrick."

"Why not?"

He actually looked disappointed, and Lessia shook her head at him.

"Because we need him on our side. The people of Ellow—well, most of them—love and respect him. We need him to believe us so that they'll fight with us."

"Another leader can take his place." Merrick's brows rose in challenge. "He hurt you. And his guards are planning on hurting you again. I usually don't even give one chance, and this man is pushing my patience."

"This is not about me." Lessia tilted her head as he frowned. "That's why I didn't set after Frelina right away. It's about Havlands, about every innocent person here. We need him to save them."

Merrick's teeth ground so hard she was surprised Raine and Kerym didn't hush him. "You're wrong, you know."

"What am I wrong about?"

"Everything is about you."

Her face heated when Merrick's eyes burned into hers, and she couldn't stop herself from leaning into him, resting her head against his shoulder.

A deep breath rumbled through him as he lay his head atop hers, and that sense—that sense of home—came over her.

Even in this small, dark, and terrifying place.

CHAPTER THIRTY-ONE

Merrick's fingers traced over her palm when she woke, and even though hunger gnawed at her stomach, it was soon replaced by the lightheadedness—the borderline euphoria—that told her they'd been locked up here for a few days by now.

Maybe even a whole week.

Tucking in his legs, Merrick made space for her to crawl over to the small stream of water that dripped down one of the walls.

Lessia greedily opened her mouth, using her tongue to capture as many drops as possible and trying to ignore the stings of pain that accompanied it from the Vincere that mixed with the dirty water.

At this point, the dirty stream was the only thing keeping them all relatively conscious, although Lessia was becoming unsure whether it was for the better.

Raine and Kerym had become grumpier by the hour, and not even Merrick hissing at them to focus—as once the soldiers came back, they'd need to be ready—could quiet their grumblings.

She could tell Raine regretted ever coming with them, and while his constant complaining would have usually annoyed her, she'd been awake last night when sobs shook his large frame, and his whispered "I'm sorry. I'm so sorry, Solana" had nearly broken her.

He'd probably been under the influence of that liquor every day since her death, and right now, all the feelings he'd repressed were coming right back.

She tried to smile at him as she made her way back, but as she bent her neck toward him, something whistled through the air, leaving a stinging kiss on the skin between her shoulder and throat.

"What..." Lessia lifted her bound hands to her neck, but she couldn't reach it.

Cocking her head instead, she sensed some type of dart, or at least something with a sharp tip piercing her skin, as Merrick collapsed before her.

Blinking slowly, she tried to move toward him, but her limbs went sluggish, and darkness began pressing at the corners of her eyes, soon filling her entire vision.

But it wasn't like falling asleep.

No, she was aware of the hands that unclasped the chains she was bound in.

Could feel the arms lifting her, dragging her boots on the hard floor as they moved her, and hear the men's breathing, the words that seemed slurred to her, talking about something she couldn't quite understand.

Lessia didn't know how much time had passed, but after a while, she was placed in something.

A chair?

It must be, she decided when cold metal wrapped

around her wrists and ankles again, and something leathery wrapped around her face.

But not over her eyes.

Instead, the strap tightened across her forehead.

As if to hold her head in place.

If she were able, she would have frowned.

It wasn't like she could move anyway...

She could feel and hear, but it was as if she couldn't communicate with her muscles.

Even her eyelids remained closed, no matter how hard she tried to pry them open.

"She done?"

A male voice broke through the clinking of fetters.

"She'll need some time to be fully aware."

Another male voice.

One she unfortunately recognized.

One that she'd heard speak but never seen the face of.

It was one of the guards who'd overseen her torture during the election process.

Lessia's heart fought against whatever they'd injected her with, the slow beats pushing to accelerate, for adrenaline to rush through her blood.

If that man was here, this couldn't be good.

"He's waking up."

She already hated that too-high-pitched voice.

And who was the "he" who was waking up?

Lessia's eyelids fluttered as her heart gained more momentum, and she could finally get her fingers to twitch.

"So is she."

"They're strong—even her only being half-Fae."

Lessia pressed her tongue against the back of her teeth as she regained more motion.

First her hands began flexing.

Then she could feel the ground beneath her feet.

Warmth flooded her veins, her pulse thrumming against the cold metal.

And finally...

Finally her eyes popped open.

Lessia had to snap them shut when bright light blinded her, and the shackles rattled as she instinctively reached up to rub her eyes, the jangled sound mocking her as it halted her movement.

Trying again, she opened her eyes a fraction, and the warmth that had begun heating her blood ignited to a burning flame when she took in the scene before her.

Merrick sat half dressed in a chair a few feet from her, thick chains with white powder sprinkled over them wrapped around his entire bare torso.

Several shackles also held his arms and legs in place, but when his eyes found hers, there wasn't an ounce of fear in them.

Only relief.

Relief that slackened his features as his gaze dragged over her, then to the rest of the brightly lit room, and as she tried to follow it, she realized why.

The leather strap around her head wouldn't allow her to move it; her gaze was allowed only forward, into the corner where Merrick's chair was placed...

"No," she breathed, realizing what Merrick had already understood.

"You see now, don't you." A hand landed on her shoulder, and the rage within her rose with each tap of the four fingers. "I was there during your torture and when they made you choose between the traitor and the blond whore. It was clear as day that you hurt more by making a choice between your friends, so I thought..."

The soldier continued to tap her shoulder as if he was building anticipation. "I thought it could be fun to play a little game." His nails dug into her skin. "See how long it takes you to break, watching us slowly kill the Death Whisperer."

"I'm going to kill *you*," Lessia snarled as she fought against the head strap.

The man laughed. "I don't think so. You're going to be a good little halfling and stay in your chair."

She could hear him move about behind her chair, and she pressed her feet down into the ground to try to tip it over, try to make it fall, but it wouldn't move an inch.

She snarled again.

It must be bolted into the ground.

"Lessia."

Whipping her head up from trying to get out of the bind, she met Merrick's eyes.

He smiled at her.

Fucking smiled.

"Don't do that," she hissed. "Don't do this to me."

Merrick smiled wider. "You're stronger than you think. And I am also stronger than you think. I've been tortured before. By much worse enemies than some weak humans." He threw a lazy wink behind her when someone grumbled.

Lessia shook her head, but before she could speak, two men walked up, one on either side of her chair, keeping their backs turned on her the entire time they stalked toward Merrick.

And even though it couldn't have been more than six

or seven steps, it felt like an eternity passed while she desperately met Merrick's gaze over their cloaked heads.

She made herself breathe in through her nose and out through her mouth as one of the men lifted his fist and, without warning, slammed it right into Merrick's face.

Even though she could tell the man had used most, if not all, of his strength, Merrick's face barely moved, and a low chuckle escaped him. "That's all you got?"

The man struck again.

And again.

And again.

Every time, Merrick only laughed, his eyes dancing as he continued to meet Lessia's across the room.

As the soldier lifted his hand once more, the other placed his own over his fist.

Walking up to Merrick, he leaned in close. "We heard about the blood oath to your king... It would seem the Death Whisperer wasn't as dangerous as we were always told. Leashed like a pup for years..."

Merrick gave him a crimson-stained smile, a drop of blood snaking its way down his strong jaw as he shrugged. "You're welcome to try me."

The man clicked his tongue. "I think I shall."

He jerked his head toward the other soldier. "Remove the chains from his left arm, but keep the one on his wrist."

Lessia frowned as she continued to stare into Merrick's eyes, and she didn't miss his quick glance down, the tightening at the corners of his eyes as the man followed the orders.

A sense of foreboding despair settled on her chest, and it only worsened as the soldier continued to work on the bindings and the man who'd spoken walked out of Lessia's line of sight.

She tried to collect herself as Merrick's features remained passive, to make her locked muscles soften enough for her to speak.

"Y-you and me," she got out, and Merrick smiled again.

A real smile.

Not the glacial one he'd offered the guard.

She forced her lips to form a shaky one back.

But when that guard returned to the spot beside Merrick and he held two sharp blades in his hands, there was no way she could keep it.

As the one who'd removed the shackles stepped back, the hooded soldier laughed darkly and dragged the tip of the blade over Merrick's now-exposed arm. "You can still see the outline of the oath. But it's definitely faded. Perhaps it'll even disappear after a while..."

Lessia held her breath as she pushed away the thought beginning to form in her mind.

They wouldn't.

Then the man laughed again, and her heart froze in her chest.

"It's the mark of a traitor for the Fae, right? Why a snake, of all things?"

Merrick kept his mouth closed, his eyes fixed on Lessia.

"Answer me!" The knife moved to Merrick's throat, and Lessia couldn't take it when drops of blood trickled down his chest, pooling between those taut muscles.

"Stop it!" she screamed. "Yes, it's the sign of a traitor! Rioner bestows it on us if he deems us to have betrayed him or the crown. It's the crest of another noble family that the Rantziers defeated in a war a long time ago. They commanded snakes, and Rioner became obsessed with them. He keeps them as pets and will use them to kill if it pleases him."

"So elaborate." The man yawned. "I guess you Fae live so long you need to find things like this to entertain yourselves..." He brought the knife back to Merrick's arm, balancing the tip against the skin right beneath his elbow.

Right where the snake tattoo would have begun coiling had it still been there.

"I don't have that kind of time. But..." He pressed the knife until it broke Merrick's golden skin. "You betrayed Ellow as well. Helping a spy in our election... That's what I consider a traitor."

"Please," Lessia whispered as she watched the blood well up around the edge of the blade. "Please don't do this."

Merrick's eyes caught hers when she lifted them, and once again he gave her a smile.

A smile she could barely make out through the tears beginning to cloud her vision.

Still staring into her eyes, he spoke in that lethally low voice she'd been used to before everything changed between them. "Mark me. Hurt me. I truly don't care. But you should know..." Merrick licked a drop of blood off his full lips. "I will come for you. And once I do—it'll be worse than your darkest nightmares. I'll show you exactly why they call me the Death Whisperer."

Lessia could see the shudder going through the man not holding the knife.

But the other one didn't flinch, and that a smirk must twist his features was evident when he responded, "So cocky. Is it because you're Fae or because you're an idiot?"

Merrick's canines scraped against his bottom lip as he cocked his head. "No. It's because I'm *that* deadly."

"M-maybe we shouldn't." The other soldier walked up to his friend's side. "What if Loche..."

"Loche will not care," the knife-wielding man snarled. "They betrayed him. Both of them! He only said to keep them alive."

He spun around to face Lessia, his cloaked face bent, but she could still feel his loathing stare burn over her, and the fact that Loche wanted them alive barely registered as he took a step toward her.

"Both of them," he mumbled as he took another step. "You're both traitors, and everyone should know."

"Stop," Merrick growled. "You were doing this to me. Not her."

The man didn't slow his pace as he threw over his shoulder, "I've made no promises. We shall mark you both."

"Human," Merrick seethed. "You'll beg for your nightmares if you touch her. And when you're dead, your head severed from your body, your soul will continue begging for them for all eternity."

"Theon... I don't know about this. Loche cared for the halfling at one time."

The man halted at her feet before spinning around to face the soldier who had hesitantly followed him. "I don't care. Hold her shoulders."

"But..."

"Now!"

Lessia swallowed as the man walked around her and took her shoulders in a hard grip, holding her against the wooden backrest as the other cut off the arm of her tunic.

"Lessia, look at me," Merrick ordered, and her heart shattered at the pain in his voice.

But she made herself sit straight, her chin up and eyes clear of tears as she met Merrick's dark gaze.

It didn't matter what they did to her.

It didn't matter that she had stopped obsessively pulling at clothing to hide the dark mark only a few days before.

It didn't matter she'd enjoyed wearing dresses again—even if those dresses had been more revealing than she'd perhaps have chosen herself.

It didn't matter.

She didn't scream when the blade cut through her skin.

Nor when warmth began running down, dripping onto her thigh.

Nor when the man triumphantly emphasized each letter he carved into her newly healed arm:

T

R

A

I

T

O

R

She didn't even flinch when he poured coal dust into the wound, rubbing it in with his calloused hands.

She only looked into Merrick's eyes, watching as emotions fought over his features.

Anger.

Fury.

Guilt.

Worry.

Love.

She was certain that was what it was.

Because she knew that pain.

Knew it as well as an old friend.

The devastation of watching a loved one hurt.

She didn't brace herself when the men retreated from her chair and returned to Merrick without a moment's delay.

If he allowed himself to feel every moment of pain watching her go through it, she wouldn't deny him the same bravery.

Her eyes remained locked with his over the crouched backs of the guards, refusing to even blink the entire time they worked on his forearm.

They continued to stare at each other even as the men cleaned off the blade, even as they held a short conversation before announcing they were leaving them there to ensure their Fae blood would heal them enough for the coal to seal within their skin.

Neither of them spoke as the men left the room.

What was there to say?

They'd lived with a traitor mark before.

They'd do it again.

CHAPTER THIRTY-TWO

Lessia didn't fight the guards when they tied the blindfold back in place before they released her from the chair and secured her hands in front of her body with thick iron that pressed on the raw wound winding down to her wrist.

She didn't fully understand why they did it—they'd already subdued her again by blowing Vincere into her face, which made her bound arms twitch painfully as they shoved her out of the room.

Perhaps they were being extra cautious.

She could sense Merrick's presence somewhere beside her, his scent layering over her like a warm blanket in winter, and Lessia drew a shaky breath.

It would be all right.

For some reason, she believed it.

Merrick made her believe it.

He made her... believe in herself.

And for some reason, Loche wasn't out to kill them.

At least not yet...

They'd convince him.

She'd convince him.

She would.

That much she dared promise herself.

"Oh, are we too early?" A voice cut through the silence, the soft purr of it perking Lessia's ears.

Her brows furrowed.

She knew that voice.

"Who are you?" Theon, the guard with a tight grip on Lessia's arm, demanded.

"Vali sent us. He thought you might need some company after being out here all alone for so long," a more melodic voice chirped.

Another voice Lessia recognized, and she had to force her expression to remain neutral, her gait not to falter as shock jolted her.

The voices belonged to Soria and Pellie.

"Vali?" Something clapped to her right, and if Lessia had to bet, she guessed one of the guards just slapped the other on the back. "What a good man. We only need to return these two to their cell, and then we'll have some fun. You may wait upstairs."

"Oh!" Pellie exclaimed. "Are they Fae? I've never met a Fae before. What did they do?"

"Bad things. That's why we're taking them back to their cells. Head on up now." Theon's grip on her arm tightened as he pushed her until she stumbled forward.

"Move faster," he hissed into her ear, drops of spit landing on her cheek. "I'm going to enjoy myself today. More than I've already done."

"No, you're not." The seductive purr in Soria's voice vanished, and Lessia barely had time to react before air rushed, and a sickening thud of something hitting flesh filled her ears.

A moan sounded somewhere beside her, and her ears picked up two bodies slumping to the ground, one likely Theon, as the hand around her arm released its grip.

Gentle fingers touched her face, and Pellie urged, "One second," as she worked on the knot at the back of Lessia's head.

Once the fabric fell to the stone beneath their feet, Pellie's arms wrapped around her neck, and Lessia's face was crushed into her copper hair.

"Lessia! We missed you so much," she said with a sob. "We thought you were dead."

"My turn." Soria grinned as she dragged her sister away, pulling Lessia into a softer version of the hug—and without suffocating her with hair, as she kept her own copper hair cropped short.

"We did miss you," she whispered as she pulled back, her blue eyes glossy in the light from the chandeliers dangling from the arched ceiling.

"I... m-missed you too," Lessia stuttered as she stepped toward Merrick, her eyes flying across his tall body, making sure he wasn't injured.

Well... more injured.

Once he'd rolled his eyes at her, she turned back toward the auburn-haired sisters.

Lessia's confusion must have been evident because they both grinned back at her, and Soria threw out her hands. "Liar. You have probably barely spared us a thought."

Rubbing her neck, Lessia flicked her eyes to Merrick, but the Fae was of no help as he only shrugged back.

"I'm sorry," she said quietly.

They were right.

She had barely thought of them since she joined the election.

But they had never truly been friends...

She and Ardow had saved them a few years ago, but it hadn't only been out of the goodness of their hearts.

They'd needed distractions as they began bringing the children over, and Soria and Pellie were perfect.

Both beautiful, strong, and deprived of a life young women craved.

Pellie shook her head. "We're teasing you."

Licking her lips, Soria nodded. "She's right. We heard whispers in the taverns that traitors had been captured on Asker, and we thought..."

"Must be Lessia, mustn't it? And we owe you." Pellie put an arm around her sister.

"We do. You saved us."

"And we don't like to owe anyone."

"We don't," Soria confirmed. "And now we're hopefully even?"

"Especially since we saved that scary Fae male of yours." Pellie gestured toward Merrick, who'd been watching the sisters talk with his mouth hanging slightly open.

Lessia held back a smile.

They were a lot.

Always talking, always playing, always up to do something fun.

But she'd never imagined they'd risk their lives for her this way.

"Well, shall we get going?" Soria pointed up the spiral stairs behind her. "It's still a day's walk to the capital from here."

The rattling of chains reached Lessia's ears, but for once, it didn't immobilize her.

"Soon. We need to save two more." Lessia dropped down onto her knees by the knocked-out guards.

Eyeing the wooden makeshift weapon the sisters must have grabbed from the forest, she shook her head and began digging into Theon's pocket, ignoring the pain shooting up her arm when the chains around her wrist scraped against her new tattoo.

More metal clinking told her she'd found what she was looking for, and as soon as she pulled the keys out of his trousers, she got to her feet again and walked up to Merrick.

The traitor's mark was stark against his skin as she unlocked the cuffs around his wrists, but she refused to look away from the large black letters.

When Merrick quietly took the key from her to free her wrists, she kept her eyes on the identical tattoos marring their arms, following each swerve of the characters, every drop of dried blood peppering his golden skin and her slightly fairer arm.

Traitor.

Wasn't it what they were, anyway?

She was a traitor to the crown in Vastala.

To her own flesh and blood.

And she would betray Loche without a doubt if that was needed to save Havlands.

Lessia blinked a few times.

But the thought remained.

She would if it came to that.

One of Merrick's fingers stroked her cheek, and when it reached her neck, she lifted her gaze to his.

His eyes searched hers, and when they didn't find

what she was sure he was looking for, a half smile lit up his face.

"It's the same one," he said softly.

You and me.

That's what he'd said when she'd panicked.

When only his touch could bring her back from the darkness.

She nodded, and his half smile widened into a full one.

It wasn't the snake mark—the mark they'd shared with countless others who'd gone against King Rioner...

It was their mark.

And regardless of how ugly it was or what it said about them... it was theirs.

Merrick's and Lessia's.

"How long are you going to keep us waiting here?" Raine grumbled through the stone, breaking the loaded silence—the conversation she imagined she'd been holding with Merrick's eyes.

Rolling her neck, she snatched the keys from Merrick and, after trying a few different ones, managed to unlock the thick stone door.

Raine leaned one of his hands against the wall, his back arched because of the short chains fastened in the ground and his head hanging between his shoulders.

Kerym barely reacted, still sitting on the floor, his dark hair shining in the light from the lanterns bordering the hallway that spilled into the cell.

They looked like Lessia felt—tired, dirty, and very, very hungry.

Approaching Raine first, she undid his restraints as swiftly as she could, then crouched to do the same to Kerym.

He reached out to stabilize her when she wavered, the lightheadedness from earlier returning in full force now that the adrenaline was leaving her blood, and before she had time to react, Merrick's arms slipped in under her own, guiding her to the spot next to Kerym.

After grabbing the keys from her, he finished what she'd started, and when Kerym rose on shaky legs, she made to do the same, grateful for Merrick's hand, which shot out to help her when black spots flickered before her eyes.

"*These two* are our rescuers?" Kerym leaned against the doorframe as he nodded toward Soria and Pellie, who watched the Fae intently. "We're truly rusty in the ways of war."

Soria's brows crashed, and Pellie let out a disapproving sound, but neither responded as they took a few steps back to allow Raine and Kerym to get out of the cramped room.

Raine tried to double back to help Merrick when the latter bent down to drag the two guards into the cell, but after he hissed, "They're. Mine," in the lowest voice Lessia had ever heard him speak, Raine backed up, his hands in the air.

Merrick's eyes landed on hers as he began to shut the door—keeping himself on the side with the guards—and Lessia knew she should have been afraid of the look in his eyes, the one that told her exactly what he planned to do once the stone door slammed shut.

But she wasn't.

She gave him a nod, and his features softened for the briefest second before they disappeared behind the closed door.

They all remained quiet, trying not to listen to

strange noises coming from within the thick wall—the ones Merrick's whispers might have been preferable to—and while there wasn't fear in the sisters' eyes when they tracked Raine and Kerym as they leaned against the wall, there was something else...

Curiosity, Lessia realized.

They weren't strangers to death, nor to revenge, based on the vague responses Lessia had been given when she found out their mother had died in strange circumstances, but perhaps they hadn't lied when they said they hadn't encountered full Fae before.

It wouldn't be too surprising, given that their mother had kept them locked up in the attic for most of their lives—too afraid of the sisters leaving her once they realized there was a whole world out there.

The smell of iron joined the wet stone when Merrick finally opened the door, but although blood painted his left arm and chest, it was all his own, Lessia realized as he walked over to her.

For a second her thoughts drifted to the harsh sounds that had bounced against the door, wondering what he'd done to the men, but upon remembering the screams from the rebels Merrick had killed back in Ellow, she pushed it from her mind.

That lethal look still remained in his eyes when Lessia caught them, but it softened with every second they stayed locked with hers, and when she kept her chin raised and shoulders down, his taut posture eased—at least a little bit.

"Let's find our weapons and get out of this damned place." Merrick's fingers laced with hers before he gently tugged her down the hallway, with Raine and Kerym following closely behind while Soria and Pellie started up the stairs, stating they'd wait for them by the fire.

As Merrick peeked through the doors lining every few feet of the hallway, Lessia found herself watching him instead.

She sighed deeply when she realized he didn't look much different than he usually did.

His hair was perhaps slightly more disheveled—a little dust dulling its shine—but it definitely wasn't as dirty as her own, which hung limp around her face, and the skin on his bare torso still had that slight glow that she'd always been envious of, especially in the winter, when her own almost turned gray.

Even the tattoo seemed to complement him—the black letters somehow contrasting beautifully with his tan, making the ugly word almost seem... alluring.

"Why are you pouting?" Raine nudged her as he overtook them, seemingly eager to find the weapons.

Or perhaps the flask their captors had also taken from him.

Then his eyes snagged on her outstretched arm, and when his gaze slowly moved to Merrick's arm and then back to hers, his face went white.

"I'm sorry," Raine mumbled as Kerym's hand clasped her other wrist, fingers gently squeezing.

Lessia shook off the hand, trying for a smile instead of letting the lump threatening to form in her throat take hold.

"I'm pouting because Merrick still looks like the gods themselves just carved him, and I look exactly like I've spent a few days in a gross cell," she joked, trying to get the Fae to shake the horrified expressions on their faces.

Merrick halted so abruptly that she walked right into him.

After glaring at Raine and Kerym, who continued walking, stating something about "continuing to look," he spun around to face her.

Gripping her face in his hands, he tilted it upward, his eyes traveling slowly over it—as if he was savoring every inch.

His gaze left a warm trail in its wake, and Lessia couldn't help her cheeks heating in response to his darkening eyes.

"You're beautiful," he declared quietly. "You're always beautiful."

She thought about arguing.

She could smell herself, after all—see the dirt layering over her skin, the golden-brown strands that appeared more brownish now, and the pale, marred skin the guards had carved into.

But something in his gaze had her swallow the retort.

And when he lifted her arm and pressed his lips against the tattoo, kissing the letters one by one with a feathery touch, she released a trembling breath.

Offering her one of those devastating smiles—one of the ones where he seemed to turn into a completely different person—Merrick wrapped an arm around her shoulders and tucked her against his hard frame.

"Found them!" Raine called out, and she let Merrick guide her toward the room Raine and Kerym had slipped into, farther down the corridor.

Lessia snorted when they walked over the threshold, finding Raine deep into a cabinet filled with bottles, his sword carelessly lying on the floor beneath him.

Kerym threw Merrick a leather tunic that had hung

on a chair in the corner of the room. As he released her to pull it on, she walked over to the shelf where her ruby dagger glinted, and relief warmed her gut when the one her father had given her lay farther in.

Lessia tucked them into her waistband and picked up Merrick's heavy sword from where it lay on a shelf above her dagger.

After trailing her fingers over the red gemstones decorating its hilt, she turned around to offer it to Merrick, and she nearly jumped upon finding him right behind her.

"Thank you." Merrick's hand brushed hers as he accepted the sword. "It was my father's. It's the only thing I have left of him."

Lessia gave him a weak smile as she pointed to the dagger with the amber stones. "This was my grandmother's. My father gave it to me when I turned twelve."

Merrick nodded. "It suits you."

"Thank you."

Lessia's eyes went to his sword again.

Then to the dagger Merrick had given her that day in the woods.

Her eyes widened.

"But if... if this sword was your father's... what about the dagger?"

Merrick's eyes sparked. "It was my mother's."

Lessia choked on a breath, and her hand flew to the dagger.

"I am so sorry! Here..." She started pulling it from the scabbard attached to her belt.

"Don't." Merrick's hand wrapped around her own.

"Please," he added. "It was a gift."

Lessia was still shaking her head when a loud crash sounded above them.

And when a cry followed it, they all started sprinting toward the stairs.

Merrick first, with Lessia on his heels and Raine and Kerym behind her.

"My magic isn't fully back, but I can see flickers of minds. There're a lot of soldiers up there," Raine hissed when they came to a halt beneath the stairs, their heavy breathing echoing between the stone walls. "As in *a lot*. And..." He hesitated for a moment, stealing a glance at Merrick before continuing. "The regent is there."

Lessia's gaze flew up to the ceiling as she took a calming breath, trying to soothe the pulse thundering through her.

She would do this.

She would.

Determination joined the unease roiling in her gut, and when she met Merrick's eyes as she tilted her head back down, she nodded once.

"Time to burn," he whispered.

CHAPTER THIRTY-THREE

She'd thought she'd have to fight Merrick to take the lead up the stairs, but as soon as she lifted her foot to take the first step, he moved to the side, allowing her room to pass.

The pounding footsteps above them rumbled right through Lessia, the dust falling from the ceiling tickling her nose, and when Loche's deep voice reverberated down the spiral staircase, she almost turned right back around.

Only because Merrick's hand clasped around her own did she find the strength to continue upward.

"You are surrounded," Loche called out. "And we have your friends, so do not try anything, or they both die."

"My magic is still not back," Kerym hissed. "I'll have to fight the normal way if it comes to that."

Trying to pull on her own, she found her veins still filled with that horrible clogged feeling, and she could tell Merrick's magic wasn't back, either, from the sound that rumbled in his chest.

Lessia threw a glance over her shoulder when Raine whispered, "I am getting some back. Do you want me to try to take out his guards before we ascend?"

Flicking her gaze from him to Kerym, she hesitated but finally shook her head. "Me using my magic was what ruined everything last time. Let's... let's try without first. But... be ready."

As she turned forward again, Merrick rushed his steps so that he climbed the final ones beside her, and Lessia prayed they wouldn't have to control Loche's mind the way they had on that cliff.

She would do it if needed.

But she wasn't sure if she could bear it.

If it would be the thing that finally changed her forever.

Her blood roared in her ears as she took the last step, and every muscle in her body went taut when gray eyes snared hers.

Lessia's heart skipped a beat as she took the regent in.

He looked the same.

Dressed in his usual black leathers and with his dark hair out of his face, he was lethally handsome. And as his perceptive gaze flew over her, that sense that he read too much into her every movement made apprehension coat her skin.

When a smirk—the one that had infuriated her so much during the election—played across his lips as she pressed herself against the wall, she tore her eyes away.

Instead, Lessia shot a quick look across what seemed

like a dated living room, with a small couch and table, but she couldn't make out Soria and Pellie anywhere, and her stomach churned when those terrifying masks Loche's guards wore followed her every movement—like a flock of deadly black birds spread out behind their leader.

"Hello, Lessia." As she forced her eyes back to his, Loche's sharp gaze flew down to the hand Merrick still held on to as he casually leaned his back on the wall beside her, and he clicked his tongue before continuing. "Death Whisperer. Not bothering with the glamour anymore?"

Merrick flashed his teeth back. "Seems we're past that point."

"We are, aren't we?" Loche nodded to himself, holding up a hand when his guards—who stood posted at almost every inch of the wooden walls in the large sitting room—stepped closer. "No need. I'm confident Lessia and her little band of Fae warriors won't try anything. Especially since her friends in *the cave* would not fare well if something happened to me... or if I seem a bit too accommodating."

Cursing silently, Lessia shot Merrick a quick look, and he dipped his chin the tiniest bit before locking his gaze ahead.

From the outside, Merrick appeared calm, his legs crossed and shoulders lowered, but Lessia could see the vein straining on his neck—could feel how his fingers rhythmically brushed the back of her hand.

He was anything but.

Raine and Kerym growled softly as they took up the spots next to Merrick, keeping a hand on their blades and fixing the regent with their glares.

Despite it all, she pursed her lips.

They probably didn't appreciate being called little.

"Look at that."

Her eyes snapped up when Loche spoke once more.

"It's almost the full brotherhood." Loche cocked his head, his smirk not once wavering as he dragged his gaze over the four of them. "Are you here to declare war against me, Lessia?"

"N-no," she got out.

After clearing her throat, she quickly continued. "We've come to warn you."

Loche let out a low laugh that had her clamp her lips shut. "Warn me... Do you have a death wish? I told you I'd kill you myself if you ever set foot in Ellow again."

Lessia hushed Merrick when he let out a low growl.

"I know," she said as she took a step forward.

The only step she could take, as Merrick had her hand in a death grip.

"Loche, the rebels are planning a devastating attack. And not just from the sea—there are people all across Ellow who are part of this. And... and that's not the only threat Ellow—we—are facing. Another realm of Fae is heading here—the Oakgards' Fae—and Rioner is working with them. He's going to help them take over Ellow. There is a curse... I don't know all of it, but he believes you're destined to destroy the Rantzier family and bring him to his knees, so he needs to take you out."

Not a single muscle in Loche's body, nor a single feature of his face, shifted.

Lessia's pulse quickened as she eyed him, and the thumps within her accelerated when he eyed her right back.

"He knows." Merrick sidled up next to her. "Don't you?"

Sucking his teeth, Loche waved for his guards to retreat out the door behind him—into the gray light shining through the small window to his right. "I need a moment with them alone."

As a few guards lingered, their steps hesitant as they followed the others, Loche hissed, "That was an order."

Loche didn't waste a second when the door slammed shut behind the last one.

After a quick look out of the dusty window, he stormed up to them.

Merrick immediately shifted her behind him, so that he was the one who met Loche's glacial eyes when the regent halted a few feet away.

Shaking his head, Loche laughed again. "So, you finally came to your senses."

Merrick straightened so that the one inch or so he had on Loche became evident as he snarled, "Do not test me, human."

"Merrick." Lessia tugged on his hand when whispers started to boom through the room, growing louder when Kerym and Raine snickered. "Please."

She was surprised he could harness his magic so quickly.

Her veins were still filled with the dry, lead-like feeling the Vincere unleashed, not an ounce of magic simmering beneath her skin.

His nostrils flared as he turned his head to look at her, but when she repeated "Please," Merrick finally retreated a step, although he remained an inch or so ahead of Lessia, his muscles coiling beneath his leathers.

There was a coldness in Loche's eyes—one that made her hair stand on end as she met them. "So... you're with him now?"

Lessia opened and closed her mouth a few times, unsure of how to respond, and the unease crawling over her skin mounted with each silent second that passed.

She hadn't even spoken to Merrick about it yet.

As she sliced her eyes to the Fae, his night ones already waited for her, and whatever thought had started to form in her mind evaporated at the depths of the feelings shining in his dark gaze.

You and me.

"Noted," Loche snorted, and she moved her gaze back to him.

"I guess this should hurt me?" Loche dragged a hand through his dark hair, messing it up in the way she'd loved during the election process. "It's strange... knowing the feelings I had for you, knowing they were there, but not feeling them." He shrugged. "Probably for the better, anyway, if you could sway so quickly."

"Excuse me?" Lessia dropped Merrick's hand as she took a step toward Loche, shoving a finger into his chest. "You left *me*! You let me fucking crawl after you. I told you I loved you, and you... you told me to erase me! You do not get to judge me, *regent*."

Loche's gaze slowly rose from the finger poking his jacket to her eyes, and when he raised one of his hands, she couldn't stop herself from recoiling.

But he only used his fingers to brush a strand of hair that must have lain across her forehead, and she watched quietly as he frowned at it before tucking it behind her ear.

As Loche's eyes traveled down, she saw the exact moment he noted the tattoo.

His eyes rounded for a second before he locked down the shock, but there was no mistaking how his hand shook as he ran his fingers over the aching letters, and she swallowed loudly when his teeth snapped together.

"Do not touch her." Ice dripped from Merrick's voice as he pushed the regent back a step. "You lost that privilege that night. Get back before I kill you."

Loche offered Merrick a lazy smile. "I don't think you will. See... I don't think she'd forgive you if you did."

Merrick's growl shook the entire cabin.

Or whatever this place was.

Out of the corner of her eye, Lessia could see Raine and Kerym inching closer, their eyes flitting from the seething Merrick to the seemingly unbothered Loche, and she quickly stepped in between the two males.

"Stop it," she ordered as she placed a hand on Loche's chest. "Loche, this isn't about me! It's about Ellow—all of Ellow. Everyone here is in danger!"

"But it is about you," Loche said slowly, as if he were testing out the words. "I can't feel it now, but I can remember the desperation—why I asked you to remove the memories, the feelings. This... this is all because of you."

"What do you mean?" Lessia stared at him, then turned to Merrick, and whatever fought over his features didn't reassure her.

Not one bit.

"You weren't supposed to come back." Loche began pacing back and forth before them, his unbothered mask slipping as her hand dropped to her side. "I'd set up everything perfectly to ensure it. I made sure the three of them were in the cells together so that when you ran, it'd be easy for you to take them with you. Having Zaddock overhear... I knew he'd understand—that he'd think I'd been acting too quickly... Why are you back, Lessia?"

"I told you!" she responded, her voice sounding more high pitched than she'd like. "Rioner has a plan to kill you! To take out all Ellow and give it to the Oakgards' Fae. I couldn't let that happen, could I?"

Loche slammed his fist against the wall, and the cracking of the stone fractured something within her even before she met his broken gaze. "I should have realized you'd be too damn noble!"

Stalking up to her, he ignored the warning rumbling in Merrick's chest. "Do you not think I know what Rioner has planned? I might not remember what memories you took away from me, but if I loved you and you loved me... you must have known me better than that."

Her mouth fell open when Loche dragged his hands down his face, and an emotion she'd never seen him carry before flitted across his features.

Guilt.

Raw guilt.

"I risked everything for you," he said, emphasizing each word. "My land. My people. For you. And even now... even when I don't feel what I know I felt, when I don't remember... I can't. I can't sacrifice you."

"Sacrifice..." Lessia threw out her hands. "I have no idea what you're talking about! Why are you risking anything for me?"

Merrick let out a choked sound, and she stumbled back when she met his dark eyes.

Wide dark eyes.

In a face white as a sheet.

"He just figured it out." Loche eyed the hand he'd struck the wall with, wiping the trickles of blood running down his knuckles off on his trousers.

"Merrick?" she demanded.

Lessia met Raine's and Kerym's eyes over Merrick's shoulder when the Fae remained quiet, his jaw clenching so hard she wondered if he was about to crush his teeth.

They looked as confused as she felt, wrinkles lining their foreheads as they stared from the regent to the frozen Death Whisperer.

"What is going on?" Lessia whipped her gaze from Loche to Merrick, and when still neither deigned to respond, she stepped into Merrick's space and waved her hand before his glassy eyes.

"Merrick, you're scaring me," she told him shakily.

His eyes finally focused, finding hers as he lifted them.

But when his hands landed on her shoulders and he clasped them in a way that made her feel as if he never wanted to let go, pure, undiluted dread roiled within her.

"The curse isn't about Loche," Merrick said in a monotone.

CHAPTER THIRTY-FOUR

Lessia blinked as her eyes left the swirling dark ones before her.

She blinked again as hard gray ones found hers.

And again when first hazel ones, then blue ones, met hers, only to quickly glance down at the dirty wooden floor.

"If... if it's not about Loche," she said slowly, unwilling to let the thought touching the border of her consciousness become clear. "Then who?"

The hands on her shoulders pulled her closer to a body, one of them dropping and another wrapping around her waist, pressing her against quivering muscles as if to protect her from the outside world.

"The one that's loved by Fae and human."

Lessia's eyes met those gray ones again, and she must have only blankly stared at him because Loche repeated himself. "The one destined to take down Rioner is the reluctant ally, the one loved by Fae and human."

"Yes... loved by someone like me? A half-Fae, half-human." Lessia frowned as she stared at the group. "The reluctant ally... Like all recent regents in Ellow, Loche has honored the allyship with Vastala."

"I'm not a reluctant ally, Lessia." Loche sighed as he flung a glance outside the window. "I *wanted* a closer partnership with the Fae. I wanted us to work together. I wanted peace. I wanted... not this."

Merrick's hand around her waist clenched and unclenched as Raine mumbled, "Rioner misunderstood the curse."

Loche nodded. "It doesn't refer to half-Fae, half-human. It refers to someone loved by both."

An unwelcome feeling crept across her skin, something lurking just beyond her awareness.

She shook her head.

No.

There was no way.

"Merrick," Lessia whispered, needing him to reassure her.

Needing him to tell her she was strong enough for this.

Just... needing him.

As if he could read her mind, he glanced at the others quickly before removing the arm around her waist and taking her hand, lifting the arm with the traitor mark branded into it.

His fingers traced the snake that was barely visible beneath the black letters. "The blood oath."

Their gazes intertwined, and even though she wanted to look away, she couldn't when he continued, his voice lowering so much she wouldn't have been able to hear him if everyone else hadn't remained quiet—

barely pulling air into their lungs, as if the whole room were holding its breath.

"The one bound by blood oath is a reluctant ally."

"But..." Her bottom lip trembled, and she couldn't finish.

Couldn't ask.

Not this.

"Loved by Fae and human." Loche's voice broke in, and despite the pull of Merrick's eyes, she turned around to face him.

His face was expressionless when he stated, "I loved you. It's why I asked you to remove my feelings. I knew Rioner had his suspicions about me, and it wasn't until one of my spies got ahold of that part of the curse that I understood he'd misinterpreted it..." Loche scratched the scruff on his chin. "You were hiding something. It was so clear, and I suspected all along you were spying for him. I don't remember exactly when I realized, but at some point I understood it must be unwillingly."

"Loche..." Lessia's voice was laced with grief, and she couldn't help but move toward him.

He waved a hand dismissively her way. "No one could miss how Merrick stared at you when you weren't looking. Well, apart from you, of course." He threw her an empty smile. "When I realized just *how* reluctantly you were bound to the king that day, I had to act fast. Rioner would have understood if I pushed too hard to keep you in Ellow, so... I had to throw him off."

Take. Them. Away. Take my feelings away. Take every memory of us.

You are hereby banished from Ellow.

The memory came crashing down on her.

That pain… that pain in his eyes hadn't been because of her betrayal.

It had been because of what he had to do to himself.

To them.

Lessia took another faltering step toward him when a shuddering breath left someone behind her.

She turned her head over her shoulder, and her eyes collided with Merrick's.

No one could miss how he stared at you when you weren't looking.

Already then?

But he'd hated her…

You and me.

His eyes seemed to speak to her, and she had to fight with everything in her to break the draw of his gaze when Loche cleared his throat. "Apparently it didn't work, since you're here and not as far away as possible from the war I expect to descend on Havlands."

Lessia winced, her voice nearly betraying her as she responded. "There was no way I'd leave everyone I loved behind."

"I'm guessing that's one of the reasons I loved you." Loche's gaze curiously swept over her. "So strange to know I did, but not know why. I mean, you're beautiful and all… or you probably will be once you've bathed. But you seem… just quite average?"

Lessia started when Merrick flew past her, pushing Loche up against the wall, his face twisting with rage. "Do not speak to her that way. I don't care that you did what you did to protect her. You hurt her."

When Loche laughed darkly, Merrick's hand wrapped around his throat. "I told you not to test me. I do not give a fuck who you are, regent. You do not disrespect m..." A muscle in Merrick's jaw twitched. "You do not disrespect her."

"Yours..." Loche spluttered as his face shifted colors, red tinting his cheeks. "Sh-she didn't even respond to my question... question if she was with you," he wheezed as Merrick's eyes flared.

"Stop it!" Lessia screamed as she ran up and pulled at Merrick's arm. "Merrick, stop!"

He didn't spare her a look as Loche coughed a laugh again. "See. Sh-she still cares for me."

Whispers exploded through the room—like a thunderstorm had drawn in without them realizing, and for the first time since she'd met him, a flicker of fear reflected in Loche's hard eyes.

"Raine," Lessia pleaded, whirling around to gesture toward the two Fae warriors who'd stood idly by this whole conversation.

"Please!" she yelled when Raine and Kerym hesitated.

"Shit!" Raine swore, and with a jerk of his head that sent his red hair flying, he and Kerym closed the distance to the raging Merrick.

It took both of them to get Merrick off.

When they finally succeeded, Loche fell to his knees, a hand grasping at his throat as he fought for air.

Merrick panted as well, his chest heaving where he stood between his friends, his face so cold it had goose bumps rise across her skin.

Lessia's head snapped between the two males, and when Loche reached out to brace himself against the wall and got to his feet—clearly not injured beyond his pride—she stormed up to Merrick.

Raine and Kerym snickered as they backed away, but

when she shot them a dark glare, they must have seen something in her eyes, as they swiftly shut their mouths.

"What. The. Fuck. Merrick," Lessia hissed as she reached him.

His features contorted into a mask of boredom as he shrugged. "I didn't kill him."

She couldn't help her lip curling to show off her canines when he began picking at his nails.

Picking at his nails!

"Do not do that again," she snarled, adding "Merrick!" when he continued only to look at his hands.

He finally glanced her way.

"Promise me?" She glared right into his indifferent eyes.

"No." Merrick raised his brows in challenge when she stepped even closer. "I won't make a promise I can't keep."

She was about to smack him when Loche hoarsely announced, "My guards are probably storming this cabin soon. We should get going."

"Get going?" Lessia still glared at Merrick, her eyes following the tension building across his shoulders again —probably at Loche's voice.

"Well, I assume you won't leave again, regardless of what you've just found out, so I need to bring you to the castle as my prisoners."

Lessia spun around, wondering if she needed to smack some sense into Loche as well, when he tilted his head, his mouth lifting into a listless smile.

"You won't actually be prisoners. Once we're at the castle, you'll be free to roam it as you see fit, as I have only the most loyal guards there. On the way there, however, we'll encounter a lot of people who doubt me, including some of those rebels you spoke of. I don't expect them to understand the decision I made... and you're still considered traitors to Ellow. I can't exactly host a welcome ball in your honor."

The castle...

Lessia shivered as she remembered the long white hallways.

The loneliness she'd felt living there.

The fear as the pressure of the king's commands built upon her chest.

But it was where they needed to go.

And it was where she'd left that stone...

She inclined her head. "What do you need us to do?"

As Loche told them what to expect once the guards came in, including that he'd made sure one he trusted had taken Soria and Pellie to the cave, she turned back toward Merrick.

His face slackened with each moment she stared into his eyes, and when the door finally opened behind them and the guards stormed in, putting them back into chains and tying them down onto horses, Merrick didn't say a word.

Still, she refused to let her eyes leave his the entire way back to the capital, even as thoughts other than what she'd found out about him fought for dominance in her mind.

No one could miss how he stared at you when you weren't looking.

CHAPTER THIRTY-FIVE

Rubbing her frozen arms and holding back a whimper when the movement sent a jab of pain through the one Loche's guards had branded, Lessia stared at the room she'd spent months in during the election.

It looked exactly like she'd left it.

Well, apart from her clothing not hanging in the closet anymore.

She tried to shake the eerie feeling of being here again, the one that had clouded her mind as soon as they'd ridden in through the metal gates of the castle courtyard.

But to no avail.

It had remained the entire time they dismounted the horses, when Loche sent the majority of the guards away, when the few who remained released them from their restraints, when Loche informed her she could take her old room while the others stayed in the same hallway, and when she walked through the large sitting room and up the familiar spiral stairs.

"Are you all right?" Merrick poked his head through the door connecting her room with his, and she jolted when the memory of him refusing to let her change rooms that first day struck her.

Back then, she'd thought he'd kill her the second Rioner gave the order.

But if what Loche said was true...

Her brows knitted as she nodded, and Merrick must have sensed the confusion because he didn't return to his room to get in the bath he'd muttered about when they mounted the stairs.

Instead, he walked into her room, closed the door leading to the hallway, and opened his arms.

Lessia walked right into them.

She might have been annoyed with him for losing his temper with Loche.

Not because Loche didn't deserve a bit of a telling off—because honestly he did.

But because they needed him.

They needed him on their side. Needed the stone she didn't see anymore atop the dresser where she'd left it.

Needed his fleet of soldiers, who would not respond to a call other than his.

Still, whatever burned in Merrick's eyes right now...

She couldn't refuse him closeness if that's what he needed.

Merrick's arms tightened around her when she relaxed against him, and he whispered against her hair, "It's going to be all right. I promise you Rioner will never hurt you. He won't ever come near you again."

Oh.

She had barely spared the curse a thought on the way here, her mind too occupied with what she'd discovered about Loche and Merrick.

Pulling back, she eyed the Fae before her, and her insides twisted when she realized the feeling that made the silver in his eyes shine so bright was fear.

Merrick was scared for her.

But she had no inclination to overthrow Rioner...

Nor to divide a people she'd never been part of.

Could they be wrong?

You need to kill him.

If not for yourself, for your sister...

For those like you.

Her eyes widened when the small voice touched her thoughts.

If he'd hurt Frelina...

She gritted her teeth.

Of course he had.

Like he'd hurt so many close to her already.

Of course the king would initiate the damned curse out of his own stupidity—out of his own hatred and narrow-mindedness.

Because there was no way Rioner wouldn't punish Frelina when he realized who she was. And he wouldn't spare her father either.

Not when he'd see it as the ultimate betrayal.

As if love ever could be a betrayal...

A chill—and not like the one she'd endured on the ride here, when Loche's guards wouldn't even allow her a jacket against the freezing wind and wet air—coated her skin.

She might not have *had* an inclination to usurp Rioner.

But now...

Did she have a choice?

Lightheadedness washed over her, and she didn't have time to react before Merrick scooped her up in his arms and gently set her down on the bed.

Taking the spot beside her, he leaned his elbows on his knees and covered his face in his hands. "I know what you're going to ask me."

She nearly smiled then.

He always knew.

But when the muscles in Merrick's back tensed, she bit it down and placed a hand on one of his knees. "Then you know I don't have a choice."

Merrick's head jerked up. "You have a choice. You have the path that we were on! The basta—Loche is already on your side. And we'll get your sister away from him."

She shook her head. "But that path was never more than a fragile hope. It's what everyone's been telling me the past few weeks. It's *why* Raine and Kerym joined us. This is bigger than me. Even if I am the one who can end it. I need to let Rioner know that he's wrong about Loche, even if... if it means I won't be able to fulfill the prophecy. I could save a whole people, Merrick."

Merrick gripped her face with his hands, his eyes darting between hers.

"Fuck them, Lessia," he growled. "I don't care if every single one of them dies. I don't care if the whole realm burns to the ground and not a single grain of dust remains. I am not letting you go anywhere near Rioner."

"He's right, you know."

Lessia's and Merrick's heads snapped to the door, and while Merrick dropped his hands from her face, one of his arms snaked around her waist, pulling her closer as Loche strode into the room.

"I didn't risk everything for you to just... hand yourself over." Loche walked up to her desk, his gaze lingering on the melting icicles hanging from the window casing.

"But we're also not going to let my people die." His sharp gaze returned to hers. "We're going to have to kill him. Together."

"Kill Rioner?" Kerym strutted through the door, his hair still wet, and a few drops landed on Lessia as he plopped down on the bed and shook it out like a hound. "Sounds much more fun than watching the oh-so-noble Faeling sacrifice herself."

"Of course, you'd also be a martyr." Raine leaned against the door, a full glass of wine in his hand, which he lifted toward Loche before taking a deep sip.

Loche's narrowed gaze sliced across the room before settling on hers. "He has your sister?"

Lessia nodded, her heart clenching at the thought of Frelina.

Frelina in those cellars...

Her jaw tightened.

No, she couldn't go there.

"Why?" Loche demanded.

"This should be fun." Kerym crossed his arms over his chest as he settled in with his back against the wall, feet dangling off the bed.

"He's my uncle," Lessia responded quickly.

No point in dragging this out.

Loche would need to find out sooner rather than later.

"He's your uncle?" Loche repeated slowly.

"Yes."

"Your uncle kept you locked up for years and then bound you to him like a puppet?"

It was as if lightning blazed in Loche's dark eyes, and Lessia averted her own as she mumbled, "He didn't know. My father—his brother—kept us hidden."

"Alarin..." Loche threw his head back and groaned. "I should have seen it. You have the same hair."

Lessia grimaced. "He didn't remember me. I... I might have removed his memories."

"Seems like you have a bit of a habit of doing that, then." Loche raised his palms when Merrick snarled beside her, his fingers hardening against her back as if he was fighting against balling his hands into fists. "It was only a poor joke."

It was quiet for a few moments as Loche seemed to fall deep into thought, and the only thing that echoed across the room was Raine swallowing more gulps of wine.

As Lessia watched a drop of it lodge itself in Raine's reddish stubble, she wondered whether she should ask for a sip to calm her empty stomach, and as if she'd conjured it, her gut roared in response.

Loche's eyes darted to hers. "Let's discuss more over dinner. It seems my guards didn't just take it upon themselves to dole out punishment in a form I'd never approve of but also kept you starving."

"Fucking locked us up in a cupboard," Kerym muttered.

Loche nodded, staring at her as he stated, "They'll be punished."

Merrick snorted.

Loche eyed him, and his eyes widened for the briefest

moment before he drawled, "I'm guessing the Death Whisperer had more creative ways than I do to deal with them."

She couldn't muster a smile, even if it felt like that was what Loche expected, and as the others began rising, heading toward the lower floor, Lessia gestured for them to go ahead.

She needed a bath.

And to be alone with her thoughts instead of with four males who all seemed entirely used to getting what they wanted.

When Merrick lingered, she gently shoved him out the door, even as her hand reached for him of its own accord to pull him back.

Lessia stared at it as she flexed it, trying to push the sense of loneliness away.

She needed time *alone.*

To process.

Think.

Plan.

And for some reason, whenever Merrick was anywhere near her now, she couldn't focus on a single other thing than the tingling feeling racing up and down her spine and the damned fluttering that started in her gut as soon as his eyes bore into hers.

CHAPTER
THIRTY-SIX

Lessia rolled up the sleeves of the leather tunic Merrick must have sneaked back into the room to lay on her bed.

While it was much too large for her, she was grateful, especially with the cutoff sleeve of her own tunic displaying the traitor's mark for all to see.

And when she pulled some air into her nose... she was also something else.

Warmth welled within her as Merrick's wild scent wrapped around her—embraced her as if he were right there, his arms holding her close to his chest.

She couldn't help but lift the front of the shirt to sniff it, pulling more of the intoxicating scent into her nose, fueling that feeling it invoked—a sense of freedom, of shaking off shackles, guilt, and masks.

As she caught her movement in the mirror outside the bathing chamber, Lessia blushed when her eyes met those of the reflection.

Her already heated cheeks turned bright crimson

when wild amber eyes looked back at her as if she were a predator that had just been caught by surprise by its prey.

She brought her fingertips to her burning skin as she took a few steps closer to the mirror, brows snapping together as she observed herself for the first time in what felt like an eternity.

She looked... older?

No, that wasn't possible.

Half-Fae who could wield magic, who took more to their Fae side than human, started aging unbelievably slowly once they turned eighteen—when they were fully grown—precisely like the full Fae.

After that they could become thousands and thousands of years old if the gods smiled at them.

Unlike her, who...

Lessia shook her head, pushing the thought away.

Looking deeper into the amber eyes, she realized it wasn't so much age as it was... resolve.

Something seemed to have settled in the eyes that used to flick so nervously from side to side, either from guilt or from not being entirely comfortable in her own skin—from not knowing where in this world she belonged.

She drew a deep breath.

That, at least, she thought she knew now.

Where she belonged.

Where home was.

Lessia tried for a smile when sorrow jabbed at her chest, sticking her tongue at herself when it still looked more like a grimace before turning around to follow the mouthwatering aromas drifting up the stairs.

Her wet hair slammed against her back as she took

the stairs two by two in her hurry to fill the stomach she'd mistreated so severely these past months—with too little food, disgusting food, or, whenever she got the chance, too much food.

She was glad she knew the way to the dining room, as she didn't pass a single servant, only a lonely guard whose hidden eyes tracked her, his dark mask turning ominously as she made her way down the dimly lit corridor.

Lessia drew a breath before she walked over the threshold, preparing herself for a dinner filled with thick tension.

She was not wrong.

It was as if a weight hung across the room, the uncomfortable silence so palpable she wondered whether she should try a bite of it instead of the plates of vegetables and meat placed out on the wooden table.

Every pair of eyes drew her way as she made her way over, but it wasn't Loche's piercing gaze nor Raine's raised brows that had her face nearly melting off.

It was Merrick's dark eyes dragging over her body, the slight flare of his nostrils as he must be picking up her scent mixing with his, the fingers gripping the table so hard the others had to catch their glasses from falling over, and the heat that followed like a shooting star on a clear winter night.

She felt lightheaded again.

But for an entirely different reason.

And it didn't help when a thrill raced down her back, a flame igniting within herself, and the heat in Merrick's eyes turned to hunger.

Swallowing, Lessia set her sights on the empty chair beside Kerym, but as she neared, the Fae violently shook his head at her, eyes flicking toward Merrick. "Absolutely not. I don't plan on getting killed today. You go over there."

Her cheeks burned as she did everything she could to move smoothly to the other side, toward the chair beside Merrick, without lifting her gaze or losing control.

She failed miserably.

Bumping into the side of the table, she nearly brought the entire thing with her, and only because Merrick flew from his seat, correcting the table in his stride and then catching her, did she not drop down on her ass on the gray carpet.

Lessia exhaled sharply as his arms wrapped around her, and she couldn't help but lift her eyes to his, knowing exactly what he could smell right now.

What Raine and Kerym could smell.

She groaned silently.

What was happening to her?

Merrick made no sound as he guided her to the chair and placed a plate of steaming food before her.

She began shuffling the food into her mouth as fast as she could, trying to erase the past seconds from her mind when warmth trailed over her face.

And not the scorching heat that was Merrick's eyes, but softer—still probing, but gentler.

With the fork in her hand, she sneaked a peek at Loche.

He sat leaning back in his chair with two soldiers hovering a few feet behind him—how she'd missed those two walking in, she didn't know—swirling a cup of wine.

His gray eyes moved from her to Merrick and back again, the corners crinkling, before he took a long sip.

Setting down the cup, Loche leaned forward. "You will be happy to know your friends are safe and doing well."

A small part of her fractured heart pieced itself together as she noted the sincerity in Loche's eyes.

"Thank you," she whispered.

"You might not want to thank me yet." Loche filled a glass and pushed it over to her. "I believe Zaddock has nearly driven Amalise crazy with his protectiveness. She has been... how do I say this nicely? Not the most joyful whenever I've checked in on them."

Lessia pursed her lips, ignoring the wine before her.

She'd seen how Zaddock had looked at her friend.

And Amalise...

Well, Lessia would be surprised if he had managed to melt the walls of ice she'd built around her heart after her lover died.

"Can I... can we see them?" Lessia asked, the wish to hold Amalise—to have just one of those nights she, Ardow, and Amalise used to have, where they ate food Ardow cooked, drank wine, and just hung out—so strong it nearly took her voice.

One night without all this tension, confusing feelings, and males she didn't understand.

Ardow and Venko must be at that cave now.

Lessia tried to console herself with the fact that they'd be together at least.

That Amalise would get to meet Venko—Venko, whom Lessia might have spent every minute getting to know just for the smile he put on Ardow's face, but whom she'd met under the most unfortunate circumstances and would now probably never truly be friendly with.

Especially with everything she'd found out today...

"I guess they'll have to come here should war descend upon us. The caves will be reserved for the children and elderly—those who cannot fight."

"The caves?" Raine asked as he waved for the bottle.

Loche nodded as he offered it, gesturing for a guard to bring another one when only a few drops made it into Raine's glass. "They tell me you've been there, Lessia. I didn't realize it was one of our spots..." He uncorked another bottle when the guard set it down on the table. "It's..." Loche hesitated. "It's my sanctuary. My family and friends live there. It's the most important place in the realm for me."

A lump formed in her throat when Loche searched her eyes, and the Fae males around the table quieted as if they could smell the shift in the air—the sorrow and guilt no wine could ever drive away.

"Did... did I bring you there? Or did you follow me there as part of being a spy? If so, we might need to make other plans for those who will not fight." He frowned, and the lump grew at the uncertainty muddling his gray eyes.

She'd never seen him like this.

She didn't like it.

Whatever warmth had remained from her entering the room washed away, leaving Lessia's veins cold and empty, and she could sense Merrick stiffening beside her.

"You brought me," she said softly when Loche continued to stare at her. "It was a wonderful place filled with wonderful people. It's why I risked sending them there. I-I thought they'd be accepted."

"Geyia has taken them in as if they were her own

children." Loche tapped his glass absentmindedly. "She liked you... I think?"

Lessia was about to respond when another guard stalked into the room, immediately bending down to whisper something in Loche's ear—not realizing Fae had much better hearing than humans and that everyone around the table could hear every word.

Loche, more accustomed to the Fae, rolled his eyes as he impatiently waved the guard back a few steps. "Just tell us all. Our guests will hear you anyway, and from what I've heard, that one"—he gestured toward Raine—"can read minds, so hiding anything is useless."

The guard's mask jerked, and while Lessia still couldn't see his eyes, she could smell the wafts of fear drifting from him.

"He will not read your mind, Loche," Lessia quickly threw in. "We are following the treaty while in Ellow."

"She's right. Besides, I'm not a *mind reader.* Like Lessia, I am a mind-bender." Raine wiggled his brows at her. "I can just control more of you at the same time."

Loche hummed, and Lessia could tell he wasn't convinced by the familiar squint of his eyes—that too-seeing gaze lingering on her for a moment longer than she liked.

"While we're sharing, my magic is slightly more special than what these two bores have." Kerym grinned as he crossed his arms over the table. "My twin and I are the only ones I know of."

"The Siphon Twins," Loche muttered. "Your magic sounds like the worst."

"Oh! You've heard of us. I wasn't sure if humans..."

Kerym quieted when Lessia gave him a pointed look,

her eyes moving to the soldier who nervously shifted his weight from foot to foot where he stood behind Loche.

"Shall I go on, regent?" Loche's guard's voice was slightly muffled behind the mask.

As Loche nodded, Lessia moved on her chair, and a shock rippled through her.

Looking down, she realized the movement had lined up her leg with Merrick's, and while they both were dressed in similar leathers, the heat radiating from him seemed to pass right through the fabric—right into her core.

She released a slow breath as she lifted her eyes, trying to subdue the energy pulsating through her and refusing to let them seek out the ones they wanted, especially when she could sense their burning stare on her face.

Instead, she stared so hard at the guard that his shape blurred, and it was all she could do to try to listen to his muted voice—or any of the other muffled sounds, as the world appeared to have become dangerously hazy.

"Our spy confirmed that the rebels are attacking in two fortnights from today. They plan to begin in the middle of the night—taking everyone by surprise. The ships will come first, and as people gather together on each isle to fight back, those on land will bring them to their knees. They..." The guard hesitated for a moment.

"Go on," Loche demanded.

"They will come to Asker last. They plan on filling their ranks with the people from the islands—those who bow to them—so they have the numbers when they storm the castle. Their leader w-wants the sea to be painted red from the blood of those that refused them so that you will know what's coming your way."

Lessia could feel the blood draining from her face, and even as Merrick's hand landed on her thigh, it felt as if someone had opened a window in the room—as if they were dining on a cliff in the freezing wind.

"Do we have a better view of who the rebels on land are?" Nothing in Loche's posture or face betrayed any interior turmoil, but when his eyes brushed hers... she recognized what flickered there—what he tried so hard to push down.

Helplessness.

Worry.

Guilt.

Dread.

A realization dawned on her.

The reason there were no soldiers in the castle wasn't because she and the Fae males were there.

It wasn't because he needed to keep her return concealed, hide that he'd let the traitor live.

It was because Loche didn't think he'd win this.

And he would not take his men with him.

The crack within her rib cage should have echoed through the room, and she was surprised when the guard didn't even pause as he responded to Loche's question.

"We don't. We know of a few, but even with those, we are not certain whether their whole family is in on it or not. We still have orders not to mention anything about rebels on land?"

Loche gave a sharp nod. "We will not say anything. We can't have the people of Ellow turning on each other even before war has broken out. But we need to spread the word of the attack outside of the council. I'm certain they'll use the people on their islands as protection if not. It's time for the ships to pick up those too young, sick, or old for war. Tell them to bring them to Asker, and we'll figure out how to transport them to the cave. After that, the ships must spread out and provide the isles with weapons and whatever else they can spare."

"And here on Asker?" The soldier straightened as Loche's eyes narrowed. "The same plan? But regent..."

"There will be no more discussion." Loche slammed his hand on the table. "You are dismissed."

His hand shook as he swiped a glass off the table and downed its contents, barely swallowing before he refilled it with the bottle the guard had brought up.

"Loche." Lessia leaned forward and touched his wrist, her eyes widening when he flinched.

Actually flinched at her touch.

She started lifting her hand, apologizing, when his landed atop hers.

"Don't," he whispered, eyes filling with that confusion again as they met hers.

That heartbreaking confusion the lethal ruler of Ellow, the feared and respected and loved leader, shouldn't have.

So she didn't.

Even when Merrick's hand left her leg and an emptiness like a vast abyss opened within her, she tried to let some of the conviction she had left within her flow into Loche.

When she dared to glance at Merrick, his eyes appeared unseeing as they lay on the hand resting over her own, and the urge to pull away, to crawl into his lap to get that starry darkness back—perhaps even draw another smile from him—nearly overwhelmed her.

But she couldn't bear it when Loche opened his mouth to speak again.

"I am not scared of death. I knew I wasn't destined to grow old, not in the business I'm in and the way I got here." Loche's eyes bore into hers, and it was as if they were the only two in the room when he continued.

"But I don't want to see my people bleed. We've barely healed from the last war, and I'm afraid this one might be the end. We do not have enough ships to protect Asker, the castle, *and* the isles, so there will be no fleet—no soldiers here when they come. I refuse to be like the leaders before me—like the council—and take the fleet to protect myself. I will fight. And when I die... it will be for the people who elected me—for the world I promised them. If the decisions I made caused me to fail... then death seems like a fitting punishment."

The decisions he made...

The decision to save Lessia over the land he loved.

She squeezed the hand not holding on to Loche's arm so hard it began shaking.

It was her fault this was happening.

If Loche died...

No.

She had promised herself never to be responsible for another soul's death again.

And his was tied to too many.

Hers was not.

"We need to speak to Rioner." Lessia's voice didn't waver as she met the eyes of each male around the room. "I will not be responsible for a whole people perishing."

Merrick let out a hissed breath, and she turned to him, her eyes burning at the emotions crossing his face.

"I can't. I can't put my life over thousands. You must understand that?"

Merrick only shook his head, his jaw twitching as he broke their stare to share a look with Raine and Kerym, who avoided her gaze when she tried to find understanding in their eyes.

Loche's hand tightened over her own, and her head whipped back to his. "He will kill you, Lessia. But that doesn't mean this will end. The rebels are not under his command. And the Oakgards' Fae coming here still need a place to live. The curse is merely an excuse for Rioner to keep Vastala as he prefers it."

"He is right," Merrick gritted, although Lessia could tell it was somewhat grudgingly. "Rioner will not change course now. He will see this through regardless of whether he needs to kill you or the regent."

"That fucking king." Kerym shook his head. "We should just kill him and then change the course for him. Lessia's father is next in line for the throne, since Rioner never had children. Alarin would put a stop to all this."

It was quiet for a moment, and an idea, a tiny seed of a thought, began to grow in Lessia's mind.

Killing Rioner was necessary.

And they'd need to be close to him to accomplish that...

Close to many things she needed to accomplish before it was too late.

"Yes." She stared right into Loche's imploring eyes. "We should kill him. As soon as possible."

Something deep rumbled in Merrick's chest, and when she turned his way, she could tell he was furious.

But not with her...

No, once she quieted, one of his hands landed on her

leg again, and she immediately felt more grounded and confident that this was the right decision.

Something else was driving that primal Fae rage to the surface.

Something that perhaps had to do with the dark-haired ruler who still had her hand in a firm grip, whose eyes seemed never to leave her face, that sense that he wanted—needed—to figure her out tracing over her skin like curious fingers.

Lessia quickly pulled her hand free, and while Merrick's growl quieted, she didn't miss how Loche's eyes dipped before he shot to his feet, declaring that they'd have to make the plan for how to kill the Fae king tomorrow, as he was tired from the long ride.

And she didn't miss the glossed sheen overtaking the gray when he had to turn back around for the sword he'd forgotten, resting against the leg of the table, and noted the hand Merrick still kept on her leg.

Pressure slammed into Lessia's chest so hard she sounded breathless when she declared she needed to go as well, and she stumbled as she tried to keep her legs from sprinting after the regent.

She thought the weight might splinter her ribs when Merrick called out after her, not in the cold, demanding voice he used in training but in one tinged by worry.

But she didn't turn around.

She needed to fix this.

Now.

CHAPTER THIRTY-SEVEN

Lessia didn't hesitate as she walked up the two sets of stairs leading to the balcony where she and Loche had had one of their first honest conversations.

She didn't know how, but somehow, she was confident that was where he'd be.

When the glass double doors stood ajar and a broad back greeted her where Loche sat on the railing, his legs dangling over the drop of hundreds of feet into the wild ocean, her lips curled in a sad smile.

It felt like an eternity ago they'd talked about Ardow and Amalise here...

When she'd evaded his questions as best she could while also fighting her growing curiosity about what made the terrifying regent tick.

She shook her head as she silently made her way onto the balcony, leaning her arms against the frozen, but no longer snow covered, railing and letting her eyes rest on the moon's broken reflection in the angry waves.

The whole election process felt like it had taken place in a different life.

When Loche had thrown a smirk or scowl her way at any moment he could.

But when he had also been vulnerable—sharing memories she knew must still pain him.

When she had found common ground with one of the people she least expected.

When she'd dared open her heart again...

Only to have it ripped from her chest and thrown out as if it were trash.

And now?

She wasn't sure what to feel toward the dark-haired, gray-eyed confusion of a man.

There was only one thing she knew for certain...

"What has you frowning like that?" Loche stared at her, his keen eyes following her every movement, eerily similar to how they'd tracked her all those weeks of the election.

Lessia shrugged as she moved her gaze out back over the sea. "Painful memories."

Fabric rustled as the wind blew through their clothing, and she gripped her hair, twisting it a few times and pulling it over a shoulder when the strands continued to cover her sight.

"I'm sorry if I was the cause of them," Loche said. "I hope you know I must have done it because of the love I had for you."

Nodding, she let her fingers glide over the smooth ice, picking at a spot where a crack had begun forming.

"I can still feel it."

Lessia stiffened when Loche moved closer, one of his

legs swinging over so he straddled the railing, his body now turned fully toward her.

"I keep watching you, and *I know* it shouldn't stir any feelings. I remember you removing them—I still feel them being ripped from my mind. But for some reason, your voice snakes its way into here when you speak." Loche tapped his heart.

"And those eyes..." He sighed. "It's like lightning strikes me when they meet mine, and I think... I think my body remembers, even if my mind doesn't."

Her throat tightened as she turned his way, and she took a step back when the intensity of his gaze deepened.

"I'm sorry," she offered quietly.

"Were we happy?" Loche's dark brows snapped together when she took another hesitant step away from him. "For a while, at least?"

Lessia hesitated.

Had they been happy?

The wild ride in the forest replayed in her mind.

The dancing.

The library.

The cave.

Their conversation on the bed when she'd found out Frelina was alive.

"As much as people like you and me can be," she finally replied.

She tried to muster a smile, but her lips wouldn't cooperate when Loche's features twisted, understanding that she wished he didn't have lowering his chin.

She sensed he was about to ask her something else, so she quickly blurted out, "There is something in this castle that can help us in the war."

Loche eyed her for a moment. "And what is that?"

"It's something you gifted to me that I-I didn't have time to take when I left."

"I don't remember gifting anything to you." Intrigue flickered once more in his eyes as he added, "I don't think I've ever gifted anyone anything before."

Her heart clenched at his words, but she forced herself to continue. "It's a stone that glows softly? It belongs to the Fae, and you told me I needed something to light up the darkness when you offered it to me."

"And what does this stone do?"

Lessia narrowed her eyes.

Something else crossed Loche's features.

Something calculating.

Something far too similar to what she'd seen of him in the early weeks of knowing him.

But they were on the same side.

What harm could there be in telling him?

"It calls to the sea wyverns. It was a gift from the gods to help us communicate with them, help us call upon them in moments of need."

Loche tilted his head.

"I have a stone that controls the wyverns," he repeated.

"You do." Lessia nodded, her eyes flitting between his. "I expect it will only work for a Fae or someone with Fae blood, but whoever wields it can call them here to aid us. We'd be able to protect the people of Ellow from both rebels and the Oakgards' Fae."

"And you want me to give it to you?" Loche asked, and for some reason, his tone made apprehension race over her shoulders.

"Yes?" She frowned at him when he jumped down

from the railing, closing the distance between them. "It can save us, Loche. All of us."

"Is that why you came back?" Loche's voice was so cold she expected a white cloud to follow as he opened his mouth.

Another crack worked its way through her chest.

His voice was like ice, but those eyes...

They were filled with sadness.

"No." Lessia reached out to grip his hand. "I came back for Ellow. For you."

Loche's eyes softened, and he took another step—right into her space.

"You came back for me?" he rasped, tilting his head down.

"I—"

Well, shit.

The air whirling across the balcony became heavy, and she placed a hand on his chest when Loche asked, "Can you give me my memories back?"

"Loche, I..." Lessia pressed against his taut muscles to get some space between them.

His face fell. "You can't?"

She opened and closed her mouth a few times, her eyes pleading with his.

Understanding filled his grays. "You won't."

Releasing her hand, Loche stepped back, fighting to put on the mask of indifference they both liked to wear.

Except...

She didn't carry that mask anymore.

She didn't want to.

She didn't have to.

Because...

"Do you love him?" Loche had reached the balcony

door, one of his hands resting on the knob as he waited for her answer.

Her silence appeared to be answer enough because Loche forced one of those smirks to overtake his features as he nodded. "I think I'll hold on to that stone a little longer, if you don't mind. Don't need you all to take it and run should something *better* come along."

A shocked scoff left her as Loche whirled around and disappeared down the hallway.

But she didn't follow him.

That might not have gone exactly as she had planned... but it had the outcome she'd wanted.

She'd needed him to know.

Needed to tell him *first.*

She owed him that much.

Some of the massive weight on her shoulders lifted as she made her way back to the dining room, and she had to hold back her feet from falling into a run when she turned the final corner.

She wasn't sure how much time she had left in this realm—not after what she'd found out today—and she was not wasting another moment of it avoiding life.

Avoiding love.

She'd spent enough years doing that.

Lessia was surprised that the air was still thick with unspoken tension when she walked over the threshold into the room where the fire burned softly in one corner and the table—still filled with food—stood in the other.

Frowning, she took in the three males: how taut their shoulders were as they sat silently in their chairs, how jerky Merrick's movements were as he absentmindedly lifted a glass to his lips, how they all froze as she walked up to them.

"Did something happen?" Lessia asked as she rested her hands on the back of Loche's chair. "Or are you practicing your brooding?"

Kerym began laughing, but after Raine, of all people, gave him a dark look, he grimaced and focused on nursing the wine in his glass.

"How did it go with the regent?" Raine asked, his voice worryingly low.

She tried to catch Merrick's eyes, but the Fae kept his gaze on the table, his features not betraying a single thought that might be crossing his mind.

Lessia winced, her eyes drifting down to the hands clenching the wooden backrest. "I think he needs a bit more convincing that I came back for him, not just for the stone."

A loud crash had her whip her head up just in time to catch a glimpse of silver as Merrick stormed out of the room.

She gaped after him, watching as the doors swayed slightly from the haste of his steps.

Turning back to the two Fae warriors, she shook her head. "What just happened?"

"What do you think happened?" Raine stared at her, and the look in his eyes chilled her to her bones.

Lessia scolded herself as she thought back to her words.

I think he needs a bit more convincing that I came back for him.

She dragged her hands down her face.

She should have phrased that better.

"I didn't mean it like that," she got out. "I didn't... come back for Loche. I just meant that I came back to help him and Ellow."

Still, Merrick hadn't even let her finish before he left the room...

"He is losing his mind!" Raine rose so fast that his chair also fell over.

"We shouldn't," Kerym warned. "He'll kill us. As in actually kill us, Raine."

"He might very well be dead before that, so I'll take my chances," Raine snarled back. "I'm sick and tired of watching you two dance around each other, especially when it's hurting someone I love."

"Hurting?" Lessia's brows furrowed. "Who is hurting?"

"Merrick, of course!" Raine stalked up to her, forcing her to bend her neck to continue meeting his furious hazel eyes. "This will be the one and only time I break a promise to him."

Lessia's mind spun as she stared up at one of the deadliest Fae in their realm.

And when he leaned in and snarled "Merrick is your fucking mate," she had to grip the chair not to let her knees give out.

CHAPTER THIRTY-EIGHT

"No." She glared back at Raine. "That's not possible."

"Why would it not be possible?" Raine asked, his voice shaking from so much held-back anger that Kerym rose from his seat and slipped up beside him, slamming one of his arms into Raine's chest to keep him from attacking her—or whatever he was planning to do.

"Because males sense their mate from the first moment they meet them!" Lessia bit back, flashing her teeth at Raine when he growled at her. "My father told me you catch their scent, and that's that. It's impossible to miss. He found my mother when she passed him on a *ship*! You two should know better than anyone!"

She wasn't prepared for the males' faces contorting with pain.

Raine's glass shattered in his hand, and Kerym's hand fisted so hard where it lay across Raine's chest that it looked as if it belonged to a wraith.

"I'm so sorry!" she hurried out. "I didn't mean to hurt you."

"We're not hurting for us," Kerym responded, his hand flexing and eyes so full of agony that the sense traveled right into Lessia's chest, wrapping around her heart and keeping it captive.

"You truly don't know," Raine mumbled, and she backed away from him when tears brimmed in his eyes.

No.

Lessia shook her head.

It couldn't be true.

Because if it was...

"Rioner was there the first time Merrick was in the same room as you. It was the day he forced you to swear the blood oath to him." Raine ground his teeth before he continued.

"Merrick tried to hide it, but once that scent reaches your nose... it's pure instinct... primal. We have no control over it, and he fought for his life to get to you in those cellars... but he was bound by the oath, and Rioner threatened to make him kill you if he didn't back down."

Kerym's blue eyes flooded as she sliced her blurry gaze to his, and his voice trembled far too much to belong to a feared Fae warrior. "At first, Rioner thought it was enough to keep you separated, but then..."

She wanted to cover her ears with her hands as she continued to step backward.

Didn't want to hear this.

"He thought it was an even better punishment for Merrick to have to be near you. But to never fully lay eyes on you—to have to hurt you, make you scared of him! Did you never wonder why the strongest Fae in the realm was sent to watch over *you*? A half-Fae already blood-sworn to him." Kerym shook his head.

Raine pulled a long drink of wine before adding, "And... imagine Rioner's joy when you went and fell in love with someone else."

Her heart shattered.

And not into those cracked pieces that might be put together again.

But into millions of tiny shards, impossible to ever heal.

Raine blew out a deep breath as he tracked her, the torment stark in his gaze. "It would have killed a lesser Fae. But Merrick is strong. Stronger than most. And you hadn't started sealing the bond then... It's different now, so I had to tell you."

Lessia halted her retreat. "Started sealing the bond?"

Kerym's eyes flitted between her and Raine when a low growl found its way into her voice.

"He didn't want to, Lessia." Raine took a step toward her. "He wanted to 'fight fair.' Win your heart without using the bond, so *you* made the decision, not fate. But that's not how the bond works... you are affected as well—it's not one-sided! So after you bit him..."

It felt as if her eyes would pop out of their sockets.

That feeling after she bit him back on Raine's island?

That energy.

That strange sensation of not being able to stand still?

Had that been the mating bond sealing between them?

Kerym's eyes flew across her face. "You're not mated yet, but you started to accept him once you tasted his blood."

Lessia blinked rapidly, trying to process what they were saying.

Her father had told her only that the female needed to formally accept the bond...

She withdrew another step as Raine tried to approach her again.

"Stay back." Lessia put up a hand, an overwhelming urge to scream overtaking her. "I-I can't."

"I know this is a lot, Lessia." Raine tried to soften his voice, but she could see right through the urgency keeping it sharp. "But if you reject him now, you will weaken him significantly, and for a long, long time. It'll be too dangerous for him to fight in a war."

Lessia turned around and ran.

The white walls blurred as she pushed herself to run as fast as her legs would take her, any ounce of fatigue or hunger from the past days forgotten.

She jumped three steps at a time up the stairs, and using the railing, she flew around the corner, running right up to Merrick's door.

Fighting the urge to kick it down, she twisted the doorknob, and a snarl—louder than she'd meant—ripped from her throat when she found it locked.

Lessia banged on the door until she heard the lock click and a livid Merrick popped his head through the crack.

She didn't hesitate.

Using both her hands, she pushed him with everything in her so that he stumbled back into the room.

Whirling around, Lessia slammed the door shut again—so hard that the wood creaked—before spinning back toward the Fae who watched her wide eyes.

She took a slow step toward him, her voice slipping

into the low, dangerous purr that usually surfaced only when she used her magic. "When were you going to tell me?"

Merrick threw a glance over her shoulder, his face hardening.

She drew one step closer. "No. You're not going to be angry with them."

Another step.

"What did they say?" Merrick growled.

Lessia took the final step, aligning their heaving chests and glowering right into Merrick's eyes. "Oh, you know... They casually informed me that you're my *mate*."

Merrick's jaw clenched.

"And that you've known the entire time. As in the *entire* time." Her nostrils flared. "That you've been *hurting* for years because you thought you'd be some kind of unsung hero and let me choose."

"It didn't start like that," Merrick snarled. "I was fucking blood-sworn to the king. He forbade me to tell you! Do you think I enjoyed following you around, reporting on your every move, when all I wanted was to snatch you away and hide you from the rest of the world?"

"No, I don't think you enjoyed that," she snarled right back. "But you could have told me weeks ago, Merrick. For weeks I've gone around thinking I've lost my mind because I can't stop thinking about you—because my skin fucking vibrates when you touch me! And you let me!"

Merrick's eyes flared. "This is what I didn't want! I don't want you to want me because of fate. You've made it very fucking clear what you think of the gods and the fate they bestow on us. Do you think I wanted to force another thing on you?"

"I don't want you because of the stupid bond!" she screamed. "I want you because you make me feel alive! Because you believe in me when I don't believe in myself. Because you try to make dumb jokes to make me happy. Because you make me fires to keep the darkness at bay. Because you hide your smile when I've made you proud in training. Because when I fucking stab you, you lecture me about missing your heart!" She shoved him back again. "You knew there was something deeper, something even stronger, pulling us together! And you fucking reject me when I kiss you! What is wrong with you!"

Merrick gripped her hands when she went to push him again, pulling her flush against his hard chest, where his heart beat so hard Lessia wondered if she should be worried.

"What is wrong with me?" he hissed. "What is wrong with me?"

Merrick released her, backing up against the wall, his hands dropping by his sides and his gaze dropping to the floor. "What's wrong with me is that I'm the fucking Death Whisperer, Lessia!"

She followed him, her heart thundering in her chest. "I don't give a shit!"

In a blink, he was before her again, towering over her as he growled, "Do you know how many I've killed? Do you understand what my magic is? I walk the fucking thread that keeps our world separate from the afterlife—and not the one where those gentle souls go. No, my whispers belong to those too evil to pass through fully—the ones who are angry and who only want to drag more souls into the agony that is now their world."

"I. Don't. Care," she hissed between clamped teeth as she placed her hands on his chest.

"I don't," she repeated, louder this time.

Merrick panted as he stared down at her, his eyes darker than she'd ever seen them, and shook his head. "What do you want from me?"

What did she *want* from him?

She nearly reached for one of her daggers to stab some sense into him.

"The fucking truth, Merrick." She shoved him once more. "I want the truth and not you trying to spare me from fate or whatever else you might think to take upon your own shoulders. I want it all! I want to fucking share it with you."

"Stop pushing me," Merrick warned.

She did it again.

In the next second, her back was against the gray stone, Merrick's hands wrapped around her arms as he crowded her against it, his face an inch from hers as he hissed, "Do you want to hear how I can barely be in the same room as you without losing my mind from your scent invading my every fucking sense?"

One of his hands clasped around her neck, fingers pressing against the pulse that beat wildly there.

Bending his head, Merrick slowly dragged his nose along her neck, inhaling so deeply it sent goose bumps rippling across her exposed skin.

His eyes slammed into hers as he straightened again, a jolt running through her so strong that she jumped—heating every single inch of her body.

"Do you want me to tell you that every time I helped you up from the floor when we trained, I had to physically restrain myself from pushing you down again and having my way with you? From claiming your fucking perfect lips and ripping those damned leathers off, making you scream from something other than frustration?"

Merrick released her arm, moving the hand to rest on the wall beside her head as he stepped even closer, pressing his hard body against hers until her breath caught in her throat.

His eyes flashed as she pushed against him, and when a low whimper fell from her lips at the hardness digging into her thigh, Merrick swore loudly.

"Do you want me to tell you I nearly ripped that fucking dress Loche gave you to shreds and that I was only able to stop myself because you wore something with my scent with it?"

The hand around her neck squeezed softly before moving down, fisting the jacket she wore, and Lessia couldn't stop a moan when he roughly pulled at it, twisting the fabric until it shrieked.

"Do you want me to tell you I wanted to fuck you senseless on that table tonight—regardless of who was watching—when you walked in wearing my shirt?"

A muffled sound escaped her when Merrick's grip tightened further.

Heat burned in his eyes as he bored them into hers, and that hunger she'd seen earlier returned, filling the entire darkness.

Only now, it was entirely primal.

Raw, primitive need that she knew reflected in her own eyes.

A rough breath left him before he cursed "Fuck it" and ripped the jacket to shreds.

They both panted as she shrugged off the torn pieces,

standing half bare before him, with heat pooling in her core—heat as she'd never felt before—which she was sure he could smell from the way his eyes sparked as they roved over her.

"Fuck, Lessia," he breathed, and she squirmed until their chests heaved against each other and Merrick's eyes darkened so much she could barely make out any silver.

"If you don't tell me to stop, I am going to fuck you until your screams echo so loudly within the castle walls that his damned soldiers might try to tear the door down," Merrick rasped, his gravelly voice melting her core until a fire burned so bright there, she thought she'd never have to worry about darkness again.

"Please," she whispered. "Please don't stop."

Merrick's eyes flitted between hers as he swore again.

Then his hands moved to her bare shoulders and slowly—so fucking slowly—down her arms.

When Merrick reached the traitor's brand, he pulled off his tunic—as if he couldn't stand seeing hers on its own—and, dropping to his knees, he kissed every single letter, his teeth gently scraping against them, eliciting another moan from her.

Looking up at her, Merrick growled softly, "Do you want me to tell you every instinct inside me is telling me to kill him? Not because he loved you or because you loved him. But because he fucking hurt you?"

His kisses moved from the brand to her stomach as he helped her out of her trousers, and Lessia's head fell back against the wall, her eyes closing as his tongue traced a path from her navel up across her breasts to her neck, where he lingered, sucking on the sensitive skin, before drawing higher, stopping right at her mouth.

"Do you want me to tell you I've loved you since you stood up to Rioner and me on that cliff?"

Merrick's hot breath hit her mouth, and she opened her eyes to the darkest night ones she'd ever seen.

"Do you want me to tell you I've fallen more in love with you every day, watching you fucking fight for your life?"

His hands came up to cup her face, and she didn't think her heartbeat could quicken any further, but what Merrick said next nearly brought her to her knees.

"Do you want me to tell you no one—mate or not—has loved anyone the way I love you? That I would laugh as the world fell apart as long as you stood by my side? That even if I could only have one fucking night—one night pretending you're mine—I'd take it?"

His lips brushed hers with the most infuriating featherlight touch.

"Because I would. That's how fucking bad I want you. How bad I need you."

Lessia crashed her lips against his, grinning when Merrick growled against her mouth, and the sense of falling she'd had ever since she'd looked into his eyes for the first time shifted into a complete free fall—as if she'd walked right out from a cliff and the sea wasn't there to catch her.

And she didn't care.

"I love you," she breathed back when she came up for air, the heat within her becoming almost unbearable as it rushed through her blood. "And one night is not nearly enough. I told you. I want *everything*. I want to be your fucking mate, and I don't know the right words, but I accept our bond—I welcome it—I'm proud of it."

Merrick blinked at her before he let out a shocked laugh that sent another wave of fire through her. “You...”

His words clipped when she wrapped her palm around his smooth hardness, gliding her hand from his base to the tip.

She had no idea when his clothing had disappeared...

But she wasn’t complaining.

“I need you,” she whispered as her hand traveled the length of him again, her core clenching at his size.

The solidness.

The silky skin.

“No.” Merrick’s arms wrapped around her, and when he lifted her, she hooked her feet around his back, her entire body quivering as he fused them together. “I’m the one who needs you.”

She squeezed his base in response, and the sound that left Merrick was nothing short of feral.

“Fuck.” His forehead fell against her own as he stormed toward the bed, and she cried out in pleasure when he somehow managed to rip her undergarments to threads while doing it.

Merrick didn’t allow a single inch between them as he laid her down, himself on top, and the air thickened with anticipation as he rose on his elbows, his eyes drinking her in as if he was committing every part of her body to memory.

Lessia dragged her thumb over the tip of his cock, savoring the wetness already forming there, and Merrick growled again—a pure guttural growl that made her squirm beneath him.

Gripping the hand encircling him, he dragged it over her head.

Then he grasped her other one.

When both lay above her head, he wrapped his fingers around her wrists and pressed them down into the mattress.

"I don't think you need t-to teach me how to please you," Lessia panted as she fought the grip, needing to touch him again—or perhaps herself, as he was slowing this down too much.

Merrick's eyes closed for a moment. "Gods, Lessia."

Opening them again as he pressed his hard length against her, he groaned as it slipped against her wetness. "I think you're right."

She writhed under him again, rubbing her legs together and pushing up against him, trying to find some —any—relief, and Merrick laughed roughly.

"I am taking my fucking time with you." He lowered to nip at her lip, still holding on to her hands. "I've waited a damned eternity for this. Please don't deny me."

As if there were anything she would deny him.

She'd meant it.

She loved him.

Utterly and completely.

Not just because of the mating bond.

Perhaps even despite it, she loved him.

With everything in her.

Lessia stopped squirming, biting her lip as she rasped, "I promise never to deny you anything."

She got the response she'd hoped for.

"You... fuck, you're incredible." Merrick's mouth fused with hers, his tongue sweeping across her lips until she opened for him, and his weight pressed down on her, his cock finally rubbing against her sensitive bundle, the pleasure so intense she cried out.

"Fuck, Lessia." He growled as his muscles went taut. "You feel so fucking good."

"Merrick," she whimpered, her eyes drowning in his. "Please. I want you."

He shut his eyes, his face freeing from whatever hardness remained. "Say that again."

"Look at me," she whispered, and when Merrick opened those beautiful eyes, she echoed, "I *want* you."

He cursed again—some words she knew and some she'd never heard—as he shifted her beneath him, lining himself up exactly where she wanted him.

Lessia lifted her hips, and the first part of him eased into her.

Truly eased, because as Merrick pressed further, stretching her in the most delicious way, it was as if he was made for her.

They held their breaths until he was all the way in, and as his strong hips met hers, they released it together.

You and me.

The words echoed in her ears as Merrick pulled out and drove into her with one single stroke.

It was so simple.

But so true.

So clear that it was him and her.

Merrick and Elessia.

Two broken souls healing into one.

She could hardly take in the love that brightened his eyes to almost all silver as he continued to fuck her—pressing into her in the most perfect rhythm.

It was as if his body moved in sync with her heart, the exquisite hardness of him twitching within her tugging at her every emotion, the hands caressing every bit of skin he could reach, healing every broken part of her.

Merrick's eyes didn't leave hers as he increased his speed, the slapping sound of skin meeting skin driving her nearly mad, and jumbled words left her lips as she dragged her nails down his back, trying to force him closer, drive his cock deeper.

And when he whispered "Elessia" and his fingers laced with hers...

She couldn't hold back anymore, her back arching, allowing him to thrust that final inch into her depths, filling her until silver flecks danced before her eyes.

With his name on her lips, she came undone, and as Merrick followed right after, she held on to him, her hands tangling in his hair, as the Death Whisperer whispered her name again and again.

He said it almost as if in prayer.

As if she was his goddess and he was entirely, utterly devoted to her.

A tear made its way down her cheek when they both gasped for air, and she promised herself never to forget his smile as he licked it off before burrowing his face into her neck.

CHAPTER THIRTY-NINE

Merrick traced circles on her skin as they watched the stars wink outside the rounded window beside the bed, and she sighed happily as she pressed closer to him, lining every inch of her naked body with his.

Her heart rate had finally slowed, its steady thumps beating in rhythm with Merrick's, and when she sensed the warmth of his gaze traveling across her face, she shifted so she lay on her back, allowing her to look up at him.

"Hi," she whispered as he only stared at her, his eyes still nearly pure silver, those flecks dancing in the light from the lanterns placed every few feet of the room—on the nightstand and in the windowsills, and one right at the door leading into her own room.

"Hi."

His lips lifted into a smile, and whatever words had begun to form in her mind melted away like the ice on the cliffs beneath the windows in spring at the sight of it.

Lessia couldn't help but lift her fingers to his face, tracing them over the fullness of his lips, up toward his high cheekbones and the forehead free from lines.

He looked so... happy.

"I am happy." Merrick's hands moved to her face, cupping it as he bent down to kiss her again.

Lessia had to catch her breath when his lips left hers, those waves of heat rolling through her once more as she rasped, "Are you reading my mind?"

One of the corners of his mouth curled. "No."

Lessia popped a brow. "Then how did you know that's what I was thinking?"

She fought a shudder of pleasure when his fingers traced a path from her cheeks down her neck, then caressed her chest, moving farther down until thrills of delight shot up her spine.

"Merrick," she moaned as her eyes shut. "Are you trying to distract me?"

His teeth scraped her ear as he bent down to whisper "Would that be so bad?"

She blinked as another surge of need welled within her.

No.

No, it wouldn't.

Lessia let out an involuntary sound when his touch left her, but then he shifted so he lay atop her, his arms caging her as they rested on either side of her head, holding most of his weight off.

"I feel your emotions." Merrick's eyes were immediately there when she opened her own. "Always have, but it's even clearer now. And after... after watching you for so many years, I am pretty well versed in your different facial expressions."

He kissed her, and this time it wasn't a gentle brush but a more urgent one—his lips fusing with hers, his tongue demanding as it danced with her own.

Her eyelids fluttered closed as she responded, whimpering into his mouth as an overwhelming need overtook her, making her limbs heavy and eager—all at the same time.

"I need you to know," Merrick whispered into her mouth, and she stopped her writhing when the pain in his tone broke through the need. "I wish to die every time you hurt. And when it's because of me... Fuck, I nearly jumped off a cliff when they made me torture you. I—" His voice broke. "I can't say how sorry I am for what I've done to you."

"Merrick." Lessia placed her hands on his cheeks, forcing his averted eyes to hers. "It wasn't your fault. Raine told me what Rioner did—that he knew about us... *I* am sorry you hurt for so long."

"You're sorry..." Merrick shook his head so violently her hands dropped from his face. "You're too damn good for me. You're all fucking light and goodness and *life*. While I'm all darkness and evil and death. I don't understand how you were chosen for me."

Placing her hands on his rumbling chest, she dragged her nails down his taut muscles until he shivered above her and some of the pain faded from his eyes. "That's because you're a damned idiot."

Lessia grinned when Merrick's brows flew up.

"A."

Her fingers reached his hips, and she slid them over the sharp angles, a fire building within her core again.

"Brooding."

She traced farther down, savoring the groan falling from his lips.

"Damned."

She gripped his hard cock again, and Merrick growled so deeply the bed shook from it.

"Idiot."

Squeezing him from root to tip, she glared right into his glazed eyes. "And I love every single inch of you." Her eyes dipped down. "Maybe especially these ones."

Merrick inhaled sharply when she slowly pumped her hand up and down again.

Before she could react, he reached down to grip her wrists, and with one deliberate movement, he lifted her hips and thrust himself inside her again, her cries mingling with his groans as he filled her.

"You're going to be the end of me," Merrick rasped as he pulled out, only to slam into her again, any words and responses leaving her mind at the feeling of him—the delicious thickness of him—completing her, consuming her every thought and sense.

The slap of his hips meeting hers echoed through the room, and she dragged her nails down his back, ignoring that the scratches from earlier had barely healed.

She wanted him closer.

Wanted more.

Just... wanted him.

"I want you more," Merrick growled as heat flooded her core, and when she clenched around him, he cursed again, the words barely reaching her ears as he thrust into her with such force the bed thudded against the wall.

Her cry split the air as he angled himself to get even deeper.

"I want to fuck you until every inch of your body smells like me." Merrick slammed into her again, and her eyes rolled back into her head.

"I want to fuck you until I'm so deep inside you you're never getting rid of me." His lips collided with hers, and when he drove into her—merciless, unforgiving—she bit his lip until iron touched her mouth.

"I want to fuck you until everyone in Havlands realizes you're mine." Another ruthless thrust.

Lessia's hands tangled in his hair as his words pushed her over the edge, and she barely heard him growl "You're so fucking perfect. So fucking perfect" as he pushed up inside her once more.

Merrick held on to her as she shook from the aftermath of the pleasure, his cock still buried deep inside as her eyes flew open.

"Do you have any more in you?" he rasped when she gave him a soft smile, and she could barely believe it when that scorching heat blasted within her again, pangs of pleasure shooting up her spine as he shifted inside her.

A corner of Merrick's mouth lifted before his lips clashed with hers again, and he ordered, "Wrap your legs around me."

A silent pant dropped from her lips as she did what he told her, and she swore she saw stars when Merrick purred "Good girl" as he moved them so that she straddled him, his back against the wall and feet planted on the floor.

She moaned his name when his hands landed on her hips, guiding her back and forth, the position somehow driving him even deeper.

"Hold on to me," Merrick rasped into her ear when

she cried out again, desperate for the release, desperate for him to get deeper, desperate for him.

For everything.

All coherent thoughts left her as she locked her arms around his neck, and he thrust up into her, faster, harder, deeper than she'd ever experienced.

"You."

Merrick's hands squeezed her hips as he pulled out of her, his tip teasing her wetness, leaving her nearly feral when it danced over her entrance.

"Are."

A hand dipped between them, immediately finding her most sensitive spot.

"So."

Her eyes slammed shut with pleasure when his thumb pressed against her clit, the other fingers gliding farther down, hovering right above where his cock still taunted her, nudging but not entering her.

"Fucking."

His other hand trailed over her stomach until it found one of her aching breasts, pinching the hard bud until she gasped.

"Good."

Her head fell back when Merrick thrust into her, and that warmth in her core exploded into a wildfire, consuming her every nerve—her every thought.

Only because Merrick's arm wrapped around her, holding her up, didn't she fall into a heap of satisfaction as his warm release followed right after her own, his chest vibrating from the curses he let out, ending with her name falling from his mouth.

Merrick leaned his forehead against hers, and the Death Whisperer kept her eyes hostage as their hearts hammered so hard against each other that she was surprised neither of them cracked a rib.

"That..." Lessia had to pull some air into her lungs before she could continue. "Was fucking amazing."

A smug smile spread across Merrick's face, and he cupped her face as he kissed her, tugging at her bottom lip with his canines until she couldn't help but moan again.

"That." He trailed his lips across her cheek until he reached her ear, his whisper prickling across her heated skin. "Was nothing."

She couldn't believe it when another rush of anticipation roiled in her core.

He was still inside her, for the gods' sake.

Merrick's hot breath moved from her ear down to her throat, and when his canines sank into her skin, not breaking it, his lips only sucking—teasing her like a sublime promise—she squirmed so much his cock hardened within her again.

He laughed hoarsely when her eyes widened. "Let's never leave this room."

Lessia was about to agree when Raine's voice floated through the door. "I am so sorry to do this, but you need to leave the room."

Nestling his face into her neck, Merrick groaned. "Go away."

"Trust me," Raine called. "I want nothing more. But Alarin sent my eagle back, and Loche received a note from Rioner. It's not good."

Lessia stiffened.

But if Alarin had been able to send an eagle back, could it be that bad?

He wasn't imprisoned, so maybe Frelina wasn't in Rioner's claws.

Unless he's killed her...

Lessia shook her head as the thought popped into her mind.

She couldn't be dead.

There was no way.

"That fucking king," Merrick hissed under his breath as he gently shifted Lessia onto the bed. "I swear I'm going to kill him."

Lessia believed him when she met his eyes.

And she knew it was wicked, but another thrill whispered over her shoulders as Merrick jerkily pulled on his clothes and growled to Raine that they'd be right there.

Rioner needed to die.

And with Merrick by her side, it was more likely to happen.

CHAPTER FORTY

Low voices drifted underneath the door to Loche's office when they reached it, and while she hadn't been here since that horrible day, Lessia didn't hesitate as she pushed the door open.

With Merrick's hand in her own, she walked over the threshold, refusing to let the guilt surface when Loche's eyes immediately flew down to their intertwined fingers from where he sat atop the desk.

She had nearly broken upon hearing how Merrick had suffered watching her with him, and she wouldn't be the cause of another single moment of torment.

It might hurt Loche for a while, but the feelings he had right now weren't those of heartbreak—not when she hadn't given in to remove the hold her magic had over his memories of them.

They were only thoughts of what could have been, the what-ifs she refused to let her mind linger on.

And perhaps that made her a bad person...

But Merrick was her priority.

Mate or not, she couldn't bear seeing the light that now burned in his eyes—even as they were forced from the bubble of his room—go out.

Raine and Kerym grinned at her, leaning against the bookshelf lining the wall to their right, but when Merrick snarled softly, they quickly averted their gazes.

Although neither could hide their smile nor how their nostrils flared as she passed them to sit in one of the chairs by the fireplace on the other side of the room.

Merrick's snarls grew louder, possessiveness sneaking into the primal sound, and it was Lessia's turn to bite back a smile.

They'd nearly not been able to leave the room when she'd refused to wash up, declaring that she planned to ensure his scent always cloaked her from now on.

Merrick had had to go and throw some cold water on his face, as he'd been unable to stop himself from lifting her up again, kissing her with such passion she'd nearly passed out from the lack of air.

But her smile fell when she sat down with Merrick standing behind her, his hands resting on her shoulders and fingers brushing the skin beneath her neck, and Loche unceremoniously shoved a piece of paper into her hands.

It seemed as if the person had been in a great rush—the paper wrinkled and the letters sloppy—but she'd recognize her father's handwriting anywhere, and her blood ran cold when she read the only word he'd sent back from their warning of what had happened with Frelina:

Run.

Lessia snapped her head up, and Merrick's grip tightened as he stared back at her, that muscle in his jaw flexing.

"What does he mean?" she whispered, unsure whether she truly wanted to know.

"I'm fairly certain he means get the fuck out of this realm." Loche tapped his fingers against the solid wood of his desk as he dangled another piece of paper before her. "I received this letter at the same time as Raine's eagle broke through one of the windows, waking up the whole damn castle."

Lessia glanced at the two Fae males by their side, and she really didn't like the tension pulling at their features.

Snapping the letter from Loche's hand, Merrick ignored the regent when he scoffed at him and sat down on the armrest of her chair, allowing her to read the note with him.

Regent,

I've understood you're harboring the fugitives we both sought to punish.

I am confident that this is a misunderstanding, but I'd like to ensure the alliance between Ellow and Vastala remains intact.

My ship will be waiting for you tomorrow at dusk, in the spot we met when you were elected.

Should you not show, I will take it as an act of war and act accordingly.

King Rioner Rantzier

"He's worried," Merrick mumbled as he stared at Raine and Kerym.

Kerym nodded. "It would seem so."

They all froze when the door flew open, but it was only one of the guards who had been posted behind Loche at dinner.

His masked face nervously turned from Raine and Kerym by the bookshelf to herself, Merrick, and Loche by the desk until Loche waved him into the room.

The clinking of glasses interrupted the thick silence, and Lessia realized the guard carried a tray filled with cups of liquor.

"Thought we might need something stronger than wine to deal with this." Loche inclined his head when the guard offered him one first. "Thank you."

Accepting the glass, Lessia took a sip when Loche raised his, letting the warmth drive away some of the cold that seeped through her veins after reading the threatening letter.

The other Fae did the same, Raine downing his in one go, as usual, while Merrick sipped slowly, and she could nearly not tear her eyes away when he licked his full lips as he set it down.

"Why is he worried?" Loche demanded as he placed his glass on the table, once again thrumming his fingers against the dark surface, tapping an ominous melody that started an ache in Lessia's head.

Merrick didn't bother looking his way as he responded; instead, his eyes fixed on Lessia's, and his hand moved to clasp her shoulder. "Because of us, I expect."

He threw his other hand toward Lessia and then to Raine and Kerym. "He probably believed Raine and Kerym to be dead, and I was blood-sworn to him for so long he forgot that I'm a threat. And powers like those Lessia and Raine wield have always frightened Rioner."

Merrick's eyes found hers, and his hand moved to her neck, his thumb brushing her cheek as he lowered his voice. "I'm guessing he started to piece things together when he learned about Frelina. He must have realized whatever Alarin knew, we now know, and he's scared you're about to compel Loche to go against him before his plan can be executed."

"So... he's coming to take us out?" Kerym moved to stand beside Loche, a smirk slipping across his features. "I can't wait to see him try."

Loche's eyes hardened. "Should I be worried for my people?"

Raine broke in. "I doubt it. He likes to pretend he's this noble leader, so he wouldn't try anything. Not by himself. But you should be worried for us—he surely has something up his sleeve if he's proactively proposing to meet."

Loche nodded, and for a moment, it was silent—so silent Lessia felt it press down on her, squeeze the air from her tight lungs, as if Rioner had already used his magic on her, replacing her breath with water, as she'd heard he liked to do if someone talked back to him.

But as she leaned into Merrick, letting his touch distract her for the second she needed to draw a steadying breath, she forced the fear out of her mind.

"Then we need to come up with an advantage of our own." Lessia stared right at Loche as she said it. "We need that stone, Loche."

Loche's eyes trailed from the hand Merrick still kept around her neck, down to where her body aligned with the Fae's, then finally up to her own, and she almost shivered from the frost filling his grays.

"I've told you. I am not giving you the one thing Ellow might use to survive two wars. I already risked my whole land—my people!—for you once, and..." He shot a look at Merrick, his eyes emptying. "That clearly was a mistake."

Merrick and Lessia flew to their feet at the same time.

But as Merrick noticed her slitted eyes, he let her step forward, although the snarl he unleashed shook the floor as she took the two steps needed to get into Loche's face.

"This isn't about me, Loche." Her low voice shook as she tried to keep herself from growling at him. "We need this! Ellow needs this! Your people need this! You need this, for gods' sake—he still believes you're the one who's to betray him!"

"No. He"—he gestured toward Raine—"said I don't need to worry for my people, so why should we use it now? I prefer to hold on to it until I know you won't just leave Ellow to its fate."

Lessia ground her teeth. "Loche, he has my sister. Perhaps even my father. He'll surely come with half an army to ensure no harm will come to him. We need the wyverns to maintain an advantage."

"That's exactly why I won't give it to you. What if he has your family somewhere else, and you conveniently disappear with the stone to rescue them?" When Loche scoffed, she couldn't stop her magic from surfacing, the golden of her eyes reflecting in his.

Lessia hesitated only for a second.

She was confident Rioner had something up his sleeve.

They needed that stone.

"Give. Me. The. Stone," she purred. "Now."

Her eyes widened when Loche's didn't glaze over—when his features didn't morph into the mask of obedience she'd expected but hardened further as he tsked at her.

"See, I realized my mistake when we were on that balcony..."

Merrick's body lined up with hers as he advanced, and Raine and Kerym also drew closer, the tension filling the room so palpable Lessia was certain her daggers could cut through it.

Loche didn't seem bothered by the three Fae warriors glowering at him as he continued. "I am man enough to admit I had a weak moment... but I was too curious as to why I'd risked everything for you. But now—"

Loche jumped from the table, straightening to look down upon her. "When you refused to give me my memories back, I realized you're not on my side... Not fully. Not anymore." He picked up a small vial from the table. "That's where this comes in."

Not thinking, Lessia reached out for the gilded flask, but Loche backed up a step, a low laugh escaping him. "I don't think so."

"What is it?" Kerym walked up to her side, his face straining as he glared at the regent. "I can't drain him. It's like..."

Merrick's whispers burst through the room, but Loche only continued laughing, the sound bouncing between the walls as the whispers drifted away, only to be replaced by a frustrated snarl from Raine.

"Amazing! I wasn't sure it would work."

The smile pulling at Loche's features didn't light up his face in the way that had once mesmerized her.

Instead, it twisted it into one of those masks Loche liked to bear, the cold, lethal mask of a regent who didn't care for anything or anyone other than his duties.

"What did you do?" Lessia whispered as the light in her eyes dimmed.

Loche cocked his head. "I did what I had to do for those I love."

Merrick's arm circled her waist, and he pulled her to him as he shook his head. "You damned idiot."

"You get it now, Death Whisperer?" Loche raised a brow.

"What the fuck is going on, Merrick?" Raine asked, and a twinge of worry brushed her skin as Lessia met his eyes and worry crinkled the skin around them.

Merrick stared right at Loche as he answered. "The liquor. There was something in it that rendered our magic useless."

Lessia sucked in a breath, but it wasn't fear that made her body shake.

"What the fuck is wrong with you?" Shaking off Merrick's arm, she got into Loche's face again. "Rioner is coming *tomorrow*! When will it wear off?"

"A day or so, I believe... but I am not too certain."

When Loche smirked, she saw red.

Lifting her hand, she prepared to slam it right into his smug face when Merrick caught it.

Whirling around, she flashed her teeth at him.

"What are you doing?" she hissed when he wouldn't let go.

"He's caught on."

Lessia didn't turn around when Loche spoke.

She couldn't.

Not when she realized it wasn't anger distorting Merrick's face, but...

Relief?

Relief mixed with the tiniest bit of gratitude.

"Merrick?" she demanded, but when her eyes lifted to the other two Fae and they watched her and Merrick with sorrow-filled but knowing looks, a thought flickered to life within her mind.

No.

Lessia slowly turned her head toward Loche, then back to Merrick again. "You did this in some twisted way to protect me?"

"Rioner let you go. You are not a fugitive, so you need not be there tomorrow." Loche tried to appear bored when he responded, but she knew him too well by now—knew that slight twitch of his eye meant a storm of emotions raged within him.

"But they do?" Lessia swept out an arm toward the Fae. "You're willing to sacrifice the strongest Fae in Havlands—who are on your fucking side and could save your people—for *me*?"

"You are meant to kill him, Lessia." Merrick's voice was low, and it would have been soothing if there were room for more emotions within her. "He's also protecting his people by protecting you."

But the anger that had taken root seemed to burst through every pore, and she took a step back when Merrick reached out for her hand.

"You're on his side?" she hissed between her clamped-shut teeth.

"We're all on the same side." Loche moved so he stood next to Merrick. "We want Rioner gone. And you're the key to that. I banked on Merrick not letting you go without the protection of the three of them, and without their magic..."

"Not *letting* me?" she repeated slowly, the crimson hue dancing before her eyes.

"You just fucked up, regent." Merrick threw his head back. "I do not decide what she does or doesn't do. She is her own person, and she makes her own decisions. While I am hers and she is most definitely *mine...*" He emphasized the last word by sending a death glare Loche's way. "I do not own her. No one owns her."

She opened her mouth to argue when his words sank in.

I do not decide what she does or doesn't do.

He didn't.

Unlike Loche, he didn't try to force her hand.

Merrick tried to give her all the tools to make decisions for herself—like when he trained her or gave her new perspectives on her gift and life.

But never had he forced her to do or not do anything.

A rush of love broke through the fury within her, and she threw Merrick a grateful look before boring her eyes into Loche's once more. "Rioner has my sister. There is no way I am not coming. And besides, do you think I'd let any of them walk right into the death trap that is Rioner's ship? Especially now, when their magic doesn't fucking work?"

"You're doing exactly what he wants, then." Loche's upper lip curled. "We'll lose this war before it's even begun if he kills you. How can you not see you're key to all of this?"

"He doesn't know the prophecy is about me!"

When Loche sighed, she bared her teeth at him.

He was such an idiot.

What had he been thinking?

How would they face Rioner now?

The three males he feared were still strong fighters without magic, sure.

But they weren't the extraordinary warriors she'd heard tales of growing up.

If Merrick's magic didn't tinge the air and Raine's didn't brush his mind, Rioner would get suspicious.

Unless...

Lessia brushed some hair out of her face, a seed of an idea beginning to sprout in her thoughts.

After a glance at Merrick, she started pacing back and forth in the small room.

Loche was a damned bastard for taking away their magic—the one thing Rioner was frightened of—the day before they were to meet him.

But...

Rioner didn't know what Loche had done.

He might think he understood what she was trying to do—why she was here.

But he also must know by now the love she, her father, and Frelina held for each other—the lengths they would go for each other.

That she'd take all the torture in the world and still not speak of her family ties.

That her father would risk everything for them.

And she didn't expect Frelina to break easily, either, should Rioner use the same methods on her that he'd done with Lessia.

"Rioner wants to look like the righteous leader he definitely isn't, right?" Lessia threw a look at Raine and Kerym, who both nodded. "Given the note, Rioner knows of Frelina and my father... so he must believe I am about to betray him."

"What's your point?" Loche glared at her but quieted when Merrick snarled, "Shut your mouth, human. Or I'll do it for you. You've already fucked up enough."

Ignoring their chilling glares, Lessia halted. "What if Loche isn't the one who's keeping fugitives?"

Loche frowned, but a smile curled Merrick's lips as understanding—understanding in the way he had; he always understood her quicker than others—filled his eyes.

"Rioner knows Lessia will probably do anything to get her family back."

She nodded when Merrick spoke, and when he stepped toward her, she didn't back away but met him halfway, slipping her hand into his as he reached her.

"And how do we manage that?" Loche drawled, although she could see he'd also started to understand the direction of her thoughts.

"We pretend you are all under my control. That I've compelled you all to follow my lead. That I am the one ruling Ellow." Lessia met each pair of eyes before continuing. "That I'll hand you all over if Rioner releases my family. He won't be able to resist having you all under his control again. And when you step onto his ship..."

"We kill him." Kerym grinned at her. "It's a good plan."

Raine shook his head. "It's *a plan*. Not a good one."

Merrick let out a concurring sound, but when Lessia fixed him with a sharp stare, he gave her a nod. "If this is what you want to do, we'll do it."

"Come on!" Kerym slapped Raine's back when he continued to mutter something incomprehensible. "It would be boring if there weren't any risks."

"It still puts you at risk," Loche mumbled. "Rioner isn't dumb. He'll be suspicious."

"Then we have to be convincing." Keeping Merrick's

gaze, she swallowed any uncertainty. "We'll have to make him believe it."

She would have to make him believe it.

But she'd fooled him before.

All the years she'd been bound to him, she'd evaded any questions that might have led him to understand who she truly was.

Merrick stared back at her, and he didn't need to tell her what he was thinking.

Worry and fear tangled with pride and love in those storming eyes.

"Do you have more of whatever you gave us to mute our magic?" Lessia moved her glare to Loche when that flame flickered to life inside her again, and when he nodded, an ember of relief fought with the fury at what he'd done as she stared into his gray eyes.

"We all will need some on us," she stated.

Raine was right.

It was *a plan*.

And a lot could go wrong.

But if it didn't...

They might have a chance to save Ellow.

CHAPTER FORTY-ONE

Lessia tugged Merrick's hand as they walked the familiar streets of Asker, heads down and hoods up to avoid attracting attention from any of the townsfolk walking the streets.

Still, Lessia had to steal a peek at him—revel in how different everything was.

It wasn't because she was hiding from Merrick that she now walked these streets with her cloak over her face and shoulders taut.

She couldn't even fathom that there had been a time when she had.

When she'd been frightened of him...

Merrick's eyes found hers, and when he arched a brow, she smiled at him and rushed her steps.

They should perhaps have slept—used the few hours remaining until Rioner showed up to gather strength—but she hadn't been able to settle down after they'd talked through the plan a few more times as a strange, unfamiliar feeling began to fester within her.

Attributing it to all the risks and pitfalls that came with her perhaps not-so-thoroughly-thought-out plan, she decided she needed a distraction.

So while Loche went to find more of the liquid—which apparently was a version of Vincere the leaders of Ellow had gotten their hands on during the war and had refined until, undetected, it would suppress the abilities of Fae, neutralizing their advantage should the alliance break apart—and Kerym and Raine joined one of Loche's guards to find any smaller weapons they could hide on their bodies, Lessia had asked Merrick to come with her to her old house.

He hadn't asked why, and for that, Lessia was grateful.

She had no idea why she wanted—needed—to go there, but something within her urged her to see it, urged her to go back, especially if it was for the final time.

A hollow ache spread in her chest when they reached the metal door and a silky cobweb, glittering from the pearls of water stuck to it, covered the door handle.

She tried to remind herself that Loche had already sent for Amalise, Zaddock, and hopefully Ardow and Venko, who should be with them.

After he'd agreed to Lessia's plan, they'd decided they could use reinforcement if anything went wrong when they met Rioner.

Especially if some of the older children joined them now that her own, Merrick's, Raine's, and Kerym's magic was stifled.

Lessia tried to put the guilt of bringing them into this mess out of her mind when Merrick gently lifted the spider silk out of the way and with a firm press of his hand opened the creaking door.

She watched him as he surveyed the space—dark eyes trailing up the spiral staircase leading to the bedrooms, to the empty shelf hiding the hallway with the other bedrooms—the one that'd been filled with soft taps of feet as the children hurried into their rooms whenever they'd been out of bed later than they were supposed to—to the door beside the staircase, the one leading to her office.

"So this is your home?"

Merrick eyed her as she nodded, unable to speak due to the large lump bobbing up and down in her throat, and the slight smile on his face faltered.

"You miss it."

There wasn't any accusation in his tone, no sorrow at her missing a time when he hadn't been in her life—at least not in the way he was now.

Lessia nodded again.

She did miss it.

So damned much.

Even if she'd been blood-sworn to Rioner the entire time she'd called this house home, living with that dark cloud over her head, it was the first time since she'd left her family that she'd been truly happy.

It was the place where she'd found a purpose—something to atone for the horrible thing she thought she'd done.

It was the place where she began trusting people again—where she'd dared let people into the shattered pieces that were her heart.

Merrick bowed his head—that awareness flashing in his eyes—and his lips lifted again.

"You'll have that again." He pulled her to him, and after placing a whisper of a kiss on her lips, he rasped, "Better. I'll make sure you have it all. If you'll let me."

She smiled against his mouth. "I'll let you do anything you want."

Merrick blinked.

Then he claimed her lips with a fierce urgency that drove any lingering wistfulness from her mind.

She would have it again.

Better.

Because she'd have Merrick as well.

You and me.

It was as if his voice was forever embedded in her mind, and even when he kissed her senseless, his sharp teeth rasping against her skin as he moved down to her neck, she could hear it in every breath, in every moan, in every growl.

"Where?" Merrick's arms wrapped around her, lifting her up, and she giggled at the wild look in his eyes as he scanned the house for a bedroom with the same seriousness as he usually searched for danger.

"My bedroom is upstairs, but..."

Merrick had started stalking toward the stairs but froze at the final word.

The worry in his eyes faded when she winked at him. "So impatient."

Nuzzling his face into her neck, he growled softly. "Make fun of me again... and I might need to punish you."

Her face heated, both at his words and at the sharp need that surged within her at the thought of him...

No.

Lessia swallowed.

She'd stopped him for a reason.

Merrick seemed to read her mind because he set her down again—even with the wildfire of silver glimmering in his eyes. "There is something you need?"

"Yes, I..." Lessia started walking toward the office. "I don't know. Something was telling me to come back here."

That feeling roiled within her again.

Urgent.

Impatient.

Needy.

Like a tap on the shoulder by a restless child.

You need to see.

She frowned as the feeling turned into a whisper within her mind, and her steps lengthened as she fixed her eyes down the dim corridor.

Merrick followed her down the hallway to the other side of the house, opening the door to the freezing office for her when they reached it, and she could sense him tensing when she passed him—whatever he picked up from her probably irking him as well.

While she strolled along the walls, dragging her fingers over the backs of the books lining every inch of the shelves, Merrick worked his magic on the fireplace, and soon the room glowed in soft gold and red tones, the heat spreading quickly within the small room.

As Merrick looked through some of the papers she'd left on her desk, Lessia's eyes snagged on a leatherbound book.

But it wasn't the intricate gold binding nor the thickness that caught her attention.

It was the crossed daggers—one with rubies decorating the hilt and the other with amber stones—carved into the bottom of the spine that had her sucking in a breath.

As she grasped the book, something ignited within her.

Something ancient waking her magic to life deep down inside, despite the Vincere-like liquid traveling her veins—something foreboding, something she couldn't explain, telling her she needed to do this now.

Alone.

It was all she could do to clear her throat and shakily ask Merrick, "Could... could you get me some water?"

She didn't dare turn around when she sensed him hesitate—certain he'd read too much into her surely blanched face and wary eyes.

"Please?" she whispered, and finally, she heard Merrick's feet move toward the kitchen.

Still, she didn't dare open the book until the stairs creaked, and she was sure he wouldn't storm back in and interrupt.

With her heart in her throat, pounding so hard she had to blow out a few breaths to ensure she could still hear Merrick walking somewhere above her, she opened the book.

First, Lessia thought she must have made it all up.

It was a children's book.

One she didn't recognize but which must have been Ardow's, since it came from the Fae.

The stories described in it were the ones her father had told her growing up.

Nothing in the book warranted the feeling tugging at her, the pages only filled with words and the odd drawing.

But as she leafed through it once more, she realized

something was scribbled in the gutter on the last page, something that made her heart stutter in her chest as it caught her eye.

Her family name.

Lessia threw a glance behind her before tilting the book and reading the first paragraph as quickly as she could.

The Rantzier rule will end, its people disband, by the hands of the reluctant ally—the ally that should have stood by their side, that should have fought with them, that should have protected them. It's the one loved by Fae and human, the one you may not slay for the war that fragile death would bring, who will finally bring the Rantziers to their knees.

It was the curse her father had already told them of, back on Raine's island.

But unlike her father's words, the prophecy didn't end there... and tears burned behind Lessia's eyes as she continued reading.

Surrendering it all, they will choose to perish with them.

For only in their ultimate sacrifice can a new world be born—the world they have dreamed of, battled for, and wept over.

Lessia read the last two lines over and over until the words blurred so much she couldn't make them out anymore.

Numbness spread within her as she let the book fall to the ground.

The ultimate sacrifice.

That must mean...

As she swallowed hard, Lessia swatted at the book with her foot until it slid under the shelf it had been standing on.

She laughed hollowly.

The fucking gods.

They must have seen the one day she'd been happy despite everything they'd thrown at her.

The one fucking day.

Merrick's smiling face, his bare chest, his heated eyes as his hands gripped her hips, danced before her own.

She felt like screaming.

Screaming so loud it might reach those damned gods wherever they resided.

Everything in her wanted to follow that book.

Hide somewhere no one could find her.

Fall into a heap of hopelessness.

Break apart, and let someone else take charge.

Let someone else try to take on Rioner.

Or perhaps just let him win...

Merrick would do it.

She knew she only had to ask, and he'd take her as far away from this realm as possible.

But when he walked into the room, his narrowed eyes trailing over her, she found that last bit of strength —the one that had helped her survive that day she thought she'd killed Frelina, the one that had kept her from giving up in Rioner's cellars, the one that had forced her to continue moving after Loche banished her—and whirling so fast she knocked the glass out of his hand, she jumped up on him, slamming her lips against his with such a frantic hunger that he didn't question her.

Instead, Merrick held on to her as he swept the paper from the desk behind them and laid her down on it.

Her fingers locked in his hair when he tried to pull back, and even though he could have easily untangled her hands—could easily overpower her—he didn't.

Merrick let her lead.

As if he understood that she desperately needed to right now.

That she clung to any whisper of control she had left, refusing to listen to the voice inside her telling her it didn't matter.

The gods had decided her fate anyway.

Squeezing her eyes shut, she dragged him down on top of her, kissing him harder, until they were a mess of heavy breaths and moans and need.

"Get them off," she begged when his hands roamed over her, cupping her breasts, then moved down her stomach to tease the skin between her jacket and trousers, only to go back up again, making her squirm with want. "Please, Merrick."

"Fuck. Say my name like that again," he rasped as his fingers dug into her hips.

"Merrick," she whispered. "Merrick, Merrick, Merrick."

He responded with a growl, and her eyes flew open when his breaths hit her stomach as his teeth dug into the waistband, his hands leaving her heavy breasts to drag her trousers down to her knees as he moved to stand between her legs.

Merrick's eyes met hers when he pushed her knees up, and she couldn't look away as he slowly relieved her of the trousers, then removed her undergarments and gently nudged her legs farther apart by sliding his large hands down each of her thighs.

Lessia fought a shudder as the heat in his eyes mirrored that of her own body, and she wrapped her fingers in his hair again when he began kissing his way down her legs, the anticipation making them shake, nearly clamping around his face in her need for release.

She cried out when his mouth found its intended purpose.

His first touch wasn't tentative—not even gentle—as if he knew exactly how much she needed to see those stars, and he swore something she couldn't make out in the haze as he began devouring her.

Lessia arched off the table as his mouth closed on her, his tongue alternating between flicking and lapping, sliding over her until she cried out in pleasure at the perfect, aching sensation.

Her eyes shut when he growled against her, her legs shaking so hard Merrick's hands flew up to steady her.

"More... I need..."

She wasn't sure what she needed, the words jumbling within her mind.

Merrick knew, though.

As he drove his tongue deep into her, that heat racing up her spine turned into an inferno, her core throbbing so hard every breath leaving her turned into a moan.

And when Merrick's teeth scraped against her sensitive bud, his tongue circling it after each bite as if to soothe it, the fire within her burned hotter, so hot that she pressed against him, pulling at his hair to get him closer—desperate for more.

And when he playfully moved to nip at her inner thigh, and the gentle bite turned into something more—a possessive, territorial marking that made them both swear loudly—the pain mingling with the desire drove every thought from her mind and pushed her over the edge.

As she convulsed beneath him, Merrick straightened

from where he'd knelt before her, and she cried out again when he, in one fluid motion, escaped his own trousers and thrust into her, pressing her back against the table as he rolled his hips, stretching her so perfectly as he filled her that she couldn't help but scream his name.

His lips brushed her ear as he drove into her, so deep that stars—like the silver flecks in Merrick's eyes—danced before her closed ones once more, exploding into pure light when he whispered, "Mine. You're. Fucking. Mine."

Merrick held on to her as they both came down, and while he didn't say a word when tears slid down her cheeks as she stared up at him—only swept them off with his thumb—she could tell he knew that she was hiding something.

That it hadn't just been pure lust driving her to this.

As her eyes flitted between his, her harsh breaths the only thing reverberating around them, she wondered whether she should tell him.

Let him share the burden.

But then that crease she hated formed between his brows.

And she knew.

Merrick wouldn't stop her.

He'd let her go through with this because he would never take her choice away.

Not like Rioner.

Not like Meyah.

Not like Loche...

Lessia pulled Merrick down again, hiding her scrunched-up face in his neck.

Telling him wouldn't change what would happen.

So she didn't.

Instead, she whispered, "You're mine," and clung to him with every nerve inside her aching and only one sentence echoing in her mind:

Please don't be the last time.

Please don't be the last time.

CHAPTER FORTY-TWO

The ship rocked back and forth as one of Loche's guards—the only one he'd decided to bring—steered it between the narrow dark cliffs on the outskirts of Asker, and Lessia clasped the railing harder, savoring the cool drops peppering her face from the wind whipping around the ship.

They hadn't dared take one of the larger ships in the harbor—not with Loche and her traveling together, at the risk of people seeing them—so they'd taken one of the older warships that Loche kept for missions he needed to undertake without the townsfolk's knowledge, one he kept hidden an hour's ride from the capital.

But Lessia didn't mind.

While old, it was beautiful, carved from the oaks that used to stand proud on every isle in Ellow but which now had only started to regrow, as so many of the trees had been destroyed in the latest war.

The sail was plain buff, not the usual Ellow sails—the white with an embroidered crest, either that of the large circle and the thousand smaller ones around it, the symbol of Ellow, or the crest of one of the noble families, as they typically funded the creation of the ships to protect their islands.

Should someone spot them, they'd probably assume it was a merchant ship, as that's what most of the old warships were used as nowadays.

As long as they didn't travel too close, that was, of course.

The Fae warriors hadn't bothered with their glamours out here at sea.

Lessia tried not to wonder whether those ships would soon have to be put to their old use, forced to brave the storming seas where waves would once again be tainted red from the blood spilled on either side.

Hopefully, it wouldn't get to that.

Hopefully, they could quell the rebellion and come up with a plan to stop the Oakgards' Fae invasion.

Hopefully, no more innocent blood would be spilled.

After all, the curse had mentioned a new world.

A world she'd dreamed of.

A world she'd wept for.

A world she'd fought for.

Lessia looked down at the wild sea.

It would be worth it.

Even if she wouldn't be there to see it, it would be worth it.

Unsheathing her daggers, she crossed them over the railing like they'd been crossed in the book, her eyes resting on the glittering gemstones adorning each hilt.

Surrendering it all, they will choose to perish with them.

That's what the scribbles had stated.

She almost scoffed.

Choice...

As if she had one.

As if the gods had ever given her one.

The sound of swords clinking against each other mingled with the rushing waters beneath her, and the eerie melody rattled her bones.

Fate.

She knew she should be grateful for it.

It had brought her Merrick, after all.

Had offered her a soulmate.

But like all the others on this ship, his and her fate was cruel.

Twisted.

Devastating.

But...

Perhaps *perish* didn't have to mean death.

Although... from what she knew of the wicked gods, it surely did.

Her teeth slammed together.

Fuck fate.

That's what she'd said when Meyah kidnapped Frelina.

Wrath traveled over her skin.

She was so damned tired of being controlled.

If it wasn't the leaders of the realm, it was the gods.

Lessia let out a trembling breath when she sensed Merrick somewhere behind her.

Blinking rapidly, she pushed the rage and dread deep down inside her, grateful for the practice she'd had over the years of doing the same whenever thoughts of her sister or parents—or her time in Vastala, for that matter—decided to surface.

A forced smile lifted her lips when she glanced up at

the Fae as he took a spot beside her, but it quickly slipped when Merrick's brows quirked, his eyes catching the slight wobble of her bottom lip before she could get ahold of it.

"I know you're keeping something locked up within you, and I won't push you... but Lessia, I'm here. I'm with you. I'm always with you." Merrick's gaze drifted out toward the sea, and as she followed it, she realized they were facing east, the way Amalise and the others would hopefully soon come.

Loche had informed their friends of what was happening—at least as much as he could in writing—and when Raine had sent his eagle to the area surrounding the cave, it had reported activity, a ship being boarded by several people.

They'd left early, driven by the hope that they'd be able to strategize with the group before Rioner's arrival.

It would be quite helpful to have the backup should this go sideways...

Especially since the Fae warriors and her magic had yet to return.

"Do you think they'll arrive in time?" Her eyes returned to her daggers, remaining slightly averted, as she didn't trust the tears that stung her eyes.

The heat of Merrick's gaze told her his eyes followed her own, and she didn't pull away when he moved to stand behind her, leaning his chin on her shoulder and caging her in with his arms. "I don't know."

She nodded.

Others might be annoyed with Merrick for his unforgiving truthfulness.

But she loved him for it.

He wasn't one to offer false hope, so when he told her

she was strong enough or pushed her to train harder, she knew it was because he believed in her.

Believed she could do what she'd set out to do.

Lessia's grip on the daggers tightened.

"We stick to the plan either way." Merrick's voice lowered, his stubble scraping against her cheek as he spoke. "Rioner doesn't know about you, and you know how to put on an act. I watched you all those years... No one could tell the weight you carried so bravely."

"But what... what if I fail?" She kept her eyes forward, hating herself for the quiver that worked its way into her question.

But what if she did?

It wasn't just her sister and father on the line...

It was all Ellow.

Perhaps even all Havlands.

"Then we fight." Merrick clasped her closer to his chest. "You can handle yourself, and besides... I will not leave your side."

Then we fight.

She'd known this day might come.

Where the work Merrick had put into making sure she could protect herself might have to be put to use.

And while she knew she'd gotten better...

She hated it.

Hated the violence.

Hated to know that she might have to kill for the chance to survive.

Hated that that's what this world—her world—forced her to do.

As her eyes fell on her hands again, she was surprised the fingers clenched around the shafts of the daggers weren't shaking but... steady.

They weren't even white from holding on too hard.

Perhaps...

Perhaps she was ready after all.

"I never thanked you enough for giving me this dagger." The smile she threw Merrick as she spun around to face him came easier. "It's... it's beautiful."

Merrick's lips curled, a half smile playing across his face as his hand brushed the hilt of his sword. "Like you. That's why I gave it to you."

As she stuffed both the daggers into their sheaths, her brows crashed.

"This was a mating gift, wasn't it?"

The corners of Merrick's lips lifted higher. "It was."

"But..."

Merrick wrapped his arms around her again, leaning his hands on the railings as he kissed her, softly this time—with no urgency, as if they had all the time in the world. "No but."

Well, damn.

She hadn't given him anything.

"You have given me everything." Merrick leaned his forehead against her own, his eyes refusing to let hers break away. "Everything, Elessia. If I die tonight, I'll do so having everything I ever asked for and many things I never thought to."

Her throat constricted at the raw emotion in Merrick's eyes, at the slight tremor of his voice as he yet again whispered "You've given me everything," and she was just about to respond when an apologetic voice broke in.

"I am so sorry, but we have a slight issue." A mixture of amusement and concern filled Raine's voice as he spoke behind them.

"Damn it, Raine," Merrick rasped, a sharp edge carving around his words that Lessia couldn't help but agree with.

Did he always have to interrupt?

As he spun around, he kept an arm around her, and they both stared at the three males approaching them.

Raine kept his eyes everywhere but on Lessia's.

Kerym grinned at her, and for some reason, she didn't like the male's smile at all.

Loche's expression was even worse.

Walking a few steps behind them, he looked as if he were on his way to his execution, wide eyes fixed on his feet and shoulders slumping.

"What issue?" Lessia asked, the worry tightening the males' eyes rushing into her own body.

Kerym's gaze slowly slid over the arm Merrick kept around her waist, his look pointed when she stepped closer to Merrick, wrangling her arm around his back.

"Fuck," Merrick snarled beside her, and her brows snapped up when he stepped away from her.

Lessia attempted to follow, her brows flying even higher when he held up a hand to stop her, such a thunderous expression on his face it didn't take much for her to falter.

"What is going on?" Her head whipped back and forth between Merrick and the others until her gaze snagged on Raine's flared nostrils.

Oh.

Lifting the collar of her jacket to her nose, she breathed in.

Merrick's scent was so strong that she almost swayed.

Her body reacted instantly, and that heat—that overwhelming heat—licked her veins.

"Your continuing to react like that will also be a problem," Kerym laughed, and she couldn't stop the warmth traveling up her neck, spreading across her face like wildfire. "Although I guess we can't blame you, since it's barely been a day."

"Kerym." Merrick's warning growl was so cold even Kerym's smile fell off his face.

"He's right, though." Raine approached them, his large body tenser than Lessia had ever seen. "If Rioner gets one whiff of her, he'll realize what you've been up to... And while we might get him to believe Lessia is the one controlling us—emphasis on the *might*—from what I've seen in her mind from their last interaction, he will not believe her to be so wicked that she used magic to compel you to share a bed with her."

Lessia wished the heat crawling over her skin might melt her into a puddle so she could disappear between the planks beneath her feet.

"He definitely will not." Loche also drew closer, even though his eyes still wouldn't meet hers. "And he will also begin to question the assumption that I'm the one to take him down if the... halfling"—Loche appeared to force the word out—"isn't in love with me anymore."

"No," Merrick snarled as he stepped toward the regent. "You won't go near her."

"I forgot how possessive you become." Raine shot her a sorrowful smile. "I'm honestly surprised the regent is still alive."

"Merrick!" The sound of Kerym slamming into Merrick danced across the sea, and Lessia watched with wide eyes as the former tackled him to the floor, vicious snarls ripping from their throats as they each got hits in.

"M— Fuck!" Kerym panted. "You k-know we..."

"No! He. Won't. Touch. Her."

Kerym crashed into the floor as Merrick overpowered him, blood trickling from his nose as he glowered at the feral silver-haired Fae.

"You know we're right," he wheezed as Merrick lifted a hand again, his other wrapping around Kerym's throat.

"You do," Raine echoed. "It's for her safety."

Merrick's chest heaved, his face a shade darker than she was used to, as his eyes moved from Kerym to Raine and finally to her.

When she felt her face fall, his teeth slammed together, but he finally dropped the fist angled to Kerym's face.

"Fuck. Fine!" Refusing the hand Raine offered him, Merrick jumped to his feet, and with a flick of his hair, he stalked away.

Lessia was certain he'd go somewhere—anywhere else on the ship—not to have to watch, so when he stopped after only a few feet, his arms crossed as he leaned back against the railing, apprehension layered over her like a shadow.

She didn't want to put him through this again.

Every nerve within her began firing, wanting to argue, to run, to do anything else.

But as she glanced at the horizon, noting how the sun had already begun its descent, its pink-and-orange light mingling with the blue of the sea, she realized there wasn't time to come up with another solution.

It felt as if a cloud drew in when she sought Merrick's eyes again, as if every feature of his face darkened when pain sparked to life in his gaze, and despite the jacket she wore, she shuddered as if the chill wind brushed bare skin.

"I'll go first," Raine muttered.

"I'm sorry." Lessia continued to hold Merrick's gaze as Raine approached her.

Merrick shook his head, but when he tried to pull his eyes away, she wouldn't let him.

You and me.

They were the only words allowed in her thoughts when Raine wrapped his arms around her—as unwillingly as she felt—and rubbed his hands down her arms.

You and me.

Moving them to her face, Raine hissed, "Should have had another damned drink first," and she couldn't help but snort when he dragged his fingers down her cheeks.

Merrick's mouth quirked—as if it needed to mirror hers.

She had to admit... it was the tiniest bit funny how disgusted Raine looked when he pulled her into a hug, his cheek sliding against hers as he fought a recoil.

"Done," Raine exclaimed, moving away from her so swiftly she might have been offended had the situation been different.

"My turn, Golden Eyes." Kerym wiggled his brows, ignoring the rumble in Merrick's chest as he swept her off her feet, cradling her like a babe and nuzzling his nose against her neck.

"Whew, you really smell like Merrick." Kerym winked at her. "Must have been some trip to your house."

"Kerym," she hissed between her teeth. "Set me down."

"Or what?" Kerym spun around with her still in his arms, his face coming so close she wondered if she'd have to slap him.

"Don't worry." He grinned at her, a wild, reckless edge to the smile. "Merrick would throw me off the boat if I kissed you."

She wrinkled her nose when he breathed onto her skin instead of kissing her, the hot air layering like a gentle mist across her neck.

Kerym chuckled darkly once he finally set her down. "You know females usually react very well to me being close to them."

"I'm sure," Lessia muttered, her muscles locking, knowing what was next.

Slow footsteps reached her ears, and this time, when she tried to find Merrick's eyes, she couldn't.

His face was bent down, the lines so hard she hoped he wouldn't chip one of those sharp canines, pressing his jaw together.

She had to look away.

Seeing him like this was too much.

Too similar to those months during the election.

Too painful now that she knew the hatred tugging at his features wasn't because of her...

But because he couldn't be with her.

"Please know this brings me no joy." Loche's low voice reached her ears as she sensed him hovering behind her.

"I know." Lessia nodded as she made herself turn around.

With her hands clenched by her sides, she stepped into Loche's already open arms, swallowing when his familiar scent wrapped around her.

She couldn't stop her heart from leaping when he crushed her against his chest—not because of the memories of when he'd last held her like this but because of the shuddered sigh leaving him, the slight twitch of his chest and the ember of sorrow lacing his wintery smell.

And when his chest jerked again, her arms snaked around his waist, and she hugged him back—holding him as he fought the shakes racking his body and closing her eyes when a near-silent sob, one that even the Fae around them wouldn't pick up, escaped his lips.

They clung to each other as the words they hadn't had time to speak, that might never leave their lips but were thought all the same—the sorrow, the guilt, the grief, the friendship, the understanding—the bond they'd always share softening until the sharp edges that had jabbed at them rounded.

Until Loche's back straightened and the pit in her gut sewed itself together.

When they pulled back, Lessia didn't fear meeting his eyes.

She was right.

The grays burned with the same sharpness they always did, but the smirk on his face wasn't that of protection—of masking the emotions he harbored inside—but of challenge, of playfulness.

Loche raised his brows as he gently nudged her into a hard chest that she, without looking back, knew belonged to Merrick. "Looks like Rioner is early as well."

Lessia peeked over his shoulder, and sure enough, a large ship had just emerged from the depths of the ocean from one of the tunnels she'd heard Rioner could conjure

—allowing the ship he sailed on to travel in hours what took other ships weeks.

Loche's smirk broadened when her eyes flicked back to his. "Get that mask of yours ready, little liar."

Lessia bowed her head as she gave him a final look.

Then she turned to Merrick, and she wished she could freeze time just then because the love that shone in the Death Whisperer's eyes knocked every sense out of her.

Brushing her fingers against his, she molded her features into the disguise she needed to wear tonight.

A smug smirk curling her lips.

Hard eyes staring unseeing out over the wild sea.

A lifted chin and lowered shoulders with a back so straight a soldier would have been envious.

A ruthless leader seeking only power.

A mirror version of the uncle standing in the bow of the ship opposite them, his elaborately decorated cloak billowing behind him and that crown she'd once snorted at glittering atop his head.

CHAPTER FORTY-THREE

King Rioner's dark ship moved through the water as if it were it and not the waves that controlled the movement.

And with Rioner's water power, perhaps it was.

Going against the wind, the ship turned sideways, the wood creaking softly as its sails folded and its pace slowed.

The black ship was unbothered by the rushing torrents beneath it as it sidled up to their vessel, the deck towering a few feet above their own as it came to a halt.

From the corners of her eyes, Lessia could see that the males had taken up the positions they'd decided upon this morning.

Merrick and Loche right behind her—Loche to her left and Merrick to her right.

Kerym casually leaned against the mast beside Merrick, his legs crossed but face betraying him—the smirk lining it a tad too forced to be natural.

When Lessia shot him a glare, he wiped it off

completely, his features shifting into the same mask Merrick wore—boredom mixed with sharpness, the one Lessia had come to know intimately during the election.

Raine stood on Loche's side, his face the same as his two brothers, but she didn't miss the flask he stuffed into the breast of his tunic before his hand fell to his side.

With a final look at Merrick, unsure whether to feel glad or worried that not a single emotion danced in his eyes, Lessia turned back toward the ship.

Her uncle's eyes appeared to have followed her survey of the males, and although he wouldn't meet her own straight on, she felt when they landed back on her, the cold trail they left in their wake helping her keep her guise in place.

Especially when her father was dragged to Rioner's side, a rope of water rushing around him, the steam rising from it telling her why her father kept recoiling from its walls.

Still, when Alarin's eyes found hers, he made a rush for it, his head shaking and mouth forming one word:

Run.

Lessia shook her head imperceptibly back.

She was done running.

Fate would catch up with her whether she wanted it to or not.

And this time, she wanted it to.

Wanted to face it head-on.

Tell it exactly what she thought of it.

Clenching her jaw, she stepped forward, as they'd discussed.

"I see you've finally figured it out, *uncle.*" Lessia let her lips pull into a frosty smile as she kept her eyes on Rioner, refusing to let the fear and worry she could smell from her father fester in her mind. "Took you long enough."

A cool laugh floated toward her over the sea. "You cannot expect me to assume my brother of all people would stoop so low as to produce *halflings*?"

Lessia sucked on her teeth. "I guess not. You appear to lack any type of imagination."

Rioner stepped toward her, and her eyes landed on the many guards behind him.

All dressed in the same uniform as her father, they stood posted every few feet of the ship, their sharp teeth glinting like the curved swords they held in their hands and their hair tied back as the Fae preferred during war, showing off their pointed ears and chiseled features.

Still, even with the determination tugging at every angle of their faces, their eyes were wary as they moved —almost too fast for her to catch—between her father and their king.

"You apparently don't."

Her gaze flew back to Rioner when he spoke.

"I must have severely underestimated you." He threw out an arm to the frozen Fae and regent behind her. "They are all under your control?"

Lessia dipped her chin. "I realized I was tired of running. And besides, *uncle*, like you, I have royal blood —a leader's blood—running through my veins. I thought it was time to do something with it."

Rioner placed a hand atop the ornament decorating the bow.

Ironic, Lessia thought.

It was a wyvern.

With its maw open and a stream of water bursting

through it, the creature seemed to stare right at her as Rioner tapped his long fingers against it.

"So you... what? Decided to take control of Ellow after all?" A thin wrinkle between Rioner's dark brows was the only thing betraying that he wasn't merely bored but... curious.

Lessia walked up to the railing and placed her hands on it, forcing her eyes to remain on the king when she felt Merrick's presence shift, his hot gaze glued to her back and a slight tremor of fury filling the air—probably because of how close she now was to her uncle.

"I did participate in that damn election. If it hadn't been for Loche, I would have won it... if it hadn't been for the foolish feeling..." Lessia tilted her head as she made herself spit out the word: "Love... I wouldn't have been so weak in the first place. I guess you can say it was thanks to you that I learned my lesson."

Rioner hummed, his hand still whispering over the head of the wyvern. "Love is a strange thing... I am guessing it's what drove your father to betray me in the first place."

Lessia's breaths came in sharper when Rioner's eyes lifted.

But the king didn't meet her own, ever so carefully keeping his averted.

Which she knew was good—he didn't suspect anything was amiss with her magic.

Didn't know her powers were currently useless.

"See... I am not certain you're telling me the truth, Elessia." Rioner's smile struck her like a ball of snow in the chest. "I saw you crawling on that floor. Begging him to love you. I saw you almost give up when you removed his memories..."

Lessia bit her cheek so hard blood flooded her mouth.

"A moment of weakness," she got out. "One I don't intend to repeat."

"Not even with your *mate*?" Rioner's brow arched, and Lessia fought not to react when her father sucked in a breath from where he stood a few feet behind the king, the stream of water still circling him like a thick, whirling rope.

Lessia's nerves flared with energy as she echoed his expression. "The Death Whisperer? Yes, it was quite easy to control his mind when I realized what he was. He led me right to the others after that."

Digging her nails into her palms to fight the pain inside her--the pain straining somewhere in her chest, the pain shattering her heart—she continued. "I can see why you had him bound to you for so long. He can be quite useful."

She couldn't look backward.

Especially when Rioner's laugh pierced the air. "You truly are a Rantzier. Absolutely ruthless."

Lessia pursed her lips. "I knew I needed something you valued to get my father and sister back. I assume you have her somewhere on the boat as well?"

Her heartbeat thrummed in her ears when Rioner glided his hands across his railing, leaning over the ship for a second before lifting his face again.

"I do." He fixed the crown atop his head, a lazy smile on his face. "And what will you offer me in return?"

"I'll give you the Fae warriors. I'll compel them to follow your every order. Or I can ask them to swear you another blood oath, should you prefer." Lessia jerked her head their way. "And... I've understood Loche is a threat to you, so... I will take him out. Let you do whatever you want with Ellow."

Rioner's smile widened. "I can agree to that."

Releasing a quiet breath, Lessia nodded, her taut shoulders relaxing a single inch.

Until Rioner spoke again.

"I just need to ensure you're truly telling me the truth and not tricking me into taking those three onboard only to overthrow me."

CHAPTER

FORTY-FOUR

Each beat of her heart slowed as she stared at her uncle.

The king didn't seem to notice as he waved toward a guard, whispering something in his ear that had the guard slam his heels together before retreating into the ship's hull.

"What do you require as proof?" Lessia silently cursed herself when her voice wavered, rising a little too much at the end of her question.

Rioner waved his fingers, and her eyes snapped to her father.

Pulled by the water, he moved forward until he stood beside Rioner at the railing, his eyes desperate as they met hers.

"Alarin, I have use for your special skills." Rioner flashed his teeth when her father snarled at him. "Now, now. I have the younger one downstairs, and I won't harm her as long as you... cooperate."

Lessia huffed a sharp breath. "Careful, uncle. My

friends back here are under instructions to show you no mercy should you do something to my family."

"What a waste of a temper and skill on a halfling," Rioner mumbled. "You would have done well in my court."

Lessia was about to respond that he was the one who made the decision to freeze out the half-Fae, but she pressed her lips closed when Rioner continued.

"However, betraying someone when he doesn't love you anymore is easy. When he's forced those feelings away... I wonder what happens when he can't anymore."

Lessia froze.

And the low gasps behind her, mingling with a low hum from Merrick's chest, told her the males were as surprised as she was.

They'd thought Rioner might try to test her.

But they'd bet on him forcing one of the Fae to hurt the other. Or perhaps hurt themselves.

But this?

Chuckling, Rioner waved for her father again. "I see this shocks you. But if you're truly like me, Elessia, then the human's feelings shouldn't matter. As I was saying. Alarin, be so kind and give the regent his memories and feelings back, would you?"

Her father threw her a helpless look, and magic tinged the salty air when she only stared back at him.

Lessia couldn't stop her body from turning around, watching Loche's eyes glaze—this effect was the one thing her father's magic and her own had in common—before they returned to shiny dark gray, but filled with...

Pain.

Agony.

Sorrow.

Heartbreak.

That's what marred the regent's sharp eyes as they snapped to hers.

And when they traveled to Merrick...

"I will not change my mind." Lessia spun around, praying that Rioner's gaze would follow her, not the telling sign of Loche's grief as he beheld her mate. "He rejected me. He can feel the same—worse—for all I care."

"Lessia..."

She braced herself when Loche's uncertain voice drifted her way, and without allowing herself to look at him, keeping her voice as cold as the king's before her, she ordered, "You know your place, Loche. I am your master now, so... Be. Quiet."

She nearly winced when her father's eyes widened, his face blanching as he stared at her.

But if even he believed her...

It was working.

"You have your proof." Lessia continued in a harsh tone. "Now, where is my sister?"

Rioner dragged a finger over the water rushing around her father, pulling a drop from it and eyeing it before letting it back into the ocean beneath the ships.

"All in good time, Elessia." His cloak flew out behind him as he began pacing back and forth, the thud of his boots against the wood thrumming through her blood.

"Kerym." Rioner's eyes moved behind her. "It's been a while, friend."

"We were never friends."

Lessia stiffened when Kerym spoke, but his composure remained relaxed, his face not betraying the anger she knew simmered beneath the thick leathers he wore.

"I guess you're right." The king shrugged. "It was your brother who was always more loyal."

"Keep Thissian out of this," Kerym snarled. "I was the one stupid enough to fall into the halfling's claws. He has nothing to do with this."

"Oh, and here I thought you liked me," Lessia made herself purr, even as bile rose in her throat. "Wanted me to warm your bed and all."

Rioner's eyes flashed when they darted her way before he caught himself, and she could tell the grin spreading across his face wasn't forced.

"I'm sure the Death Whisperer loved that." Rioner laughed darkly. "Seems you also inherited my fondness of sweet torture, niece."

She couldn't help it.

Her eyes sliced to Merrick.

You and me.

The words struck something within her.

Something she hadn't seen before.

Or perhaps hadn't been looking for...

Almost tangible, like a tether, something within her whispered the words back to him.

You and me.

And she could feel it.

Could feel Merrick's love for her as if it were the air traveling into her lungs.

She had to stop herself from smiling when the warmth bolted up her spine, and from the muscle working in his jaw, she suspected he was doing the same.

But then Kerym growled, and Lessia's head snapped forward, her breath catching in her throat as she stared at a Fae being dragged toward the railing by the guard Rioner had sent away before.

A Fae who looked like the reflection of the one beside her.

He was identical to Kerym, only...

Bruises painted almost every inch of his face purple and blue, and from the curved back she glimpsed within a water cage like her father's, she could tell he was in great pain.

So could Kerym.

"Kerym, don't." The words spilled out of her mouth, but it didn't matter.

Kerym flew forward, jumping over the railing onto the black ship.

As snarls burst through the air and Merrick and Raine left their spots behind her, Rioner caught him in a stream of water, angry blisters rippling across every inch of Kerym's skin as he fought against it.

But it proved useless.

Kerym sank to his knees a few feet from Thissian's cage, his chest heaving as he called out for his brother—the brother who didn't react, didn't even raise his hanging head, as if the pain was too great—as if the shame was too much.

Tearing her eyes from the horrible sight, she stared at the king again, and her stomach sank at the smug expression on his face.

He'd heard her command.

And he'd realized Kerym had ignored it.

"Elessia," Rioner tsked as she scrambled forward, racking her brain for what to do—how to help. "I had my doubts as soon as I saw these males behind you, but I certainly thought you would put up a bit better of a fight." He shook his head. "Guess I was right about you halflings all along. Useless, spineless, waste-of-space creatures."

Her growl was muffled by the snarls escaping Merrick and her father.

Even Raine bared his teeth, his body vibrating from the rumble that racked it.

"Do not speak to her like that," Merrick snarled, his voice so defiant she was surprised Rioner didn't take a step back.

"You're giving me orders now, Death Whisperer?"

She wanted to slam her fist into the king's smug face.

Wipe that fucking smirk off it, especially when he grinned at her mate.

But Merrick didn't bother responding.

Instead, he walked backward until he stood beside her, his hand sliding into hers, squeezing it and sending waves of warmth through her.

Determination.

Courage.

Love.

We fight.

To the end, she wanted to tell him.

She'd fight for him to the end.

Water splashed up the ship's sides as Rioner let out another hollow laugh. "I am going to make you watch, Merrick. My men have missed playing with her since she left my dungeons... I think I shall create a special cell. Where you can see her—hear her screams—but never again reach her."

"You will not touch her." Loche walked up to her other side as Merrick snarled viciously, the air around them heating with rage. "It's time for your rule to end, king. And I shall watch as she climbs your throne and changes Vastala into the great realm it always had the potential to be."

The world seemed to still when Merrick and Loche stepped up to shield her.

Two males—one Fae and one human—standing shoulder to shoulder to protect her.

"No," she whispered.

But it was too late.

Rioner's gaze widened.

"You," he whispered.

Her eyes snapped to Loche's rounded ones when he turned his head.

Then to Merrick's consuming darkness, the never-ending fall that was the night swirling within them.

She barely heard Merrick's violent curse as Loche spun around and crashed his lips against hers, the kiss so urgent he drew blood as their teeth slammed together.

"Take it," he urged into her mouth as she felt him press something warm into her hand.

Then chaos erupted.

Her hand was ripped from Merrick's, her lips from Loche's.

A blistering pain shot up her arm, and whatever Loche had given her vanished.

Water invaded her lungs as she screamed.

Filling them, the icy gushes stole her breath away until darkness pressed all around her.

Until it swallowed her whole.

Until she slipped into unconsciousness, clinging to the only words she remembered.

You and me.

CHAPTER FORTY-FIVE

He was going to fucking kill him.

Which him?

The whispers constantly filling his ears echoed the question as Merrick fought against the wild waters around him, his eyes tracking the darkness to find light—to find the surface.

Both, he snarled back.

He wouldn't discriminate.

He'd kill the king *and* Loche.

Rip their stupid heads off their bodies.

Make them scream as loudly as the souls in his mind.

Make them beg for mercy.

But as he imagined all the ways he'd kill those bastards, the softest, the most beautiful cry drowned the raging whispers.

Muted them like she always did when she spoke, when she touched him, when she looked at him.

You and me.

He heard Elessia's scream as if she were right beside him as he swam toward the slight glow above him.

Merrick screamed it back.

Screamed it into the darkness of the sea.

Into their bond.

But the bond, once a scorching thread—one that had nearly killed him—was now merely a frayed whisper.

She was gone.

Merrick's head burst through the surface.

And sure fucking enough.

The ship that had bobbed next to their own had been swallowed by the sea.

The whispers from the fucking souls always trying to break into this world filled his ears once more, pressing to be let out—to hurt and kill and destroy.

And he didn't care to leash them when the first pair of eyes meeting his own were those damned gray ones of the regent.

Merrick snarled as he fought the water to reach the stupid human.

He was going to kill him for putting his lips on *his* fucking mate.

For being dumb enough to not only take away their powers but to step up beside him when they knew—when they fucking knew!—the curse talked of a Fae and human loving her.

Then he was going to kill the fucking king for daring to take Elessia away from him.

He would destroy the world until he found her.

Kill every fucking soul that dared get in his way.

And if he found her harmed...

The whispers turned into shrieks—so loud that

Loche covered his ears where he treaded water before him.

He'd promised her that she'd never see the walls of that dungeon again.

If the king made him break it...

Merrick let the souls around him get a taste of roaming this realm—pushing the boundaries of what he once considered sacred.

There would be no more Havlands to save.

ACKNOWLEDGMENTS

First of all, to you—the reader. Thank you for loving the start of this series and the characters as much as I do. I wouldn't be able to do this without you, and I'll never take your support for granted.

Thank you to my husband who patiently lets me write at all hours of the day and night, even when I leave in the middle of dinner because creativity sparks.

To my friends who always cheer me on and who read my books even when it's not their genre—thank you for being the best support.

To Amanda, my amazing friend and PA. Thank you for always being there, whether to bounce ideas, let me vent my insecurities or keep me on track. I'm so grateful for you.

To Elyse, my amazing editor. Thank you for always lifting my books to the next level (and for teaching me boat terms!).

To my amazing Street Team and friends, thank you for helping me spread the love for my books and for the amazing conversations. You give me energy every day.

But just because she was broken . . . it didn't mean she was useless.
She just wasn't the same as she'd been growing up.
She was something new.
Something forged in pain.
Something born out of guilt.
Something bound by love.

KEEP READING FOR A SNEAK PEEK AT THE NEXT STAGE OF ELESSIA'S STORY . . .

CHAPTER 1
LESSIA

Merrick grinned at her as he opened his arms, and Lessia couldn't help but break into a run to reach him where he stood upon one of the cliffs beneath her childhood home, his silver hair dancing around his face in the warm summer breeze.

The sun blasted her skin as she pushed herself to move faster, and she had to fight to keep her eyes from closing against the bright light as her feet dug into the sand to close the distance between them.

But as Merrick's arms wrapped around her waist, she gave up and let her lids fall shut, allowing her other senses to take in the male she loved.

Merrick.

Her mate.

His wild scent whirled around her, and she couldn't get enough of how it filled her nostrils—nor how it filled her with that sense of freedom, of casting off shackles, of being utterly and entirely herself.

"I missed you," he murmured into her hair, and his

heart began pumping faster, the drums tapping against her own chest and filling the air like a soft melody.

Pulling back, she finally opened her eyes to his, and the ones that usually held the darkness of the night sky were now nearly pure silver, the flecks appearing to whirl as they flickered over her.

"I missed you too," she whispered before she crashed her lips against his.

The groan ripping from him nearly sent Lessia to her knees, and only because his strong arms held her did she not tumble down onto the white stone beneath them.

Gods, she had missed him so much.

Lessia wasn't sure how long it'd been, but any time away from him was too long.

She'd gotten too used to him always being there.

I'm here.

I'm always here.

Lessia smiled against his mouth, interrupting the kiss, and when Merrick pulled back to search her eyes, she let her lips pull even wider until he also broke into a grin.

"I'll never get used to that." Merrick shook his head so wildly his hair flew around it, sparkling against the blue sky behind him. "I'll never get used to you being mine."

Lifting her hand to caress his cheek, her palm rasping against the silver stubble growing there, she responded, "I'm always yours. Always."

Merrick brushed his lips against hers again. "As I'm always yours."

"Are you coming or what? We've waited forever!" A voice broke through the clear air, and Lessia hadn't thought her smile could go any wider, but her cheeks began hurting when her sister impatiently waved at them from behind Merrick's tall frame before she sprinted up the trail toward their home.

After a final look at Merrick, who nodded and released her, she grabbed his hand and began dragging him the familiar path up to the stone house where she'd grown up—where she'd spent her first twelve years of life.

Large green bushes flanked the road, and the birdsong she remembered loving as a child filled her ears as copses of trees popped up on either side.

The sound of small animals rushing across the forest bed joined the chirping and the wind rustling the leaves, and Merrick pulled at her hand when a rabbit crossed their path, to stop her from stepping on it.

Lessia drank in every sound, every smell, every familiar curve of the road.

She'd missed this island so much.

Thirteen years...

That's how long it'd been since she'd last been here.

Her favorite place.

Her home.

She felt Merrick's eyes on her and quickly tried to shake the melancholy that had begun filling her upon remembering the night she'd left, upon remembering the mother who'd made this place a haven.

The mother who was no longer.

The hand wrapped around her own tightened its grip, and when it pulled her to a stop once more, gently tugging at her to turn around, she let it.

"It wasn't your fault, Elessia." Merrick tried for a smile, but the darkness that now filled his eyes betrayed him.

And when a second voice—another familiar one, but this one filled with anger and resentment and disgust—broke the gentle melody floating around them, his grin collapsed completely.

Lessia spun around even before her father could finish his sentence, her heart shattering at the twisted grimace on his face.

"Of course it was her fault." Alarin took a step toward them, and Lessia's blood ran cold when she realized his white tunic and breeches were splattered with something dark...

Something red?

Despite the warning blaring within her, Lessia sniffed the air.

Iron overtook all the summer scents that had twined around them before.

Blood. It was blood that painted her father's clothing—blood that ran down his hands, dripping onto the light stone lining the path as he continued to walk toward them, his amber eyes crazed as they flitted between her and Merrick.

"She killed her sister. And then she killed her mother." Alarin stopped a few feet away, but drops of spit still landed on her face as he forced the words out. "She's a monster."

"No." Lessia stumbled toward him, but Merrick's grip on her hand held her back. "No, Father. Frelina is alive! I just saw her."

Her father's face crumpled with pain, before his arm shot out behind him. "If she's alive, how do you explain the graves?"

Lessia didn't want to look, but she couldn't stop herself from following her father's shaking hand, and when it revealed two white stones—one with *Frelina Rantzier* carved into it and the other *Miryn Rantzier*, both with dark stains marring the shiny fronts—a scream burst from her lips.

"You should feel pain," her father spat. "You killed my mate. My daughter. You should suffer like I have."

No.

No, this was all wrong.

Lessia shook her head, barely able to see through the tears that welled up in her eyes.

Still, when her father unsheathed a sword hanging by his waist, she didn't shrink back.

Instead, her eyes fixed on the graves of her sister and mother.

Two of the people she'd loved the most.

She did deserve this, didn't she?

If they were dead...

If they'd truly left this realm to move on to the afterlife?

It must be her fault.

Out of the corner of her eye, she noted the sword flying through the air, the whistling sound brushing her ears, but it wasn't until Merrick's hand ripped from hers that she snapped her head up.

Tears spilled down her father's cheeks as his arm fell to his side. "Now you'll know."

Know what? It was as if her thoughts refused to collaborate.

But then a gurgling sound—a horrible, wet, blood-curdling gurgling sound—reached her, just before a loud thump accompanied it.

Turning her cotton-filled head, she found Merrick's body crumpling to the ground, the sword he ripped from his gut clinking as it fell to the stone. His arms and legs splayed out in strange positions across the grass-peppered path, almost as if he'd taken a great fall.

Lessia wasn't certain if the sound that split the air came from her own mouth.

It was animalistic, a primal roar of pain that should break worlds apart, that should carry all the way to the Old World... perhaps even to the gods.

And when that thread she'd just begun to notice, the flicker of awareness between them, went dark, something broke inside her.

Hands flying to her chest, she fell to her knees beside her mate.

"Merrick!" Lessia's voice sounded as if from far away, as if it wasn't her own anymore, as if the pain was too great to let anything else in. "Merrick!"

She dropped her hands to his face and forced it her way, but the eyes that met hers...

There was no light behind them.

No dancing silver flecks.

No deep darkness.

And his face?

There were no hard lines that she loved to watch soften.

There was no twist of his mouth to hide a smile.

"Merrick!" She snapped her head down to his chest, but no heart thumped against it, and no air drove it up and down.

Another eerie, spine-rattling sound exploded through the air.

"Now you know," her father echoed. "Now you know how it feels. What you did to me."

She couldn't look at him.